More retu
me as I shrank bac
dirt and shredded vegetation. I heard three shots from behind me, the muzzle blasts smacking me in the back of the head, and then Phil was yelling at me to get up and get back inside.

On my elbows and knees, I scrambled backward until Phil reached out and grabbed my belt, hauling me back through the door. I knocked an elbow painfully against the jamb as my rifle almost got caught up. More bullets smacked splinters off the door overhead as we drew back inside the house.

"Can't go that way," I panted.

"There are more on the street," Jordan said. "They're canalized by the courtyard out front, but we're not getting out that way, either."

ESCALATION

MAELSTROM RISING BOOK 1

Peter Nealen

Also By Peter Nealen

The Maelstrom Rising Series
Escalation
Holding Action
Crimson Star
Strategic Assets

The Brannigan's Blackhearts Universe
Kill Yuan
The Colonel Has A Plan (Online Short)
Fury in the Gulf
Burmese Crossfire
Enemy Unidentified
Frozen Conflict
High Desert Vengeance
Doctors of Death

The American Praetorians Series
Drawing the Line: An American Praetorians Story (Novella)
Task Force Desperate
Hunting in the Shadows
Alone and Unafraid
The Devil You Don't Know
Lex Talionis

The Jed Horn Supernatural Thriller Series
Nightmares
A Silver Cross and a Winchester
The Walker on the Hills
The Canyon of the Lost (Novelette)
Older and Fouler Things

Prologue

Missiles Fly Over the East China Sea

Chinese People's Liberation Army Navy ships exchanged antiship missile fire with the Japanese Kaga *task force off the coast of Fuke-jima in the early hours of Wednesday morning. It is unclear whether or not the Chinese ships had actually passed into Japanese waters, though Beijing denies any such incursion. Japanese Navy spokesman Rear Admiral Hideo Hayashi insisted that the Chinese ships entered the* Kaga *task force's exclusion zone, the fifth such incursion within the last three months, though he did not deny that the Japanese ships fired first.*

The Chinese deny that any major damage was done, claiming that their point-defenses shot down all incoming missiles. However, sources claim that the frigate Yiyang *was observed listing seriously and possibly burning.*

Violence Spreads to Palawan

The battle over the Spratly Islands has spread to the Philippine Island of Palawan. While the PLAN remains offshore, Filipino authorities are insisting that the increasingly effective paramilitaries operating on Palawan are in fact Chinese proxies. Senator Joniel Bautista has even accused the People's Republic of China of smuggling PLA commandos onto the island. Paramilitaries have seized control of Puerto Princesca International Airport, and a combined force of Filipino and Vietnamese troops have been attempting to regain control of the airport for the last three days. The death toll continues to rise.

1

Korean Unification Talks Continue to Stagnate

Representatives from the ROK and the DPRK met again on Tuesday, only to go into recess for the fourth time without progress. While the official statements from both governments insist that talks are continuing, there have been no changes in the last six months. Sources say that Pyongyang is under increasing pressure from the People's Republic of China to remain in Beijing's orbit, and that any unification that does not include a close partnership with China will have serious consequences. Meanwhile, increasing Japanese navy patrols near the Korean coast have Seoul worried about taking sides between the increasingly hostile Asian powers.

Day Four of Coup in Kiev

As the fourth day of the pro-Russian takeover of the government in Kiev comes to an end, the level of violence is still strikingly low. More Russian armored columns have advanced out of the annexed Donetsk region, taking up security positions around the capitol city. More have pushed toward the west, ostensibly to bolster Ukrainian border control points with Romania and Poland. While Ukrainian Patriotic Union holdouts still hold Odessa, Vinnitsya, and Lviv, they appear to be simply holding their positions. It is believed that the attempted capture of Ukraine Alone politician Kyrylo Stasiuk by European Defense Council special forces in Kharkiv last month contributed to the turn in public sentiment toward Russia. The EDC troops are estimated to have killed nearly a hundred people in their botched attempt to escape after Stasiuk's security and Kharkiv police cornered them in the Kharkiv Palace Premier Hotel.

More Russian Forces Observed on Estonian Border

The Estonian Defense Forces remain on high alert, as more units of the 138th Guards Motor Rifle Brigade and the 268th Guards Artillery Brigade began conducting maneuvers around Volosovo, less than 45 miles from the border. While Russian authorities insist that the maneuvers are simply scheduled training, recent Russian moves in Ukraine and Abkhazia have made the Estonians and Latvians increasingly nervous. Estonian Prime Minister Evelin Ainsalu has repeatedly requested support from both the United States and the European Defense Council.

Russia Issues New Protest Over US Deployments to Poland

Russian Ambassador Evgeniy Suvorin repeated the Kremlin's protests about US military deployments to Poland when he met with Secretary of State Gordon today. "Given the tensions that exist in Eastern Europe at this time, placing additional NATO troops in a country that has grown increasingly hostile to Russia cannot be seen as anything but adding fuel to the fires of instability in a Europe that is already suffering." In the press conference afterward, Suvorin refused to answer questions about Russian moves in Ukraine.

Night Clashes Across Saudi Border as Violence Increases in Anbar

Artillery fire thundered over the Iraq-Saudi Arabia border last night, while Iranian Azarakhsh ground-attack aircraft bombed Saudi positions near King Khalid Military City. Unconfirmed reports suggest ground incursions near Rafha, and Saudi attacks north into Kuwait. Meanwhile, a new rash of bombings across Ramadi, Fallujah, and Baghdad targeted Iraqi Security Forces and Shi'a civilians.

Turkish Forces Consolidate Gains in Iraqi Kurdistan

Kurdish Peshmerga attacks on Turkish positions near Zakho were beaten back yesterday, while fighting in Duhok continued, with Turkish forces having secured approximately half the city so far. Turkish forces are pushing out of Soran, as well, though Peshmerga forces have successfully ambushed a column making its way through the Ali Bag Canyon. There are unconfirmed reports of hundreds of civilians being slaughtered in Soran, in retaliation for Peshmerga attacks on Turkish

3

headquarters in the area. KRG officials have asked for assistance from the United States, but there are reports that they have approached the Islamic Republic of Iran for help, as well.

French and Belgian Crackdown

European Defense Council Security Forces continued their roundup of far-right groups following the burning of three South Asian enclaves outside of Paris, and one in Brussels. Some commentators have remarked that the EDCSF are not discriminating between traditionalist groups and true extremists, but the EDC denies it, insisting that there is no longer any room in Europe for nationalist violence. When questioned about the connection between the burning of the enclaves and the rash of bombings and truck attacks across Brussels, Antwerp, Reims, Metz, and Paris the week before, EDC spokesperson Clara Hausler refused to answer and ended the press conference.

Senator Billings Killed in Bombing

In the third such killing in the last six months, Senator Tyrone Billings of Michigan was killed by a VBIED outside his Ann Arbor home last night. This comes after three months of threats, following Billings' vote against S.8853, the "Hate Speech" law that would bring the US into line with European Union standards. Most of Senator Billings' security was killed in the blast. Police have no leads.

Shots Exchanged in Slovakia

American peacekeepers exchanged fire with European Defense Council troops in the Slovak town of Slovenský Grob, early yesterday. While the Pentagon insists that the brief firefight between US Marines and a Swedish contingent of the EDCAF was a case of mistaken identity, the EDC has issued official protests and demanded the US ground commander be harshly disciplined. Reports that the Marines were attempting to intervene in what some have described as a "massacre in progress" have been dismissed by all official spokespeople.

4

However, what appears to be photo evidence has already leaked to the internet, purporting to be images of Swedish troops watching as militia rounds up Slovak civilians and lines them up against walls, with other dead bodies in the background. The Pentagon has refused to comment, while EDC spokesperson Raymond Thibault has denounced the photos as blatant forgeries. Pentagon reporters confirm that the Marine unit has been recalled from Slovakia, and is currently in Germany, in transit back to the United States.

Chapter 1

The bad guys suddenly started moving about an hour after sunrise.

We had eyes on two sides of the house from our hide site, and so it was impossible to miss when the front door slammed open and half a dozen men rushed out, bearded and armed to the teeth. The only one who wasn't in a rush was the guy with the Talib beard, wearing all Russian camouflage and talking into a radio. We were so close that I could actually pick out a few of the Albanian words.

I was already nervous about being within a hundred meters of the target building, but having what looked an awful lot like a terrorist react force come rushing out made my guts pucker. Only training and discipline kept me stock-still, though my hand was already on my OBR's firing control, finger hovering near the trigger. If we'd been made, it was going to get really loud and really messy, really fast.

We were also probably all going to die in the process. Not to mention the hostage whom I was already pretty sure was tied up inside that house.

"Deacon, Weeb," Scott Hayes' voice said in my ear. "I think I see what's got 'em all stirred up. There's company coming."

I didn't answer right away. I was keeping my eyes fixed somewhere just above Camouflage Jacket's shoulder as I inched my off hand toward the push-to-talk clipped to the strap of my chest rig.

None of us had wanted to set up so close. Phil had been downright adamant that we needed to find some other way of handling the situation, as the night had worn on and we'd had to get closer and closer just to see the house through the trees. The hills we'd hiked in through were heavily forested, and just the crunch of leaves under our boots had been excruciatingly loud.

And if I could hear the guy who I was pretty sure was Ibrahim Baruti, then he could hear me.

I reached the button and pressed it once. I didn't dare try to talk; squelch breaks were going to be about all I could do until the Kosovars, ethnic Albanian jihadists who had fled Serbia after the recent unpleasantness there, went back inside or we got in a firefight. But the single break would tell Scott, in his cozy little lay-up site in an abandoned barn, ten miles away, that I was listening.

"There's a formation of four M5s coming up the road," Scott continued. He was watching the drone feed from the little tricopter buzzing around at treetop level over the town. "Can't tell yet whether they're heading for Marianka or Zàhorskà Bystrica, but it looks like the bad guys are getting ready for them in Marianka anyway."

Shit. I could feel Dwight glance at me from his position immediately to my left. Everybody was on the same radio channel, so he'd heard it. Dwight being Dwight, I knew he had something to say about it, but you don't talk when you've only got five guys ghillied up and covered in leaves, less than a hundred meters from the enemy.

Three more bad guys came running out of the house just then. One had a PKP machinegun over his shoulder. Another had what looked an awful lot like an RPG-29. They ran toward the far end of the town, while Baruti walked around the front of the house, leaving us in the clear for a moment.

And leaving me with a decision to make.

"What the hell?" Dwight whispered, momentarily relieved of the necessity to keep absolutely silent. "I thought the peacekeepers were locked down after Slovenský Grob?"

"They were," I whispered back. "I guess that the lockdown got lifted since the poor bastards who decided to do the right thing got hauled back Stateside."

"Or they're here for the same reason we are," Dwight muttered. He was watching the house intently, his thick, pugnacious features hidden under his ghillie hood and a thick application of camouflage face paint. The Mk 48 was in front of him, draped with another camouflage net that he'd brought along for just that purpose.

I glanced at the house. It made sense. Our intel didn't have much good to say about Colonel Banks, who was commanding the Brigade Combat Team assigned to peacekeeping duties in Slovakia. By all accounts he was a ladder-climber, and, shall we say... less than enthusiastic about sticking his neck out. He sure hadn't done a damned thing to step up for Lieutenant Randolph after Slovenský Grob. But a hostage situation that was already in its third week *might* be enough to get him to pull his thumb out and send his men on patrol.

Carefully, I keyed my radio and subvocalized into my throat mic. "Weeb, Deacon. Does it look like that platoon is looking for our target?" If they were, that was going to both simplify and complicate matters at the same time.

"Negative, Deacon," Scott replied. "These guys don't look like they're on the hunt. This looks like a presence patrol. They're buttoned up tight and rolling like they don't really have a care in the world. I don't think they're expecting trouble from the locals."

"These ain't exactly locals," I murmured in reply, even as I scanned the yard and the nearby houses. Sure enough, there was quite a bit of movement. Those M5s had kicked the anthill, and they probably didn't even know it yet. "Looks like a lot of Albanians and Arabs." Those Slovaks still in Marianka—I didn't think there were that many left—were keeping their heads down.

"You get the idea," Scott said with a touch of exasperation. "I can see more of the streets than you can, and these guys are about to walk into a hornet's nest."

I heard a faint rustle of movement behind me. "We're here for the hostage," Jordan muttered.

"Yeah," I whispered back, even as I started to get my hands under me to get up. "But we can't just sit here and let those kids get slaughtered, either."

I didn't get up immediately; I was planning in my head as I watched the town and added up what I knew about the enemy's dispositions.

We couldn't get into position to flank the ambush being set up on the road, not in time. Judging by what Scott had said, the American vehicles were already on the outskirts, and it would take us twenty minutes to work our way through the woods. They'd be smoking hulks by then.

We didn't have solid confirmation that the hostage was in that house, but we were going to have to take the chance. We might not be able to head the ambush off, but we damned well could create a hell of a diversion.

"Dwight, you and Greg are the base of fire," I whispered, as I got up on a knee behind the bush that we'd been hiding under. "The rest of us are going to hit that house. If we make it to the door without being spotted, give us a five count and then open up. Try not to shoot where the hostage might be."

"That's some great advice, right there," Dwight grumbled, settling himself more solidly behind the Mk 48.

The rest of the team was starting to move, though still keeping low and moving carefully. It wasn't quite time to go loud just yet.

"This wasn't the mission, Matt," Jordan whispered again. "We're here for the hostage. If we're blown now, then they might just kill the hostage."

"And if he's in there, we kill two birds with one stone," I whispered back. "Otherwise, we cause some noise and escape in the chaos. They won't know for sure that we weren't just a security element for the peacekeepers."

"They're not that stupid," Jordan hissed.

"Guys," Greg whispered. "The cell hits point to this place. Matt's right."

One of the functions of the drone that Scott was controlling from the barn was cell phone tracking. What had narrowed our search down to Marianka in the first place had been multiple targeted cell phones pinging around this very house.

"Jordan just doesn't want to risk it to protect a bunch of white boys in the Griffins," Phil said. He was crouching at the edge of the bushes, his rifle already held across his knees, his eyes trained on the house.

"Fuck you, Phil," Jordan hissed back, a real note of anger in his voice. His face was painted green and brown, but was black as the ace of spades underneath the paint. "That shit ain't funny."

I was starting to get pissed. This wasn't the time nor the place. We'd been prepared to quickly plan the hit based on our recon, but this was turning into a debate, not a planning session. We were all too old and too experienced to fall into this bullshit.

"Knock it off," I whispered. "It's my call. We're hitting the house. If England's in there, we pull him out. If not, we cause as much noise and chaos as we can before we get out, then fall back to Rally Point Hotel. Any questions?"

There weren't any. I'd known that there wouldn't be. Their initial reaction had been something of a rational one; we were five guys about to go charging into a hotbed of Kosovar and Syrian militia. None of these bastards were in Slovakia for good reasons, regardless of the European Defense Council's platitudes about the "plight of refugees."

And the fact of the matter was, that every one of us was a warrior. We weren't going to sit by and let more Americans get slaughtered if we could help it.

And we were more confident in our own training and skill than we were in the current US Army's.

I started out, moving out of the bushes and skirting the treeline, trying to get some distance between my precious personal hide and Greg's and Dwight's line of fire. The sun was still fairly low in the partly cloudy sky, so the light was dim enough that I was pretty sure I was still hard to see, looking more like a green and brown swamp thing than a man as I moved against the thick vegetation behind me.

The house was two stories tall, with a red tile roof and plastered walls. Surrounded by a waist-high iron and brick fence, it was something of a sprawling estate for Marianka; clearly the original owners had been well-off. But they were long gone, and it looked like Baruti had appropriated it for his own headquarters.

There was another treeline running down the edge of the field to the corner of the fence, and I slipped into it. Phil and Jordan followed in trace, maintaining a spread-out file, weapons held ready as they scanned around us. I was doing the same thing;

11

we hadn't had time to build much of a picture of the enemy's pattern of life since the sun had come up, but the drone's intel was painting a grim picture. This well-to-do suburb of Bratislava had been turned into enemy territory pretty quickly.

I wasn't running, but I wasn't moving slowly, either. With the peacekeepers getting closer by the minute, we were on the clock. Despite my insistence, I hated going off half-cocked like this. The rest of the team knew it, too, which was why I'd gotten as little pushback as I had.

We reached the fence without incident. I could hear yelling in Arabic and Albanian on the other side as I took a knee, facing down the fence line, my OBR held ready while I waited for Jordan and Phil to catch up.

I heard the rustle as they joined me, then Jordan's hand came down on my shoulder. "Up," he whispered.

I rose slowly, easing head and weapon over the top of the fence. We were right behind the guest house in the corner of the back yard. I couldn't be sure that it was unoccupied, but the windows were dark. We'd still probably have to clear it quickly. None of us wanted to leave a pocket of bad guys behind us as we crossed the open yard to the main house.

As I covered, Phil put his rifle atop the fence and vaulted over it. It was an easier barrier than some of the walls we'd trained on, based on compounds in the Middle East and Afghanistan. Jordan followed, and then I was the last one over.

For a brief moment, we crouched in the shadows between the fence and the guest house. I peered around the corner, seeing a single figure loitering on the back deck of the main house, carrying a FAMAS.

Whether it had come from a captured weapons cache or had directly been supplied by the French portion of the EDC was anybody's guess.

Jordan was at my elbow. "The house looks clear," he whispered into my ear. "The front door's open, no lights, just crap piled in the hall and the living room." He'd peered into the window while I'd been scanning our target.

"Deacon, Weeb," Scott's voice crackled in my ear. "Time's up. If you're going to go, you'd better do it now."

So, I leaned out around the corner and put a bullet into the guy on the deck.

The thunderous report of the 7.62 echoed across the hills around the town, shattering the early morning calm. The dark-clad man with the FAMAS bullpup staggered, staring down at the widening dark stain on his chest for a brief fraction of a second before he crumpled, crashing to the deck with a thump and a muffled clatter as he landed on top of his rifle.

I was already up and moving as he hit the floor, sprinting around the side of the guest house and heading for the steps leading up to the deck. A figure loomed in the doorway, and I caught a glimpse of a weapon. I started to slow, bringing my own rifle back up to fire, but a shot *crack*ed past my shoulder and took the man in the chest. He fell backwards, into the house.

Then I was up onto the deck, my OBR leveled at the door, Jordan right on my heels, as Dwight opened fire on the front of the house with a long, roaring burst of 7.62.

The back wall was mostly big picture windows and the door. There was no point in pausing; there was no cover. Fortunately, Jordan was right there with me, and so we didn't even slow down as we punched through the door and into the house.

I stepped over the fallen body in the doorway. The man was in his death spasms, choking on his own blood. I still kicked the old Skorpion machine pistol away from his hand as I passed, just in case.

We were in a sort of living room, or at least it had been. The sectional couch and chairs were still there, as was the coffee table. The pictures on the walls had been torn down, and the place was trashed. There were piles of propaganda leaflets on the coffee table, as well as porn and what looked an awful lot like drugs. A partial wall closed half of it off from the rest of the house, though the opening into the kitchen/dining area was wide open.

I went left, Jordan went right, and Phil darted in behind us, following me along the left-hand wall. He'd paused to take that shot on the way, then rushed to catch up with the two of us. A two-man entry was preferable to a one-man, but the more guns in the fight, the better.

More gunfire echoed outside. It sounded like Dwight and Greg were in a medium-range firefight with somebody up near the front of the house; not all the fire was going in one direction. We rapidly closed on the doorway; the living room was clear.

Jordan had hung back closer to the door, having moved only far enough to get his back to a wall instead of a window. He had a lot wider field of fire than I did, even as I quickly crossed the room, angling toward the end of that partial wall, with Phil right behind me. Jordan snapped his OBR up and fired, pumping three shots rapidly into the dining room. The reports were deafening inside the enclosed space of the house.

He ceased fire just as I reached the end of the wall, and then I was committed. Taking a breath, I stepped around, snapping my own rifle toward the nearest corner.

There was a stairway ahead of me, leading up into the second story, and a short hallway next to it, leading to the entryway and more rooms on the ground floor. There was also a body at my feet. A few feet away, I saw another Kosovar fighter with a SIG 550 in his hands, crouched and aimed in at the corner that I'd just rounded.

He was half-slumped against the wall, his rifle pointed off to one side, and off balance. He'd apparently dived for cover as Jordan blew his buddy's brains all over his jacket, but that momentary loss of balance was all the advantage I needed.

I drove my rifle toward him, barely picking up the offset irons alongside the shortdot scope, and blew a chunk of his heart out of his back. The second shot, that scorched his beard with the muzzle blast as the bullet blew the back of his skull off, spattering blood and brains against the wall behind him, was little more than insurance, but it had been so instinctive that the twin reports almost blended into a single, catastrophic noise.

The dead man was still sliding down the wall, his rifle slipping from nerveless fingers, as another figure appeared at the top of the stairs, his eyes widening as he saw the weird, leafy apparitions with rifles standing over his fellow militiaman's body. He lifted the FAMAS rifle in his hands. I had a split second to shift targets, throwing myself sideways as I did so. Staying still was a good way to get shot.

14

He triggered a burst into the wall above Phil's head, just before both of us blasted him. He staggered, wobbled for a second, then fell face-first down the stairs, actually doing a somersault before he hit the floor at the bottom.

More gunfire erupted behind me as Jordan shot at somebody toward the front of the house, but Phil and I were already driving our way up the stairs, stepping hard on the body at the base of the steps as we went.

Press the immediate threat.

I drove up the stairs two at a time, only slowing as I neared the top. I really didn't want to get my head blown off by sticking it up without at least my own muzzle between my noggin and the bad guys.

Phil was right next to me, and we popped over the landing with our rifles leveled at the same time. The short hallway at the top of the stairs was clear, for the moment. We both surged the rest of the way up, as more gunfire thundered and echoed from the front of the house.

More shots cracked from the door to the right. I started to angle toward it, though there was yet another open door right to the left. The barking reports of gunfire were coming from that one, that made it a threat.

I didn't have to say or even signal anything. Phil, who was closer, moved right to the door, pausing just long enough to know that I was right beside him, then pushed in.

He was already shooting as he crossed the threshold. I was so close behind him that my muzzle was right over his shoulder, but the man leaning out of the window, firing back at the treeline was already down, leaving a red smear on the white wall. His rifle had fallen out the open window.

It took less than three seconds to ensure that the room was clear, and then we were coming out, this time with Jordan in the lead. He went straight across the hallway, bursting into the room we'd bypassed, and I was halfway across the threshold when he called, "Clear!"

We barely paused, just turning and burning back down the hall.

As I came out, I glanced down the stairway, in time to see two men in dark clothes, chest rigs, and turbans start up the stairs. I threw myself across the hallway as they opened fire, bullets chewing into the ceiling and sending bits of plaster raining down on us, and returned fire. My first shot smashed into the smaller man's collarbone, sending him reeling as the follow-up shot tore his throat out.

The *snap* of the bullet made the taller, skinnier guy flinch. Which was when Jordan leaned out of the door and shot him in the skull. His head snapped backward as he crashed onto his back. Red started seeping from the turban wrapped around his head.

Everything went quiet all of a sudden after that. We still pressed on to finish clearing the house, even as Scott said in my ear, "Deacon, Weeb. The patrol's halted short of the town. Looks like they're setting security and calling higher for instructions."

Of course they are. I acknowledged with a double squelch break. I shouldn't have been surprised. The current US Armed Forces seemed to be even more hogtied in red tape and armchair quarterbacking than it had been when I'd been a Marine.

There wasn't time to worry about it, especially as Dwight's voice broke in. "Deacon, Teddy. Y'all kicked the anthill. There's probably a platoon heading your way. I can keep 'em back for a bit, but you need to wrap it up and get out of there."

I didn't answer immediately, because we were moving into the next room, at the end of the hall. It was as empty as the second one had been. I held up a hand to hold for a moment. "Deacon copies all," I said, as chagrined as always that I was breathing as hard as I was. Close quarters combat gets the heart pumping harder than any run. "Top floor cleared. We're going to check the rest of the first floor, then exfil."

I had a sneaking suspicion that we weren't going to find Specialist England, or if we did, we weren't going to like what we found. It was too quiet for anything else.

But as I nodded to Phil, he flowed out into the hallway and headed for the steps.

He hooked around the base of the steps as I stepped out to cover the opening onto the living room. Jordan tapped me as he went past, and I turned to follow.

16

Two more bodies were slumped at the front of the entryway. The door was standing open, with what might have been yet another corpse lying on the front steps.

There were two rooms on the side, a master bedroom and a bathroom. It took seconds to clear both. No more bad guys, and no sign of the hostage. In fact, it didn't look like he'd ever been there.

"This is Deacon," I sent. "We're on our way out." I'd barely gotten the last syllable out before Dwight opened fire again, the rattling roar of the Mk 48 tearing the brief quiet to shreds.

It took moments to retrace our steps to the back, even as we started hearing heavier ordnance going off to the west. It sounded like the militia had started engaging those Griffins anyway, and unless I missed my guess, they were getting some .50 caliber love in return. Of course, the M5s had 50mm main guns, too, but the gunners were probably locked out of those for the time being.

In a way, I thought, even as we vaulted the fence again and faded into the treeline, the paralysis of the US peacekeepers was a good thing. After all, it wouldn't be good if they found out we were even in the country.

Chapter 2

"Friendlies coming in," I called over the radio.

"I've got you," Tony replied. "Come ahead."

It was almost dark. As thick as the woods were in that part of Slovakia, we'd had to move very carefully to avoid the locals, not to mention the occasional peacekeeper or militia patrols. It had taken slow, methodical movement, slipping from cover to cover, often halting to stay put and just watch and listen.

Phil got to his feet and started toward the ancient barn. Built of plastered stone and graying, aged timber, the roof was starting to sag and the base was overgrown, but it was still solid. I suspected it had been standing for at least a couple of centuries. It probably would still have been in use if not for the turmoil that had engulfed Slovakia over the last few years.

I carefully scanned the surrounding woods and the open field beyond for a moment, despite the fact that I knew that Scott had security set and the drone up. The abandoned farm sat right at the no-man's land between the Belgian peacekeeping sector and one of the few, small, Loyalist Slovak Army sectors. While what was left of the Army that hadn't gone over to the Nationalists after the initial riots was still outwardly loyal to the shaky government in Bratislava, that loyalty was in question among many of the peacekeepers, especially the Germans and Belgians. None of this would have been happening if the Slovaks hadn't already had enough of both Brussels' financial demands and the forced immigration, mostly of young Kosovar, Bosnian, and Syrian men. To that end, most of the EDC peacekeepers made no secret of the fact that they didn't trust the Slovak Army.

Which made the uneasy borders between zones the best place to hide out, even though it had meant one hell of an infiltration from Hungary.

Seeing no movement, nor the hulking silhouettes of armored vehicles on the road, in the fields, or against the treeline, I followed Phil toward the barn.

Tony was right at the door, though set back in the shadows, his PSQ-20 thermal fusion NVGs down in front of one eye. He was on a knee, his own Mk 48 held over his thigh. Unfortunately, the NVGs weren't all that conducive to staying down in the prone. They tended to sag, making it extremely uncomfortable to crane your neck to see.

I slipped inside, making sure not to step in front of Tony's muzzle. Not because I expected the thickset former SF Weapons Sergeant to shoot me by accident, but because it just wasn't a good habit to get into. And if somebody *did* pop out of that treeline, that split second it would take to get out of his way could be fatal to us both.

Scott was hunkered down in the darkened corner, away from the doors, behind a nest of comm gear and the drone control console. It hadn't been fun, lugging that crap in from Hungary, but it had been useful.

He looked up as I crossed to join him. His vaguely Asian features were still camouflaged, despite the fact that most of us had sweated most of the cammie paint off on the infil. Knowing Scott, he'd pestered the rest of the Bravo Element to reapply their cammie paint before he'd even gotten the comms set up all the way.

I was sure that David and Chris had appreciated the reminder, and told him just how much they appreciated it in no uncertain terms. After all, nobody in this team was an amateur.

"Dry hole," I said, as I sat against the wall, leaning my rifle next to me. Dwight, Jordan, and Greg filed in behind me and found positions in the barn where they could easily switch out with the guys on security when the time came. "But you knew that already." I grabbed one of the water bladders that Scott had filled and purified and drank greedily. It had been a long movement.

"But it might have pointed us in the right direction," Scott said. My assistant team lead was all business in the field, despite the Japanese manga I was pretty sure was shoved into his pack somewhere. He turned the tablet he was using around and tapped the screen to shift windows. I peered at it, seeing a satellite map of southwest Slovakia on the dimly-lit screen, with several bright red dots pulsating on it.

"Shortly after you hit that ambush, Borinka lit up like a Christmas tree," he said. "At least three more Persons of Interest, too. I don't think they were expecting to get hit so soon."

"I wasn't expecting the leash to get taken off the BCT that quick, either," I replied. "Are you still tapped in? Are they finally on the hunt?"

He shook his head. "I am, and they're not. The official line is that 'other avenues are being pursued.' They've been authorized to start patrolling their AO again, but the ROEs sound like they're stricter than ever. And that appears to be at the behest of the EDC."

I snorted in disgust. I remembered a time when the US was the top dog on the block, and sure as hell would never have kowtowed to the French and Germans. Of course, that had been when I was a kid. The fact that everybody was at each other's throats back home had pretty much made that a thing of the past. Half the government would kowtow to Satan if it pissed off the other half.

Which was why the Triarii existed in the first place.

We weren't a PMC. Not really. Some of the op-eds back home that called us a militia weren't that far off. Colonel Santiago had started building the network that would become the Triarii in order to counteract some of the lawlessness that was becoming par for the course back home. As he started to understand just how bad things had gotten, the network's purview grew. And grew. And now we were the paramilitary force that we were, starting to fill in the blanks outside the borders of the United States as well as inside.

Why "Triarii?" I know. I thought it sounded weird the first time, too. But the triarii were the third rank of the old Republican Roman Legion. The oldest, most experienced, and most ferocious fighters, who were the last-ditch rank, the last guys to get stuck in, when the hastati and the principes hadn't done the trick.

Once I learned that, it made sense. We were the third rank. We were the last ditch.

Which was why we were in Slovakia. The Colonel had decided that it was a good test of our expeditionary capability, on top of which, he was pissed about the fact that an American soldier had been snatched off the streets of Bratislava and was being held hostage while the US peacekeepers in the country sat on their hands.

"Well, then," I said, "We're still on mission." If the Army had indeed taken up the hunt, we were under orders to back off and observe. The Colonel didn't want us potentially butting heads with the Army. For rather obvious reasons, revealing our presence by making contact wasn't high on our list of "good ideas."

While cell phone tracking had advanced a lot in recent years, it still wasn't a precise science. We could pick up when a phone pinged off a tower, which gave us a location, and Scott knew how to set the drone to simulate a tower, allowing us to do some triangulation. But it was still going to give us only a general idea of that location, and that was assuming that we were tracking the right phones.

I took the tablet and studied the readout. There were definitely some phones on there from the target list that the intel cell had put together. Mostly Syrians. This was going to get interesting.

I checked my watch. We didn't have a lot of time; as soon as the first shot had been fired, Specialist England's life expectancy had taken a nose dive. But we wouldn't do him a damned bit of good if we went in exhausted and started making mistakes. None of us had slept in almost thirty hours.

"Rest plan for three hours," I said. It wasn't going to be enough, but it was going to have to do. "Everybody down except for security on the doors." It was a risk, but we needed the rest.

We'd plan and move in the wee hours of the morning. It was a tight planning cycle, but it was one we'd trained hard for.

It said something for the Triarii special operations—or *Grex Luporum*—training cycle that even a guy like me could become a team leader.

***

I was never a Recon Marine. Don't get me wrong; I tried. Not just out of spite, either, not that my parents would have understood. Nor would it would have made anything worse than it already was. The screaming when I had announced that I was going to enlist in the first place...let's just say that it's a good thing I was a hundred miles away at the time. Mom couldn't throw anything at me.

See, I didn't come from a military family. I came from the opposite. Both my mom and dad were hard-left lawyers, and I was going to be a good little activist clone. Until I wound up with a roommate in college who was a Marine Sergeant bucking for a commission.

Bart didn't put up with my bullshit, and challenged every assumption I made. Within three months, we were fast friends and I was already talking to the Marine recruiter.

I don't think I've actually talked to my folks since then. In my more bitter moments, I think that that's not necessarily a great loss.

My enlistment wasn't anything to shout about. I did four years as an 0331, a regular grunt machinegunner. I tried to get to the Recon screening, or MARSOC Assessment and Selection, probably six times each. My command wouldn't hear of it.

That was why it didn't take much persuasion to get out after my four years were up. Just before I had to decide whether I was going to go on terminal leave or sign the reenlistment papers, Bill Vagley, who had gotten out six months before me, told me about the Triarii.

I'd known that I didn't have the background or the qualifications for the Grex Luporum Teams. They were looking for guys with at least four years in a special operations unit.

But I'd been determined. The Triarii were my second chance, so when I got called out for applying for the Grex Luporum—Wolfpack—teams without the requisite experience, I doubled down. I swore up one side and down another that I'd do whatever I needed to; I'd catch up. Brian Hartrick, the chief cadre, had been skeptical, but let me try out, just for having the balls to do it in the first place.

The next six months had been the most grueling of my life. But I passed.

It hadn't been an easy road from there to my own team. Hartrick was still my section leader, and if there was anybody who wasn't going to give me an inch of slack, it was him. He'd made me pay for signing up for the teams in selection, and nothing had really changed afterward.

Now, it seemed that the team leader who'd gotten in through sheer brass was spearheading the Triarii's first overseas op.

If I'd only known.

***

I woke up painfully as Scott shook me. An hour and a half of sleep is never enough, and when you've spent most of the previous thirty hours planning, preparing, hiking a very long way, and getting in a firefight, it's even worse.

Stifling a groan, I sat up. "Everything's quiet," Scott whispered. "The cell pings haven't moved. Hopefully that doesn't mean they already killed him."

"Only so much we can do," I whispered back. "Get some shut-eye. I'm going to start planning." He nodded in the darkness, lit only by the faint glow from the tablet's screen, and lay down against the wall of the barn.

I took the tablet, wincing. Everything hurt. Not that I had expected to wake up bright eyed and bushy tailed. That hadn't ever been the case in the infantry, and it sure as hell hadn't been in the GL teams.

Borinka wasn't far from Marianka. It was smaller, little more than a one-street village nestled between wooded hills, overlooked by a ruined castle.

I glanced around the barn, double-checking that everybody who was supposed to be awake was, and then I hunkered down over the tablet and started to plan.

***

A little over two hours later, we were all awake and Alpha Element was getting ready to go back out. I'd given my quick brief, and everyone had had a chance to look over the terrain. The general mission profile was the same as it had been; we were just a little bit lighter on ammo and a lot shorter on sleep.

"As long as we can find the hostage this time and not get sidetracked trying to save everybody," Jordan grumbled.

"Are you really sure you want to save the hostage so bad, Jordan?" Phil asked. "After all..."

"If you finish that sentence, I will cut your fucking throat, Twig," Jordan snarled. "I'm not even playing."

"Damn, Jordan, why you gotta be so sensitive?" Dwight drawled. "It's a joke, man."

"Racism ain't no joke to me," Jordan snapped. "I've had enough of Phil's 'jokes.'"

"Really?" Scott put in. "Fuck, it's like fucking high school again. Grow up, both of you."

"Motherfucker," Jordan began, but I cut him off.

"Knock it off," I hissed, exasperated. It wasn't the first time Jordan had pulled this shit, but it needed to be the last. "Not the time, nor the place. Phil, quit poking the bear. Jordan, grow a fucking Rhino liner and shut the hell up." I glared at him, though it was hard to see in the darkness of the barn. He returned my stare, though I could feel it more than see it, but finally relented.

"Fine," he said. "As long as Twig shuts his fucking mouth."

"Enough of this shit," I snarled. "We're in the field, on a mission. Fucking act like it."

"Come on, guys," Greg said, with his usual earnestness. "Game faces."

"Shut up, Greg." Greg was once of the nicest, most cheerful guys around, certainly in the teams, but the last thing I needed at the moment was for this to turn into a team meeting. He was right, but we needed to get moving and get to Borinka.

Scott was finishing packing his ruck. We weren't going to leave anyone in the barn this time; he and the Bravo Element were relocating to a site near the ruined castle. The rear security element, consisting of Dave, Chris, and Reuben, were already joining us near the front door.

"Is Jordan getting his panties in a wad again?" Reuben asked.

"Leave it, Reuben," Scott muttered. The last thing we needed was for Jordan to start feeling like he was being ganged up on. Reuben wouldn't get overtly racist just to push buttons, like Phil would, but he'd made it abundantly clear during the entire workup that he figured getting bent out of shape over skin color was stupid.

Of course, Reuben hadn't had his mom beaten to death by white supremacist thugs, but he still had a point.

I was just glad that Dave hadn't stuck his oar in. Our resident shit-talking Mexican with Short Man Syndrome would just have poured gasoline on the flames.

"We're moving out," I told Scott. Not only would it put the simmering dispute to rest, at least for the time being, but we were short on time. It was going to be a long trek back toward Borinka, and we needed to take advantage of every moment of darkness.

I pointed at Phil, who nodded silently and slipped out through the barn door.

Chapter 3

Even given how early it was, the Slovakian countryside was eerily quiet.

During the initial infiltration into the country, we'd heard a constant drone and rumble of aircraft, drones, and vehicles. The peacekeepers, sans the Americans, had been out in force. Now, following the fight in Marianka, it was like the country was dead.

Or breathlessly waiting for something.

I signaled Phil to halt when he looked back. He was a bright silhouette against shades of gray in my PSQ-20s, the thermals outlining him clearly. He signaled his acknowledgment and took two more steps before sinking to a knee next to a towering beech.

The woods were thick, though there wasn't a lot of undergrowth, which made movement fairly easy. I joined Phil in a few moments, sinking to a knee beside him, my rifle over my thigh. With a faint rustle of dry leaves and gear, the rest of the Alpha Element joined us over the next couple of minutes, forming what we could of a circular perimeter on the slope of the hill.

The terrain reminded me a lot of northern Virginia. Hilly and covered in thick woods. The thick carpet of leaves made footing on the slopes somewhat treacherous at times, especially carrying our rucks. It had slowed us down, though we'd still made better time than we had the previous day.

For a few minutes after Dwight had sunk down in the roots of another beech, about two meters uphill from me, none of us moved. We just stayed put, breathing quietly, listening. Only after I was reasonably sure that we weren't close enough to any human habitation to be heard did I key my radio.

"Weeb, Deacon," I called, as quietly as I could. "Are you in position?"

"Deacon, Weeb," Scott replied. "We're in position and we just sent the drone up. We should have some info for you soon."

"Roger," I answered back. "We're halted about five hundred meters from the treeline. Holding here for a bit."

The trouble with doing this op on a timeline, with the sharply limited resources that we had, was that locating one man, even in as small a town as Borinka, got difficult quickly. *Especially* since we didn't want to risk detection before we found him.

If we'd had more teams, we might have been able to get eyes on a bigger portion of the village. Same with more technical assets. Hell, even a local intelligence network would have been useful. But we hadn't had time. And the necessity of sneaking into Slovakia, when the Triarii are often characterized as right-wing terrorists by half the US government, had also necessarily lowered the footprint we could afford. The Hungarians didn't give a damn about American or European perceptions; they'd cut the cord with the EDC the same way the Poles had. They'd been more than happy to let us pass through. But that ended at the Slovak border.

So, my plan was to use the drone to narrow down where we needed to look. It wasn't ideal, but it would have to do. We'd stay hidden in the woods while Scott looked the town over from the air, remotely.

We settled in to wait. I could already feel the morning chill seeping through my sweaty cammies.

***

"Deacon, Weeb."

I hadn't been dozing, but the voice in my ear still startled me a little. The woods were quiet, and I hadn't seen a thing move beyond my teammates occasionally shifting position, birds flitting from tree to tree, or leaves occasionally falling from trees. Scott's voice on the radio broke a deep silence that had gone otherwise unbroken for some time.

"Send it," I answered.

"I've got a couple of possibilities," he reported. "There appear to be militia in the center of town, near the church. Two technicals in sight, and it looks like they've got some kind of checkpoint or something there; I've counted at least twelve armed men. Looks like they took over the church, too."

I didn't say anything, but I clenched my teeth a little at that news. I was pretty sure that the church in Borinka was Catholic, and that these bastards...weren't. Being a recently-baptized Catholic myself, the thought of what a bunch of jihadists were doing in a Catholic church pissed me off.

I could deal with that later. Right at the moment, the focus needed to be on finding Specialist England before he got his head sawed off.

"The cell tracker is picking up a lot of pings toward the east side of town, however," Scott continued. "And I'm pretty sure I've spotted sentries outside of Building 345."

I turned to Greg, but he was already holding out his own tablet. We had two of them; one per comms guy. Not ideal; I would have preferred a laminated printout, especially since a printout didn't glow in the dark, but having printed photomaps for every town and village in southwestern Slovakia that we might have to search hadn't been practical.

Of course, I questioned the practicality of humping the solar charger for the tablets around the hills and woods, too, but we had to do *something*.

Greg had already pulled up the imagery for Borinka, which Scott and I had marked the night before. Each building had a number assigned, making for easy identification of landmarks.

Building 345 was a two-story building with a walled courtyard in front. That was going to be interesting.

"Are they concentrated in just those two places?" I asked.

"It looks that way," Scott said. "It's kind of weird."

I nodded, even though Scott couldn't see me over the radio, as I studied the imagery. It was a little odd, especially given some of the reports we'd gotten before insert of fighting between Slovak militias and the Kosovars, Bosnians, and Syrians who had been forced into Slovakia by the EDC. Why would they split their forces like that, unless they were trying to keep something hidden away?

"There's something else," Scott continued. "I went ahead and did a wide circle with the drone before we narrowed the search area to Borinka. There were two US patrols out and about with M5s and Strykers in southern Stupava, but the Belgians in the next sector, on the north side, don't seem to be moving at all. The checkpoint is manned, but that's it."

That was even weirder. The Belgians had been some of the more aggressive peacekeepers so far. It wasn't like them to turtle. Of course, like most of the EDC military contingents, the "Belgians" didn't have many actual Belgians in their ranks.

The parallels with the later Roman Empire were striking.

Under the circumstances, though, it meant that we had an opening. If the Belgian peacekeepers were confined to their FOB for annual sensitivity training, or whatever, then they'd be that much farther behind the ball if their commander decided they needed to intervene in Borinka.

I kept studying the imagery, thinking. Twelve armed men plus two technicals observed from the drone in the center of town suggested to me that there were a lot more out of sight, especially since sunrise had just hit an hour and a half ago.

"We'll check out 345 first," I decided. "If he's not there, it's going to be a lot easier to pull off and break contact than if we go charging into the middle of town."

I was showing Phil the imagery as I spoke, and he nodded silently. Phil wasn't just my pointman because I didn't know where else to put him; like Jordan was a medic because he'd been an 18D, Special Forces Medic, or Greg was a comm guy because he had an affinity for it. Phil was good at the job, and he was good at navigation, even in thick woods and in the dark. He was better at it than I was; I'd lost track of direction and pace count a couple of times during the night, only picking back up once we hit a known rally point or landmark.

We weren't using GPS, for the obvious reasons.

After a couple of minutes checking his map and compass, Phil got to his feet and started out. I followed, feeling my knees pop as I did so, every muscle protesting the movement. We'd been sitting there in the morning cool for long enough that everything had stiffened up.

I could almost hear Dwight groan as he got up, just as I glanced back. Dwight was past fifty. If any of the rest of us were hurting, he was probably hurting twice as much.

Phil led the way uphill, though he angled his route to lessen the slope somewhat. None of us were young anymore, and hiking "cross-compartment" wasn't something any of us relished.

We worked our way over the shoulder of the hill, and then I could catch glimpses of Borinka through the trees below us. Most of the roofs were red tile, glaring through the gaps in the trees.

Phil kept us to the thicker stands of beeches and oaks, avoiding the narrow meadows between. The clearings weren't large, but with peacekeeper drones overhead, we didn't want to expose ourselves to the sky any more than necessary. Especially not in daylight.

He slowed as we got closer to our target, placing his feet carefully so as not to make noise, pausing every few steps to watch and listen. Visibility was sharply limited by the trees, but it was quiet enough in the woods that noise was going to travel far.

That was how we knew we were in the right place.

A raised voice sounded up ahead in Albanian. The man's words were sharp, like a command. I couldn't make out the words said in reply, but the voice was definitely American. Slightly high-pitched, like a young man, and with a tone that suggested a combination of fear and weariness.

Phil looked back at me, his eyes bright within the green and brown mask of his camouflage paint. I nodded. *Jackpot.*

He moved forward to another tree and eased himself down onto a knee. I joined him moments later, peering through the trees toward the red-roofed house just a few dozen meters from us. There was movement back there, but I couldn't see enough to be sure of what was happening.

I knelt next to Phil, who was staring hard through the trees. "I think they're letting him piss outside," he whispered. "This could be our chance."

31

It was almost too good to be true. If they were out there for a couple more minutes, we could swoop in and grab England before they even knew we were there, and be in and out without having to actually go into the house.

It wasn't to be, though. Even as Greg joined us and I got a semi-clear glimpse of England, still in his OCP cammies, and the bearded, tracksuit-wearing militiaman escorting him, the militiaman got tired of waiting on England and grabbed him by the collar, snatching him around and shoving him toward the house. England squawked with the sudden movement, and I was pretty sure he'd just pissed all over himself. Moments later, they disappeared back into the house, which had a second-floor entrance against the hillside where we crouched.

I didn't speak as the rest of the element converged on the tree. There was nothing for it; our golden opportunity had evaporated, and now we were going to have to do it the hard way. No point in complaining. I'd seen enough, between my handful of combat experiences in the Marine Corps and the fighting Stateside in recent years, to know that things often just went pear-shaped, without any rhyme or reason that we could necessarily see or plan for. You just had to roll with the punches.

Once all of us were gathered, I tapped my head, and every other one of us started dropping his ruck. Taking full rucksacks into a close-quarters fight was not my idea of a good plan. We needed to be agile and mobile, and seventy-pound packs were not conducive. We'd retrieve them again on the way out.

There were all sorts of ways that plan could go wrong, but another lesson I'd learned in recent years was that there's no such thing as a perfect plan.

And I had no idea just how true that was going to turn out at the time.

Once we'd all dropped our rucks, hastily camouflaging them with spider mesh and leaves, I looked around one more time and then tapped Phil on the shoulder. Go time.

He rose smoothly to his feet and moved toward the house. I gave him a couple meters, then followed.

We slipped through the trees like shaggy specters, moving from trunk to trunk, watching for sentries or booby traps.

32

Intel and recent news reports had suggested that the Kosovars and Bosnians were just as eager to blow people up remotely as their Syrian co-religionists were. And there had been a few ops the peacekeepers had run that had gone badly wrong because of perimeter IEDs around target houses.

The woods actually made such traps far easier to conceal. A trained eye could pick out disturbed leaves and undergrowth, but haste and the pre-combat adrenaline dump—coupled with the poor training most of the peacekeepers had gotten in observation—could lead a soldier to easily miss the indicators. There was just a lot of visual noise in the woods, that training geared toward desert and urban environments for the last twenty years didn't necessarily prepare a man for.

But we got within meters of the house without spotting any traps. No pressure plates or mines, so far. It might not last, but I was thankful. Mines and IEDs give me the screaming willies. I'd been involved in more than one hit against People's Revolutionary Action terrorists that had used them extensively, and they never got easier to deal with. Miss one detail, and you were pink mist.

The door in the back had a glass window filling the upper half, so Phil veered toward the corner of the house as he came out of the trees, and I followed, falling in next to him. He'd noted the position of the door handle, and shifted to that side. It would make it easier to open without exposure to the window.

Greg and Jordan pushed past us to cover our six o'clock, while Dwight joined me and Phil. Jordan and Greg would come in after us, but we didn't want to all be focused on the door if one of the militiamen decided to go for a stroll in the woods, just in case.

Phil had his rifle pointed at the door, and I paused to glance around for a second to see that we were all set, before I stepped out and reached around him to check the door. If England's escort had locked it behind them…

But it unlatched quietly and swung open easily. I threw it the rest of the way open and Phil went through as I slapped my off hand back on my OBR's forearm and followed him, my muzzle dropping level over his shoulder as we went.

We were in a short corridor, with an open door to the right, a closed door to the left, and what looked like an open common area straight ahead. Phil moved to the open door, pausing for only the fraction of a second it took for me to drive my knee into the back of his leg, almost catapulting him through the door with me right on his heels.

The room was a bedroom, fully furnished but filthy. It looked like a bum had been squatting there for a while. It was also empty. We swept the room with our muzzles, then turned and started back out, even as Greg and Jordan kicked in the opposite door with a crash and Dwight, who had swept past the door to cover the open space ahead, fired a short burst.

The thunder of the shots hammered at the walls and reverberated through the house. I came out to see the red-bearded man wearing a light-colored jacket and an AK chest rig poorly stuffed with FAMAS mags stagger back against the wall before falling on his face, leaving a red splatter on the white plastered wall behind him.

That tore it. We were made. Without missing a beat, I kneed Dwight with a snapped, "With you," and we drove forward into the common area.

Clearing with a 7.62mm light machinegun wasn't ideal, but it was what we had.

The common area was as deserted as the trashed bedroom had been, and there was more trash and needles on the coffee table in the center, along with some very sketchy-looking stains on the chair and couch. Those details were taken in at a glance as we both turned toward the stairway around the corner.

A man was running up the steps, an MP7 in his hands, and I double-tapped him. With vicious thunderclaps blending together into a catastrophic clash of sound, two 7.62 bullets smashed into the man's chest and head, sending him tumbling backward down the stairs in a welter of blood spatter, his limbs suddenly loose as he crashed down the steps.

There was another door next to the stairwell, and the two of us pushed toward it, with Phil and the rest in tow, Phil posting up on the stairs as Dwight kicked the door hard enough that it cracked the jamb and then Phil and I went inside.

I'd half expected it to be empty, given that nobody had stuck their head out after the gunfire outside. I was right; it was piled with boxes and dark. I flicked on the lights just long enough to make sure that there wasn't anyone hiding the shadows, waiting for us to turn our backs, and then we were moving again.

England's life expectancy had started dropping precipitously as soon as the first shot had been fired. If we didn't find him fast, the odds that we were going to find him alive at all were going to shrink to zero. Especially given the people who were holding him.

Even so, we didn't just race down the steps. That was suicidal, and you didn't get selected for the Grex Luporum teams by being a suicidal moron. We cleared the turn and proceeded at a measured pace down the stairs, leading with our muzzles, careful not to expose ourselves unnecessarily.

None of us were wearing body armor. Risky, yes, but when everything is going in on your back, you've got to make some compromises.

Which was why, as we neared the base of the steps, where the stairwell opened up on what looked like a very open floor plan, Jordan lobbed a flashbang over our shoulders.

It wasn't unexpected; Jordan wouldn't have screwed us that way. We had, in fact, discussed the tactic and trained for it. It took careful timing, which doesn't always work in a combat situation, but this time, it did. Sort of.

There was a man crouched behind a couch, aiming a G36 at the steps as we came down. I spotted him just as Jordan pulled the pin, and I snapped my rifle toward him and fired. I was definitely at a disadvantage, despite having the high ground of the stairs. He had a better angle on me than I had on him.

I was a split second faster. My rifle roared, spitting fire in the dimness of the stairwell. The first round punched through the couch and into him, making him flinch and sending his own burst into the ceiling over my head, showering me with pulverized plaster. Only Hartrick's ruthless training kept me from flinching, even as the trigger broke on the second shot and Jordan's flashbang went off.

We'd trained to slow our roll and look away when the flashbang detonated, but the necessity of finishing my target kept me from doing that. I ate the bang, the brilliant flash stabbing through my skull while the concussion rocked me and made my teeth snap together with a painful *clop*. My head immediately started aching, and there was a big green blotch in my vision, but I drove through it as Dwight and I hit the bottom of the stairs and split, sweeping the ground floor with our muzzles.

Dwight was already shooting as I hooked around the bottom of the stairwell, my equilibrium rocked and trying to see past the spots in my vision. A silhouette filled my sights and I took a half-second to identify the fact that the man had a pistol in his hands, even though he was blinking like he'd just looked straight at the sun. I shot him, putting a single round in his skull from fifteen feet away, and was tracking to my left even as he dropped and Greg came up beside me.

The back of the main room of the bottom floor was set up with a hanging screen, a camera on a tripod, and various crates of weapons, along with a flag I recognized as belonging to the Greater Western Caliphate, the organization that had "replaced" the Islamic State in Europe. Two men with jihadi beards stood there, flanking England, who was already on his knees in front of the camera.

One was pointing his submachinegun at us, and Greg got to him first. Greg's muzzle blast slapped me in the side of the face from less than two feet away, as he put a bullet into the man's chest, and then a follow-up into his head. I was a touch slower, but was already lining up the other one.

That man had a black-bladed knife to England's throat, and was yelling something in Serbo-Croatian. I cut him off with a bullet.

My rifle coughed, and his head snapped back with a crimson spray spattered against the screen behind him. He slumped down, dragging England with him, the knife falling from nerveless fingers.

I was on him in seconds, Greg following me with Phil right behind him. I kept the dead man covered, even though I knew he was dead, then knelt to pull England away from him.

"Specialist England!" I shouted, my voice slightly too loud on account of my hearing having been brutalized by not only the gunfire but also the flashbang. He was going to be just as deafened, though, and even if he wasn't, I didn't especially care. Not the time or the place to worry about decorum. "Are you all right?"

Ordinarily, I'd have personal questions to ask him, that would have verified his identity. We didn't have access to that kind of information, however, even if it had ever been recorded. The regular Army wasn't doing too good with preparations for separated personnel at the time. Besides, his photo had been pretty conclusive. This was him.

He wasn't responding, but he was clearly breathing, staring up at me in shock. I didn't know what this kid's MOS had been, and frankly, I didn't care. I dragged him out from under the dead terrorist and quickly ran my hand over him, checking for blood. Nothing. I hauled him to his feet.

"Time to go, kid," I said. The words were barely out of my mouth when Dwight yelled from the front of the house.

"We've got company!" He was cut off by the thunder of gunfire. "Shooters coming from next door!"

"Upstairs," I barked. "We'll go out the back, the way we came in."

Dwight and Jordan were blazing away from the front, suppressing the oncoming militia. With my off hand twisted in the back of England's blouse and my muzzle pointed at the ceiling, I started for the stairs, Phil moving fast to get in front of me.

We pounded up the steps, and that was when I realized that Scott was calling me over the radio. From the tone of his voice, he'd been yelling for me for a while, but the gunfire and my battered hearing had conspired to keep me from hearing him.

"Deacon, Weeb!" He was practically yelling into my ear.

I groped for my transmit switch and keyed the radio as we got to the top of the steps. More gunfire was echoing from below. "Go, Weeb," I called.

"You'd better hardpoint, buddy," Scott said. "I hope you found the package, because you kicked the hornet's nest. There are militia coming out of the woodwork all over the town.

You've got a couple minutes; I think they were all up to the northwest, but they're coming, and they're heading into the woods, too. You're not going to get out before they're on top of you."

I didn't have time to respond. A silhouette appeared in the doorway as I shoved England into the common area and out of the line of fire. I slapped my off hand back onto my rifle and fired a split second behind Phil.

The man with the black balaclava covering his face and a short-barreled rifle in his hands staggered backward as our bullets tore into him. He didn't fall immediately, apparently because of the second man behind him. We kept shooting, our rifles thundering in the narrow hallway until both dropped.

A small object sailed through the doorway, bounced off the wall, and landed right in front of the two bodies, rolling to come to a rest just against the wall before it exploded, blotting the hallway out in an ugly black cloud with a tooth-rattling *thud.*

Chapter 4

Instinct, hard-wired by brutal training and even more brutal experience, was what saved my life.

As soon as that frag had hit the wall, I had thrown myself out of the hallway, flattening myself against the wall behind Phil, who had ducked back at the same instant. I got the first syllable of, "*Grenade!*" out before it blew.

Fortunately, Greg had seen it, too, and thrown himself back down the stairs, colliding with Dwight on the way and sending both of them tumbling in a heap to the landing. But they were alive and clambering back up, even as Jordan continued to lay down covering fire from the base of the steps.

I didn't dare hold position for long; that frag hadn't been a final solution. There were going to be more militiamen coming in after it. I stepped back out and drove down the hallway, Phil getting up and coming with me, our rifles up and pointed at the back door.

Acrid smoke was still swirling in the narrow space as I stepped over the mangled bodies lying in the doorway and pushed outside, Phil right behind me.

I almost collided with a man in a thick jacket and Islamic cap. He stared in shock for a second, his FAMAS off-line, while my OBR's muzzle jammed into his upper chest.

I pulled the trigger in a near-panic, hammering three rounds into him at contact range, just as fast as the trigger would reset, leaning into the weapon as the muzzle blast blew bits of fabric and chunks of flesh, blood, and bone everywhere.

I kept tracking up as he fell backward, my last round blowing off the top of his skull before he dropped out of my sights and exposed the man right behind him. He was already staggering and starting to fall; my bullets had punched clear through the first man and into him. I still finished him off with a headshot, just before a long, panicked burst of automatic fire tore into the side of the house and shredded the air over my head with a painful, staccato ripping sound.

I threw myself flat as I returned fire, knowing that I wasn't going to get anywhere close. The best I could hope for was that a few rounds going in their general direction was going to give them pause.

More return machinegun fire raked the ground next to me as I shrank back against the wall, kicking up little showers of dirt and shredded vegetation. I heard three shots from behind me, the muzzle blasts smacking me in the back of the head, and then Phil was yelling at me to get up and get back inside.

On my elbows and knees, I scrambled backward until Phil reached out and grabbed my belt, hauling me back through the door. I knocked an elbow painfully against the jamb as my rifle almost got caught up. More bullets smacked splinters off the door overhead as we drew back inside the house.

"Can't go that way," I panted.

"There are more on the street," Jordan said. "They're canalized by the courtyard out front, but we're not getting out that way, either."

Stepping back behind Phil and Greg as they covered the back door, I found my radio transmit switch. "Mike Five Zero," I called, "Golf Lima Ten-Six."

"Go ahead, Deacon," Victor Draven, the mortar section team leader replied a moment later.

"Immediate fire mission," I told him. "Targets Alpha One Seven Seven, Alpha One Eight Seven, and Alpha Two Three Three." Part of the planning process had involved setting pre-arranged targets for the mortar section that had infiltrated with us, and was currently set up about three kilometers away. If anything, they'd had a more grueling movement than we'd had; even 60mm mortars ain't light, never mind the rounds themselves.

"Stand by," Scott broke in. He sounded a little breathless, and there was a different sound to his transmission. I strongly suspected that Scott and the Bravo Element had already broken down and were on their way down the hill from the ruined castle.

40

"Do not fire on Alpha Two Three Three. I say again, do not fire on Alpha Two Three Three!" There was a brief pause. "There is an American patrol entering the town from the northwest. Avoid firing on the northwest of the town."

I keyed my mic twice to acknowledge that I'd heard. More fire was hammering at the sides of the house, and Jordan was shooting from the landing again. "This is not a good defensive position, Matt!" Dwight bellowed over the noise.

"I know," I replied. We were hemmed in by buildings to either side, with the woods behind us and an open street—clearly covered by fire—in front of us. Dwight had pushed up into the common area and was barricaded at the top of the stairs with his Mk 48 pointed at the back door as we pushed past him. "We'll hold here until the mortars can clear them out or at least make some of them go to ground."

I knew it was risky. Mortars weren't always the most accurate; during that dust-up on the coast of Lebanon a few years back, I'd lost five friends when one of 3/1's mortar sections dropped five hundred meters short. But we were five guys and a hostage surrounded by way too many bad guys. We needed all the firepower we could get.

That brought me up short. Leaving Dwight and Phil to cover the back while Jordan and Greg covered the front from the landing, I moved to the stairs and tore the FAMAS out of one of the dead Kosovars' hands. Getting his chest rig off took a bit more effort, but I stepped up to England where he was crouched as far back in the corner as he could get.

Squatting down, I held out the French bullpup. "You ever fire one of these?" I asked.

He shook his head, his eyes wide, but he took the weapon. I was pretty sure he was a support soldier, but he had to have fired a rifle at *some* point. He didn't speak for a moment, in large part because Dwight ripped off a burst out the back door. A 7.62mm machinegun gets *loud* in enclosed spaces.

"I haven't," he croaked. It was almost more of a squeak. He was scared stiff, despite having just been rescued from certain, painful death. Granted, the contempt that I felt for him was based on my own hopes that I would have fought rather than

41

let myself get scooped up by a bunch of Albanian jihadi savages, but he needed to harden the hell up fast.

"Mag well, mag release, bolt release, selector," I said loudly, pointing out each control. "You call yourself a soldier, so it's time to cowboy up. You're one of my shooters until we deliver you to your command." Probably to face a very thorough inquiry, but that wasn't my problem.

He nodded shakily, looking down at the rifle in his hands and not making eye contact. I shoved the chest rig jammed with FAMAS mags at him, then moved to look over Phil's shoulder.

Just then, there was a brief lull in the gunfire, and I listened hard. Yes, I could hear it, just barely. A faint but rising whiffling sound.

If you've ever been under a mortar barrage, you'll remember that sound until your dying day. It'll make your butt pucker the same way until then, too.

I resisted the urge to drop flat, knowing that they were friendly. Of course, "friendly" has a very loose definition when it comes to incoming fire.

With a *crump* that shook the house, the first round hit in the street, just two hundred meters to our west. It was quickly followed by several more, as fainter *crumps* sounded to the north and south of the narrow valley. The incoming small arms fire slackened further.

"Time to go," I announced. I keyed the radio again. "Mike Five Zero, Golf Lima Ten-Six," I sent. "Repeat all." Once again, I was taking chances, but with the initial rounds close enough to the targets, and not falling on our heads, I was breathing a little easier. We weren't *likely* to get dropped on by our own guys.

"Roger," Draven replied. A moment later, that same nerve-shredding whiffle was sounding overhead again, but we were already pushing for the back door.

"Weeb, Deacon," I sent. "We're moving to the near RV point. We'll link up there."

"Roger," Scott gasped in reply. He had to be moving fast. Knowing Scott, he was anxious to get down the hill and get stuck in. He had to already be chafing about just having to watch, the day before. "Air is on the way. Crossed into Slovak airspace five minutes ago."

Holy hell, had it been five minutes already? Time gets funny when you're in the middle of a firefight.

Phil led the way out the back door, though he preceded his exit with a high-concentration smoke. It wasn't going to keep the bad guys from spraying bullets into the cloud, but it would give us *some* concealment on the way out.

He pushed out into the smoke with me on his heels, dragging England behind me, just as the next round of mortar strikes landed. The impacts and explosions shook the ground and rattled the windows of those houses that hadn't already had theirs shattered. Black smoke and dirt fountained up into the morning sky as we pushed out of the cloud of white obscurant and into the woods.

I could distantly hear the squeal of tracks. I glanced northwest, but there were too many trees and too many houses between our side of Borinka and the Army patrol coming in. Or at least, approaching. Despite the gunfire and mortars, I doubted that the patrol was going to actually move into the town right away. The rules of engagement were way too strict for that. They'd set up outside and monitor the situation while they waited for word from FOB Keystone as to whether they were allowed to load their weapons or not.

It briefly occurred to me that we *could* try to link up with the patrol and drop England with them. Questions would be asked, but we'd have to deal with far more of them if we showed up at Keystone with him. Granted, we'd have to fight our way through what increasingly sounded like dozens, if not closer to a hundred, insurgents to get there.

No, better to break contact under cover of the mortars and the incoming gunships, and then find a way to get England back to the Army later.

We were all out of the house and pushing up the hill when things went *really* pear-shaped.

There was a sudden, wild exchange of gunfire ahead, and Scott was practically screaming in my ear. "Deacon, wave off! Contact, contact, contact!" He couldn't say anything more, but by then he didn't have to. There was a cacophonous, crackling roar in the woods above us. Scott and the Bravo Element had to have just run into a sizeable force moving through the forest. Probably moving to try to cut us off.

At almost the same time, a massive explosion at the northwest end of Borinka shook the ground, making the trees wave as the shock rattled my teeth. I looked over to see a towering cloud of dust and smoke rising over the far end of the town.

I already knew what had happened. The American peacekeepers had gotten a little too close, and the bad guys had had an IED waiting for them.

A moment later, I heard the familiar *bang* of an RPG, and a moment later, ugly black smoke started rising above the red tile roofs.

Borinka had turned into one hell of a mousetrap. Except we were Triarii. Not mice.

"Push," I told Phil, as a bullet slapped bark and splinters off the tree just in front of us. I pivoted, dropping to a knee and returning fire, the second of my hasty pair of shots taking a man in a Multicam jacket and track pants in the chest. He twisted and fell.

Phil was already moving, pressing toward the stand of trees where we'd left our rucks. Under the circumstances, donning the heavy packs might have seemed like a bad idea, but we needed everything in those packs if we were going to get out of Slovakia and back to Hungary alive.

Short of turning ourselves over to the Army, of course. Given the state of things back home, that could either be a good idea, or a death sentence. It largely depended on the news cycle of the day, and the leanings of the commander. It was depressing, that the unrest and sociopathic violence back home had even spread its rot into the Armed Forces overseas, but those were the days we were living in.

I had no idea, at the time, just how bad it could get.

We started leapfrogging, as the enemy picked up their fire again, laying down our own covering fire as we went. Those with rifles tried to keep it to single shots and pairs, looking for targets before we fired, but Dwight was doing what a machinegunner was supposed to do. He was raking the treeline below us with long, ravening bursts of fire, smacking plaster off of walls, shredding leaves, splintering trees, and forcing the enemy to get their heads down or die.

Phil reached the rucks first, dropping to a knee and searching for a target while I ran to join him, my fist clenching the strap of England's chest rig as I propelled him forward. He'd fired a few rounds, but the unfamiliar rifle and his own disorientation was making him almost as dangerous to the rest of us as the enemy.

Jordan and Greg passed Dwight, who was still laying down the hate toward Borinka. In retrospect, there were probably still some Slovak civilians living there; I just hoped that they'd had the good sense to keep their heads down as soon as things started cooking off. After all, they had to have had *some* warning when the bad guys started taking over their houses, patrolling their town square, and laying IEDs on their road.

More gunfire rattled and echoed through the woods above us as Dwight ceased fire and lumbered the rest of the way to the stand of trees. The bad guys seemed to have backed off a bit for the moment, but even so, it sounded like Scott and the rest of the team were in a bad spot up there.

"Deacon, Weeb," Scott called. The noise of gunfire was almost drowning him out over the radio, coming through my earpiece as well as echoing down the hillside. "Hold your position; we're coming to you!"

Before I could answer, I spotted a figure dashing from behind a building toward a tree, downslope. I didn't have much of a shot through all the vegetation, but I pivoted and fired. I might have hit him, but I was pretty sure I missed. "This is not a good position, Weeb!" I replied.

"Friendly!" Chris was yelling from upslope. Phil already had his OBR pointed at him, and shifted as he came through the trees, the jute string and leaves on his ghillie flapping with the movement. He was pelting down the slope while more gunfire hammered uphill. A moment later, Scott came down after him, while another long burst echoed through the forest. That would be Tony.

"Dwight!" I barked. "North!" There was still a substantial threat in the town, but if the bad guys were breathing down Bravo Element's necks, that was going to be the most immediate problem.

Chris skidded to a halt near us, dropping to a knee, his breath heaving as he brought his rifle up. Scott joined me a second later, as a new group of ten or fifteen shooters in a rag-tag assemblage of camouflage, tracksuits, and civilian clothes came boiling out of the gap between Building 345 and 346. Jordan was on his belly behind a tree, and dropped the first with a single shot before shifting to the next one, even as Greg and I opened fire, killing three more and scattering the rest.

Scott was panting as he reloaded. "There's at least a company up there," he said, his chest heaving. "They walked right into us as we were coming down the hill. Fucking trees."

I didn't reply right away, having to duck down as a burst of 5.56 fire stitched the trees just overhead, raining splinters and bits of leaves down on our heads. And just as I opened my mouth to say something, a new sound drowned out a lot of the gunfire.

The heavy, metallic *thunk, thunk, thunk* of an M5's 50mm gun was pretty unmistakable. The peacekeepers had decided to stop sitting there and taking it.

Things had just gotten a lot more complicated.

Chapter 5

Muzzle flashes flickered in the woods above us, and bullets smacked into tree boles and kicked dirt and leaves up around us. Tony swung his Mk 48 up and ripped off the rest of his belt in reply, the stuttering roar seemingly amplified by the strobing flame spitting from the machinegun's shortened barrel.

The volume of fire was just too high, though. There was no way we were getting up over the ridge; the bad guys were pushing hard to get above us, and they were going to cut us off. I glanced over our position. It wasn't good. We had a little bit of cover there in that stand of trees, but there was high ground on one side and houses on the other, with far too little standoff. We were dropping the bad guys as they showed themselves, but there were a *lot* of them. Too many to just be hanging out in Borinka just because.

This had been a trap, and England had been the bait.

"The birds are about ten minutes out," Scott said between shots.

"We might not last ten minutes!" David yelled.

Unfortunately, he was right. Let the militia get the high ground in these woods and we'd be done for. "Back to the town," I snapped. "By twos, fall back." We were going to have to find a different way out.

I was also worried about those Army cats in the armored vehicles up the road, for a couple of reasons. I was pretty sure they'd gotten hit, hard. The black smoke that I could just see through the trees, rising into the sky to the northeast, suggested that at least one vehicle had been the victim of a catastrophic kill. Possibly more than one.

On the one hand, having American soldiers engaged within weapons range of us was a problem, simply because I didn't want my team on the receiving end of 50mm HE shells. We hadn't exactly coordinated with the Army. The Triarii don't risk that, as a rule. Or we didn't at the time.

But just like in Marianka, I didn't want to just let those kids get slaughtered. Our country might be coming apart at the seams, but they'd still signed up to defend her, and hadn't asked to get thrown into a snake-pit of a "peacekeeping" operation, with one hand tied behind their backs and their fellow peacekeepers watching them with an eye toward slipping a knife between their ribs.

I did some quick mental calculation and called Draven again. "Mike Five Zero, Golf Lima Ten-Six. Adjust fire from Alpha Alpha One Eight Seven, left five hundred, drop thirty, fire for effect." It was a quick and dirty solution, but I thought it might be close enough.

I was going to use every trick I had up my sleeve.

"Roger, left five hundred, drop thirty," Draven replied. A moment later, though the distant *pop*s of the discharges were drowned out by all the other weapons fire around us, the 60mm shells came screaming down out of the sky and impacted on the hillside above us, shaking the ground with heavy *thud*s and blowing vicious black clouds of dirt, debris, and smoke into the sky. The fire from above slackened considerably.

With that brief respite, we moved fast, sprinting in long bounds back toward the target house. It wasn't ideal from a defensive standpoint, but it would provide *some* cover and concealment, more than we had out there in the woods.

I ended up behind Jordan, who had taken lead. We moved from tree to tree, having to pause about every other bound to fire at somebody in one of the windows ahead or ducking around a tree to the east or west. The little bastards were everywhere. There had to have been two or three hundred militia crammed into tiny Borinka.

And I was pretty sure that none of them were Slovaks.

We got to the back door, where we'd first made entry, the rest of the team fanning out around us to cover our backs. Scott had corralled England and was keeping him close, sparing him as much attention as possible to keep his rifle pointed in a safe direction.

The door was still open, the jamb chewed and splintered by bullet impacts and the grenade explosion. Those two corpses were still in the doorway, too. With a quick breath, Jordan and I plunged inside behind our rifles.

The hallway was clear, and we quickly flowed into the first room while Phil and Reuben took the door across from us and the rest moved toward the common area. A quick glance confirmed that the room was as empty as it had been when we'd left.

It might seem a little redundant, clearing a building we'd evacuated only minutes before, but you just never knew. We'd given up the real estate, and it was entirely possible that some of the bad guys had taken it back in our absence.

Within a minute, the house was confirmed clear. The bodies were right where we'd left them. Scott shoved England into the same corner where he'd been ensconced before, and I got on the radio. "Whiskey Six-Four, Golf Lima Ten-Six." I wasn't sure if the birds were in range yet, but the sooner I could get in contact with them, the better.

"Go ahead, Golf Lima Ten-Six." I'd worked with our lead gunship pilot, Gene Keck, before. The guy had more rotary combat time than just about anyone else in the Triarii. He'd been flying birds in Afghanistan in *2002*, for crying out loud.

"We are hardpointed in a two-story building," I sent. I rattled off the rough coordinates that I'd read off the map. Again, after the GPS system had gotten spoofed *twice*, once resulting in an entire platoon of Rangers in Syria getting decimated, we didn't trust it. "Look for green smoke in the courtyard." I pointed to Chris, who dug a smoke grenade out of his rig and headed downstairs. "Beware of mortars from the north; Mike Five Zero is set up and supporting us from there. Advise you stay over the town itself. Also, be advised, there are Green Force vehicles under fire at the northwest end of the town. Appears to be at least one vehicle burning. Watch your fires in that direction."

"Acknowledged, Golf Lima Ten-Six," Gene replied. He sounded even older than he looked, though that was probably largely because of the cigarettes he chain-smoked constantly, even while flying. It drove his crew chiefs nuts, but he was old enough and experienced enough that he just didn't give a damn anymore. "We are two minutes out. I have black smoke…and I have your green smoke. Heaviest concentrations of enemy personnel?"

"In the woods to our north and in the center of town," I replied. I was briefly tempted to just let Gene and his Dash Two level the whole town, but that was probably going to get a lot of Slovak civilians killed along with the Kosovars and Syrians. Strictly speaking, the blood would be on the militia's hands; you don't hide in civilian populations and then get to proclaim your innocence when the civilians get mowed down when the enemy has to go in after you. I knew that. But it still wouldn't sit well with me to just have the birds mow down Slovak civvies if we could help it.

I wasn't there as a peacekeeper. I was there as a hunter, doing what needed to be done. Hearts and minds didn't matter a damn to me. Didn't matter a damn to my team, either. Not our job. Not our concern. But there's what's pragmatic, and there's what's right.

"Roger that," Gene replied. "Keep your heads down. Thirty seconds."

Ten years before, AH-1Z Vipers in non-governmental hands would have been unthinkable. Times change. And Colonel Santiago had some serious connections.

Ours were painted a dark, olive green snakeskin camouflage pattern, in contrast to the Marine gray that I'd gotten used to during my Active Duty days. But they were still the same lean dragonfly shapes roaring over the hills, almost brushing the hilltops. I saw the first one before I heard it, glancing out the east-facing window in the common area.

Gene and his wingman came in fast and low, rockets stabbing from their underwing pods, streaking down on faint smoke trails to impact in the woods with bone-shaking *crumps* that made the mortar strikes seem like firecrackers in comparison. Shockwaves rolled over the town, shattering windows and carrying debris that smashed into walls and ceilings in billowing clouds of smoke and fragmentation. The two gunships roared overhead, so low that the snarl of their rotors shook the house around us.

In the aftermath, I could hear the low, growling buzzsaw noise of miniguns off to the east. That would be the troop carriers. They'd started as Sikorsky S-70s, the same basic airframe as the military's old UH-60 Blackhawks. They still weren't as fancy as the newer UH-87s, or the V-280 tilt-rotors, but they did the job. Hearing them meant that our ground reinforcements had come in with the gunships. Bradshaw's thirty-man infantry section was prepping their LZ.

That didn't lessen the problems we had ahead of us, but it meant that we had more options.

The M5s were still firing, the rattle and thunder of 7.62 and .50 cal fire being regularly punctuated by the much heavier and louder 50mms. They had to be tearing that end of Borinka up. I was content for the moment to stay where we were, with plenty of houses to act as cover between us and those big guns, but if they decided to start advancing, we'd have a problem.

I moved to Greg and grabbed his shoulder. "Have you still got the peacekeeper fills?" I asked.

He nodded. "Why yes friend, it just so happens that I do," he said. I rolled my eyes. Greg's irrepressible cheerfulness could get downright goofy at times, and never so much as in the middle of a firefight that was steadily blasting a small Slovak village to rubble.

"Contact that patrol if you can," I said. There would be questions asked, questions that I hoped to avoid answering. If certain people found out how the Triarii ended up with up-to-the-minute US military crypto and comms plans, there would be hell to pay. But for the moment, we needed to go ahead and burn that capability, just so that we didn't end up in a firefight with our own people.

Nominally our own people, I should probably say. There was good reason why we were referring to regular US forces as "Green" instead of "Blue." "Green" means "allied." "Blue" means "friendly."

There's a difference.

Greg swung his ruck off his back, moving toward the window and away from the hallway as the staccato thunder of

20mm cannon fire raked the hillside outside. The small arms fire on the ground had slackened somewhat. Presumably, even fanatical Islamists wanted to keep their heads down when the sky started raining fire and high-velocity metal.

"Any US forces in Borinka, this is Golf Lima Ten," Greg called. "Any US forces in Borinka, this is Golf Lima Ten."

He tried for several more seconds, listening and frowning a little. Finally, he twisted the dial to transmit in the open and repeated the call.

I waited, standing over him, my rifle in my hands and pointed generally toward that back door. We were out of the fight at the moment; the bad guys weren't trying to rush the house with those Vipers overhead. If they got reinforcements, that might change, so I wasn't relaxing. But we'd gotten a breather, between the mortars and the birds.

Greg handed me the handset. It was connected to an actual Harris PRC-152, which was why we were able to talk to the Army, despite their having newer PRC-188s. Or would have, if we were on a covered channel. The fact that he'd had to switch to transmitting in the clear didn't bode well for our crypto source. "Doomhammer One Five," Greg told me, unable to keep a grin off his face as he said it. I just shook my head as I took the handset. I remembered coming up with goofy, "warrior" callsigns for the company commander's consideration in the Marine Corps. Some things never change.

"Doomhammer One Five," I said as I keyed the handset and Greg chuckled. "This is Golf Lima Ten Six."

"This is Doomhammer One Five," a harried-sounding voice replied. "I take it that air is yours?"

"It is," I replied. If not for those birds, this probably wouldn't have been a good idea. There had been attempts to spoof American comms before. It didn't get much play in the media—it went against the narrative of absolute American technological supremacy—but it had happened. "What's your status?"

"We're kind of stuck at the moment," he replied. "I've got a mobility kill blocking the road behind us, and a catastrophic in front of us. We might be able to get past and push to the east, but we're blocked to the west."

"Casualties?" I asked.

"Just the guys in the lead vehicle," was the reply.

I frowned at that. With the intensity of the firefight, I would have expected more than that. Unless they hadn't dismounted before entering the village.

With a sudden sinking sensation, I was sure that was the case. It would fit with the level that training had sunk to in recent years. I'd learned tactics from the Triarii that I'd never heard of while I'd been in the Marine Corps. Basic stuff, too; the kinds of things that once you understood them, it seemed suicidal to abandon them.

One of those tactics being, you don't go into an urban environment with armored vehicles without having infantry supporting them, rooting out the anti-tank teams hiding in the buildings and spotting the IEDs alongside the road.

"I've got mortar and air support for a few more minutes," I told him. "Can you see the green smoke ahead of you?"

There was a long pause. "Negative," he answered. "Visibility to the east is down to a few meters."

"Push past the wreck and come east," I told him. "We are hardpointed in the building with the green smoke out front." I paused. "I have reinforcements coming from the east, but you'd better get dismounts out and come to us, if the west route is blocked."

"Dismounts," he repeated, sounding a little rattled. "Right. Dismounts." I couldn't see him, but he seemed to shake himself. "Golf Lima Ten Six, do you have comms with Gatekeeper?"

I frowned and glanced at Greg. "Gatekeeper?" I asked, keeping my thumb off the handset's transmit button.

"FOB Keystone's main TOC," Greg answered. I nodded. This could get dicey.

"Negative, Doomhammer One Five," I replied.

There was another long pause. "I was hoping that you did," he said. "Neither do we. That's why we switched to open comms."

If I hadn't been in the middle of one of the biggest combined arms fights I'd ever seen, that would have had a lot more impact. In retrospect, it *should* have had a lot more impact

53

than it did. It was the first indicator of just how badly things had gone. But I was focused on trying to get out of that hellish little village in one piece, and hopefully get the other Americans out with us.

"We can sort that out later, Doomhammer," I said. "I suggest you get moving while I've still got air overhead."

"We're en route," he said. The thunder of the fight had died down, and I could just hear what sounded like the squeal of tracks in the distance.

"Roger," I answered. "If you see men with American kit in plain olive drab, hold your fire. They are friendlies. They won't fire on you if not fired upon."

He acknowledged, with a pretty blatant question in the tone of his voice, but I let him hang and handed the handset back to Greg. "India Quebec Five Six, Golf Lima Ten Six," I called over my own radio.

"Send it, Deacon," Tyler Bradshaw had been a platoon sergeant in the 173rd Airborne, once upon a time. I'd met him when I'd first joined the Triarii, and had been happy to see him again when his infantry section had been assigned as our trail element.

"We've got the Green Force element from the west side of town pushing to link up with us, Flat," I said. Reportedly, Tyler had gotten his callsign from getting everything prepped for a hit, only to get into his vehicle and give the go order before discovering that his vehicle had a flat tire. "Recommend you go firm at the east side of town and wait for us. Their commander sounds a little shaky; I can only imagine what the guys on the triggers are thinking."

"Roger that," Bradshaw replied. "We're setting in to cover your withdrawal. We have eyes on your position from here."

I clicked the mic twice and turned my attention back to the outside. The enemy had backed off under the Vipers' onslaught, but that could change at any moment. I'd seen it happen in Africa.

And elsewhere.

"Dwight, Phil, hold on the back door," I said. "Greg, Chris, Jordan, with me." I looked around. "Dave, keep an eye on the package." So far, England had hardly made a sound since we'd snatched him, and he wasn't going out of his way to join the fight, either. Given his performance so far, that might actually have been a good thing, on reflection.

The four of us headed down the stairs, passing Tony and Reuben, who fell in with us as we descended to the ground floor. We didn't bother to re-clear it that time; Tony had had eyes on the front door the entire time, and would have cut anyone coming in in half with the Mk 48.

The green smoke grenade was burning itself out. I pulled another one out of my chest rig and popped it, tossing it against the courtyard wall. The noise of the advancing vehicles was getting louder, but they weren't there yet, and with those boys and girls already rattled by losing a vehicle and its crew, I didn't want to take chances.

With Tony and Reuben taking up supporting positions by the door, the rest of us pushed toward the gate.

It was open; the bad guys hadn't closed it the last time they'd tried to rush the house. Or maybe a couple had made a run for it when we'd come pouring in and had started killing everyone with a gun. Didn't matter. I didn't have to pause on the way out to open it, but it also meant that we had slightly less concealment.

I crouched by the opening and eased my head out to peer down the street. It was currently deserted, the enemy having retreated to shelter. The shadow of one of Gene's Vipers raced over the street and the buildings on the south side, as the rotors kicked the drifting smoke and dust into fantastical whorls with a deep-throated snarl.

The burning vehicle was around the curve, downhill and toward the west, but it was belching thick black smoke skyward. There might have been more smoke behind it, which probably was left over from the IED and the disabled vehicle in the rear of the formation.

I could see the questing barrel of the lead M5's 50mm cannon ahead as the low, tracked vehicle lumbered up the street. To their credit, the Army boys had dismounts out, and though they were still keeping way too close to the track, they at least had weapons out and were scanning the buildings around them.

55

Not quite thoroughly enough, though. Or at least, they weren't looking far enough out.

I saw movement above and to the south, and snapped my rifle in that direction, hoping that *my* movement wasn't about to attract the wrong kind of attention from the jumpy kids in OCP camouflage, wearing way too much armor and gadgetry down the street. I steadied the scope briefly, focusing, searching the second-floor windows of the orange-painted, plastered house…

The man pointing what looked an awful lot like a Panzerfaust 3 was set back from the window; I couldn't see much more than the tip of the warhead. I was in a bad spot. And I didn't have comms with Doomhammer right at that moment.

"Greg," I started to say, but Greg was already on it.

"Doomhammer One Five, Golf Lima Ten," he called, the handset to his ear. "RPG, second floor, two o'clock!"

The turret started to move, but they were going to get hammered before they could bring that gun to bear. Without much else in the way of options, I put my reticle on the edge of the window and fired, pumping five shots as fast as I could pull the trigger through the opening. Hopefully I could at least keep his head down.

I just hoped that the mech infantry out there didn't get the wrong idea and think I was shooting at them.

The nipple of the Panzerfaust's warhead disappeared from the window. A moment later, the M5 surged forward, the 50mm gun traversing faster than I had expected it to, and blew a gaping hole in the wall where the window had been with a tooth-jarring concussion. Fragments, dust, and debris rained down into the street as I ducked back into the courtyard.

"Affirmative, Doomhammer One Five, that's us," Greg said into the radio. "We'll come out when you come on line with us, and move to the east, out of town." He paused. "Doomhammer says thanks," he announced, hanging the handset back on his ruck strap.

"'Doomhammer' needs to tell his kids to keep their eyes out and look farther away than twenty-five meters," I muttered.

With a deep rumble and the squeal and rattle of the tracks, the lead M5 pulled up next to the gate. There were only three vehicles left; the one M5 and two Strykers. There wasn't going to be a lot of room inside any of those vehicles.

Not that I had any intention of getting inside one of those massive rolling targets if I had the choice.

The M5 Powell looked a lot like a tank, except that it wasn't one, not quite. It was lower to the ground than the old M2 Bradley it had replaced, and could only carry four troops in the back, but it had the 50mm cannon instead of the old 25mm Bushmaster chain gun the Brad had mounted. This one was covered in hex-pattern black, green, and brown camouflage, that stood out on the street lined with white, orange, and red buildings.

The big, angular vehicle, which couldn't quite figure out if it was an IFV or a tank, sat and rumbled, while the commander's hatch opened and a young-looking man wearing a commander's helmet stuck his head out. He heaved himself up out of the hatch, revealing that he was wearing all the kit that he was required to wear on patrol, and struggled over the coaming before clambering down to the ground.

The soldier's load seems to fluctuate with the coming and going of leadership, both civil and military. After the GWOT was thought to have sort of petered out—don't be fooled; it didn't—it seemed like things were starting to get a little better; the strict requirements for armor had been slackened, and the troops were allowed to lighten their load a little bit.

The Slovakia mission had changed that again. With the commanders in-country unwilling to risk their troops on what most Americans back home considered a sideshow, and the uneasy relationship with both the EDC countries and the locals, the rules of engagement had gone full turtle again. The young man was wearing his helmet, front, back, and side plates, neck guard, crotch guard, and even the shoulder guards that had gone out before I'd joined up. He staggered when his boots hit the ground, and he'd been riding in an armored vehicle the whole time.

Glancing around, his short-barreled M37A2 in his hands, he looked nervous. He dashed toward us, ducking into the courtyard next to me. "You Golf Lima Ten?"

"Yeah, that's us," I said, holding out a hand. "Deacon."

"Sergeant Killian," he said, grasping my hand. We were both wearing gloves, but I wasn't going to strip mine for a handshake then and there, and apparently, neither was he. His handshake was firm enough, though he kept glancing around at us almost as nervously as he was the rest of their surroundings. We were clearly way too non-standard to be Army or Marines; we were wearing plain green fatigues under our ghillies, the birds in the air didn't have standard Army paint schemes, and nobody in the Army was carrying LaRue OBRs as standard equipment. "Who are you guys?"

"We can discuss that later," I said, "when we're not in contact." I pointed to the east. "We've got foot mobiles set in at the east end of town to cover our extract. Once we're clear, we can talk."

He stared at me for a second, but then just nodded. Apparently, pulling his ass out of the fire counted for a lot. I was sure there were going to be uncomfortable questions later. We could deal with them when the time came; I wasn't going to leave fellow Americans high and dry in the middle of an ambush, no matter what it cost me.

"How do you want to work this?" he asked.

"I'll bring the rest of my team down, and we'll move out together," I said. "The birds can cover us until we get clear of the town."

Once again, he looked at me, and I could see the wheels turning. But he was enough of a pro that he wasn't going to ask. Not the time, nor the place.

Scott was already bringing the rest of the team down out of the house. Killian's eyes took us in; the OBRs, the Mk 48s…and the missing Specialist England, carrying a captured FAMAS. His eyes widened a little at that, but he just turned and started barking orders to his dismounts before starting to laboriously clamber back up onto his M5.

A few minutes later, the vehicle lurched into motion again, this time with my team flanking it on either side of the road and fifty yards ahead. Together, Triarii and US Army peacekeepers started to move out of Borinka, while the Vipers circled overhead, their engines growling like birds of prey.

We were almost out of the woods. Or, I thought we were.

I was sorely mistaken.

Chapter 6

We were on the wrong side of the ridge when we finally halted.

There was no real road leading out of Borinka to the east. We'd had to follow the cleared powerlines; the woods were too thick for the vehicles to traverse.

As soon as we'd gotten clear, Bradshaw and I had linked up, and then we Triarii faded into the woods, though we stayed close enough to support the Army survivors. We'd turned England over to Killian; hopefully with him in Army hands, we could fade sooner with fewer questions asked.

At first, the regulars had stayed close to their vehicles, out in the open. Bradshaw and I had traded incredulous glances at that; had nobody taught these kids *anything*? Killian had picked up on it quick enough, though, and snapped at his fireteam leaders to get their men into the trees. Their woodscraft still sucked, mostly, but it was an improvement.

Now we were halted, the three vehicles forming an outward-facing triangle, in a clearing overlooking Bratislava itself. The Vipers had peeled off, their rocket racks empty and their fuel getting low, skimming the treetops toward the northeast to skirt around the capitol city before turning southeast toward Hungary. Bradshaw and I had already sent the S-70s off to stand by just over the border. Some of the guys didn't look all that convinced, but Bradshaw and I both agreed that we couldn't just leave American soldiers hanging while we flew off.

Some of that was because something Killian had said over the radio had slowly come to mind as we'd moved away from Borinka. Something that really, really bothered me.

I walked over to his track, where he was giving his final instructions for the halt to his squad leaders and fireteam leaders. I stood aside, my OBR cradled easily in my hands, and watched for a moment.

It was to his credit that Killian was briefing all of his subordinate leaders at once. He was pushing out as much information as possible, and keeping it simple instead of relying on a game of telephone. Under different circumstances, it might be considered micromanaging, but here and now, it was just common sense. He didn't want time wasted with passing word. He wanted to make sure all of his guys were fully informed.

I say "guys" but there were a couple of females in the unit. With one exception, they were keeping their heads down. That one exception was the halfway good-looking redhead who was hovering near the briefing and eyeballing me suspiciously the entire time.

It was interesting to watch, actually. There had been a couple of females who had come to my weapons platoon while I'd been on Active Duty; mixed-sex combat units had been shown to be a bad idea for some time, and the forced integration hadn't gone well *anywhere*, but the powers that be couldn't—nay, *wouldn't*—admit that they'd screwed the pooch, so they kept pushing them in, where most of them would last until they got hurt or pregnant.

Or both.

Looking around that bunch of scared kids with rifles, I saw something that I had noticed many years before. One of the big concerns with mixed-sex combat units was the very real biological response that young men have around females, particularly pretty ones. They lose their heads and fall all over themselves to impress the young women. Not only is it a distraction, but it breeds jealousy and division in what *needs* to be a tight-knit group.

But in this kind of physically demanding job, something else crops up, and I was seeing it in spades here. It was entirely possible that one or more of the men were sleeping with the females. It was almost certain, actually. But there was an underlying current of sullen resentment that overwhelmed everything else.

I figured I knew why. The women simply *couldn't* carry as much as the men. And being in a mech unit, it meant that they couldn't pull as much of the weight when it came to maintenance, either. Which meant that, more often than not, the male soldiers had to step in and take over from the women. I'd known a couple in the Marine Corps who had requested transfers out of the Weapons Company because they were simply ashamed at having to defer to much bigger, much stronger young men. Some of the others had stuck with it out of pride until they got hurt, or, far more often, used their sex as their excuse, and delighted in getting the young male Marines to carry their weight for them.

I'd been fortunate enough not to have to go to combat with any of the latter. Under these circumstances, I hoped that these kids could keep things together.

I hoped Killian could keep things together.

He sent his small unit leaders packing, and turned to me.

"You asked if we had comms with Gatekeeper," I said.

He nodded, pulling his helmet off and running a hand over his buzzed scalp. "Yeah," he said tiredly. "We halted just short of the town, and Lieutenant Fink called back for further instructions." He grimaced. "You know how it is; we can't intervene without permission from higher, especially after Slovenský Grob a couple months ago." He glanced at me keenly as he said it; he was fishing for any kind of information about us, but I didn't give anything away. "That was when the SINCGARS went dead. We've had no contact on any covered channel since then. I've even tried satcom. Nothing."

I shook my head even as I frowned. Losing comms was nothing new; I'd experienced it regularly. Radios just weren't perfectly reliable, especially in the woods and hills. But to lose *everything*? That was weird.

"Weird" in a place like Slovakia wasn't something to make any combat soldier comfortable. It was already making the hackles rise on the back of my neck.

"We've got no comms with them, either," I said, leaving aside that we hadn't established any with FOB Keystone in the first place. I turned toward Greg and waved him down. He left his ruck against a tree and jogged down into the clearing. "What's the comm situation look like?" I asked.

Greg actually looked worried, which was something new for him. You'd never know it, looking at him and listening to him, but Greg had been blown up by an IED while he'd been a Ranger in Afghanistan. His face had been turned to hamburger, and he'd spent months in the hospital having his face and throat rebuilt.

Somewhere in that process, he'd decided that he was going to be positive. I suppose it was a natural reaction to surviving something like that. It was probably part perspective, part gratitude. But it had made him an irrepressible optimist, as well as being cheerful to a fault.

So, when Greg lost sight of his usual "everything will work out all right" outlook, it was time to get a bit worried.

"We've got weak, long-distance comms with Kidd," he said quietly, glancing at Killian. The Sergeant First Class frowned a little; he didn't know who Kidd was. Which was only natural; Kidd was our supporting commander back in Hungary. He'd led the advance party from the States, and was coordinating all of this. "Satcom's not working at all, and apparently it's the same for him. He can't get in touch with anyone back home, either."

Okay, this was officially bad. Really, really bad. Something had gone haywire, and with a creeping chill I started to wonder if it wasn't something truly catastrophic.

It had only been a matter of time, after all. With shooting wars going in the Pacific, the Middle East, and Central Asia, and Europe and the US both coming apart at the seams, it was only natural that things were going to escalate at some point. The only question for us had been when, and how.

Those were still questions. We were in the dark, with no answers. I turned to Killian. "You mentioned a Lieutenant Fink," I said.

Killian shook his head. "He was in the lead track," he answered. I nodded, tight-lipped. I'd seen the smoke. Killian's platoon commander was dead.

"Do you have any SA on the other peacekeeping units in the area?" I asked. I was remembering Scott's report that things were oddly quiet in the nearby Belgian sector.

But Killian was still shaking his head. "There's isn't much communication between sectors," he said. "*Especially* lately. The handful of times we've interacted with any of the EDC units…well, it's been tense."

I suspected that that was putting it mildly.

"Don't spread this around to your boys and girls," I said quietly, "but I think that something has gone really wrong. We need to get you back to Keystone. Posthaste."

I knew that I was on somewhat shaky ground right then. We'd gone in to rescue one dude. We'd done that. And Killian had armor, heavy machineguns, and a 50mm cannon to back him up and get him home. We didn't. Furthermore, we didn't exactly belong there, or at least, I didn't think that his command would think so.

But as still as I kept my features behind my sweat-streaked camouflage paint, I think Killian might have picked up on something, because he looked at me oddly, with a sort of blend of hope and relief. "I won't object," he said. "I don't know who you guys are, but you're obviously better at this stuff than most of my kids are. Hell," he said tiredly, running a hand over his face, "you're better at it than *I* am." He squared his shoulders and looked me in the eye. "Look, I don't know who you are. And I don't care. You could be Delta, CIA, DEVGRU, contractors, hell, you could be the fucking *Triarii* and I wouldn't care." *That* was comforting. Apparently, we were persona non grata with the Army at the moment. Which was strange, given that this was really our first operation overseas. Who knew what was getting said at the current events briefings, though. "We'd still be back there, stuck on that street in Borinka if not for you and your air support, so you have my thanks."

It suddenly struck me just how tired Killian looked. He was out of his element, and he knew it. And here we were, a bunch of hard bastards who had come out of the woodwork and smacked the hell out of the bad guys who'd ambushed his unit, and appeared to know what the hell we were doing. We must have seemed like a Godsend to him.

He glanced downhill. "It's a fairly straight shot down to the 502," he said. "Though we haven't been allowed to take tracks on it. Too much damage to the civilian highway."

64

But I was already shaking my head as I pulled my map out of the pocket set behind the magazine pouches in my chest rig. He glanced at my gear enviously; I was rolling a *lot* lighter than he was, at least without my ruck on. I spread the map against the Powell's armor plate.

"It's just a hunch, but I don't want to take the highways right now," I said. "I've got a feeling that it'd be a bad idea. Comms go down all the time, but they don't go down this hard unless something's gone seriously pear-shaped. Let's stick to backroads, shall we?" I traced a line of unimproved roads threading their way through the woods and over the ridge to the north. We might not have had comms arranged with FOB Keystone, but we damned sure knew where it was. Set in the fields between Lozorno and Jablonovè, it was well away from Bratislava itself, purportedly on the insistence of the EDC. "It'll be safer."

"There could be more militias back there," Killian objected.

"Maybe," I replied, not mentioning that I thought the militias were really going to turn out to be the least of our worries. Militias don't, as a rule, have the capability to jam military comms. "Though I doubt it. The militias have been targeting the Slovaks more than the peacekeepers." Again, with some notable exceptions, most particularly just an hour before, in Borinka. "They've got no real reason to hang out in the woods, far from major population centers. They've been secure enough squatting in the cities under the EDC's protection."

Killian gave me a sharp glance at that. I probably shouldn't have shown my hand that early, but I hadn't quite realized just how little information the Army was getting with its current events briefings.

He probably hadn't seen the reports on the killings in Trnava, while the Belgians had just stood by and watched. It had been Slovenský Grob all over again, only without an American unit stepping in.

"It's going to take a few hours, over some of this terrain," I said, "but if the local trucks can negotiate these roads, your vehicles should be able to, as well."

"Are you guys planning on riding with us?" he asked, looking around at my team and the infantry section, at least where they could be seen. Bradshaw had pushed more of his men out, deeper into the woods, expanding the perimeter as much as he could. We both wanted as much warning as possible if we were going to get hit.

"Not if we can help it," I replied. "It's close woods, and close terrain. Just because I'm *hoping* that the militias aren't out in the hills, doesn't mean I'm not going to be prepared for them to be. Cramming everyone on vehicles might take less time, but the woods are just like an urban area. We don't want to recreate the Battle of the Teutoburg Forest in miniature, here." He gave me a blank look, and I couldn't help but shake my head. Granted, I probably wouldn't have known about the Varian Disaster either if it hadn't been for Bart Cooper, but it still astounded me sometimes how little other people knew about such things. Particularly warfighters.

Hell, that battle hadn't been all *that* far from where we were. Varus had taken two legions into close terrain and thick woods, and hadn't come out again.

He looked down at the map, though, and nodded. "How long do you expect the movement to take?" he asked.

"We might get there by midnight," I replied. We were looking at a seventeen or eighteen klick movement, over terrain that wasn't exactly flat. It wasn't the Alps, but it wasn't going to be fun, either. And that was leaving aside the ever-present possibility that one of the vehicles was going to break down.

Or that we were going to get into another firefight.

He sighed heavily. "If we're out of contact that long, there's going to be hell to pay," he said.

"So, keep trying to get comms with Gatekeeper," I retorted. "It's going to be a lot worse if we drive into another ambush and get another one of your vehicles blown up, along with however many dismounts are in or on it."

His lips thinned a little; he was grateful for our intervention, and clinging to our help like a life-preserver, but on some level, he couldn't be happy about getting lectured by a scruffy-looking ginger with cammie paint in his beard and completely non-standard equipment. I probably wouldn't be in his place, either.

Not that I cared overmuch. I was a Grex Luporum Team Leader. I had bigger concerns than Killian's ego.

I glanced around. There were a handful of soldiers on security, though most of it seemed to be covered by the vehicle turrets. A couple of the dismounts had been wounded, either by fragmentation or bullets, and their platoon medic was treating them. "How soon can you be ready to move?" I asked.

He followed my gaze. "Fifteen minutes?"

I almost asked him if he was asking me or telling me, but bit my tongue. That would definitely not go over well, and while I'm no diplomat, we kind of needed each other. Especially since I'd sent the S-70s away.

Great thinking, Matt. You just had to dive in and be helpful, didn't you? Could have finished the mission and gone back to Hungary, but no. You had to take a mech infantry platoon under your wing.

I shook off the doubts. There had been a time when I would have essentially said, "I've got mine," and gotten on the birds and left Killian and his platoon to sort out their own fate. It would have been the pragmatic move.

But I'd been one of the Triarii for a few years. I'd seen too many cases where some police or National Guard unit's higher command made the "pragmatic" choice, and let men and women die because of it. I was sick of it, and if I ever had the chance to make one of those cowardly bastards pay, I was pretty sure I was going to take it.

So, there I was, with a short platoon of mech infantry hitched to my wagon, in presumably hostile territory.

"Fifteen minutes," I echoed. I turned and headed back up toward the trees, where the rest of my team was set in, most of them sitting against their rucks, rifles held across knees and pointed outboard, mostly back toward Borinka. Greg didn't hesitate to follow me; apparently, even the most gregarious Ranger I've ever known wasn't all that keen on hanging out with our lost patrol.

Scott was crouched next to his own ruck, and looked up as we approached. "I don't know about this, boss," he said quietly. His voice wouldn't travel much past where Tony was down in the prone next to his ruck, his Mk 48 sitting on its bipods, pointed back down toward the power lines. It certainly wouldn't make it to Killian's ears. He glanced down toward the vehicles, his eyes pensive.

"They lost two vics and at least half a dozen people," I said, though I knew why he was reticent. "Killian's not going to look a gift horse in the mouth. We saved their asses, and he knows it."

"Maybe," Scott replied quietly. He wasn't as taciturn as Tony, but my assistant team leader was always quiet and soft-spoken. It was usually attributed to his Japanese art hobby. "And five years ago, I would have accepted that. But these days…"

I just nodded as I followed his gaze toward the troops in the clearing below us. Scott hadn't been on my team from the beginning. He'd been on another team that had worked directly with some local law enforcement for a while before being set up for a fall with the Feds in Philadelphia. Coming after he'd been screwed by his platoon commander, ending his career at 2nd Recon Bn, he didn't have much trust in officers in the regular armed forces, or for anyone outside the Triarii, for that matter.

But I was fairly good at reading people. "I don't think Killian's got a knife out for our backs," I said. "If his CO had survived, it might be different, but he's almost as scared as his soldiers. And they're fucking terrified."

Scott nodded, though he still looked a bit skeptical. "Yeah," he said, "and I think I know why." He looked at me. "Something ain't right here, brother. There's losing comms, and then there's losing comms."

I didn't have an answer for him, but he was right. The need to stay focused on the problem at hand was keeping the growing sense of dread suppressed at the back of my mind, but the fact that Killian and his platoon *still* didn't have contact with Keystone, and the fact that even we had no satcom, was more than a bit worrying. It would take something big for that to happen. Something coordinated.

"One thing at a time," I said, as much to myself as to Scott. I crouched down and pulled out the map to give him an overview of our route. "Let's get to Keystone, first."

***

We were ready to roll ten minutes before Killian's platoon, to my utter lack of surprise. But with the infantry in the woods and the vehicles on the road, we finally started moving.

Chapter 7

"Deacon, Flat," Bradshaw called. I turned and looked back. "We need to halt again."

"Dammit," I muttered, before keying my radio and replying, "Roger that." I signaled to Phil, but he'd heard it, and was already pushing toward a stand of trees where he would have good concealment while maintaining a clear field of fire both down the valley in front of us and toward the top of the ridge to our left.

For my part, I headed back downhill, toward where the three Army vehicles were stopped on the road. Again.

I passed the rest of my team and the handful of Bradshaw's guys whom he'd split off to join us on the left-hand side of the road, while he kept the bulk of his section on the right-hand side. It was too dark to see much in the way of facial expressions, but the general demeanor was tired and frustrated. I could relate.

We'd been moving at the pace of a depressed snail for the last six hours. While we hadn't taken any contact, the tension was getting thicker and thicker with every step. We'd heard fast-movers roaring overhead, some distant artillery fire, and once had seen a formation of four EDC NH90 helicopters heading toward Bratislava. Drones were buzzing over nearby towns, but fortunately, the trees kept us out of sight.

Something had prompted me to insist that we take cover when the birds had gone over. Technically, the US Army was in Slovakia in cooperation with the EDC peacekeeping mission, so the Belgians, the Germans, the Swedes, and the French were allies. But the loss of comms, the complete lack of reaction to the firefight in Borinka, and the tension that Killian had described when dealing with any of the EDC forces were weighing on my mind. Something had gone wrong, and until I knew what it was, I wasn't comfortable with contacting anyone who wasn't an American.

Bradshaw, of course, was on the same page. Killian hadn't needed much persuading, though I had heard some loud grumbling from his troops about having to do all this sneaky stuff. I was less and less impressed with the quality of the Army's personnel, those days. Killian had cracked down on it, but it was obvious from what little I'd seen that he was fighting an uphill battle.

How dicked up was his command, that even after the casualties they'd taken, his kids were acting like spoiled college students?

I met Killian at the prow of his Powell, as Bradshaw came down out of the trees to join us. The contrast between the three of us was marked; I was wearing greenside kit and carrying a ruck, with a ghillie hood over my head, shoulders, and rucksack, a painted LaRue OBR, with a short-dot scope mounted, in my hands. Bradshaw was in plain green fatigues, with a similar chest rig to mine, an assault pack, and boonie hat overshadowing his thermal fusion NVGs, a much plainer M5E1 in his hands. Killian looked twice our size, without a pack on his back, thanks to all the camouflaged armor he was wearing, his M37A2 looking about half the size of our rifles. And he was carrying less ammo, for all the bulk of his gear.

"What is it now?" I growled. We'd just halted what felt like half an hour ago.

"We've got to stop again," he said, his voice raised just enough to be heard over the rumble of the M5's engine. "I've got three soldiers who are about to collapse."

I grimaced, though it was too dark for him to see the expression, and he wasn't wearing NVGs. Bad call on his part, but he had presumably been using the Powell's thermal imager to see. "We're already behind schedule, and it doesn't seem to be getting any more permissive out here," I said.

Killian didn't say anything, but spread his hands. I got the impression that he didn't really want to say what was going on; he didn't want to admit that none of his soldiers could keep up with us, particularly burdened by body armor as they were. We were carrying more weight in our rucks, but a rucksack is easier to move in than plates and Kevlar. But the fact of the matter was, the Triarii had higher physical standards than the Army did. "There's only so far I can push them," he said.

Bullshit, I didn't say. *You're their commander now. You push 'em as hard as they need to be pushed, because this isn't a fucking war game. This is about survival.*

"Then get them on the vehicles," Bradshaw said harshly. "If they can't keep up, then they ride. Matt and I will cover the dismount piece. If we're going to get to Keystone before daylight, we've got to step it out." I glanced at my watch, shielding the faint green glow with my hand. He was right. The sun had set three hours before, and we'd been moving most of the day before that. The halts had just gotten more frequent and lasted longer.

Killian looked uncertain and nervous. "If I do that..." he started to say.

"If you do that, then yeah," I said, "you're turning over a chunk of your security to total strangers, working for you don't know who. I get it. Tyler gets it. But if we wanted to double-cross you, we'd just have left you to the Kosovars and Syrians in Borinka." I sighed. "We're on the same side, Sergeant Killian. Whether your command knows it or not."

Or likes it.

He still hesitated. I realized that I didn't know what kind of monitors were supposed to be feeding audio and video back to the TOC at Keystone. I knew that even the Marine Corps had gotten stupid with such things even before I'd joined. It had been a large part of the reason why I'd had no trouble declining to reenlist in favor of joining the Triarii.

Finally, though, he nodded. "I'll get them to mount up," he said. "We can be ready to move in...twenty minutes?"

I knew that it was going to be more like half an hour, but just nodded. "Fine," I said. "We'll move when they're loaded up."

I glanced to the north. It was too dark to see far, especially with the woods towering over the road, but I almost thought I could see a brighter glow in that direction. And I'd been smelling the faint tang of smoke for the last couple of hours.

It wasn't woodsmoke, either.

***

It was more like forty-five minutes before everything got up and moving. I could only imagine the ass-chewing we'd have gotten in Weapons Company if we'd ever taken that long. But these kids just weren't in shape for this kind of movement. They were strung out well past their endurance.

I blamed their command. Which included Killian, despite what he might have had to work with for a CO.

"We're ready to go, Golf Lima Ten Six," Killian called.

"Roger," I replied. "Keep your vehicles to about three miles per hour. We'll be in the woods above and around you." Three miles per hour was a little quick for a patrolling pace, but we had time to make up. And with the amount of noise—not to mention the thermal profile—that the vehicles were making, if we went *too* slow, it was just going to invite attack.

I was already back up in position, and I tapped Phil, who got smoothly to his feet.

"Nice little rest," he said. "I could go all day, now." Being Phil, he was being a smartass, but he wasn't too far off. We didn't train to take forty-five-minute halts after less than forty minutes on the move.

We got about ten steps before he froze, and I followed suit, holding up a fist for Greg behind me. I'd heard it too. We made sure we were well under the trees as the drone buzzed overhead. I looked for it through the thick boles and leaves, catching little glimmers of thermal glow. It was off to our west, over the hilltop. I just hoped that it was at the wrong angle to spot the armor down on the road.

As soon as it had passed, I tapped Phil again. On the off chance that Killian's vehicles had been spotted, we needed to get some distance, quick.

It might have just been paranoia. The only real adversaries that were supposed to be in Slovakia were the Slovak Nationalists, who were stronger out east, toward the central part of the country, and the vicious, mostly jihadi militias that had flooded into the country when the EDC and the Slovak government had nullified the general plebiscite that had demanded that Slovakia secede from the dying European Union.

There had been no threat indicators that suggested we needed to worry about conventional troops in western Slovakia.

But that sense of dread was still nagging at me, getting stronger and stronger the longer satcom stayed down, and the longer Killian went without being able to contact Gatekeeper. Until I knew more, I was going to treat *everything* as a threat.

I knew Bradshaw was on the same page. I hoped Killian was getting there. Clearly, his troops hadn't gotten the idea yet.

I just hoped they figured it out before too many more had to die. Or that I was wrong.

But as we paced through the trees, scanning carefully in every direction, weapons following eyes, I was still afraid that I wasn't.

***

The smoke was getting thicker and thicker in the valley. And it didn't smell wholesome.

"Golf Lima Ten Six, Doomhammer One Five," Killian called me. "We still don't have any comms with Gatekeeper." He paused. "Something's wrong. We should be able to talk to them. We're not even getting them on the phone."

I didn't ask why the hell a combat patrol was rolling with phones on the local cell network. Everybody had gotten sloppy in that regard for some time. It was a backup, everyone said, but it became too easy to turn it into a primary.

"Roger, Doomhammer," I said. We had halted again in another meadow, just on the back side of the last hill before the open valley where Keystone sat. There was definitely a stronger glow in that direction, though it *might* have just been the FOB's lights. They hadn't been blacking the base out lately, from what Killian had said. "I'm taking a leader's recon up to the edge of the woods to take a look. Keep your vehicles here, and keep security up."

I know that *I* would have been insulted if an outsider reminded me of that basic continuing action, but at that point in time, I didn't care. It had taken a long time for his soldiers to pile out of the vehicles once we'd halted, and they weren't acting like the professionals they were supposed to be. They were tired, they were in pain, and they didn't know why they were supposed to be acting like they were in hostile territory. They'd gotten away from Borinka, hadn't they?

I'd actually heard one of them say that. To his credit, one of the others promptly bitched him out about it. Not all was lost with these kids. But the fact remained that they were way behind the power curve, and they needed to catch up before the enemy did.

Alpha Element was already gathered at the northern treeline, rucks on the ground, ready to go. I turned to Scott. "I'm taking Alpha, and we're going up over the hill to get a look-see. I don't expect to be longer than an hour, but if we are..." I finished out the contingency plan. It was something that we might all consider to be common sense, particularly after months of training, but when you're splitting your team, it pays to make sure all the bullet points get hit. To make damned good and sure that everybody really was on the same page.

Assuming such things in a combat environment was how stuff got missed or miscommunicated, and people got killed.

He recited the plan back to me, just to make sure. I nodded, and he clapped me on the shoulder. I pointed to Phil, who led out, with me, Greg, Jordan, and Dwight in tow.

It was easy going after the last few hours with rucks on our backs. Losing the weight meant that, despite the fatigue that was really starting to set in—it had been a couple of days now since my last full night's sleep—it felt like a breeze to slip through the woods.

But that didn't mean I relaxed. I was getting more and more on edge, as the tang of smoke got thicker and nastier, and the glow to the north intensified.

Phil got to the top of the hill and slowed, getting low and moving from tree to tree. He paused, but looked back at me and shook his head, making a "negative" gesture with his hand. No eyes on. The trees were too thick. We were going to have to push closer.

I still signaled for him to halt. It wasn't going to be a good idea to just go running in. I wanted to stop, listen, watch, and take stock.

We gathered up in a tight perimeter. I placed Dwight next to Phil, pointing that Mk 48 downhill. The belt-fed always needed to go where the most likely threat was going to come from, and while Keystone was in that direction, I had the screaming heebie-jeebies at that point, and wasn't going to take chances.

It said something that nobody had confronted me about my case of the willies. Phil and David, at the least, would have said something. Which told me that everybody else was sensing the same thing.

There was a brooding threat in that otherwise idyllic countryside, that got heavier and heavier the longer we went without comms with anyone except our own guys in Hungary. And those were weak and spotty, since the satcom still wasn't working. Which told me that something big *had* to have happened; satcom doesn't just go down and stay down. It's not like regular radio that is reliant on the ionosphere to transmit over distance.

Something had to have happened to the constellation we were using. Which was big, bad medicine.

The smoke was getting thicker, though the wind was blowing from the southwest. Whatever was burning, it was big. And it stank of petroleum, rubber, and less wholesome things.

"Let's go," I whispered to Phil. Without a word, he got up and moved forward.

We crept down the hillside, moving as carefully and silently as we could in the dark. The carpet of old leaves underfoot made that interesting, but we still moved with only faint rustles. Our only communications were hand and arm signals.

The glow to the north was intensifying. And even before we came to the edge of the trees, I could see what it was. And that my worst fears had been realized.

"Holy shit," Dwight muttered as we set in within a tight stand of trees at the edge of a cornfield. We still had to look through another line of trees along an irrigation canal between us and the road, but even that couldn't obscure the horror we were looking at.

FOB Keystone was burning. Fierce flames blossomed white in my thermal fusion goggles, belching a thick column of black smoke into the night sky.

Chapter 8

I tore my eyes away from the burning base, forcing myself to look past the conflagration and scan for more immediate threats. While it was a no-brainer that we weren't going to go rolling up to the gate, not after that, it never paid to get so fixated on one disaster that you didn't see the next disaster coming.

Sure enough, there were plenty. The hulking shapes of several tanks and armored fighting vehicles squatted on the road, about five hundred meters from the ruin of FOB Keystone. I could only get glimmers on thermal through the vegetation and the drifting smoke, but I was pretty sure they had foot patrols out in the fields, too.

Mid-sized drones were buzzing along the road at treetop level, apparently keeping an eye out for anyone approaching the base. Drones would extend a commander's visual range by a considerable margin, being able to see past where his vehicles' sights were cut off by terrain and vegetation.

A pair of helicopters appeared suddenly, bursting through the smoke with a whirl of rotor wash, snarling as they circled the smashed, burning FOB. My eyes narrowed as I watched them. I couldn't ID the armor squatting on the highway, but those were definitely Tiger attack helicopters. Which made them either French or German.

I turned my eye back to the FOB. The front gate—or what was left of it—was facing the highway. It was a crater, backlit by the fires. I'd seen detailed imagery of the base before we'd inserted. We'd taken high-definition photos from high-altitude drones; the Army wasn't so ass-backwards that they were posting publicity photos of their FOBs and security measures on the Internet, though I'd seen stuff almost as dumb. That gate had been solid, a serpentine of T-walls and HESCO barriers. It had to have taken some serious boom to flatten it.

There were other gaps in the T-wall outer barrier, chunks of the hardened concrete sections having been blasted to rubble. Whatever had happened, there had been a lot of explosives expended to do it.

Which drew my eye back to the tanks and other armored vehicles squatting on the road. If those were EDC Tigers in the air overhead, who were they?

"We're moving back," I whispered. "Slow and careful. Let's not get spotted now."

"You think those tanks had something to do with the FOB getting blasted?" Jordan asked. His tone was flat, offering no clue as to his thoughts. Knowing Jordan as I did, I knew that he was more than likely to object if I assumed anything one way or another. He was like that. He considered himself a very critical thinker, and didn't like assumptions.

"I don't know, Jordan," I replied. "But under the circumstances, I don't want to take chances with just walking up to them, not without comms." I stared at him, though he could only see the same thing I could; the blocky shape of my fusion goggles sticking out from under my vegetation-adorned ghillie hood-over.

He met my gaze for a second, then looked away. "Fair enough," he muttered.

Damn right. The chip on Jordan's shoulder was going to cause a problem, one of these days. But right then and there, less than half a klick from armored vehicles that might or might not be hostile, was not the time to deal with it. And Jordan was enough of a pro that I knew I could trust him not to push things to the point of putting us into an untenable position in combat.

But he was going to have to quit expecting the worst from everyone around him if the team was really going to hold together.

"Phil, get us back to the rally point," I whispered, glancing up at the pair of Tigers as they snarled overhead, circling around to the north. "Keep us under the trees as much as

80

possible." It wasn't just the helos I was worried about, and I was pretty sure Phil knew it.

Phil got to his feet and started back, moving even more carefully than he had been before. I glanced back at the glowing hulks of the tanks squatting on the 501, then followed.

***

I could hear the drones whining overhead as we moved back up the hill. It sounded like they were getting closer. Maybe it was just my own fears talking, making me hear the drones getting louder simply because I was scared that they were going to come this way and spot us. But that sense of urgency kept driving me forward, and I had to temper it, even as I caught myself catching up with Phil.

I wasn't the only one, either. I turned and looked back to find Greg almost on top of me. His body language was a little sheepish as he fell back again. He glanced up as I started to turn back forward, and I just nodded.

But the closer we got to the top of the hill and the meadow where our companions were gathered, the more I was increasingly convinced that I *wasn't* imagining it. The drones *were* getting closer. Which meant it was only a matter of time before we were made.

"Deacon, Weeb, we just got buzzed by a drone." Scott sounded tense, but he wasn't freaking out. It wasn't like Scott to freak out, anyway. He'd be more likely to either make a joke, or get more overtly laid-back. It was his way. "No ID."

"Weeb, Deacon," I replied, without slowing down. "Consider it hostile until we know more. Tell Doomhammer to get his vehicles under cover if he can. We're about five minutes out."

Being on the back side of the hill, Phil was starting to speed up, and I didn't try to slow him down. I looked up, searching between the leafy branches for the drone. I knew that if it was flying low enough that we could hear it that clearly, or that Scott could have seen it to know that they'd been buzzed, it probably wasn't armed; the armed drones in regular use were still about the size of the old Reapers, and tended to stay at ten thousand feet or higher. We'd never have known that it was there until a missile smacked into a vehicle.

81

But those Tigers were weighing on my mind. "Doomhammer One Five, Golf Lima Ten Six," I sent. "If you've got anti-air defenses, I suggest you get them ready now."

"We've got a couple of .50 cals," Killian replied.

"Get men on them now, and watch the sky," I said. "Just in case." I didn't want to transmit more than that in the clear. *If*, somehow, the EDC had something to do with the destruction of FOB Keystone and the jamming of the SINCGARS network, then they were probably listening in on the open channels.

Damn, if this really was as bad as I was afraid it was, we were screwed.

I caught a glimpse of the lighter patch that was the meadow ahead, just as Phil dropped to a knee behind a tree and signaled with the IR light built into his NVGs. A moment later, an answering flash signaled that Tony saw us, and we were clear to come in.

Even as Phil got to his feet, I heard the rising growl of rotors behind us.

"Down!" I hissed. It was still possible that I was barking up the wrong tree; that we had nothing to fear. Maybe Keystone had been taken out by a terrorist attack, like the strike on the old FOB Bastion in Afghanistan back in '12. In that case, the EDC peacekeepers might just be watching and searching for survivors. The tanks might just be there as security, in case the insurgents— whichever side they were on—tried again. After all, the Americans weren't the only ones who'd had problems with the jihadi militias. They had a real tendency to bite the hand that fed them.

To listen to Dwight, only an idiot would have expected anything else. And he really wasn't wrong.

But something about the whole situation was still nagging at me. Something wasn't right. It should have taken more than a handful of Kosovar Albanians and Arabs to level an American FOB. A lot more.

The two Tigers came in fast and low, their rotors lashing the trees overhead. And as they came, rockets roared off their stubby wing rails, the flashes lighting us up under the trees.

My stomach turned over as the white streaks of the rocket motors arrowed down into the clearing. All of that, trying to get those soldiers out of Borinka, when we could have just climbed onto the birds and flown back to Hungary, for nothing.

But a moment later, the stuttering, metallic hammer of heavy machinegun fire answered out of the cloud of smoke. And unless I missed my guess, there were at least three guns in that mix.

Tracers stabbed upward, and the two Tigers split away, banking sharply and heading for the trees. They'd gotten the first shot, but they must have used dumb rockets instead of ATGMs, and somehow, they'd missed. Maybe they were relatively new at engaging armor. Or maybe they'd used all their ATGMs already, and just had the rockets left.

A moment later, the Powell opened fire with that 50mm, the heavier and slower *chunk, chunk, chunk* actually making the .50s sound like popguns. Killian's gunner was too slow, though; the helos ducked below the trees and disappeared, leaving the rounds to sail off into the distance.

Hopefully they didn't hit any civilian houses.

"Golf Lima Ten Six, this is Doomhammer One Five," Killian called. "What the hell just happened? Those were EDC birds!"

"Yes, they were," I replied. "And if you want to survive, then pop smoke and move out. We'll follow, but if you're still stationary when those birds come back, or the armor on the highway comes after us, then you're going to be sitting ducks."

There was a pause, almost as if he wanted to say something. But the harsh reality of the situation seemed to finally penetrate. "Roger," he said. "How will we link up again?"

Damn. That was a question. I didn't dare send rendezvous coordinates in the clear, and just because he'd asked the question made me think that Killian had thought of the same thing. "We'll offset a couple klicks, and contact you later," I said, hoping and praying that he'd get the message.

"Roger that," he replied. "We'll see you on the flip side. Be safe."

I'd gotten back on my feet. I could still hear the helicopters in the distance, but they didn't seem to be coming back soon. That 50mm could go through a Tiger long-ways, if I wasn't mistaken, and the pilots probably didn't want to risk it, particularly after they'd missed with their initial salvo, then just about gotten gutted by ground fire.

"We need to get the hell away from here," I said. "Scott, can that little toy of yours create some distractions?"

"Ask Dave," Scott replied. "It's his toy."

"Peanut," I hissed, but David was already ahead of me.

"Yeah," he said, "it's got a limited ECM suite on it. It won't do shit for visual or infrared, but we can send some radio messages with it that they might DF on."

"Provided they don't just blanket jam everything," Greg put in.

"Since when did you start getting as cynical as the rest of us, Strawberry?" Phil asked.

"Enough," I said. I could still hear the Tigers, and I wanted to get well away from there before they came back. Or before the bad guys decided to bring an armed drone overhead and start dropping on anybody they saw moving in the clearing. "Get that thing up and start it doing its thing. Then we've got to move." I didn't have a rendezvous point picked out for Killian yet, but that could wait until we were gone.

Dave started digging in his ruck, and came out with the compact drone. It looked like a simple quad-rotor, no different than a kid's toy. But it had cost a *lot*, and there were a lot of electronics packed into it. He switched it on, pulling out the tablet that controlled it, hunching over it to shield the light.

"Dwight, go cover your son so he doesn't backlight himself for everybody within ten miles," Scott whispered.

Dwight grumbled something unintelligible, but moved to stand over David, blocking most of the faint glow of the tablet with his bulk. Dwight had been the one to give David his callsign, "Peanut," when the much smaller, and younger, man had been talking a lot of shit, which had immediately led to the jokes about Dwight being David's real dad.

David rapidly tapped controls on the tablet, then stepped away from Dwight to toss the drone into the air before blanking the screen and stuffing the miniature computer back into his ruck. "There," he said. "It's autonomous until I retake control, or it runs out of batteries."

84

"Fine," I said. "Let's move." I keyed my radio. "Flat, Deacon. We're heading out. We'll take lead."

"Roger," Bradshaw replied.

Phil was already moving. Despite the banter, nobody wanted to stick around that clearing any longer than necessary, especially with the growl of the Tigers' rotors still audible in the distance.

***

We moved fast; it wasn't a patrolling pace but more of a forced march through the woods and over the hills. We'd covered almost three klicks before I finally called a halt. We were under the trees and should, hopefully, be concealed from the air.

"Greg, see if you can raise Killian," I said, once we were circled up and security had been set. I was crouched in the center, next to Greg and Bradshaw, scanning the woods through my fusion goggles, my rifle held over my knee.

Holy hell, was I tired. We were going to have to stop for a rest soon, or we were going to start making mistakes. Despite the fact that it was early fall, and starting to cool off, especially at night, I was soaked with sweat under my gear and my ghillie hood. It was starting to chill me as I knelt there in the leaves, resisting the urge to do the rucksack flop. I'd be hard-pressed to get up if I did that, at that point.

"Got 'em, Matt," Greg reported. "There's a *lot* of noise; some of it's probably the terrain, but somebody might be trying to jam the open channels, too."

I just nodded silently. It wasn't terribly surprising, especially after that little dustup back there. Whoever had orchestrated the destruction of FOB Keystone had to know that we were using open radio chatter, and if they couldn't use it to follow us, they'd jam it so that we couldn't use it.

I reached up to my chest rig, and pulled the tablet out of its pocket. With a little time to work with, I pulled the blackout cover out of the top pouch on my ruck and spread it over me, so that the screen's glow wouldn't spotlight me in the woods like a will o' the wisp.

It took a few minutes to locate our position, then figure out a rendezvous point far enough back in the "Little Carpathians" that we'd be less likely to get discovered, while still being reachable for Killian's vehicles. It took some searching. My brain was getting sluggish.

Finally, I blanked the screen, pulled the blackout cover off, and took a deep breath of the chill air. It got stuffy under that cover. "Tell him it'll take a couple minutes, then send these coordinates," I told Greg. I rattled off the eight-digit grid coordinate, deliberately changing the second digit of each quartet by two. I just hoped that Killian would get the message. We hadn't exactly been able to coordinate our code.

Greg sent the message, then listened for a moment. "He said he's got it, and will be there in two," he relayed. I nodded gratefully. For all the problems I'd seen with his unit, Killian was smart. He'd figured it out.

I heaved myself to my feet. "Time to get moving," I said, to Bradshaw as well as my own guys. The RV point I'd set was about another five klicks away, as the crow flew. As the crow walked, it was more like seven. It was going to be a rough night.

Not that it had been great so far.

***

Killian beat us to the rendezvous. No great surprise.

What was a bit of a surprise was the fact that he hadn't just circled the vehicles and called it good. He'd made his soldiers dig in. When we hiked inside the perimeter, it was past hasty fighting positions that had been dug in between the trees, manned by two soldiers apiece. The ramparts were a little on the small side, and the holes were shallow, but they couldn't have had much time to dig before it started getting light.

He'd also moved the vehicles under the trees as much as possible and put up camouflage netting. I had to hand it to him; he was taking the situation seriously, and exhibiting more tactical acumen than I'd given him or anyone currently on Active Duty credit for.

He met us near his Powell, which was powered down, though the turret was still humming slightly. The IFV must have had some serious battery backups to run the weapons and comm systems while the engine was shut off.

"You made it," he said.

"Yeah," I replied. "Any more contact en route?"

He shook his head. "Not that they weren't looking for us," he said. "Lots of drone traffic. It just seems like none of it's ours." He took his helmet off and rubbed his scalp. "We can't raise any adjacent units, either. I know for a fact that there were three other patrols out at the same time we were. But the comms are silent."

I just shook my head. "Any number of possibilities at this point," I said. "We can talk about it later. Unfortunately, right now my team and I are running on about four hours of sleep out of the last seventy-two." I wasn't hallucinating yet, which was a little surprising. I'd seen some very interesting things that hadn't been there during Grex Luporum Selection, on slightly better sleep than I'd had lately. "We'll set our guys on security, then we need to initiate rest plan. Otherwise, we're gonna come up with all sorts of stupid stuff, and probably get somebody else killed."

He squinted at me, then nodded. "Of course," he said. "I've been there. We'll talk later."

I nodded and shambled toward the perimeter. Bradshaw already had most of his section on security, and as I started to find spots for my team, he intercepted me.

"We've got this, Matt," he said. "We got some sleep before insert. I know you guys didn't get much. We'll get you up when it's time."

I just nodded my thanks, found a spot against a tree, and was passed out in seconds.

Chapter 9

I went down hard. By the time I woke up, the light was getting dim again. The high overcast hid the sun, but it was definitely getting close to sundown.

Stifling a groan, I levered myself upright. I was pretty sure I hadn't moved at all since I'd gone down. I just *hurt*. My joints and muscles had stiffened as I lay on the ground. I wasn't eighteen, anymore.

Bradshaw heard me anyway, and came over to crouch next to me, cradling his rifle. "Good, you're awake."

I squinted at him. "What time is it?"

He checked his watch. "It's about 1830," he replied. He glanced around at the rest of the team, which was mostly stirring except for Phil, who was up and cleaning his weapon. "You guys needed the rest. But I'm glad you're up. Things have been getting a little tense."

I looked around at that. It took a minute, but I started to see what he was talking about. Several of the soldiers in the nearest fighting holes were stealing glances at us, and they were alternately suspicious and slightly awestruck. "Oh, hell," I said. "They been asking questions already?"

"A few," Bradshaw answered. "We've been stonewalling them, mostly, but the whispers have started. And not all of them are friendly."

I didn't expect that they were, especially given the treatment that the Triarii had gotten in the press. "You'd think that they'd have more important things on their minds." I glanced toward the hulking silhouette of the Powell, obscured by tree trunks and camo netting. "Is Killian up?"

"I don't think so," he answered. "Not yet. He told me he was going down about four hours ago."

With a glance at the sky, I dug into my ruck. "I've got time to eat, then." Pulling out a ration package, which was simpler but considerably better than the "Expeditionary Rations" that the Army had, I ripped it open and started eating. Italian Pepper Steak. It was odd, just eating it freeze-dried, but I didn't want to take the time to heat the water up.

As I was eating, the rest of the team got up and started squaring themselves away. I was thinking as I ate, getting my sluggish brain back in gear. We had several problems to deal with, and no good solutions to any of them.

"Have you still got contact with the mortar section?" I asked Bradshaw.

"Yeah," he answered. "They're set up about two klicks to the northeast, but they're low on ammo. They've got about one more fire mission in 'em, and then they're going to have to either bury the tubes and E&E, or start humping for the border."

At least they were still on the loose and alive. There was that.

My thoughts were interrupted by one of the soldiers getting out of his hole and coming toward us. I frowned as I watched him, glancing around at the rest. No one seemed to be calling him out. Was this because Killian was asleep?

"Are you guys Triarii?" he asked, mangling the Latin name.

"Why are you out of your position?" I asked in reply. My voice might have been more than a little harsh. "You know we're still in hostile territory, right?"

"I was just asking," he said. The kid looked about twelve to me, which meant he was eighteen or nineteen. And I was far from the old man among the Triarii, either. "We've been talking, about who you are. If you were Delta or SEAL Team Six, you'd have M37s, like us." He pointed to my OBR. "That's not any kind of US military issue. Not anymore, anyway."

I just looked at him for a second. I've been told that I have "resting mad dog face," so he started to get uncomfortable pretty quick. I finished chewing and swallowed before I said,

"How about you mind your damned business and get back on the perimeter, kid?"

"I don't answer to you," he replied petulantly. "I don't see any rank, or any unit patches."

Of course he didn't. Bradshaw's guys had stripped their fatigues sterile before insertion, and those of us on the GL teams never wore our patches, anyway. The old Roman helmet, crossed rifles, and US shield were a dead giveaway.

Personally, I thought that Colonel Santiago never should have okayed the insignia in the first place, but I was just a team leader. He had to have his reasons.

"What's it matter to you who we are?" Bradshaw asked. "We're on the same side. That's it."

"So you *are* Triarii," the kid said, a little smugly. "I'll admit, I'm kind of surprised. I hadn't expected…well…" He faltered a little as my stare turned icy. "Well, I guess…all the stories didn't quite tell me what to expect." He glanced up. "I'm kind of surprised there's an African-American with you…" He trailed off as Jordan turned his not-inconsiderable glare on him.

"What?" He snarled. "The fuck you mean, white boy?"

"Jordan…" I'd known guys who would have taken that opening and run with it, just to fuck with the kid. With Jordan, though, I knew that that wasn't what was about to happen. The kid had just knocked the chip off Jordan's shoulder, and didn't even know it.

"I, uh," the kid stammered, even as Jordan got to his feet. He stood half a head taller than the soldier, and was clearly in better shape.

"'I, uh,'" Jordan mocked bitterly. "Spit it out. Go on."

"Well, uh, the Triarii are supposed to be hard-core, uh, right-wingers," the kid stammered. He'd apparently figured out that he'd just stepped in it, but it was too late to back down, especially with a very angry black man glowering at him.

"And just because of the color of my skin, I'm supposed to, what?" Jordan demanded. "Join the PRA?"

He was *pissed*. Jordan hated People's Revolutionary Action almost as much as he hated the Fourth Reich skinheads who had beaten his mother to death during one of the regular riots in Richmond. The only reason he'd wound up with us instead of one of the black supremacist organizations that were cropping up in the major cities was because they'd all sided, to one degree or another, with the PRA.

Jordan had spent a lot of time in the Third World as a Special Forces Medic. He'd seen the kind of government that the PRA wanted, and he wanted no part of it.

The kid, faced with Jordan's rage at being stereotyped for his race, just stammered.

"Jordan, not the time, nor the place," I snapped. He turned his furious eyes on me, but I'd learned a while back not to give an inch when he got this way. I returned his glare with one of my own.

He snapped a dismissive hand at the soldier. "The fuck outta here," he said. "You don't know shit, kid. Keep your fucking racism to yourself next time."

The chastised young soldier beat a hasty retreat, but we were getting looks from the other holes. I glared at Jordan until he sat back down. We had big enough problems without getting into fights with our allies.

I finished my breakfast, or whatever you wanted to call it, and stuffed the wrapper back into my ruck. We'd pack it out. Another thing that I'd had to learn when I'd come to the GL teams was the concept of "target indicators." Hartrick had thrashed us unmercifully for leaving *anything* behind in the field.

Of course, he'd lost friends when their hide site had been compromised by a single piece of trash left outside. So, he had good reasons. Didn't make him any less of a dick.

I glanced at the Powell again, but decided that before I discussed our next move with Killian, I needed more info. I crossed to Greg, who had gotten the long-range, HF radio up before going down to sleep. He was still kind of a mess; he was rummaging in his pack for food, his rifle was leaning against the tree next to him, and he had taken his ghillie hood-over off. At least he only had one boot off.

Of course, I'd left mine on. I was probably going to regret that, in the long run. But at least I'd change my socks before we got moving again.

I squatted down next to him. "Are we up with Kidd?" I asked quietly.

Greg looked up at me and smiled. "Of course," he said. "I had to change freqs a couple times, but we're good." He handed me the handset. "He might not be in the COC right at the moment, but he probably hasn't gone far. I just talked to him a couple minutes ago."

With a nod, I lifted the handset to my ear. "Tango Charlie Five Seven Six, this is Golf Lima Ten Six," I sent. *Tango Charlie* stood for *Triarii Command*. All of our unit callsigns were very practical, downright boring. Personal callsigns got more interesting.

It took a second before Kidd's voice, scratchy and faint, came through. "Golf Lima Ten Six, this is Tango Charlie Five Seven Six," he said. "Good to hear you, Deacon."

"Likewise, Pegleg," I answered. Kidd didn't have a prosthetic leg, but his name had *required* a pirate-oriented callsign. "Have you got contact with any other stations in the AO?"

"Negative," he replied. "Believe me, we've tried. Once things went sideways with the SINGCARS comms, we tried raising every major FOB in-country. Nothing. There seems to be a complete comms blackout over Slovakia. Satcom's still down. Hell, the cell network seems to be down. Same with the Internet. It gets worse, too."

He paused for a moment. "We can't get drone coverage on you, Deacon. We've sent four over the last eighteen hours, and not one has lasted more than a klick inside the border. It seems to be electronic, not physical. They just fuzz out and we lose the signal."

My lips thinned as I stared at the woods around us, the handset at my ear. This was bad, alright. And it was coordinated. There was no way all of that had just happened by accident.

And with the satcom down, it made me wonder what else was happening in the rest of the world.

Not that we had the time or the energy to worry overmuch about that. We had a much more immediate set of problems.

"I'm sorry to say this, Deacon, but you guys are on your own, at least until the skies clear or we get more reinforcements,"

93

Kidd said. "I don't dare send the birds in blind. We could just lose them as fast as we've lost the drones."

"Understood," I answered. He was right. Losing the Vipers and the S-70s wouldn't help us any. It was probably a minor miracle that they hadn't been shot down on the way back to Hungary. And we didn't have the full expeditionary force that Colonel Santiago was building yet, so there were no armored vehicles to come get us, either. "Have you been able to make contact with anyone back home?"

"Negative," was the answer. "We've tried several HF shots, ever since the satcom went black, but we haven't gotten any reply yet." He paused, and though his voice was scratchy and distorted, when he spoke again there was a note of desperate hope in his voice. "Might be solar activity. Might just be that the satcom jamming is localized to this region, so they don't know that it's down, and so they haven't gotten the HF up."

Kidd didn't really believe that, any more than I did. The Triarii wouldn't have let two days' worth of comm windows slip by without trying secondary or tertiary comms. Something big was up, bigger than just a sneak attack on FOB Keystone.

"Copy all," was all I said, though. We had a limited time window, and while we were in a reasonably secure position for the moment, pointless wrangling over the radio wasn't going to do anyone any good. And the longer we kept transmitting, even if the enemy couldn't listen in, the more likely it became that they were going to spot the fact that *somebody* was transmitting.

Besides, there wasn't anything more that Kidd could do for us. Like he'd said, we were on our own.

While I kept my composure and maintained my bearing, my blood was running cold and my stomach was doing flip-flops. The realization that we were alone, unsupported and surrounded, with nothing more than the supplies in our rucksacks, which would last about another day, wasn't a good one. I was having to mentally focus on keeping the dread down while it was still dread, and not full-blown panic.

We'd find a way out of this. We had to. The alternative was to lie down and die. And the Triarii don't select for men who are likely to just lie down and die. The Grex Luporum teams even less so.

"We'll figure out our next move and keep you advised," I said. "That way, if we don't make it out, at least *somebody* knows what happened to us." Someone else might have thought the sentiment ghoulish, but Kidd was a veteran. He was relatively new to the Triarii, but he'd been on the ground in the Fourth Balkan War. Between the Kosovars, the Croats, and the Serbs all trying to exterminate each other, along with anyone who tried to get between them, he'd seen some shit.

"We'll be here," he answered. "I wish there was more that we could do. Stay alive."

"We'll try," I said. "Otherwise, we'll take a lot of 'em with us. Golf Lima Ten, out."

I handed Greg the handset. "That sounded cheerful," he observed.

"We're cut off," I told him. I wouldn't sugarcoat things for my team, and they wouldn't expect me to. "No drone support, no air support for the time being. Jamming, or some such."

Greg nodded. His camouflage paint had been worn off to the point that it was mainly just darkening the lines on his face, and his fiery red mustache was showing through quite brightly. He stroked it momentarily as he looked around at the surrounding woods, which probably had something to do with why there wasn't much paint left in it.

"Well, at least it's pretty country," he said. "It could be Africa or Syria."

"It is way too early for your cheerfulness, Greg," I said, shaking my head as I got to my feet and turned toward Killian's Powell. "*Especially* under these circumstances."

"It's not early," Greg pointed out with a grin as I started walking away. "It's getting late; it's almost sunset."

I flipped him off without turning back.

I felt the Army soldiers' eyes on me as I walked toward the armored vehicle. Most of them turned back front as I looked at them; some of them had probably heard the confrontation earlier. The rest just didn't want to look me in the eye.

Some warriors.

I knew that I was probably being unfair; the Army didn't encourage the kind of warrior spirit that the Triarii did, but there had to be some meat-eaters in that crew. There always were. It was just that in that kind of outfit, they tended to be the low-ranking ones who were always in trouble.

Reaching the M5, I stepped to the open hatch and stuck my head in. "Killian?"

He was awake, sitting up on one of the four seats in the back. That kind of space was why the Army had kept the Stryker in service; the Powell just didn't have the troop-carrying capacity, and it was way too expensive to field in sufficient numbers to make up for it. "You're up," he observed.

"Not that I'm enjoying it, but it was past time," I replied. I still hurt everywhere, and my eyes were gritty. I didn't expect that to change anytime soon. "We need to figure out our next move."

"Yeah," he said. "About that. Have you guys been picking up anything on the open comms?"

I shook my head. "Not that I've heard. Bradshaw would have told me if his comm guys had heard anything during the day."

He nodded. "No surprise." He pointed, indicating the vehicle he was sitting in. "We've got bigger amps than you do." He looked down at the handset in his hand. "I'd invite you to listen, but we don't have recording equipment, and there hasn't been anything for the last hour. But there's been something, real faint. It sounds like it might be somebody back at Keystone. There might be survivors."

"Or it might be a trap," I answered. "Whoever knocked out Keystone is clearly sophisticated enough that they can play all sorts of electronic games."

"Even so," he said, "we need to be sure. I sure don't want to leave somebody back there to die."

"You didn't see what was left," I told him. "The whole base was on fire. And it looked like somebody blew the hell out of it beforehand."

"Maybe," he answered. He wasn't quite looking me in the eye. It was a little off-putting, but he was arguing with someone he didn't know about going back into a hellscape that he hadn't seen. He was nervous about it. "But there were some pretty sturdy bunkers in there. Somebody might have holed up and survived."

I thought about it. On the one hand, it was a stupid risk. On the other hand, I had to agree with him. If we could get anybody else out, and didn't, I knew I was going to have a hard time with it later on.

"You know what that's going to mean driving into?" I asked him. "Those two Tigers were only the air component. There were tanks, IFVs, and infantry on the road, overwatching the ruins. I doubt they've pulled off, especially after the birds traded fire with us last night."

He looked down at his hands. "That's assuming that what happened wasn't a friendly-fire incident. I know I was pretty rattled when you told me that the FOB was gone. Maybe the pilots were, too. Shot too fast, before they'd IDed us."

"You really think that?" I asked. I sure didn't. There were too many bad things lining up.

That time, he really did look me in the eye. "What else am I supposed to think?" he asked. "That the EDC decided to declare war on the US? They're our *allies*, for fuck's sake. We came here at their request. Why would they do something like that?"

"After Slovenský Grob?" I asked. "You figure it out."

"That was one incident," he protested.

"One incident that had you on lockdown for over a month, and that created more political trouble than the Slovak uprising did in the first place," I pointed out. I sighed. I'd probably seen a *lot* more intel than Killian had, particularly lately. I hated to think about what kind of bullshit was being spun for the troops' consumption in their weekly briefs, presuming that they were even *getting* weekly briefs. I'd seen enough during my own Active Duty days.

"You may not have seen it," I said, "but the EDC's getting fucking desperate. *Especially* within the last year. The unrest in France and Germany's getting worse, and with the pushback they're getting from Eastern Europe, they know that they're screwed. The money's running out, and control's slipping through their fingers. What do you think desperate people are going to do when an 'ally' starts standing up to them? *Especially* one that they've been sniping back and forth with, politically and economically, for the last decade?"

Besides which, I'd seen enough of the European Defense Council's rhetoric to know a pack of utopian sociopaths when I heard it. There was no doubt in my mind that those soft-clothed bastards wouldn't hesitate to order thousands of people killed.

"It's crazy," he protested.

"What about the world today isn't?" I asked rhetorically. A shooting war in the Pacific, Europe coming apart at the seams, the Shi'a about to invade Saudi Arabia to crush the Sunni once and for all, Central Asia on the ragged edge of a nuclear holocaust…

The US in the middle of a civil war that its own government didn't want to admit was even happening.

There was a long silence after that. The radio squawk box near his shoulder hissed and popped, but there was nothing like regular radio traffic on it. He rubbed a palm against his forehead, looking down at the decking between his boots.

"It doesn't matter," he said, finally. "If there's anyone still alive back there, we've got to help them. They're Americans." He looked up at me. "I guess I'm hoping that still means something to you."

"Why the hell do you think I'm here in the first place?" I asked. "Your command was sitting on its hands while an American was being held hostage."

I blew out a sigh. This was going to suck. "Hold this position," I said. "My team has a lot better chance of getting in there undetected and looking around than your guys do. You roll up in these gigantic turtles, and you're going to be in a firefight. We might be able to sneak in and sneak back out." We'd certainly practiced it enough. Infiltration was a key Grex Luporum skillset, and it was one that we honed in all sorts of situations, usually against OPFOR role-players who were other GL operators.

But Killian shook his head. "No," he said. "I'm willing to concede that you guys are probably better for going in; I still don't know exactly who you are, but you're clearly some kind of SOF types. Or you were." His tone made it clear that he had his suspicions as to who we were, but he wasn't going to voice them under the circumstances. He didn't want to look a gift horse in the mouth. "But if we stay here, we're not going to be able to support you if something does go pear-shaped." He pulled up an electronic map on a screen that was mounted on a rotating armature attached to the front bulkhead. "We'll move up to here," he said, indicating another clearing, about a klick away from where we'd taken contact from the Tigers. "That way, we're within shouting distance if you end up in trouble that you need some extra firepower to get out of." He slapped the overhead with a gloved hand, indicating the 50mm above us.

He looked me in the eye, and there was some steel in his gaze. "They're our people, too," he said. "We're not going to sit back here on our hands and let you do all the heavy lifting."

I nodded. As long as they stayed out of the way. This was going to be tricky enough as it was. But I wasn't going to turn down support, given our situation.

Thomas Paine once said, "If we do not hang together, we shall surely hang separately." I held out my hand and he shook it.

"Sounds like a plan," I said. "We need to get started soon; we've got a bit of a movement ahead of us, and only so much darkness."

There was no way in hell I was going in there in daylight. Fortunately, Killian just nodded his agreement. Then we got down to planning.

Chapter 10

We'd split up. The woods between the lay-up site and the target were too thick for the vehicles to negotiate, and the route around was far too long for us to cover it on foot in a timely manner. So, we set the rendezvous, and left in different directions.

Killian must have pushed hard. The vehicles were already there when we got closer, and we had to deconflict the linkup carefully. We didn't dare use the radios too much, not that close to the wreckage that had been FOB Keystone. Once we'd made contact, we slipped inside their perimeter, finding that Killian had set up much the same way as he had before. The vehicles were camouflaged and parked as far under the trees as possible. It wouldn't hide them entirely from thermal imaging, but it would help.

Bradshaw met me and Killian by the M5's back ramp. "We're getting set in," he said. "You sure about this, Matt?"

I nodded, though under the circumstances I wasn't as sure as I should have been. This was a long shot, and I knew it. So did the rest of the team. Jordan hadn't been shy about expressing his opinion about it. Nor had Dwight. But I'd stood firm and pointed out that if there really *were* Americans in there who needed our help, it wasn't far off the mission we'd entered Slovakia for in the first place. And that, as cut off as we were, every gun helped.

Jordan was still pissed about it. Dwight had just shaken his head and shrugged. Phil had been quiet, for once. Greg had agreed, if only because it was my idea. He was just agreeable like that. Tony hadn't said much; neither had Scott. Chris had agreed, because it was the Christian thing to do, not because he liked the idea. David just wanted another chance to get stuck in. He'd joined the Army after reading too many Punisher comics, after all.

Reuben had had the most to say. "I don't care," he said. "It's a risk, yeah. But Matt's right. We stuck our necks out coming here, when there was plenty of work Stateside, because an American was in danger. This is no different. If we don't look out for other Americans, why the fuck did we join the Triarii in the first place?" Reuben was the one of us who was most likely to stick his neck out for his countrymen. He still believed that the American experiment could be salvaged, and that we were going to be instrumental in the salvage operation, through acts just like this.

I wasn't sure how many of us still thought that way. There's only so long you can watch your country tearing itself apart before you start to wonder if you're just fighting a holding action before the final collapse.

But as cynical as I'd become, I had still signed on for this mission. All of it.

"I'm sure," I told Bradshaw. "We'll drop rucks and leave them with you. I want to be light as possible for this." He just nodded.

"If we get in trouble, we'll pop a red star cluster," I said, speaking to both him and Killian. "Don't leave us hanging for too long, alright?"

Bradshaw nodded and clapped me on the shoulder. Killian just nodded.

I turned and headed back to where I'd left the rest of the team, right at the perimeter.

**

I paused in my crawl across the open field to look around and listen.

It wasn't an ideal approach, but there wasn't going to be one. Not going into a FOB. The fields had been harvested the year before, and once the peacekeepers had come in, the farmer had been paid off to leave them fallow around the base, which had sprawled almost as big as Lozorno to the west.

But there were no shooters in the guard towers now, at least not the ones that were still standing. There might be bodies in the ones that had collapsed.

The fires seemed to have died down, but smoke still drifted across the fields. It stung the nostrils and threatened to make us cough. It was quiet enough in the country night that that could have been fatal. The sound would have traveled a long way.

The team was spread out across almost three hundred yards, all of us flat on our bellies, using every bit of micro-terrain we could find to disguise us from the armored vehicles still parked on the highway to the southwest.

Of course, we hadn't just crossed the road right in front of them and then gone crawling across and open field. That would have been stupid. We'd worked our way around the northeast side of Jablonovè and then started working our way toward the back wall of the FOB.

The armored vehicles on the highway weren't what worried me. It was the drones buzzing around. Fortunately, most of them seemed to be focused on the south side of the highway or closer to Jablonovè. They didn't seem to have spotted us yet, despite the fact that we were probably standing out as blazing white thermal beacons against the cool dirt.

Phil had found an old, now dry, irrigation ditch that appeared to lead right up to the T-walls. That was our infiltration route. Getting over the wall was going to be interesting, but it looked like a few of the pre-fabricated concrete sections had been blasted down or smashed by explosions.

Phil was almost to the wall. My elbows and knees were aching, but fortunately, the fatigues were reinforced in those spots, so I wasn't too worried about skinning them when the fabric wore through. Our stuff was designed for field work, unlike some of the cammies I'd worn in the Marine Corps, that had disintegrated within a couple of weeks of hard use in the field.

I was carrying my rifle with my thumb and forefinger wrapped around the front sight, the weapon itself laid over my elbow and shoulder. I'd managed to keep from stabbing the muzzle in the dirt so far, thankfully. Clearing it before going over that wall would have been a bitch.

Phil got to the base of the T-walls and got up on a knee, his rifle held ready, scanning all around us. I would have given my eyeteeth for a diversion just then, but that would have likely required expending munitions, and we needed to conserve as much of them as possible.

It took a couple minutes for me to join him. I had to resist the urge to move faster, to turn my careful and measured movement into a frantic scramble to get to the wall and out of that exposed, open ground. Even if the drones were far enough away that they couldn't quite spot us, if there were foot-mobiles in the woods, rapid movement would attract attention. I knew that much from personal experience, as well as training. I'd shot a would-be jihadi infiltrator once because he'd moved too fast.

I finally reached Phil, who helped me up with his off hand. My heart was pounding, as hard as I was working to regulate my breathing. Crawling is hard work, and when you add the strain of trying to go unseen for almost half a klick across flat ground, it just gets worse.

With my own rifle at the ready, crouched against the base of the T-walls, I could take stock. I'd taken my NVGs off on the approach; they were just going to cause problems and point themselves down at the dirt otherwise. Now I pushed my ghillie hood back long enough to pull the skullcap mount over my head before pulling it back up again. The fields lit up in shades of gray and black in front of my eye.

Greg was close behind me, and the rest were following. Our thermal signatures weren't quite as bad as I'd feared, though if anyone with thermal imagers was looking at the field closely, they'd see us. I scanned the woods beyond, where we'd come out, and saw only the dark under the trees.

Movement above the trees caught my eye, a spark in the NVGs drifting north above the forest. A drone. It was too small to be anything else. I stayed perfectly still for a moment, resisting the urge to hiss at Greg to freeze. I'd have to make too much noise.

But the drone kept on drifting north, without altering its course to take a closer look at us. If its operator had seen us at all, he'd probably dismissed us as local livestock.

I hoped so. We were banking hard on the bad guys thinking that nobody would be stupid enough or crazy enough to come back here after what had happened the night before.

Greg caught up and struggled to his knee, taking up his own position along the wall. We started spreading out, even as Phil moved toward the nearest gap, where a T-wall had halfway tipped over, held in place by the steel cables that were strung along the inside of the barrier.

In some ways, it was risky; a series of heat sources lined up against the concrete T-walls might stand out more. But the barrier itself would provide some shelter from observation from other angles, so getting close to it made sense. Plus, while the fires had died down, there were still enough smoldering structures inside that there was a pretty decent thermal bloom inside, that might further mask our presence.

There weren't any perfect solutions. There never were. Just "good enough" solutions that hopefully didn't get people killed.

Before Scott brought up the rear, Phil was already moving, standing up under the gap opened by the tipped concrete barrier, while Dwight moved past him to cover the flank with his Mk 48. Reuben started to crouch down to give him a boost, while I grabbed Chris and moved over to the other side of the cracked T-wall to do the same. I wanted as many guns pointed inward on the breach as possible when we crossed the threshold.

Chris squatted down with his back to the upright T-wall, even as it shifted slightly. It'd had clearly been damaged by the blast that had tipped over its neighbor. I just hoped that it didn't decide to collapse on Chris and me.

Putting my boot on his thigh, I shifted my OBR to my right hand, grabbing the edge of the canted T-wall with my left, and hoisted myself up, dropping the rifle level as I came into the rough, V-shaped notch left between the sections of cement. I quickly scanned the open ground on the inside of the wall, even as Phil appeared across from me, similarly clearing the area to my right that I couldn't see.

Nothing. The "cans," prefab trailer living quarters, right in front of me were smashed wreckage, one of them still smoking over a day after its destruction. Smoke was still drifting, though not nearly as thickly as the night before. Everything else was still.

I glanced across at Phil, and nodded. He returned the gesture. Our entry was clear.

So far.

I took the lead, putting all my weight on the one foot that was braced on Chris's leg. He grunted a little, and I felt him sag, but I wedged my other foot in the notch above, barely reaching it and struggling with my balance for a second. I wasn't as flexible as I used to be.

Dwight was really going to have a hell of a time getting through. We might have to leave him and a couple others outside, on exterior security.

I got my weight on that foot, and promptly felt a pang of pain as my boot was squeezed down into the notch. No surprise, really. The job isn't supposed to be comfortable. I'd gotten somewhat inured to pain as a Marine machinegunner.

With another heave, I got myself up, having to let my rifle dangle on its sling as I grabbed the cable and the concrete, then swung a foot over the cable. If I was hoping for a graceful, silent entry, I was doomed to disappoint myself, because as soon as I got a foot over the cable, it started to slip on the pocked, dusty concrete. I started to fall toward the inside, catching myself on the cable with one hand and my other foot, even as my rifle swung and hit the inside of the concrete wall with a loud *clack.*

I hung there for a second, feeling exposed as all hell, then got my boot over the cable and deliberately dropped the rest of the way.

I almost ate shit at the bottom, especially when one boot slid off the bottom of the T-wall. Only a fast movement got my weight over my feet as I bent my knees to absorb the shock, quickly snatching up my rifle before I buried the muzzle in the dirt.

I heard Phil land next to me, but I was getting my weapon up and scanning, my heart pounding in my throat. That had been sloppy and noisy, and if there were any bad guys—or simply any shell-shocked, trigger-happy survivors, then the next few seconds could go very badly, very quickly.

But the open ground was just as empty as it had been a moment before.

Phil and I moved away from the breach, leaving room for the others to cross. As Chris hit the ground and came up beside me, I tapped him on the shoulder and pointed, indicating he should cover the sector I'd been watching, then moved back to the breach as David appeared in the V.

"Tell Dwight, Tony, Scott, and Reuben to stay outside on security," I whispered, as he paused in the notch, his boot wedged into the gap and a gloved hand on either concrete wall. He nodded, then turned back and whispered. Then he resumed his passage through the gap, making it look a lot easier and smoother than I'd managed.

I told myself that David was small. Of course it was easier for him.

It took a few minutes to get all of us over the wall. Getting out wasn't going to be fun. We might have to find a different breach point, though that was going to depend on the enemy. The place we'd picked seemed to be the least likely point to be observed.

Finally, everyone who was coming was on the ground, on a knee, scanning the hellscape around us.

The base had been obliterated. There were smashed, smoldering prefabs and the ash heaps that had been tents everywhere. Furthermore, there were craters. A lot of craters.

It looked like it had been hammered by artillery or massed airstrikes. It sure as hell didn't look like the aftermath of a terrorist attack.

The smoke that still drifted stung the throat and threatened to make me cough. It stank of burnt plastic, rubber, and worse.

I switched my radio to the open channel that Killian had told me he'd heard the faint transmissions on. "Any station this net, this is Golf Lima Ten Six. We are Americans. If you are alive and need help, send your position."

There was a long silence. My guess was that if there really was anyone left in that desolate ruin, they weren't going to be quick to trust an unknown voice on the radio.

107

On the other hand, they had been the ones transmitting in the clear. Which meant that they'd already spotlighted themselves to anyone listening. They might even already be dead or captured.

Captured by whom was the question. I still doubted that this was the Slovak Nationalists' doing, but without more information, we had to assume that *everyone* was the enemy.

"This is Chief Warrant Officer Warren," a hoarse voice said over the radio. "We are in a bunker, in hiding. Is the base clear?"

"I don't know yet," I replied. "But there does not appear to be any movement. Where is the bunker?"

"We're on the north side, next to the TOC," Warren replied. "Come get us."

"We are on our way," I said, resisting the urge to tell him to be a little more specific and a little more circumspect at the same time. He'd made no effort to verify that we were who I said we were. "Are there any other identifiers for which bunker you're in?"

He didn't respond. Great. That was going to make deconfliction to link up that much more difficult.

I moved up and tapped Phil. We were at the northeastern corner of the base, which meant that we didn't have far to go. Of course, "the north side" wasn't exactly all that specific, and none of us really knew where the FOB's Tactical Operations Center had been located. Which meant we were going to have to search every bunker we came to until we found Warren and whoever was with him.

We moved out, stepping carefully, eyes and weapons up and staying as alert as possible on what sleep and food we'd had. This kind of thing was why Hartrick had made Selection as brutally harsh as he had. We had to be able to push through when every faculty just wanted to shut down.

Phil slowed as he neared the corner of one of the trailers. The can had a massive hole blown out the side of it.

I stepped up next to him and saw why he'd stopped. There was a bunker right there, between the rows of trailers. It wasn't complicated; these things never were. Little more than a

U-shaped chunk of reinforced concrete, set upside-down, with smaller versions of the T-wall barriers at either end.

There were bodies lying on the ground just outside. And from the way they were lying there, they'd been leaving the bunker when they'd died.

Rifles up, we moved toward the bodies, as the rest spread out and took cover at the corners of the surrounding trailers, covering down every approach. I came up to the nearest corpse and looked down at it, a cold fury starting to build in my chest, a rage that hadn't been able to really come to the fore under the weight of fatigue before.

There were two young men and a woman. One of the men was in uniform; the other man and the woman were in PT gear. They hadn't been killed by the artillery. They'd been shot, multiple times. All three had head wounds that looked, even through the blurry gray tones of my NVGs, like they'd been administered at close range.

Someone had shot these soldiers, then walked up and made damned good and sure they were dead. Presumably, standing close enough that he'd gotten blood on his boots.

I glanced down the lane. More craters and wrecked trailers stood out in the faint, drifting smoke. And there were more bodies on the ground, that hadn't been in the open when the bombardment that I was sure had flattened the base had happened.

"Warren!" I hissed toward the bunker. I doubted he was in there. Whoever had murdered those kids on the ground would have made sure that there wasn't anyone left inside. Silence met my call, and I risked sticking my head and weapon inside.

The bunker was empty.

Despite the sickened hate churning in my guts, I got Phil's attention and pointed along the outer wall. We needed to move.

He glanced down at the bodies again. Phil was a smartass and a shit-talker, but even he didn't have anything to say. He just shook his head in disgust and got up, turning back toward the perimeter wall. I thought I saw his hands clenching on his rifle as he did so.

The next row looked much the same. The only difference was the brass piled at the corner of one of the trailers, and the fact that there weren't any bodies outside the nearest bunker.

"Warren!" I hissed again, a loud stage whisper that I hoped would carry without being heard beyond the wall. It was deathly quiet within Keystone's perimeter, despite the faint crackle where the fires still burned.

There was no response. But something about that bunker, the concrete cracked by a near-miss from an artillery shell, that had cratered the ground next to it and smashed in the side of a nearby trailer, bugged me. I wasn't ready to just go up to it.

I keyed my radio. "Warren, this is Golf Lima Ten Six. Are you in bunker…" I squinted. "Bunker Seven Echo?"

I thought I heard movement at that. There was a faint crackle on the radio, as if someone had keyed the mic, then decided against it.

Rifles were pointed at the dark maw of the entrance to that bunker. I suspected I knew what was going on, but under the circumstances, there was no way in hell I was going to take chances.

Finally, the radio crackled with Warren's voice. "Yes," he said, "we're in Seven E."

I didn't bother to correct his radio procedures. From the sounds of things, Chief Warrant Officer Warren was a pogue, a non-infantry type. He was out of his depth, and it could cause problems going forward.

England hadn't been much use, but if we had more than one bit of human baggage in tow, getting out of Keystone unobserved could get interesting.

But these survivors were why we were there. Just like Specialist England. "I have eyes on your position now," I told him. "We're going to move to you. You will see or hear armed men moving around the bunker. Do not shoot at them. They are friendlies. Once we have security set, I will come to you."

"R-roger," was the response. "Over."

I rolled my eyes. This guy must not have done much for the last decade plus besides fly a desk. But I pointed to Phil and Chris, and soon they were darting across the lane between

110

smashed and bullet- and shrapnel-riddled trailers to take up security positions on the openings.

Once we had a rough perimeter around the bunker, I moved in. "Warren," I called softly. "I'm coming in." Hoping that I wasn't about to get my head shot off by some jumpy private or admin warrant officer, I ducked inside the bunker.

There were five figures inside. Three were in varying degrees of PT gear or sleepwear. One was in cammies, but otherwise unarmed. The last one was kitted up, and had his M37A2 pointed at my face as I entered.

Of course, I had my OBR pointed at him, too. I wasn't taking chances, and my finger was resting on the trigger, just in case. I was partially silhouetted against the gray light outside, but he was a white outline in my NVGs, and the IR aiming laser was dancing on his chest.

"Friendly," I hissed. He lowered the rifle, and after a second, so did I. I looked around at the group of survivors. Four men and a woman. One of the men in PT gear was fat; he was going to have a hard time keeping up, or even crawling across that damned field outside the wall. Unfortunately, he was also the one with the radio in his hands.

"All right," I said. "We've got the immediate area secured. We need to find field clothes for you three." I'd never imagined that I'd be worrying about dressing soldiers like little kids, but that was the situation I found myself in. They couldn't be in very good shape after the last day and night that had already passed, and they were going to die of exposure as fall approached if we dragged them through the woods in shorts and t-shirts.

We couldn't expect to get out of this situation quickly. We had to think long-term. And that meant making sure that everybody was at least dressed to survive.

"We were all in this block of trailers, I think," the man with the rifle said.

"Doesn't matter," I said. "It looks like everyone else in here is dead, so go in, find something that'll fit, and get dressed. You've got five minutes."

The fat guy, whom I suspected from the radio was Warren, was about to protest, but thought better of it. He was breathing hard, and was obviously scared, but he wasn't completely stupid. He struggled to his feet and ducked out of the bunker. The others followed, slowly.

I grabbed the guy with the rifle on the way out. "How many mags do you have?" I asked him.

"Four," he said. "I was just coming off patrol when things clacked off."

"You're with us," I said. "Find a hole and fit in."

He nodded. "You planning on going out the north gate?" he asked.

"Didn't even know there was a north gate," I replied. "We weren't stationed here." I left off the fact that we weren't Army. He'd figure that out soon enough.

He pointed. "It's just over there. How'd you get in?"

"Climbed," I replied. I keyed my radio. "Weeb, Deacon. We've made contact, and one of the survivors is telling me that there's a north gate that might be easier to get out of. He's pointing to the west of our breach point."

"Roger," Scott replied. "We'll relocate. No more drone activity at present."

I keyed the mic twice to acknowledge. "Find a spot, buddy," I told the young soldier. He nodded, looked around, and found a gap in the perimeter he could cover.

I stayed where I was, watching the door where Warren and the other two underdressed soldiers had disappeared. Time was flying, and with it what darkness that we had left to cover our movement.

They finally came out, the fat warrant last, fastening a blouse that looked about a size too small for him. None of them had grabbed a go bag, load bearing gear, or weapon.

Unfortunately, we didn't have time to go hunting for such things. Not there. Not with presumably enemy armor sitting on the highway outside, watching. We needed to get the hell away from Keystone and back into the hills.

"Do you know of any other survivors?" I asked Warren.

He shook his head. "We've been on the radio since about midday," he said. "We haven't made contact with anyone else."

"Have you looked around?" I asked.

"No," he replied shakily. "I didn't consider it safe, until we knew more."

I nodded, looking around and thinking. I didn't want to leave anyone else behind, but we were also short on time, and I didn't think we had enough time to search *every* bunker. But the need to make sure we weren't leaving more men or women to their deaths won out. "Saddle up," I said. "Next bunker."

***

It didn't take as long as it might have. Too much of the base had been blasted flat. There were probably only about three dozen bunkers left intact, and it didn't take long to search each one.

We found more survivors, but only about half a dozen. Of those, four were clearly grunts, and had at least grabbed their weapons when things had gone sideways. At least one, I suspected, was an infantryman, but hadn't armed himself. He was noticeably being shunned by the other two in the bunker where we'd found him.

Gathered in the shadow of what had been a vehicle parking area, the overhangs blasted to pieces and the vehicles nothing but still-warm, burned-out hulks, I checked my watch. 0350. We had a couple hours at least before sunrise. But we'd need all of it, especially since it didn't look like some of our charges were going to be moving all that fast. Not everybody was up to the highest of physical fitness standards, let's put it that way.

"Weeb, Deacon," I called, even as I scanned the sky above us. I could just barely hear what sounded like a couple drones, but I wasn't picking them out, even with the NVGs' thermal capability. "We're coming out."

"We've got the north gate secured," Scott reported. "Just watch your step on the way out. It's kind of a mess out here."

I had that first infantryman with me, and he pointed the way for Phil. We moved out, my team forming a loose diamond formation around the gaggle of survivors.

We threaded our way north, through the ruined and smashed remains of the installation, having to step wide around craters and passing bodies and pieces of bodies. Some had been killed by the bombardment or IEDs. Others had clearly been shot.

113

The enemy had thoroughly swept the compound *after* the bombardment had ended.

The north gate was smaller than the main gate to the south, but it had been hit, too. I immediately saw what Scott had been talking about. Something had detonated inside the gate. There were twisted fragments of metal everywhere, including embedded in the armored glass of the guard post, and the gate itself was a warped ruin. Whatever the bad guys had used, it had been big.

Scott and the rest of the team were in a rough half-circle outside, mostly down in the prone, covering the surrounding woods. I moved to Scott and crouched down on a knee, once again watching the sky. There were two drones up there, now, and they might have been circling closer. It was definitely time to go.

"We've got too many people to get out of here sneaky-like," I whispered.

"Dash for the trees?" Scott asked.

"I think so," I said, glancing back at the rescued survivors huddled in the ruin of the gate. "It won't be much of a dash, but hopefully we can get under cover before the drones call in the cavalry. Presuming that we don't just get gunned down from the road."

"Always cheerful, aren't you, Matt?" Scott said. "You've been hanging out with Greg too much."

I punched him in the calf, hard enough to hurt, then moved back to where our charges were crouched. "We're moving to the woods up there," I said, just loudly enough that they could hear me. "You stay low, you move fast. Do not stop or slow down in the open. Understood?"

I got what might have been murmurs of understanding and assent. I hoped so. "Phil, you're on point."

Phil got up and led out. Glancing at the drones again, seeing that they really did appear to be closer, I followed.

Chapter 11

Phil got to the treeline quickly; even as tired as we were, three hundred yards isn't far, especially without the weight of our rucks. Our charges, however, weren't quite so quick. Scott, Chris, and Tony were chivvying them along as fast as possible, but it still took a couple minutes to get them all under the trees.

And during that couple of minutes, the drones were getting closer. From my position on a knee at the edge of the field, I could hear the buzz getting louder, and a glance up at the sky showed me the faint spark of the nearest drone's thermal signature getting closer. They were definitely heading our way.

"Hurry the hell up," I muttered. I was increasingly convinced that the drone operator had figured out that somebody was leaving the wrecked FOB, and was going to be alerting enemy forces at any moment. It was certainly a possibility that Killian was right; that the EDC had fired on our vehicles mistakenly, and that the drones were looking for survivors to rescue.

I just didn't think it was likely. And when I heard diesels rumbling and tracks start rattling and squealing in the distance, on the far side of the smashed compound, my heart rate picked up. Bad juju. "Come on!" I hissed. "Move it!"

I looked up as the grunts passed me, Warren and the other presumed pogues trailing behind. That drone was getting closer. To hell with it. If it turned out to be a friendly that was looking for people to help, they could bill me. I brought my rifle to my shoulder, put the laser on the dot, breathed out, and fired.

I don't think I'd actually expected to hit the drone on the first shot. I'd blasted drones with rifle fire before; they were becoming a ubiquitous weapon of irregular warfare as well as being in common use by regular forces, and there were some nasty surprises getting attached to little commercial quad-rotors back Stateside. But this was at a bit longer range than I'd engaged one before. So, I was a little surprised—and somewhat pleased with myself—when the drone suddenly tumbled out of the sky, fluttering like a wounded bird until it hit the ground.

"Move it!" I snarled. The vehicles down by the highway were definitely moving. They might have a hard time following us into the woods, but they'd have dismounts. And that hadn't been one of the bigger, high-altitude drones, either. A smaller one could be steered between tree trunks, at least for a while. It would lose signal eventually, but that might not be for a while.

We had to make tracks.

I grabbed Warren by the blouse as he passed me. "We are officially made," I whispered urgently. "So, we have to move fast. You keep up with us and you *do not stop*. Not for anything. If we stop, you keep pushing. We've got firepower, you don't. You keep your people moving until I tell you we're secure. Understood?"

"What if that was a friendly drone?" he asked. I wondered if he'd actually been listening.

"No such thing right now," I told him. "Do you understand what I just told you? Your life and the lives of the rest of these soldiers depends on it."

He gulped air, then nodded. "Yes," he said. "I understand."

I didn't quite shove him toward Phil. "Move," was all I said.

I glanced back as Scott brought up the rear. I might have seen movement around the side of what remained of Keystone's wall, but it was hard to say. We had a head start, anyway.

"Last man," Scott whispered. I signaled that I'd heard him, then turned into the woods and stepped it out to catch up with Phil.

***

It was a punishing movement, even for us. For the soldiers who'd gone most of two days and two nights without food or much water, it was almost a death march. But we didn't have any other choice.

116

The drones were still buzzing above the treetops, and I could hear aircraft overhead, fast-movers and rotary-wing both. Neither of which were unknown sounds in Slovakia at that time, but recent events lent the sounds an ominous note that might not have been there before.

The addition of the distant rumble of artillery made it worse. It might have just been thunder, except that the skies were clear.

Something big was going down in Slovakia. And I had a feeling that the destruction of FOB Keystone was an integral part of it.

Warren was flagging within a klick, even more so than any of the rest. It had taken almost half an hour to cover that distance, but that was still too quick for him, even unburdened by weapon or gear. I didn't let us stop, though. Scott had informed me that he was pretty sure there were foot-mobiles coming into the woods after us.

Phil hadn't gone straight north once we'd gotten into the woods; that would have been counter-productive. We needed to link back up with Killian and Bradshaw, and they were south of the highway. Getting across was going to be fun—by which I mean a cast-iron, stone bitch—but I had a plan for that. As it was, we were half a klick into the woods and pushing east, paralleling the edge of the fields.

Chris had moved up to "motivate" Warren. I hadn't told him to. Chris was a study in contradictions, sometimes. He was doubtless cussing Warren six ways from Sunday every time he had to pick the man up when he fell—which was often. At the same time, Chris was a bit of a holy roller, and considered helping his fellow man to be a sacred duty. Warren being the ranking officer among the survivors and the weakest meant that Chris was kind of caught between his contempt for weak officers and his eagerness to help people.

As I looked back, Chris was pulling Warren to his feet again. "Weeb, Deacon," I called. "We still got shadows?"

"I think so, Deacon," Scott replied. "They're not closing the gap, but I've seen some movement back there. Still about five or six hundred meters back."

I waited, standing under a hoary oak that blacked out the sky above me. Fall was coming, but most of the leaves were still on the trees. They were only just starting to change color.

We didn't have claymores; right then I would have given my eyeteeth for a couple. They might have discouraged our pursuers. As it was, our options were sharply limited.

I waved at Phil to keep pushing, along with Greg. I'd catch up. I waited where I was, letting the rest pass me until Scott reached the oak.

"As long as they're following us, we're in trouble," I whispered, as the two of us took a knee under the tree. Scott was breathing hard, but he wasn't flagging yet. "But if we stop and hit them, if they've got the numbers, they might just keep pushing, and it'll give them a chance to close the gap."

"They're going to keep pushing as long as we *don't* do something," Scott replied. "And they're presumably fresher than we are." He paused for a moment, looking back down the way we'd come. The density of the woods limited our lines of sight, but I could faintly hear the sounds of movement back there, only drowned out occasionally by a nearby aircraft.

"I think they've been waiting for this," Scott continued. "It's what I'd do. Station a force to watch the FOB for any survivors either trying to get out or return if they were caught outside."

"You don't think that they're friendlies trying to rescue any survivors who might have been, as you said, caught outside?" I asked.

"Nah," he said. "They'd have tried comms before now if that was the case. Some kind of comms, even if it's fucking loudspeakers. They haven't. They've just sent drones after us and men on foot, who haven't yelled or anything. That's hostile act, hostile intent, in my opinion. If you don't want someone to act like they're being hunted, don't act like you're hunting them."

I nodded. So, I wasn't the only one thinking along those lines. Every once in a while, it was good to get that sanity check.

I chewed my lip, tasting salt and grit. I didn't want to get in a firefight, particularly not while we were dragging unarmed personnel with us. We needed to slow our pursuers down, rather than come to grips with them. A firefight in the dark would just

118

give them something to shoot at. I wanted them second-guessing themselves and the darkness around them.

In the absence of claymores, we were going to have to make do with what we had.

Pulling a frag grenade out of my chest rig, I started digging in the side pouch for the 550 cord that I kept daisy-chained in there, just in case. There was never any telling when you might need 550, so I kept some in my ruck and some in my chest rig. It wasn't ideal for the purpose at hand; wire would have worked better. But, once again, you gotta make do with what you've got.

Scott glanced over and saw what I was doing. He started looking around the nearby trees, and held out a hand. Scott and I had worked together long enough that we could catch up with each other's thought processes pretty quickly, even without speaking.

I tied one end of the 550 cord, which was originally designed for use as parachute shroud lines, hence its other name of "paracord," to the ring of the frag's pin, then handed the grenade to Scott while I unraveled the "daisy chain" as he pulled it over to him and wedged the frag in the roots of one of the oaks. Meanwhile, I was running the cord to another nearby trunk and starting to carefully wrap it around the bole, drawing it *just* tight enough before tying it off.

If I pulled too hard, Scott would be in trouble.

Satisfied, we backed off and hurried to catch up with the rest of the team. Hopefully, even if they spotted the trap, it would give them pause. There would be no way they could be sure that there wouldn't be more. They'd have to slow down and search for other traps, which would give us time to open up that time/distance gap.

Scott fell in behind Tony while I pushed to catch up with the point element. Phil knew where he was going, but I was the team leader. I needed to be able to steer him if necessary.

We'd gone about another half a klick when I heard a dull *thump* from behind us.

They hadn't spotted the cord, after all.

***

119

Phil and I crouched at the edge of the trees and scanned the field in front of us.

It was getting late. First light was in about an hour. In a way, it would be something of an advantage. NVGs get less effective during Before Morning Nautical Twilight; the image gets washed out and contrast goes to hell. Even movement gets hard to see. Meanwhile, it's still too dark for the naked eye. Thermals, unfortunately, were still unaffected, though. Which meant that we still had to move carefully.

Hartrick had talked about the days when the Marines and Army could move with impunity during the night, because the Arabs and Afghans they were fighting didn't have night vision. The US had owned the night. Those days were long gone. We had to act as if the enemy had every capability that we did. Because, in most cases, they did.

Phil finished his scan and turned to me. "I can still hear drones, but I don't see any," he whispered. "Makes me nervous."

I craned my neck to scan the sky again. "There might be some north of us, blocked by the trees," I said, "but they can't be everywhere. Comes the point where we've just got to take the risk."

He nodded, the motion just visible in the slowly receding darkness. "We can try to crawl, or we can make a dash for it," he said. "What do you want to do?"

I studied the ground in front of us. We had about two hundred meters of open field to cross to get to the line of trees that separated two different fields. The trees weren't thick, but they'd provide *some* concealment. And we'd need every bit of it to get across the nearly two klicks of open fields between us and the woods on the southeastern side of Highway 501.

Fortunately, as I scanned the landscape, through the much lower and sparser hedgerow along the sides of the road that split the fields between us and the highway, I didn't see any vehicles. And, at least for the moment, the sky was mostly clear. Didn't mean it would last, but they couldn't watch *everywhere*.

"I think the faster we get over there, the better," I said. "With the numbers we've got, if we try and take it slow and sneaky, we *will* get caught with somebody in the open when a bird or a drone does go over."

"Speed is security, then," he said. He was all business at that point, his usual, and often unwelcome, "wit" shelved for the moment. That was Phil. He was an ass the rest of the time, but when it was really time to work, he shut up and worked. He looked back over his shoulder. "No time like the present, huh?"

I followed his gaze. Sure enough, it looked like everybody was in place behind us. It was time to move. I tapped him on the shoulder, and then he was up and moving.

It was a short dash, and he made it half bent over, his ghillie hood-over flapping a little around him. I pointed to Greg, who followed. The next man back was, I thought, the grunt who had been in the bunker with Warren. I waved him over and grabbed him by the kit, pulling him down so that I could hiss in his ear.

"You stay low, you move fast," I said. "Get over there and get set in on security." He nodded, and I let him go. He followed Greg, lumbering a bit more, weighed down by his body armor.

Watching him go, I reflected that we were going to have to do what we could to talk the soldiers into ditching as much of that armor as possible. If we were as far out in the cold as I thought we were, mobility was going to be at a premium in the days ahead.

I ushered the rest across until Scott caught up and took up a security position next to me, facing back the way we'd come. "No sign of our tails for the last hour," he whispered, even as Tony took off across the field, his boots thumping a little more heavily thanks to the belt-fed he was carrying. "I think it worked."

"I hope so," I replied. "You got this?"

"Go," he said. I turned, glanced around the fields, and then ran for the trees.

The last four days were definitely taking their toll. I was more worn out when I reached the trees than I should have been.

Fortunately, as I pushed forward, past Tony, who had taken a knee facing back across the open space to cover Scott, who was already starting his own dash, I reflected back on Selection, and knew that I'd catch my second wind in a little bit. Or, at least, it wouldn't get any worse.

By the time I reached Phil, having to pause a few times along the way to tell some of our charges to get back against the trees and as out of sight as possible, Scott was already in position, and sent me a one-word transmission. "Up."

I broke squelch twice to indicate that I'd heard. Even as I did, I glanced up, and reflected that under the circumstances, we needed to stop relying so much on the radio. Not only were the batteries running low, but if the enemy had any Direction-Finding equipment at all, they were going to start triangulating stray transmissions that weren't theirs.

The sheer hash of electronic noise that characterized the modern world would help, but if they'd managed to crash the Internet and cell networks in Slovakia, that was going to clean things up a lot, and make it harder for us to hide.

As I reached Phil, I took another look around and above. We seemed to still be clear. I tapped him on the shoulder. Without a word, he rose and moved to the next tree, pausing just long enough to scan again before moving to the next one past that. We were running out of darkness. Hopefully, we could be across the highway and into the woods before sunrise.

***

Bradshaw had been busy during the night. Our linkup with Killian's vehicles went smoothly. Scott took over the rest of the team, while I accompanied Bradshaw and the rescued soldiers to Killian's track.

"Good to see you back, Bowen," Killian said. He was still kitted up, though I'd seen a couple of his soldiers who weren't. It was stand-to time, too, and Bradshaw had his infantry section at one hundred percent, but there were notable exceptions in spots around the perimeter that Killian couldn't see from the Powell's position.

Killian had some discipline problems in his platoon.

We'd barely gotten to the track when Warren simply slumped down on the ground next to a tree. He was pale, clammy, and gasping for air like a landed fish. We'd pushed him to his breaking point and beyond to get away from Keystone in one piece.

Killian looked at him, but apparently didn't recognize him. The blouse he'd grabbed had belonged to a Sergeant First

122

Class, judging by the rank insignia velcroed center chest, and Warren wasn't in any shape to introduce himself or do much of anything besides try not to pass out.

"I'm Sergeant Killian," the platoon sergeant announced, looking around at the ragged assembly of soldiers while Bradshaw and I stood off to one side and watched. "And right now, it looks like we're on our own. If there's any information any of you can give us as to what happened at Keystone, or what's going on, now's the time."

The woman we'd rescued had slumped down on the ground where she'd stopped, and looked about as done-in as Warren. Most of the others just looked around at each other. A couple shrugged.

The young grunt who had been in the first bunker stepped forward. He had no helmet, but still had his body armor and his rifle. He was deeply tanned, with sandy blond hair, a prominent nose, and a pronounced underbite. "I didn't see much, Sar'nt," he said. "I was just getting back from patrol, and heading toward my can when something blew up at the front gate. It was something big; it just about knocked me on my face. A couple minutes later, they blew the north gate. After that, all hell broke loose. The IDF alarm started going off, and artillery started coming down. At least, I think it was artillery. We got rocketed a few weeks ago, and that sounded different."

Killian nodded. "I remember the rocket attack," he said.

"So," the kid continued, "they shelled the base for what felt like a half an hour. It all gets kind of fuzzy." He'd probably gotten mildly concussed by a few of the nearer impacts. "There were some bigger booms in there, too, and then they hit the ammo dump."

I winced. That must have been hell.

"It seemed like things kind of went quiet after that," he went on. "I was ready to get out of the bunker, but Chief Warren," he indicated the slumped, doughy warrant officer, who was either semi-conscious or asleep, "wouldn't let me. Said we needed to stay put until the all clear was called. That was when I started hearing gunshots.

"I looked out, then. Chief Warren didn't want me to, but I was damned if I was gonna die in a hole without having a chance to fight back." I was starting to like this kid. "There were three guys with guns walking into the lane between trailers. They weren't Americans. They didn't look like soldiers at all; they looked like some of the militia who ambushed us a month ago. They were shooting into the trailers, long bursts. I was going to shoot at them, but Chief ordered me not to." The glance he shot at the glassy-eyed warrant officer was downright venomous.

"What happened after that?" Killian asked.

"They shot at the bunker, but didn't come in," the kid said. "Then they moved on. Chief insisted everybody stay quiet and hide. We kept hearing gunfire for…I don't know. An hour, hour and a half? Then it was getting dark." He suddenly looked deathly tired. "We were hiding after that, until these guys came and got us."

Killian studied him for a moment, then looked around at the rest. "Anybody else got anything to add?" he asked.

One of the other grunts raised his hand, like a kid in school. "Sergeant Ybarra tried leading a bunch of guys he'd gathered up out through the west gate," he said. "Something heavy tore 'em apart right outside. Sounded like a 20 or 30mm."

He didn't mention how he'd seen that, but hadn't gone out with Ybarra. Killian let it slide, though his expression flickered for a moment, telling me that he'd noticed the same thing.

It's interesting, how fast you get to know somebody when you're running and fighting for your lives together.

"All right," he said. "You four, head over to that Stryker and find Sergeant Ragsdale. You five, go over there and look for Sergeant Myers. The rest of you, stay here, find a hole, and work out the rotation with the guys and girls on security."

They shuffled off, and he turned to me and Bradshaw, though not without a glance at Warren. "Artillery," he said quietly.

I nodded, my expression tight. Bradshaw's face was a mirror of my own. "Yeah," I said. "Still think this was the Nationalists?"

He shook his head. "Unless intel *completely* dropped the ball, they don't have any tubes anywhere near here. They're all out east." He suddenly looked like he'd aged twenty years in the last few minutes. "What the hell are we going to do now?"

"Not much we can do while it's daylight," Bradshaw said. "Everybody needs some rest. I don't think we should be anywhere less than seventy-five percent on security, though."

I nodded. "We need to be ready to move, though," I said. "Hopefully they're looking up north, but they're definitely hunting us now. If they find us, we've got to be able to break contact and get out in minutes."

"Agreed," Killian said, but not without another glance at Warren. I followed his gaze, thinking that I understood his note of concern.

Not everybody among us was in top shape or had the training and experience that we did. If things went south…

Well, that would be interesting.

Chapter 12

It was a long day.

Not only had it warmed up from the day before, but when I did get a chance to sleep, between shifts on security, studying the maps with Bradshaw while we wracked our minds for a plan, and the occasional comm shot with Kidd in Hungary, none of which resulted in any new information, I didn't sleep well.

I should have. I was exhausted. The last ninety-six hours had been a relentless forced march of movement, fighting, and more movement, coupled with the sheer mental stress of being hunted and knowing that we couldn't count on any help but ourselves. I should have passed right out.

But I couldn't. I drifted in and out, unable to get comfortable even in the shade of the beech I'd set my ruck against. Even when I did drift off, I kept starting awake as either artillery rumbled in the distance, or an aircraft went by overhead.

So, by the time it started to get dark, I wasn't doing much better than I had been at first light.

I didn't have much chow left. My stomach was going to be an aching void by the end of the next day. And I knew that the rest of the team wasn't much better off. Bradshaw's boys had some extra, but it wouldn't last all that much longer. We were going to have to take steps. Preferably without getting compromised, surrounded, and slaughtered.

That was going to be a good trick, with about seventy-five men and three armored vehicles.

I chewed the last of the meal replacement bar. I had three more left, not counting the two in my E&E kit. And they really weren't much of a "replacement" for a full meal. More like a snack. One that didn't satisfy and left you thirsty.

Especially after hiking, crawling, and fighting through the woods for four days.

Slinging my rifle, I walked over toward Bradshaw's position. He'd set up close, just not close enough that both of us could get taken out by one artillery shell. But neither one of us wanted to rely too much on the radios; especially as our batteries died, we were going to have to stick close, or rely on runners.

It might come to the latter, depending on how things worked out. I didn't think we were necessarily going to be able to stick together in a big lump like this.

Although, I thought as I neared where Bradshaw was sitting up next to his ruck, looking bleary as he chewed a backpacker meal that he didn't look like he was even tasting, splitting up now that we had a bunch of regular Army types under our wing might be even more difficult. I wasn't hopeful that all of them were going to make it out alive if left to their own devices. Killian was proving more competent than I'd feared, but not all of his troops were top shelf.

Of course, if I was being honest, I had to admit that some of that perception might have been my old Marine Corps prejudices at work.

Bradshaw looked up at me as I stopped, standing next to him, waiting for him to finish his chow. He grunted. I didn't speak. I was too tired for small talk.

A bulky figure came out of the trees. "Over here, Killian," I murmured. He shifted his course and joined us, squatting down as best he could in all that Kevlar and ceramic he was toting. I was glad to see that he still had his M37A2 slung and one hand on the firing control.

"Gents," he said quietly. "We need to have a talk."

There was a pause as we both just watched him, with hooded eyes. He looked back and forth between us, then sighed heavily. We weren't going to give him an inch, so he had to open the ball himself.

"Chief Warren's up," he said. "I think you can guess where I'm going with this."

"He's the ranking officer, isn't he?" Bradshaw asked, around a mouthful of food.

Killian nodded, taking his helmet off and rubbing his scalp. He hadn't shaved since this had started, and his stubble was dark. "Yeah, he is. He hasn't taken command, just yet." He grimaced. "Well, he hasn't in so many words. He's just been asking questions. And that's where things get…"

"Dicey?" I put in, leaning against a tree, my hands crossed on my OBR's buttstock.

"That's one way of putting it," he agreed, looking up at me. "Look, I'm not an idiot. I haven't asked because I really don't want to know, and I don't want to look a gift horse in the mouth. But I'm pretty sure that you're not Delta, you're not SEAL Team Six, and you're not Special Activities Division." He half-shrugged. "Though that *is* the current front-runner in the rumor mill."

We still didn't say anything. Bradshaw looked up at me. Technically, he'd been a Triarii longer than I had, but I was the Grex Luporum Team Leader, and his section was the trail element for my team. That put me on the spot.

"Your silence is just confirming my suspicions, gents," Killian said quietly. He spread his hands. "Look, I get it. And I *don't* want to bring this up. If you are who I think you are, it…well. It could cause some issues." He held his hands up placatingly. "Not from me. I'm no pogue. I know you high-speed types might think that because I ride around in a Powell, I'm half a step from joining the PRA, but I'm not." He spat, then sighed, looking down at the loam between his boots. "Unfortunately, that's not the case with everybody. And I don't know Warren well enough to know which way he's going to jump, if you are who I think you are."

"What's his MOS?" Bradshaw asked.

"Information Systems," Killian deadpanned.

I raised my eyebrows in bemusement. "Your ranking officer is an IT nerd?"

"Afraid so," Killian answered, looking up at me. "So, you can see what the hard part is. He doesn't even know what he doesn't know. But he's the ranking officer. I'm an E-7. I can't tell a CWO-3 to sit down and shut up."

"Why not?" I asked. "Look around you, Killian. Your support network is the people and vehicles in this clearing. That's it. This is hardly the time to worry about rank when it comes down to survival."

"That's easy for you to say," Killian replied, though his voice was calm. "You're outside the chain of command. I could be court-martialed afterward."

I snorted. "Who gives a shit?" I retorted. "That just means you'll be alive when they court-martial you, and when the truth comes out, if they don't give you a damn commendation, then they're even stupider than I imagined they've gotten. We are out in the cold, Killian. There's not time or space for niceties that permit stupid decisions, and an amateur trying to play field commander is just going to result in stupid decisions. And stupid decisions just get people killed."

Bradshaw heaved himself suddenly to his feet. "You know what?" he said. "Let's go talk to him. Maybe we can talk some sense into him before he does something dumb. Maybe he's smarter and more self-aware than either one of you are giving him credit for, and he's just trying to fulfill what he sees as his responsibilities, even though he knows he's in over his head."

I shoved off from the tree trunk as Bradshaw dusted off his hands and grabbed his M5E1. Killian looked a little uncomfortable; he was probably worried about what was about to happen. Under any other circumstances, I might not have blamed him.

But here, surrounded, cut off, and hunted, I didn't have much sympathy. Everyone needed to come to grips with what had happened and what was going on, or none of us were going to get out of this alive.

We might not, anyway. But I'd rather go down fighting than get killed because of indecision.

It was a short walk to the Powell, where Warren was sitting inside. He looked pale and cold; he didn't have much in the way of warming layers, having grabbed some other poor bastard's blouse. He looked up as we approached, his face cast in a weird, bluish light by the screens inside the armored vehicle. The look on his face was hard to read, until I realized that he wasn't just nervous, like Killian was. He was terrified, and trying not to show it.

"So," I said, deciding to get things going when Warren didn't seem eager to start talking, himself. "Killian here tells me that you're the ranking officer."

Warren seemed to gulp, though it might have just been the light. "Yeah, I guess so," he said. His voice wasn't as high-pitched as I might have expected it to be, but it wasn't exactly the epitome of gravelly manliness, either. He looked at Killian. "Believe me, I'm no happier about it than any of you. I'm a computer geek."

I squatted down outside the hatch. "How much ground warfare training have you had?" I asked.

"The absolute bare-bones basics," he admitted. "I qualify every year. That's about where it stops." He definitely gulped. "And yet, here I am. Responsible for three armored vehicles and something like thirty people." He looked down at me for a long moment, his mouth working. He wanted to ask the question, but he was scared of the answer. "At least, I'm pretty sure just the thirty," he said. "That depends on..." he trailed off.

"On who the obvious Americans in the strange fatigues and non-standard weapons are?" I finished for him.

"I guess, yeah," he said. "Are you with JSOC? Or the Agency?" There was a distinct note of hope in his voice. Ranking officer or no, he would feel more comfortable turning command over to Delta or DEVGRU types, or even Special Activities.

He was in for a bit of a disappointment in that regard. Not that it really mattered. The trick was going to be whether he really understood that.

"Neither," I replied. "We are working for an interested third party."

His eyes flicked between me and Bradshaw at that, and his nervousness increased. "What...what exactly does that mean?" he asked.

"Exactly what it says," Bradshaw replied. "We're not under either the Pentagon's or Langley's chain of command."

"They haven't said it, and I'm pretty sure they're not going to come out and say it," Killian said quietly. "And given what's been going on back home, I can't say that I blame them. But I'm about ninety percent sure that they're Triarii, Chief."

Warren didn't quite twitch, though he blinked, hard. He looked down at his hands for a long moment. They might have been shaking a little. "That could be a problem," he said, finally, his voice cracking a little.

"That's politics," I said. "Politics stopped mattering to any of us out here as soon as Keystone got flattened. We're in this together, whether we like it or not. You want to live? You work with us. Otherwise, we're going to have to exfil on our own, and leave you to the tender mercies of the enemy." I blew out a deep breath. "That might sound like a threat, but it's not. It's just reality. The bad guys won't give a damn whether we're Army, Marine Corps, Navy, Triarii, or even PRA. To them, we're Americans, so we're targets."

As I was talking, I was silently praying that common sense prevailed, and that this wasn't going to be an issue. That he came to understand just how precarious our position was. If he let Stateside politics govern his decision, this could get real uncomfortable, real quick.

Of course, the Triarii wasn't an *illegal* organization, not really. We had our supporters on multiple State and Federal levels. It said something about just how deadlocked government had gotten that we were the unofficial State defense force in some states, and an invading terrorist group in others, while the Federal Government was so split that nobody with any authority even wanted to mention our existence.

"I guess that depends," he said. "We'll have to see what the ranking officers say once we get out of hostile territory and back to the other peacekeepers. It's out of my wheelhouse, I'm afraid."

Killian glanced at me. I didn't look at him, but I felt his eyes, and Bradshaw's. Neither man seemed eager to jump in. *Thanks, guys.*

"That's your plan?" I asked him. "Make for Camp Leyen and turn yourselves in to the Germans?"

"That's the nearest peacekeeper base," he said. "If it's still intact, it should be secure enough, provided they can get a relief force to us. And no, I'm not suggesting that we try to push through the Nationalist forces to get there. We should hold our position and call for help."

"Two problems with that," I said. "One, the comms are down. Full-spectrum jamming. We've got some faint and fitful HF comms with our own support people, but SINCGARS and satcom are both out. Calling for help isn't going to work very well.

"Two is the more important one, though. We'd be better off slitting our own throats than walking into Camp Leyen."

"What are you talking about?" Warren asked. "I'm pretty sure the Germans don't even know that the Triarii exist. They might not like you, but that doesn't mean…"

"Chief," Killian interrupted. "We were fired upon by EDC helicopters the night that Keystone was destroyed. Tigers."

Warren either wasn't getting it, or didn't want to get it. He looked back and forth from Killian to me to Bradshaw. "Mistaken identity happens," he said. There was a quaver in his voice. He got it. He just didn't want to believe it. "Especially after a Nationalist attack like that…"

"It wasn't the Nationalists," I said bluntly. "The only people with that much artillery anywhere near here were the US, the EDC, and the Loyalist Slovak Army."

"And the EDC's been keeping the Slovaks on a really short leash," Killian put in.

Warren was clearly shaken by this time. "No," he stammered. "No, that's crazy. We're *allies*. We always have been. There's no way. It *had* to be the Nationalists." He was looking for any other explanation. "The Russians must have gotten the support to them that we've been hearing about, somehow. More artillery, maybe disguised BM-21s or something."

I shook my head. We had enough intel to know that the Russians were a threat; Russia has only ever cared about Russia, no more, no less. It didn't mean they *were* the Soviet Union reborn, though there was some worrying continuity in personnel among the leadership. If you looked hard enough, just about everyone running things in Moscow had been KGB or FSB at one time.

But they'd become a convenient scapegoat for everything in recent years. Just like the jihadis had blinded the

133

American defense apparatus to any other threats for over a decade beforehand, the Russians had become the subject of a similar fixation.

"The Russians are still focused on Ukraine and the Baltics," I said. "Trust me, our intel people have been watching them, too. They wouldn't have gotten that kind of materiel into Slovakia without *somebody* noticing." I shook my head again. "No, this wasn't the Nationalists, and it wasn't the Russians. It would seem that the EDC decided to take Slovenský Grob as an act of war, after all."

"But..." He was starting to look a little overwhelmed. His safe, tidy notions of how the world worked were crumbling. "But we *explained* that! The people responsible were punished! It wasn't US policy! How..."

"My guess is that they needed a war, given how fast the EDC countries are imploding," Bradshaw said. "It's happened before. The money for all their social programs is running out, the people have no more trust in their leaders, so they found a new boogeyman to try to get the people to stop rioting in the streets. They've already targeted every nationalist and traditionalist group in Europe as an enemy of peace. How much do you want to bet that they've been quietly doing the same thing with the US, and that Slovenský Grob was just the excuse they needed?"

Warren didn't even have an answer to that. He was still trying to process it. Having his base blown to hell had rattled him enough. I had to actually, if grudgingly, credit him some. He was an office geek; probably had been for close to twenty years. His world was computers and information systems. Not explosives and bullets and sneaking around in the woods and the dirt. The fact that he hadn't shut down completely when FOB Keystone had been flattened, had taken cover and, despite that young grunt's opinion, probably saved their lives by keeping them inside the bunker instead of trying to take the fight to a prepared and coordinated force of attackers with one rifle, was good on him. But this seemed to be a step too far for him.

"Weren't the Germans kind of giving us the cold shoulder before the EDC was even a thing?" Killian asked. "I think I remember hearing something about that. Somebody who was traveling to Frankfurt, or something."

"You could say that," I answered. I'd made sure I'd read the whole intel package on the way to Hungary. It had been long and complicated, and had stretched clear back to the 'teens, but it had been eye-opening. We'd been in an economic and increasingly military cold war with Germany ever since the "EU Army" had first been proposed. It was just that nobody wanted to call a spade a spade anymore. Everyone was terrified of what might happen if they did.

Maybe those days were over. I suspected they'd just been blotted out in the last few days of fire and death. The only question was whether or not anyone would figure it out before it was too late.

Presuming it wasn't already too late.

"The point is, we're surrounded by enemies, we're getting low on supplies, and we've been in one place too long," I said. We needed to get this little meeting over with, before a lucky drone or helicopter pilot spotted us and brought all hell down around our ears. I looked at Killian. Warren seemed to have partially shut down. "How are you doing on fuel?"

He patted the Powell's hull. "This baby's got about another three hundred seventy-five klicks in her," he said. "The Strykers are about the same. Ammo could get tight soon, though." He pointedly glanced at my rifle. "We've got some 7.62; there are still M240s on the Strykers. But the supply's limited."

"We'll make do," I said. We had trained for a long time to make every shot count. It had meant not just hours on the range, but days. Hartrick had laid down the law, though.

"If the Selous Scouts could hunt bad guys in the African bush for a month on three magazines, so can you," he'd said. "You don't shoot unless you've got a kill shot. Leave suppression for the belt-feds." We hadn't been one hundred percent faithful to that, but we were still doing alright for ammunition. Plus, Bradshaw had brought some extra, which had been passed around after we'd linked up outside of Borinka.

"It's water and chow I'm getting worried about," I continued. "We'll be all right for about another day, but then things are going to get tight." I glanced at Warren, who was still

135

staring at his hands, apparently tuned out. He'd have to snap out of it sooner or later, but for the moment, I just turned my attention back to Killian.

"I think our best bet is to find the Nationalists and link up," I said. Warren did look up at that, but he was still turning over what we'd told him, and didn't comment.

Killian glanced at Warren. He was clearly uncomfortable with the situation. Warren was the ranking officer, so Killian could be considered out of line if he took over. But Warren was out of his depth, and wasn't saying anything anyway.

"I don't have a better plan," he said. "Except to try to get to FOB Poole. But that's a long movement. I doubt we can make it in a day."

FOB Poole was the other major US base in Slovakia, set up right outside the city of Zilina, just south of the Polish border. And while I didn't say it, I doubted that Poole had escaped Keystone's fate. If they'd mobilized their guard force and QRF fast enough, they might have held their own, but given what had happened to Keystone, that was a faint hope. It's hard to prepare for an attack from people who are supposed to be your allies.

"I've got the more up-to-date intel," Bradshaw said, pulling out his own map tablet. "Last we heard, there should be a major cell in or around Vrbovè. There's been a lot of reporting on attacks and ambushes around there."

What went unsaid was the fact that most of those attacks had been directed at peacekeeper units and the Slovak Army. And we were talking about rolling in there with a Powell and two Strykers. Not exactly what would be sticking in the memory as "Nationalist-friendly" forces.

"That's sixty klicks or more from here," Killian pointed out, looking over Bradshaw's shoulder. "That's going to be a hump. We can't fit everybody in the vehicles."

"I know," Bradshaw said. "It's going to take a few days. Or nights."

"We're not going to get sixty klicks on the supplies we've got," I said. "We might make it thirty." Killian gave me a sharp look at that; he probably couldn't imagine going that far on what I'd said we had left. Of course, what was one day's chow at full rations could keep us going for a while. Just not all the way to Vrbovè. We *needed* to resupply before that. The question was, where? It wasn't like there were a lot of American supply dumps around. "We need to find a cell somewhere closer, if we're not just going to be robbing the locals."

"We ran into the most trouble around Kuchyňa," Killian put in. "Not quite so much after Slovenský Grob, but it was always tense going through there. Especially if we were rolling with the Germans or Belgians."

"That might be our ticket, then," I said, peering over Bradshaw's other shoulder at the tablet and its imagery. "It's only about a ten-klick movement from here." I stepped back. "Probably a good idea to keep the vehicles back in the woods; even if the locals have decided that Americans are now friendlies by default, there are probably going to be EDC or their proxy militias around. Let's not bring the hammer down on our heads before we have to. I'll go in with my team; it'll make for a smaller footprint, and we're trained for this kind of thing, anyway." Not that we had any contacts with the Nationalists, or any partisan linkup procedures worked out. This could get interesting.

"How soon can you be ready to go?" Killian asked. Warren was being ignored, and didn't seem to mind all that much.

"In the next few minutes," I said. "We've been ready to break out since we halted."

He nodded, looking a little shamefaced. "It's going to take us about thirty," he admitted.

"Make it quick," was all I said, as I turned to head back to my team. Harsh, maybe, but we weren't in a situation where any of us could afford to be nice.

Nice had gone out the window the moment our "allies" had started shelling one of our bases.

Chapter 13

Ten klicks isn't all that far. But when you're running on short sleep and short rations, carrying a third of your bodyweight on your back, trying to stay out of sight and alert for the enemy, covering a hell of a lot of nasty, wooded terrain, it *becomes* a long way.

I called a halt on the back side of the last hill south of Kuchyňa. There were still a lot of woods, but most of the forest around there had been clear-cut some time ago. The clear-cut was crisscrossed with vehicle tracks, but it wouldn't provide much cover or concealment. Fortunately, Killian was learning fast. He kept the three vehicles as far back under the remaining trees as he could.

Being on the receiving end of an attack helicopter's rockets tended to make a man more than a little cautious.

We didn't drop rucks that time. We'd need them, provided this went according to plan. I had that nagging worry at the back of my mind that it wouldn't; nothing *ever* went according to plan, and this op was the crowning illustration of that fact. We were supposed to be back in Hungary, getting ready to return Stateside. The plan had been to get England, drop him at Keystone, and then exfil.

Instead, we were running and fighting for our lives in what felt an awful lot like World War III kicking off.

Not that it hadn't already. Nobody wanted to call it that, except for a few of the wilder pundits. The others were calling it an "unfortunate coincidence of conflicts," or "the recent breakdown in global order."

I guess the reality was just too horrifying to think about. Easier to look at the fact that the Chinese, Japanese, and what was left of ASEAN were going at it hammer and tongs in the Pacific, Central Asia was one Pakistani *shahid* short of a nuclear holocaust, the Russian Empire was expanding violently, the Middle East was about to enter the next phase of open warfare, Europe was imploding, and the US was in the middle of what could only be called a civil war, as just a conglomeration of isolated conflicts.

Except that a lot of the Second World War had really been the same way. The Germans and the Japanese had never conducted any joint operations. This was just even more out of control.

Tired, footsore, and worn down, I still conducted my last-minute coordination with Killian and Bradshaw, before dragging my ass over to the team, rucksack-flopped in a circle just outside the main perimeter.

"Let's go," I whispered. "We're burning darkness."

"Can't Bradshaw's guys do it, this once?" Phil asked. He was still sitting against his ruck, his head back against the frame. "I'm beat."

"We're all beat," I replied. "You think they're any less tired?"

"Yeah, actually I do," Phil replied. "They haven't been on the ground as long as we have."

"Why don't you turn in your GL tab, then?" David asked. "If it's too hard for you."

"Hell, son," Dwight rumbled. "I've got like twenty years on you. What are you bitching about?"

"Are you talking to Phil, or to Peanut?" Scott asked.

"Phil," Dwight grumbled, with the exasperated growl that spoke of hearing the same joke about a hundred times too many.

"Dwight's not even my real dad," David said. "Don't worry, Phil. I'll take point, too. You can go see if you can sleep with the Stryker crew. That chick who looks like she got beat with an ugly stick might like it. She's been watching us when she's not doing anything else."

"Which is most of the time," Chris said sourly. "But I don't get the vibe off of her that she's smitten with Phil. More

140

like she thinks we're some kind of evil right-wing terrorists, or something."

"She's infantry," David said. "Can't be a liberal and be infantry."

"You'd think," Chris replied. "These days, you can't be sure, though."

"Is the knitting circle done?" I asked. "Because if you lot have enough energy to chatter like little girls, then you've got plenty to hump another fifty klicks. We may as well not even try to go into Kuchyňa after supplies."

David shut up, his jaw closing with a faint *clop*. He was the shortest of us, and also tended to eat the most. He sure as hell didn't want to keep up with the rest of the team for another fifty kilometers without chow.

"Fine," Phil said. "We'll take care of it. Let the grunts get their beauty sleep. They need it more than we do, I guess."

He heaved himself to his feet, steadied himself against a tree, and then started out. I reached down to help Greg to his feet, then followed.

We had to move downhill to the west to stay in the woods, spreading out in the sparse undergrowth. There wasn't a lot of light getting under the trees, but the fusion goggles did a good job of amplifying what was there, and the addition of our thermal signatures helped, too. We weren't going to lose each other in the dark, as thick as it was. Of course, that could go both ways, too.

We got a few hundred yards before Phil slowed and sank to a knee, holding up a hand to signal a halt. I closed in on him before taking a knee myself. I didn't need him to tell me why he'd stopped; I could tell for myself.

The smell of smoke was heavy in the early morning darkness. And the sporadic *pop*s we were hearing to the north were unmistakable as anything but gunfire.

The war had come to Kuchyňa, as well, it seemed.

We circled up and listened for a few minutes. The shots were coming at irregular intervals. There was nowhere near the volume of fire that one would expect if there was a fight going on. Whatever had happened, it was probably in the mopping-up stage.

It could simply be somebody randomly shooting off his back porch, too. We didn't *know* that there had been a fight. But given what had happened at Keystone, and what we'd heard in the distance since, I didn't think it was all that likely.

Besides, when you're sneaking around a country where you're not supposed to be in the first place, loaded for bear and cammied-up, paranoia isn't just a good idea. It's a requirement.

Finally, I tapped Phil's shoulder. Staying there and listening wasn't going to get the job done. We needed to move in and get eyes on.

He got to his feet and moved out. If he was moving slightly more cautiously, stopping more often in the cover of trees to look and listen, I wasn't too worried about it. We had a limited amount of darkness left to work with, but if we rushed right into a firefight, it wouldn't matter if it was still dark.

It took most of another forty-five minutes to reach the edge of the trees. The forest had been cut down there, on the south side of town, but a lot of bushes had grown up in the aftermath. Most of them would have come to my upper chest if I'd been moving upright, but we moved through them as best we could, crouched down underneath the tops. It was a punishing movement. It would have been even without the rucks. As it was, my back was screaming by the time we reached the edge of the reservoir that sat at the southeastern corner of town.

We had already been able to see the flickering light of fires inside the town, before we'd even been out of the woods. It wasn't the raging inferno that had been FOB Keystone after the attack; it looked more like isolated houses were burning. Another gunshot rang out as we crouched in the bushes near the reservoir, the report echoing across the valley.

We circled up in the trees. This had just gotten a lot more complicated. Not that it had been simple from the outset.

"We're going to have to drop rucks, at least for the moment," I whispered. "Scott, you've got the Bravo Element back here. I'll take Alpha and see what's going on before we try going in there and making contact."

"Roger," Scott replied. We'd be pushing daylight if this did work out, because we'd have to go in, make contact if it was feasible, then come back out and get the rucks, load them up, and then get away.

Presuming that making contact worked out well at all. It might not. It might go very, very wrong. We were on thin ice.

But we really had no other choice. We needed supplies, and we weren't going to get out of Slovakia with seventy people without working with the Nationalists. Unless the comms magically cleared up so that we could call for help.

There comes a time when you've got to accept that there is no safe way forward, spit on your hands, and get ready to win through or go down fighting.

***

The first street was deserted. Unfortunately, that didn't mean empty.

One of the houses about a hundred yards from where Phil and I had come out of the trees was burning. In the light of the fire, we could see bodies in the street. They were sprawled in attitudes of violent death, some curled in the fetal position, as if they had died surrounded and under attack.

As I scanned the scene, I realized that the street wasn't *quite* deserted. It was hard to make out past the big thermal bloom of the burning house, but there was a low, angular shape squatting at the far end, a small turret topping it with a shrouded cannon pointing toward the east. I couldn't be sure, but it looked like a German Puma IFV.

More gunfire echoed across the town, this time a rattling exchange of shots that shattered the night, punctuated by what might have been screams and yells. Kuchyňa wasn't a large town. Sound carried.

The armored vehicle stayed where it was, neither intervening nor fleeing. Almost as if it was posted on guard, to keep anyone from getting out of the town.

I realized that that might not be the case; this might just be a repeat of the Dutch at Srebrenica, standing by while the massacre went down. It amounted to the same thing, in the end. I strongly doubted that the attackers were Slovak Nationalists. With only a couple of notable exceptions, the Nationalists had been remarkably discriminating in their target selection, mostly going after the peacekeepers, the Army, and the militias. Massacring towns wasn't their usual MO.

I stayed in place, as Phil crouched at the corner of the first house, looking back at me from time to time. I didn't want to move too soon, though. Five of us getting into a firefight, with that armored vehicle sitting with a pretty clear shot down the lane, wasn't a good idea. Sure, Scott and the rest would be down in minutes, but we'd probably all be dead by then.

Finally, I squeezed Phil's shoulder and pointed to the closest window. I didn't want to go out in the street if we could help it, not until I knew more. He nodded, moving to the window and peering inside.

"Looks clear," he whispered. He tested the window; it was an inward-opening setup, and it was latched. That didn't stop Phil; he glanced behind him to make sure he wasn't about to flag any of the rest of the team with his muzzle, and buttstroked the joint between the panels. The window bent inward with a *crack*, but didn't open. He hit it again, and we had our entry.

Of course, I would have preferred to be first in, but Phil didn't wait. He hefted his rifle in one hand, put the other on the sill, and started to clamber inside. I had to move quickly to boost him when his boots started scrabbling for purchase on the wall beneath the opening. I might have shoved a little too hard; he almost fell inside, hitting the floor with a *thump* that made me cringe from outside, even though I was only a couple feet away, and it probably hadn't been audible for more than about ten more past that, especially with that ragged, sporadic firefight going on farther into town.

I followed quickly. I didn't want Phil to be stuck in there by himself. One-man clears are possible, but rarely advisable. Fortunately, nobody inside had started shooting yet.

As I hit the floor, having gotten through a little more easily than Phil on account of my longer arms and legs, I saw that all the shooting in that house was long over.

There was a corpse slumped in the front doorway. The long-haired man was dressed in a tracksuit and chest rig. He didn't have much of a face left, thanks to the shotgun blast that had killed him, but the stubborn remnants of what looked a lot like a jihadi beard clung to his shattered jaw.

144

The man who had shot him was lying in the middle of the common room, riddled with bullets, an ancient break-barrel shotgun underneath him. The splintered holes in the front wall revealed that the tracksuited man's compatriots had simply mag-dumped into the front of the house as soon as he'd gone down.

The violence hadn't stopped there, though. There was spent brass scattered amidst the shattered glass on the floor inside, and the man with the shotgun wasn't alone. His family had been huddled under the table in the kitchen behind him.

They were still there. What was left of them.

Everything in the house looked like it had been tossed. Furniture was torn up, cupboard doors hung open. The crucifix on the wall had been torn down and dashed on the floor.

Phil and I moved away from the window, spreading out to allow the others room to make entry, while we cleared the corners and the dead space. I doubted that we were going to find anyone else in the house, but there was still the possibility that we'd run into a straggler, busily looting the house while his fellows had moved on.

The bottom floor was mostly open, so it took seconds to clear it. All of us steered clear of the bodies for the moment. Jordan led the way upstairs, Greg on his heels, while Phil, Dwight, and I set security on the ground level. A moment later, they were coming back down, Jordan whispering a terse, angry, "Clear."

"There was a girl up there," Greg said, his voice haunted. For once, his usual cheerfulness was gone. "They…they weren't quick."

I just nodded, as I picked up the crucifix where it had been thrown on the floor. Setting it carefully on the table, I knelt next to the dead man with the shotgun.

While the others watched the exits, I crossed myself. *"Réquiem ætérnam dona eis Dómine; et lux perpétua lúceat eis. Requiéscant in pace. Amen."* The others kept their eyes on their sectors, though I might have heard Dwight muttering a prayer of some sort. I thought he was Baptist, but I honestly hadn't ever asked, and he hadn't been particularly forthcoming.

I hadn't grown up religious. In fact, if there was one thing my parents probably hated even more than my choice of profession, it was my newfound Catholicism, especially since I was what they would have contemptuously referred to as a "trad." But sometimes God opens doors in ways you don't expect. I probably would have gone on being a rather snooty agnostic, regardless of my political views, if it hadn't been for Caleb Mosby's death.

Caleb had been the first friend I'd ever really lost. We'd been together since boot camp. Losing him sent me into a downward spiral that could have ended badly, if it hadn't been for our Regimental Chaplain, Father Krieg. I'd known some wishy-washy chaplains, but Father Krieg wasn't one of them. Padre had been a grunt in Vietnam, Desert Storm, and Somalia before he'd become a man of the cloth. He saved my life, and my soul along with it.

That short prayer for the dead was all that I had time for. I straightened as a massive explosion shook the house around us. The entryway was briefly lit brightly by the flash as a fireball rose into the night sky, barely five hundred yards away. The gunfire died down a bit after that.

"I don't think we're going to be able to make contact with the Nationalists here," I said. "Search the kitchen for any food we can take, and something to take it in." The light outside was getting brighter, and it wasn't from the impending sunrise. Whatever had blown up, it had set at least one more house on fire. "We'll load up with what we can find and head back to rendezvous with Scott and the others."

More gunfire rattled outside. Something told me that the fighting was over; that was celebratory gunfire. Given the looks of the dead man in the doorway, and the shattered crucifix, I had a feeling I knew who had come into Kuchyňa and gone house-to-house, killing anyone who resisted. And it hadn't been the Germans.

Just their proxies.

There was going to be a reckoning. At least, I hoped there would be. I knew full well that I might not be alive to see it.

At the same time, as the rage mounted in my chest, I knew that I was going to do my damnedest to make sure that I was.

***

146

In the end, we had to fade back into the woods after only searching three houses, coming away with two duffels full of bread and sausage. It was going to have to do; most of the other food we'd found wasn't going to be all that packable. And it would require stopping to cook. I'd been a little surprised; processed food had made its way all over the world, but it seemed that a lot of the people in Kuchyňa had been a bit more traditional. Or, given the town's size, they were just more dependent on local food sources, particularly as the European economy collapsed.

Every house had been the same. The bad guys had been thorough. And all the time, that Puma had sat at the end of the street, not moving. Overwatching the carnage.

The picture was becoming clearer to me, putting the massacre in Kuchyňa together with the accounts of the destruction of FOB Keystone. The EDC was letting the militias do most of the dirty work, keeping their own forces aloof from the worst of it. They didn't have to worry so much about casualties, or the potential backlash if the regular German or French people, many of whom were simmering with unrest already, found out that their sons or daughters were slaughtering allies and civilian populations, only a couple hundred miles away.

If they thought that using proxies was going to insulate them from the war that was coming, they were doomed to disappointment.

I was determined on that point.

Chapter 14

We took the risk and moved in daylight. Bradshaw, Killian, and I had agreed. We didn't want to stay put anywhere near Kuchyňa after that. Fortunately, Draven had linked up with Bradshaw while we'd been in town, so they were hiking with us, the mortars strapped to the tops and sides of the Strykers to lighten the mortarmen's loads. They had rifles, the same M5E1s that the infantry section was carrying. They just didn't have as much ammo for them.

It wasn't an easy movement; the Little Carpathians look small on the map, but when you're humping everything you need on your back, even little mountains get to be a bitch to cover. We kept close to the vehicles as they found the logging roads and back tracks, but mountain terrain wasn't great for armored vehicles, especially when you're worried about helos and drones. In places, it was even slower going for the vehicles than it was for us with our leather Cadillacs.

We'd stopped just after noon, in a clearing just beneath the peak of Vysokà. Not because we necessarily wanted to, but because one of the Strykers had gotten stuck. The driver had apparently miscalculated, and hooked one of the drive wheels over a log.

Bradshaw had his men spread out on the outer perimeter. He'd talked me into putting our team at fifty percent; Dwight was snoring like a sawmill, Jordan was motionless, his eyes closed and his hands folded over his rifle in his lap. I was only awake because I still had a few things I wanted to check on. We had been making better time than I'd expected; depending on how long it took to get that Stryker moving again, and dependent on not getting spotted and attacked, we could well make eleven klicks by nightfall.

I knew I'd get some pushback, but I was going to insist that we keep going after that. We needed the cover of darkness; we needed to grab every advantage we could find with both hands. We were moving during the day out of necessity, but that didn't make it a good idea.

I knew Killian might get it, but expected that some of his platoon would grumble. They were mech infantry. They weren't hard-wired to try to stay in the shadows, the way we Grex Luporum guys were. They had armor and firepower, we had stealth. But with no comms and no air support, presumably badly outnumbered, they had to try to stay stealthy, too.

"Look at these little pussies," Phil muttered.

I followed his gaze, frowning. He was supposed to be down on rest plan, but he was looking down at the Army infantry gathered around the stuck Stryker. Only about half of them seemed to really be doing much of anything, and even as I watched, Killian intervened, tersely bitching a bunch of them out and scattering them to security positions or giving them other tasks to do. But a lot of them moved slowly, looking more than a little mopey as they did.

"Probably missing their pizza and Green Bean coffee," Phil went on. "Saturday movie night at the MWR."

Reflexively, I felt the same way. But as I watched them, I couldn't help but think about it. Sure, the modern military was soft. It had been when I'd been in; I hadn't even realized just how soft until I'd gotten into Brian Hartrick's clutches at Grex Luporum selection. Being stuck out in the woods without the amenities that had been a part of just about every US military base for the last twenty years had to be a shock.

But there was a deeper shock that I thought some of these kids were still processing. We'd been on the move, escaping and evading, for days now, but the reality still had to be sinking in that most of their friends and comrades, people that they'd deployed with, trained with, even patrolled with, were dead. This had to be the biggest single US loss of life in a decade or more. Possibly longer.

Of course they were traumatized. They'd survived a near-total team-kill. And it was going to get to some of them, more than it would to us, because they simply hadn't been prepared for it.

As nasty as things had gotten in the last few years, a lot of people could still go through life without thinking much about death. It just wasn't something that Americans liked to think about happening to them or theirs. Hadn't been for a long time. Having that many friends snuffed out...it was a wonder that most of them were still functioning at all.

"If everybody in Bradshaw's section were dead, you wouldn't be doing too good, yourself," I pointed out. "Quit being an asshole."

"I'm not being an asshole," Phil replied. "We can't afford to mope around like they're doing. I'm sorry their friends are dead. I really am," he protested when David snorted. "But if they don't want to be dead, too, then they need to quit crying and act like somebody's got a gun to their heads. Because somebody does."

As abrasive as Phil could be, I was afraid that he was right, in this case. It wasn't pleasant, it wasn't whatever buzzword the Army was currently using for friendship in place of leadership, but everything that the US military had done to lower standards and soften discipline was working against them. The enemy and the situation didn't give a damn about feelings. They wanted us dead, and we couldn't count on the kind of support that had been par for the course for our entire lives.

"Well, fortunately or unfortunately," I said, "they're not your concern, or mine. They're Killian's."

"You don't really believe that," Scott said quietly. I glanced over at him, but he wasn't looking at me. Scott wasn't being an ass, either. He was serious. "Killian's not a bad guy, from what I've seen, but he's not exactly a meat-eater, either. He's been keeping his head down, trying to get through his tour and move on to the next thing. Why else would he have come to talk to us about the Triarii before the meeting with Warren? He's still afraid of being the nail that gets hammered down. He's not going to rock the boat any more than he has to."

"He's got enough sense to keep his people alive, and not let our affiliation get in the way," I pointed out.

"I'm not denying he's got some common sense, Matt," Scott said. He turned to look at me. "But common sense isn't everything. Just like motivation's not everything. He hasn't got much fire in him. He's not aggressive. It's worked to our advantage because he doesn't want to argue, particularly when he decided that we're better-trained and better-prepared than he is. Any real meat-eater wouldn't have been happy about playing second-fiddle to glorified contractors."

We were far from contractors, but I got his point. And as I watched Killian, I wondered just how close to the mark he was. Scott could be pretty perceptive, when he got his head out of Meiji Japan.

There was a reason he'd gotten the callsign "Weeb," after all.

"I'll talk to him," I said. I levered myself to my feet, as much as I really wanted to take a nap. It was going to be a long time before I got another chance. "Phil, shouldn't you be on rest plan, anyway?"

"Just some last-minute observations," Phil said, grinning wickedly.

"Whatever. Shut up and go to sleep," I said.

I walked down toward where Killian was watching the Stryker crew try to get their vehicle freed from its predicament. He was frowning, his helmet shoved back on his head, his rifle slung in front of him.

"How long, you think?" I asked as I came up to him. He started a little, looking over at me as if he'd just noticed I was there. I realized, especially as I looked into his bleary, bloodshot eyes, that he was probably almost as short on sleep as I was. I was just more used to it.

He glanced back down at the stuck vehicle. "I don't know. Could be thirty minutes. Could be seven hours. I've seen it go both ways. We might have to hook up the Powell and yank it out." He glanced at the trees and the lay of the land. "That's going to be harder than it sounds, too. The terrain being what it is."

I nodded. "Probably better to get started on that sooner rather than later," I said. "We don't want to be sitting here for the rest of the day. And there sure ain't any recovery vehicles coming."

He ran a hand over his face. "Right," he said, continuing to stare at the stuck Stryker. "I've got to remember that this isn't a situation we ever really trained for."

I didn't have an answer to that that wouldn't have sounded like I was chewing him out. I was dead-on-my-feet tired, and when I get tired, what little tact I have goes flying away. Couple that with my "resting mad-dog face" and I'm not the best people-person.

I looked around. "Where's Warren?" I asked.

He glanced toward the Powell. "Still in my vehicle," he replied. "It's gotten a little crowded in there."

I could imagine. They'd already stuck the survivors from the mobility kill outside Borinka into one of the Strykers, and the other stragglers from Keystone into the other. With the exception of a couple of the Keystone grunts, we were the only ones on foot most of the time. And the Powell had a lot less troop space than the Strykers did.

"He's been trying to reach Pathfinder, up at FOB Poole," he continued. "On the comms every minute." He stopped himself, but the tone of his voice told me that hearing the repetitive comm calls was getting on his nerves.

"He needs to knock that off," I said, glancing overhead reflexively. "We don't know who's listening. Or direction-finding."

"I've tried telling him that," Killian said tiredly. "That if the bad guys can jam the SINCGARS nets, then they can listen in. He insists that it doesn't work like that. And that as long as we keep moving, they're going to have a harder time locating us."

He might have been right. I was no expert on comms; I'd avoided doing much of anything beyond the minimum necessary with the radios or other comm gear. Electronics in general are not my forte.

But I couldn't help but think that spewing radio transmissions constantly wasn't a good way to hide. Especially since we didn't know whether or not the enemy might be listening in. Of course, our personal radios were pretty much dead; Greg still had the long-range HF radio, and enough batteries for a couple more good comm shots, but the rest of them were turned off for the foreseeable future.

"He hasn't gotten anything back, has he?" I asked.

"Not a whisper," Killian replied grimly. "The question is, are the comms just down, or…"

"Or did Poole get the same treatment as Keystone?" I finished. He didn't flinch, not quite. But he clearly didn't want to hear it out in the open.

And the fact was, I didn't *know* that it had happened. Knowing what I did about our own military, the odds that the EDC had managed to coordinate two such strikes so flawlessly that both bases were reduced at exactly the same time seemed unlikely. However, Keystone had been destroyed days ago. Even if their timing had been off, and Poole had managed to put up some resistance, they'd had time to reduce it. Given the lack of American forces besides us in the Slovak countryside, and the silence on the comms, that seemed more likely. Even if Poole had held, they wouldn't be able to talk to the major bases in Poland. And if US Mil was having the same issues with Slovak airspace that we were, they wouldn't know any more about what was happening around Zilina than we did.

And given the general level of leadership I'd seen even before I'd gotten out of the Marine Corps, the likelihood of a flag officer giving the order to roll across the border without Washington's say-so were slim to none, and Slim left town.

I didn't say any of that. From the look on Killian's face, he'd already thought most of it.

"Tell him…" I stopped myself. "Politely and respectfully suggest that, since he hasn't been able to establish comms by now, he needs to stop trying for a while. We don't know that the enemy has DF equipment around us, but there are definitely drones up, and if they get too nosy about sources of radio transmissions, we could be in trouble."

Killian didn't look happy about it; I didn't know what kind of exchanges he'd already had with Warren, but as I was getting to know the man, I was seeing the little indicators that Scott's assessment was pretty spot on. Despite the fact that he knew I was right, and that Warren hadn't even really tried to throw his considerable weight around, he didn't want to confront the man who outranked him. About much of anything. It was a weakness.

We all have our weaknesses. The problem arises when those weaknesses could potentially get you and yours killed.

He was sort of hemming and hawing, looking around as if he was searching for something else to talk about rather than go back to his vehicle and tell Warren to get off the net. I was about to just go ahead and tell him, as gently as I could, to get his thumb out and get moving, when one of his soldiers came trotting over from the Powell.

"Sar'nt?" the young man called softly. Despite the fact that the vehicles were still running, our stealthy flight seemed to be affecting some of the younger hard-chargers, and they were trying to be as low-profile and "tactical" as we were. "I think we've been spotted, Sar'nt."

That got Killian's attention. He snapped his head around to face the young Specialist, suddenly all business. "Talk to me," he said.

The kid pointed skyward. "A drone went over about five minutes ago," he said. "It got to the end of the valley, then turned and came back toward us. It's circling now. It's at high-altitude, and it's small; we almost didn't spot it."

I looked up, searching the mostly clear sky. Spotting a high-altitude drone with the naked eye was going to be tough, but I'd done it before.

There. Sunlight glinted off metal. It was moving slowly, but it was definitely circling, nearing Vyoskà's peak.

Something like a chill ran up my spine. I'd developed a finely-tuned sixth sense during my varied career, going back to those interventions in Africa. And it was going gangbusters right at the moment.

I tore my eyes away from that tiny glint, quickly scanning the rest of the open sky between the trees. I couldn't see the threat yet, but somehow, I knew it was there. And it would be on top of us before we heard it, more than likely.

"Killian," I said, somewhat proud that my tone was low and even. "Get your people off the vehicles. We need to move. Now."

Something in the tone of my voice must have told him more than I said. "What?" he asked, looking up.

"Everyone," I repeated, letting some steel into my voice. "Grab their kit and their weapons and get moving northeast, minimum five hundred meters. *Now.*"

"But..." he still didn't see it. I grabbed him by his plate carrier.

"Listen, Killian!" I snapped. "We have minutes, at best. Get your people moving!" I shoved him toward his vehicle, hard, and turned back toward my team. "Scott! Tyler! Victor! Everybody up! Five hundred meters northeast! Go!"

Tony was already on a knee, his pack on his back, his Mk 48 in his shoulder and the ELCAN sight to his eye, scanning the sky. Tony never said much, which made some people think he was kind of slow, but he was usually quicker on the uptake than I was. Phil was scrambling to get up, Greg was stuffing things back in his ruck, and Jordan was rolling to his feet, shifting his pack onto his back as he went. Reuben was already up, having set himself between a tree and a sapling that he could use to pull himself up without taking his ruck off.

I moved quickly to Greg's side, grabbing the balled-up socks that had fallen out when he'd pulled out whatever it was he was stuffing back into his ruck, and jammed them in for him, my rifle pointed at the sky with my other hand. "Let's go," I said urgently. He hastily clipped the pack closed and threw it on his back. I hauled him up and shoved him toward where Phil was already pushing along the treeline, heading northeast at a faster clip than we usually adopted on movement.

If I was right, we needed to get out of the open as fast as humanly possible.

Bradshaw hadn't paused to ask questions, but had his section up and moving. When you just get a direction and distance and a command to move that way with a quickness, it communicates something. Usually that hell is on the way.

Scott and I were the last ones of the team, making sure that everybody else was up and moving, and nothing had been left that might be vital for our survival in the days ahead. Provided there were days ahead, and we didn't bite the big one in the next few minutes.

We weren't quite running when we left the edge of the clearing, but we weren't far short of that pace. I thought I could already hear the distant roar of jet engines.

The roar increased in volume, from a far off, barely heard rumble like thunder, to a banshee shriek. "Down!" I screamed, as I threw myself flat, my rucksack trying to fly over my head and bury my face in the leaves and loam beneath me. For a moment, everything went black, my breath muffled by moldy leaves and dirt.

Then the world seemed to split apart.

The shock of the bombs hitting actually picked me up off the ground for a split second before slamming me back down again. The overpressure washed over me like a hurricane, before frag, dirt, and the splintered remains of trees started raining down like hail. I tucked my legs under me as much as I could, trying to get as much of my body under my ruck as possible in lieu of actual overhead cover. I couldn't get low enough. My fatigues and my chest rig were holding me too high off the ground.

The rain of debris petered out, but I didn't get up. I couldn't hear much; the detonation had deadened my hearing. But I was waiting for the other shoe to drop.

The Dash Two strike almost seemed muted after the first. It still hurt. Being danger close to a five-hundred-pound bomb going off was going to.

I stayed down as the pattering cascade of debris slowly decreased to nothing. Dust and black smoke hung in the air between the trees. A lot of them had been stripped of their leaves by the blasts.

Only after a few minutes had passed without a follow-on strike did I pry myself up off the ground and look around.

Ugly black smoke billowed over the fiercely-burning Powell. From where I was, I couldn't see the Strykers clearly, but at least one of them was definitely burning. The vehicles were gone.

The vehicles weren't the only casualties. I could see several soldiers nearby sprawled in unnatural contortions on the forest floor. One had been thrown against a tree by the shockwave, and was bent around it in a way that no human spine was supposed to bend.

There were other bodies in less wholesome shape.

"Head count," I croaked.

For a moment, I was met with silence. My heart started racing. Had I lost my team?

"I'm up," Scott groaned. He levered himself up to one knee, patting himself down for wounds. I started to breathe a little easier. He'd been closer than I had been. Maybe we'd all gotten clear before the bombs fell.

"Up," Tony said, in a tone of voice better suited to saying, "Ow."

One by one, the rest of the team rogered up. We'd made it. Barely. Reuben had a piece of frag or a chunk of wood stuck in his calf, but it was a relatively superficial wound. He'd be a little bit slower, but he could walk on it. "It just stings," he said. "I'll be all right."

"Bradshaw!" I called, my voice echoing strangely in the woods. "Flat!"

He came back through the trees, looking a bit better than I felt. "I'm still getting a head count, Matt," he said. He looked back toward the wreckage of the vehicles. "Was Killian...?"

"I don't know yet," I answered. "My team's up. That's about where my SA ends at the moment."

"I'll see if I can find him," Bradshaw said.

"Killian!" I barked. It still felt wrong, yelling in such a situation, but we were clearly made if they'd dropped on us. Stealth would have to wait for the moment. I didn't know what kind of follow up was coming.

My hearing was still muffled and my ears were ringing. They'd recover with time. Partially.

"I'm...I'm here," Killian replied. His shout was more of a croak. I turned toward the sound and spotted him.

He was sitting up against a tree, staring back toward the burning vehicles. His face was slack, his stare fixed. I hurried over to him.

158

"Killian!" I barked, almost in his face. He blinked and looked at me, but the shock and horror in his eyes were unmistakable. I grabbed him by his kit and hauled him to his feet, running my hand over him quickly to check for bleeds. "You need to get accountability of your people," I told him firmly, my voice probably a little too loud given my own battered hearing. "Then we need to get far away from here as fast as possible. Do you understand?"

His glazed eyes seemed to clear a little, and finally focused on me. I didn't know how hard he'd gotten hit. He probably had some degree of traumatic brain injury from being so close to the blast. Hell, I probably did, too.

When he didn't answer, I shook him a little. It wasn't an ideal way to deal with a man with a TBI, who'd just watched some of his unit turned into hamburger in front of him, but right at that moment, we didn't have time to deal with the trauma in any kind of sensitive manner. We needed to get everyone who was still alive the hell out of the kill zone.

"Killian!"

He blinked. "Yeah. Accountability. Right."

"Get moving," I snapped. "We don't know if they're finished yet."

He staggered off, yelling for his fireteam leaders. I turned back to my team and caught up with Phil, who was looking more shaken than I think I'd ever seen him.

There weren't many in our line of work, in our generation, who had ever been the target of an enemy airstrike. The US had always had air supremacy; airstrikes were what happened to the *other guys*.

We were going to have to get used to a whole different reality. The old narrative about how First World nations didn't make war on each other seemed to be slipping into the fantasy that it always had been.

We pushed farther northeast, taking up security positions deep under the trees while we waited for Bradshaw and Killian to get their units together and get ready to move.

There wasn't going to be time to bury the bodies or otherwise deal with the burning vehicles. We'd have to hope that any follow-up force decided that the dead were all there had been. Hopefully, the dead would help their brothers and sisters one last time.

It was a grim way of looking at things, but it was grim world we'd woken up to. Grimmer than it had been only a few years before.

Chapter 15

Bradshaw had lost five men. I didn't know them well, but I still knew their faces. Wheeler, Dekker, Crowley, Morrow, and Hughes were gone. Three of them had died quickly. Morrow had taken a shattered tree limb to the throat, and had died slowly, choking on his own blood. There hadn't been anything any of us could do. Dekker's chest had been crushed. He died while Jordan was working on him.

Killian's unit had taken almost thirty percent casualties. Of those, about half were dead. The others were mostly walking wounded, except for a young female PFC named Bond who had lost her leg. She would have to be carried.

If she didn't die of shock before we got very far.

We stayed in place long enough to get Bond somewhat stabilized, her stump tourniqueted, and then, with two soldiers carrying her, we headed out. It was going to be a long night.

***

We didn't get nearly as far that night as I'd hoped. I think we covered about five more kilometers after dark, before having to find a hide site and lay up. The regulars were spent, ground down by the movement, wounds, and shock. We weren't really in much better shape, except that we were better-trained, and our conditioning was better. Physically, we could have kept going another five.

Mentally, I wasn't so sure.

Killian had shaken off some of his shock. His voice was a harsh rasp as he issued instructions once we halted. He didn't give his soldiers a moment's rest, not until they had dug in and set security.

In a way, it was good to see. He was adjusting, finding the hardened spine he was going to need if he and his men were going to survive this. It was just too bad that it had taken such a disaster to bring it about.

Warren hadn't said much, deferring to Killian. He was clearly exhausted and in shock. We'd barely halted before he was down on his ass, back against a tree, either asleep or damned close. How he'd made it out when so many others hadn't, I didn't know. And I knew that others, among the regulars as well as us, were going to be asking the same question.

Draven had gotten his guys out quick, and had managed to get them to cover in time to avoid any casualties beyond some battered hearing and minor frag. They were every bit as tired as we were, but they were infantrymen, even if they'd been humping mortars. Draven had quickly teamed up with Bradshaw, and the mortarmen were mixed in with the other infantry on the perimeter.

My team didn't have a sector. We were scouts, snipers, saboteurs, and shock troops. We needed to be able to move without taking away from the larger unit's security. Some of Killian's soldiers weren't happy about it; we were getting looks. Of course, so were Bradshaw's guys, but not to the same extent.

They could look all they wanted. We had our role, and it was going to keep more of them alive.

Even as we planted ourselves among the bushes and rocks in the middle of the oddly-shaped perimeter on the mountainside, I heard the distant rumble of artillery. Another section of fast-movers went by overhead with a dull, crackling roar. I spotted them briefly in my NVGs as I craned my neck to look up, just before they passed out of sight, blocked by the trees. A few minutes later, I thought I heard the distant *crump*s of their ordnance.

"I need one guy," I said quietly. "I'm going up to the crest of the ridge, see if I can get a better view." It was recon, but I wasn't going to assign anybody unless I had to.

"I'll go," Chris said. "Phil's been breaking trail all day and all night, while I've been tagging along."

"Because I'm better at it," Phil said. "Recognize."

162

"Because you're the last one we'll miss if you get blown up, more like," David replied.

"Pot, meet kettle, Peanut," Phil shot back. "If you hadn't wormed your way into the secondary comms billet, you'd be right up here. Having to be stealthy might finally shut you up."

"Come on, Chris," I said, dropping my ruck and slinging my rifle. I started uphill, toward the perimeter. Scott could sort this bickering lot out.

Draven, it turned out, had the northern, uppermost sector. I crouched down next to him and hastily explained the plan in whispers, giving him my rough direction, distance, and timeframe, along with instructions if we didn't come back within that timeframe. It mostly boiled down to, "Tell Scott, and get ready to get the hell out of here, because we're probably captured or dead." But he got the gist. And Draven was no newcomer, either. He'd been around the block almost as long as Kidd. He'd dropped mortars on Kosovars and Serbs alike in the Fourth Balkan War.

With contingency plans and linkup procedures established, Chris and I moved out.

It was a tough climb. The slope got steeper and rockier as we went up, the pines and firs getting farther apart on the stony mountainside. Both of us slipped a couple of times, freezing as a rock tumbled away down the slope from under a wrongly placed boot.

It took nearly an hour to get the top. It was barely three hundred meters, but we were tired and the terrain was unforgiving. Once we reached a good lay-up spot, I stopped, sinking to a knee and scanning the ridgeline carefully, my rifle held ready, the muzzle never far from my line of sight.

After about five minutes of just staying put, listening and watching, I was satisfied that we were alone up there. I could hear faint noises from down below; I was pretty sure it was Killian's troops. My guys would have gone silent, and Bradshaw would be ruthlessly enforcing light and noise discipline. Not that he needed to with Triarii, especially when we had regular Army pukes along with us. They'd stay silent and professional just to show the little guys how it's done.

Satisfied with our position, I turned my attention north and east.

Distant flickers preceded more faint rumbles. Somewhere below us and to the north, a multiple-launch rocket system battery opened fire, the missiles roaring northeast on fiery streaks of exhaust, the rapid-fire *whoosh* of the launch only reaching us most of a minute later. The rockets spent their fury on the far side of a hill we couldn't see over, though the earthquake rumble of the impacts echoed across the fields in the night.

"Somebody's getting pasted tonight," Chris whispered.

"Yeah," I replied. "Unfortunately, I don't think it's the bad guys."

We watched in silence for a few more minutes, while I tried to get a handle on just what we were looking at, casting back to the map in my mind. Judging by the direction, and the amount of time it was taking for the sound to get to us after the flashes, I thought that we were looking at an engagement somewhere between us and Vrbovè. Which meant that the Nationalists had advance forces out to try to forestall the "peacekeepers."

Or, we were watching another massacre, in real time.

However, as I watched, I started to doubt it. A faint growl reached my battered ears, that wasn't artillery fire or explosions. I squinted. It was a long way off, but I thought I saw the speck in my NVGs that might be a helicopter. Then another. My suspicions were confirmed when a long line of tracers reached up toward the two distant specks, forcing them to veer off.

So, somebody was getting pasted, but they were still putting up a fight.

"You think this is it?" Chris asked quietly as we watched the biggest battle I'd ever seen in my life.

I knew Chris. I knew what he was asking. I still asked, "You mean the End Times? Hell, I don't know, Chris. It's another war. There have been an awful lot of them throughout history."

"Yeah," he answered. "But everything seems to be falling apart at once. There are a lot of parallels with Revelation."

"There always are," I replied. I sighed. Chris was a zealous member of some evangelical splinter church. This wasn't the first such conversation we'd had. "There were a lot of parallels at the fall of Jerusalem, too," I told him. "It's apocalyptic literature, Chris. It's got multiple layers and meanings. That's the nature of it." I watched the next salvo of rockets streak off to the north. "Maybe it is the final war. Maybe it's no more the last war than World War I was the 'War to End All Wars.' Maybe it doesn't matter."

"Of course it matters," he said. "If the End Times are coming, we want to make sure we're on the right side."

"Well, I'm pretty sure that the EDC ain't on the side of the angels," I said wryly. "Look, Chris. It doesn't matter because all that we need to be worried about is how we're going to face our own deaths, even if they come tomorrow." Which they might. "'Thou knowest not the day, nor the hour,' remember? He told us not to worry too much about it."

Chris fell silent. This wasn't a new conversation. Like a lot of people in his particular sect, Chris was borderline obsessed with trying to suss out just which element of the modern world corresponded precisely with which element of the Book of Revelation.

I thought it was a waste of time, and a lack of faith. But there came a point where the argument became somewhat pointless. And on a leader's recon, watching the EDC and the Slovak Army hammer the Nationalists that we were trying to reach, wasn't the time to really go into depth.

After a while, there wasn't much more we could figure out from our vantage point. The battle continued to rage, but it was too far away to tell who was winning and who was losing. After I glanced at my watch, seeing that we had about three hours of darkness left, we started back down.

**

Greg had the HF radio up when we rejoined the rest of the team, and handed me the handset. "Kidd's on," he whispered.

I took the handset. "Pegleg, Deacon," I said.

"I don't have a lot of new info for you, Deacon," Kidd said. His voice was scratchy and weak, and I had to press the handset hard against my ear to hear him, even in the relative quiet of the night. "We've still got no comms Stateside. We might have gotten a whisper on the HF, but satcom's still flatlined. And get this; we're locked out of most of our email accounts. There seems to be some kind of denial of service attack across the board. We *might* have gotten something through on one of the tertiary accounts, but so far, there's been no reply. That might be because nobody back home can get access, either, or…" he paused, as if carefully picking his words. "Or, they're too busy to get access."

Given what had been happening back home for the last couple of years, the increasing frequency of riots, flash-mob violence, assassinations, bombings, and infrastructure attacks, both by foreign and domestic terror groups, that didn't bode well. If the main body of the Triarii were too busy for the command to make contact with the first Triarii expeditionary unit, something had to have gone pretty far south.

Given the coincidence of timing with the attack on Keystone and the crash of US military comms in Europe, I doubted that the coincidence was accidental.

"Roger," I acknowledged, before filling him in on what we'd seen in Kuchyňa, and from the peak above us. "This looks to me like a concerted effort to wipe out the Nationalists, and punish anyone who helped them in any way," I said. "I think they realized after Slovenský Grob that the US wasn't going to play ball, so they decided to take the American peacekeepers off the board."

"Sounds about like it," Kidd replied, his words almost drowned in a wash of static. "We still can't get air over Slovakia; we lost two more drones yesterday. But before we did, we got imagery of some major movements toward the Hungarian border. Most of the units looked Czech; I think that the EDC is forcing Prague to walk under the yoke." It would take a Triarii to understand the reference, these days. In the old Roman days, forcing a defeated army to walk under an ox yoke was a way of enforcing their subservience to the victors. The EDC had forced both Prague and Bratislava to open their borders to the continuing flow of "refugees" from North Africa, the Middle East, and the Balkans, while increasing their financial and military contributions to the EDC itself, based on the debts

166

already owed by both governments to Paris and Berlin. The Czechs had folded quicker than the Slovaks, and now both nations were paying the price, if in different ways.

"The Hungarians are treating these movements as a threat," Kidd went on, "which I'm pretty sure they are." Kidd would have been in close contact with the Hungarian Army. The Hungarians had split away from the EU at about the same time the Poles had, and had been more than receptive when Colonel Santiago had sent Kidd with our advance party to lay out what we wanted to do. "They're deploying elements of the 25th Infantry Brigade to the border." He paused again. "I'm not sure that coming this way is going to be the best idea, Deacon."

"We weren't really planning on it," I admitted, though this was one of the first times I'd really had a chance to think about it. "The original plan was to get the Army cats to Zilina and FOB Poole. Now, I doubt that Poole's still standing. Nobody's gotten comms with them. And without the vehicles, these kids are going to get slaughtered." They would have been slaughtered *in* the vehicles if we hadn't moved fast. "That leaves the nearest American forces in Poland." Despite the magnitude of the sneak attack in Slovakia, I doubted that the EDC had managed to penetrate far enough into Poland to wipe out the big US bases there, the same ones that the Russians had been complaining about for years. "We've got you guys in Hungary, but if we go there, we're going to be stuck with the same problem of returning these people to the Army that we've got now."

"Well, you're the guy on the ground," Kidd replied. "See if you can link up with the Nationalists. We've been trying to contact them in Vrbové via HF, but we haven't gotten through yet. If we can, we'll tell them to be on the lookout for you." We didn't have any solid contacts with the Nationalists, but there had been messages sent before we inserted to rescue England. "Just keep me posted as best you can," he continued. "I'll do what I can to coordinate with the Hungarian Ground Forces if you do come this way. They've got no reason to love the EDC."

"I'll be in touch," I replied, before signing off. Truth be told, I doubted that either Killian or Warren would be willing to head for Hungary. As far as the US Army knew, there were no friendly forces there. Granted, they were still operating on the old paradigm that the EDC, the new de facto successor to the European Union, were American allies. Hungary having told the EU to sit on it and spin even before the formation of the so-called European Defense Council, the Hungarians were going to be viewed by Washington with suspicion, at best. And the Army answered to Washington, no matter what the grunts on the ground might think about the realities of the situation.

I didn't seek either of the regular leaders out. There was no real change to either our situation, or our plan. We were still heading for Vrbovè the next night, provided we didn't get forced out of this position again during the day. Being limited to our feet, in a way, made things a little easier. Foot-mobiles are harder to spot from the air than steel behemoths spouting exhaust fumes.

I found my ruck, lay back against it, and was asleep in seconds.

Chapter 16

Vrbovè had taken a beating. But it was still standing.

We'd seen the smoking hulks of vehicles on and around the road, starting at Chtelnica. Entire stretches of fields and the hedgerows in between were blasted and blackened, where the Nationalists had put up a fight before either falling back or being annihilated.

Now, from our vantage point in the woods, on one of the last foothills of the Little Carpathians before the open valley where Vrbovè sat, Phil and I scanned the fields in front of us and tried to plan our infiltration.

With more time to observe, it became apparent that for all the firepower that Chris and I had seen getting thrown around the night before, most of the fighting had been fairly irregular. The burned-out husk of an AMX-10 on the side of Highway 499, north of us, was halfway in a deep crater, that must have been from an IED blast. Even as we watched, a salvo of five rockets blasted out of the trees in the distance, on the edge of Vrbovè, aimed at somewhere south. When those five were it, with no further activity before a howling barrage of artillery fire slammed into the same area, blotting out the dim outline of the house in a cloud of dust, smoke, and fire, I suspected that the Nationalists had followed the playbook of every insurgent since the advent of modern war. Shoot and scoot. The men who had launched the rockets were probably far away by the time the counter-battery fire hit.

"Damn, this is a shit sandwich, isn't it?" Phil asked.

He wasn't wrong. There were drones in the sky on multiple levels, and we could hear the distant rumble of fast-movers as well as the growl of helicopters. The helos were

169

steering clear of the town itself; the anti-aircraft fire they'd taken the night before must have shaken them up. The sheer cost of modern military equipment meant that lives were less valuable than vehicles or helicopters.

The air cover wasn't the only problem, though. There were vehicles on the roads and in the fields, mostly standing off a couple of klicks from Vrbovè itself, but with clear fields of fire on all the major thoroughfares leading in. Most of them appeared to be hastily up-armored militia technicals or Slovak Army BVP-2s, but there were plenty of German Pumas, Belgian Griffons, and French AMX-10s in the mix. There were even the low, predatory shapes of tanks squatting in hedgerow to the south; I couldn't see them clearly enough to know if they were German or Slovak. Both countries used the Leopard 2, anyway, so it would be hard to say even close up.

"Well, we don't have much of a choice but to take a big bite, do we?" I asked. Scanning the ground below us, I thought I saw a bit of a gap. It wasn't even a gap, so much as it was a covered and concealed route through the cordon that the EDC had slapped around the town. The vehicles were mostly up by the roads, probably because there was definitely some wetland near the 499, which would be rough going for armor trying to go offroad. They'd get stuck worse than that Stryker had gotten stuck in the mountains.

"Might mean getting wet, but I think I see a way in," I said. I pointed out my planned route, which was partially dependent on the enemy being as weak-minded and averse to discomfort as a lot of our allies were. Phil scanned it with his eyes, nodding slightly, once again one hundred percent the professional soldier and point man.

"Got it, boss," he said. "Leaving rucks here?"

"I don't see another way," I said. "We're going to have to do some crawling, and I don't know about you, but I'm not thrilled with the idea of trying to do that with close to seventy pounds on my back."

"Me, neither," Phil replied. "You ready?"

"Let's go." We slipped back into the trees and moved deeper into the woods to link up with the rest. I gave a down-and-dirty brief of our route and the plan.

"Don't take this the wrong way, Deacon," David said. "But the linkup plan is kinda shit."

"Oh, I know," I answered, refusing to rise to the bait and get defensive with Dave. That never ended well for anyone involved, and letting that happen during a brief like this was a bad, bad idea. "We don't have a lot of choices, though. Kidd's been trying to get through to the Nationalists in Vrbovè for the last couple of days, but either he's on the wrong channel, they're not interested, or they've been too busy to answer. Judging by what we can see out there, my money's on A and C."

I looked around at the darkened, painted faces. "Any other dumb observations?" I asked. "Or, miracle of miracles, any *smart* ones?"

"As much as it pains me, I agree with Peanut," Jordan said. "This isn't smart. There's a lot more likely to go wrong trying to contact the Nationalists. We've already managed to resupply once. We don't exactly need fuel anymore. Why not just head for the border?"

"Poland's a hundred thirty klicks away," I replied. "Hungary's almost the same distance, and across a lot flatter, more open terrain. Personally, I think we've got a better chance of survival if we can link into the Nationalists' network. *We* could do it on our own; we did it on the way in. These kids?" I jerked my thumb toward where Killian's soldiers were dug in. "They wouldn't make it halfway there. And like it or not, we've got them hanging around our necks, now. Unless anybody really wants to turn their back on the whole reason we came into this hell in the first place, and leave a bunch of Americans to the wolves?"

Nobody had an answer to that. It was tough, it was dangerous, but that was what we'd trained for. And despite the more practical considerations, I think that all of us were just mad. I know I was. I'd joined the Triarii because I'd been sick of what the Marine Corps was continuing to descend into. But I hadn't quit being an American just because I'd put on that patch.

I pointed to Phil. He turned and headed downhill and toward the town.

It was deceptively quiet; the fighting of the night before must have given the EDC pause. Given the number of blasted,

171

burned-out hulks we'd seen on the way, that shouldn't have come as any surprise. The only sounds were the distant rumble of vehicles on the ground and in the sky, along with the occasional distant *pop* of a gunshot.

Phil threaded his way down through the woods, sticking a little bit more to the south from where he and I had observed the fields and the lay of the land.

Reaching the edge of the woods and the beginning of the first hedgerow that formed our route, he got low and started moving even more slowly. I let him get a few meters' head start, then followed.

That kind of movement gets excruciating after a while. You have to stay low, below the tops of the bushes. That means bending down, which gets to be murder on the lower back after a shockingly short time, no matter how fit you are. Meanwhile, you're trying to watch every step so as not to make too much noise, while simultaneously keeping your head on a swivel to watch for threats, keep track of your teammates, and look ahead so that you don't get so focused on where your feet are *at that moment*, that you wander off into the open, or expose yourself from a direction you weren't thinking about.

Those who say that infantrymen are just crayon-eating knuckle-draggers? I'd like to see them try it. It's a thinking man's game, if you want to stay alive in places where it ain't easy.

Phil paused at the end of the hedgerow. We had to either cross an open stretch of field, if only about fifty yards, or else turn sharply north to stay in the cover of the hedgerow. That would take us much too close to the formation of BVPs and AMX-10s on the 499 for comfort, particularly in that spot.

He stayed where he was while I caught up. He didn't even whisper, but pointed due east, toward the town and across the field. He was more comfortable with taking the direct, if somewhat exposed way. I looked north, then south. My fusion goggles could just pick out a glimmer of heat signature down that way; there was an armored vehicle in the hedgerow to the south, about two fields away. There was closer cover and concealment, but it seemed that the Nationalists had mauled them badly enough that they were keeping some standoff.

Still, modern thermal sights could see an awfully long way. Better not to take too many chances. I squeezed Phil's shoulder to get his attention, pointed to my eyes, then pointed south. He looked carefully for a long moment, then nodded, and motioned to indicate crawling on his belly. I nodded.

It was going to be rough going, but low-crawling is always better than getting blown apart by machinegun fire or worse.

I looked back to make sure that Greg and Jordan were keeping up, as Phil got down and started to worm his way forward, finding a furrow in the by-then fallow field. His ghillie hood-over helped break up his outline and a little of his thermal signature, but it wouldn't have disguised him enough if it had been daylight.

Ghillies don't work the way movies and video games would have it.

With Phil a few yards in front of me, I got down on my belly, making sure that my rifle muzzle was up out of the dirt, and started following him.

Low crawling is not fun. It is painful. It is slow. Especially when you are trying to avoid detection, it makes it even slower. Hartrick liked to call it, with an evil glee, the "Skull Drag." Because you're trying to make yourself part of the ground while you inch forward with your elbows, knees, and toes.

The dirt seemed to fill my nose as I crept along behind Phil. It quickly started working its way into my sleeves, my gloves, and my belt. Not that I'd been exactly clean for the last few days, but fresh grit has a way of getting even more uncomfortable.

The dirt wasn't the worst part, though. The worst part was the feeling of being as exposed as a bug on a plate. We were in the open, and while, when I turned my head first to the north, and then to the south, I couldn't really see any of the enemy armored vehicles, that didn't mean that the skies were entirely clear, either. I couldn't look without stopping, so I just prayed that no drones flew directly overhead, or that if they did, their operators were asleep at the switch.

Phil got to the next hedgerow and scrambled up to his feet. I was just over a minute behind him. Even as I got out of the open and started to pick myself up, I thought I heard a faint, humming buzz.

"Shit," Phil whispered urgently. "Recon drone." He had his rifle up in his shoulder, pointed at the sky, but fortunately, he held his fire. A gunshot was going to draw just as much, if not more, attention. We had to hope that we hadn't been spotted, that the drone was watching inside the town.

I got up on a knee next to Phil, grabbing him by the shoulder and turning him to watch ahead, while I covered the rest of the team crossing the field. Greg had almost reached us, getting a little higher in his hurry to get out of the open.

If I hadn't turned back to cover, I might not have seen the figures coming out of the trees to the north. They weren't in what I would call any kind of formation, but they were armed. And they damned sure weren't ours.

Even so, I held my fire, just in case they were a random patrol, or even some of the EDC's troops trying to probe the edges of Vrbovè. Maybe the drone hadn't seen us. Maybe these guys had nothing to do with us.

But they weren't moving east, toward the town. They were coming south, toward us. And the buzz of that drone overhead was getting louder.

"Hurry up," I hissed. "But stay down." I wasn't even watching the others at that point; I was watching the oncoming gunmen. They were sloppy, bunched up and walking upright across the field. Not well-trained.

Not that that would be much consolation if they opened fire on us at that range, in the open. We didn't have enough cover. And if they shot like they patrolled, they would make up for their training with volume of fire. And quantity ends up having a quality all its own.

I raised my rifle as Greg got past me and struggled to his feet. I could only see a bit of his movement out of the corner of my off eye; my fusion goggles were focused entirely on the men coming closer, and they didn't have a great field of view. But after a moment, I saw his IR laser switch on from behind me, dancing toward the figures in the field.

"Turn that off," I hissed. I didn't know if they had NVGs or not, but it hadn't been a good bet to assume that the bad guys *didn't* have night vision for the last decade.

I was too late, though. One of them yelled, and then all hell broke loose.

Greg switched off the laser just as muzzle flashes flickered along the ragged line of advancing skirmishers, and he and I both dropped flat at the same time. Jordan had almost reached us, but rolled to one side, bringing his rifle around even as I searched for my sights and bullets *snapped* overhead, ripping the vegetation behind us to shreds.

My OBR's short-dot scope could be set to zero magnification, and the reticle was illuminated. Through the fusion goggles, it wasn't clear; it may as well have been a red dot. But that was about all I needed right then. I put the fuzzy blob of white on the nearest muzzle flash and squeezed the trigger.

Flame spat from the muzzle and the 7.62 thundered twice before I shifted to the next man in the line. The pale outline of the man I'd shot flopped backward, pumping more rounds uselessly at the sky. They had NVGs, but they were still spraying fire wildly at us, so they could see, they just couldn't see well. Probably old Gen IIIs or Gen IVs, without our thermal capability. Still, the muzzle flash from my rifle would be like a beacon.

More flashes were erupting across the field as the team reacted to contact. I shifted my aim to the next man to the left of the one I'd just dumped, but Greg had knocked that one off his feet, so I kept shifting my aim left, even as I crabbed to my right, trying to get away from the position I'd just announced by my muzzle blast.

Four men were down in as many seconds, and the rest were running for cover or throwing themselves flat in the aftermath, still shooting wildly back at us. They weren't even trying to aim; some of the bullets were far enough away that their passage sounded like a hiss instead of a *snap*. One was crawling on hands and knees back toward the trees, until I put a bullet into his center mass and he flopped on his face.

Taking stock, I got back up on a knee. "Let's go!" I barked. There was no point in noise discipline at that point. We'd gone loud, in a big way. "By twos, toward the town!"

Some of the survivors had reached the trees, and were spraying more fire at us. I returned a rapid five shots, aiming just below muzzle flashes as best I could, before Dwight tore into that treeline with a long burst of automatic 7.62 fire. That was my signal, and I got up and grabbed Phil. "On me!" I barked, and we plunged into the hedgerow, heading east as best we could.

So much for quietly infiltrating Vrbovè.

Chapter 17

I dashed forward, skidding to a halt as I spun around and dropped prone. The hedgerow itself had proved to be too thick for us to stay inside it while trying to break contact; Phil and I were both hugging it, but had had to push into the field to the north just so that we could get some distance.

Getting my rifle into my shoulder, I searched for targets. I wasn't going to waste ammunition on suppressive fire at that point.

I saw a brief flicker of movement, but it looked like the sheer ferocity of our counterattack had given them pause. They hadn't expected to run into soldiers out in the open, and when they'd lost at least six in the first few seconds, that was going to shake their morale. I hoped that they were running scared, but we weren't going to take chances.

Hope is not a plan, to use the hoary old turn of phrase.

Jordan pounded past me, squeezing between me and the hedgerow, almost stepping on my back. I could hear him panting, but he was in good shape—better than I was. Greg was behind him, and he was sounding a little more ragged. Greg wasn't the biggest PT stud on the team.

The two of them pushed past us and kept going, stretching out a few more meters before setting in. By the time they dropped flat, Dwight and Chris were passing.

The technical term for the maneuver was the "Australian Peel." We hadn't necessarily set out to do it that way, but the confined nature of the terrain had pretty well mandated it.

In pairs, the rest of the team peeled past, until Tony thudded past me with a gasped, "Last man."

I stayed where I was for a moment, scanning the field and the far hedgerow for the enemy. I didn't want to get up and move only to get caught in the open just as more shooters came out of the trees and opened fire.

For a long minute or two, the field was quiet and still. I could hear the vehicles revving up on the road, and distant shouts. Somewhere behind us, gunfire rattled in the night, but it sounded like it was on the other side of town.

Naturally, as soon as I levered myself up onto a knee, six men came out of the trees.

They were moving carefully; they didn't know where we were anymore, presuming they were even a part of the same patrol we'd shot to pieces. I froze, hoping that my ghillie would break up enough of my outline to lose myself in the vegetation behind me.

Maybe it did, maybe it didn't. The machinegunner who hefted his HK 21 to hip level and sprayed a long, stuttering burst of fire at the hedgerow didn't seem to be aiming at anything in particular. It was recon by fire, or simply him hosing down any place that might have an enemy with bullets.

My money would be on the latter, but at that point, it was hardly pertinent.

I dropped on my belly, my chest rig and magazines digging into my ribs, as Phil shot the machinegunner, the single bark of his rifle silencing the HK 21's thunder. The man stumbled, then fell on his face in the dirt.

Phil had already been aimed in. By the time he dropped the machinegunner, I was just getting my eye to my scope. I transitioned to the next man just as they whole group opened fire, spraying bullets at the hedgerow as they threw themselves on the ground.

I fired just as they dropped, my shot missing my target by inches. He got low, almost out of my sight, but I aimed and fired even lower, just about right at the ground in front of him. I didn't think I'd actually hit him, but I sure blasted a bunch of frag and dirt into his face, because he reared back in pain. At less than three hundred yards, it wasn't that difficult a shot. The rifle surged back into my shoulder with a heavy *boom*. My thermals showed a faint, light-colored splash, and he slumped.

I fired two more shots at the lumps I could just barely see, then hauled myself up and hauled ass toward the town behind us.

It's always a temptation, in such a position, to stay put, behind cover, and pick off as many of the enemy as you can. The problem with that is, while you might be stationary, that doesn't mean that all of the enemy are. And a small unit like my ten-man team would be too easily flanked and wiped out. They had numbers that we didn't.

So, despite the fact that there were still more of them on their feet and moving, I heaved myself up, turned, and ran. I pounded past Phil, gasping, "Last man!" My voice was drowned out by the hard, thunderous reports as he opened fire on his own, shooting fast enough that I doubted just how precisely he was aiming.

Three seconds. That is, on average, about how long it takes an enemy to spot you, bring his weapon to bear, aim in, and squeeze the trigger. Which means that it is, on average, about how long you have to get behind cover once you move from your last covered and concealed position.

Believe me, when you're running upright in the dark, with bullets already *snap*ping past your ears, three seconds feels like way too long.

I skidded to a halt, while simultaneously spinning around and dropping on my belly in the dirt. It took a frantic second to see clearly, as my fusion goggles immediately tried to slide down over my nose, but when I did, I saw muzzle flashes flickering in the hedgerow where the enemy had popped out, but none of them trying to close in. They'd learned quick. The rapidly-cooling bodies lying in the dirt and stubble between us made for a hell of an object lesson.

The angle between us was such that a normal peel wasn't really going to work. The plus side was that every one of us who wasn't moving had a shot. I picked out a muzzle flash and shot at it, making sure that I aimed low; most misses go high. It had taken some practice to make that second nature.

I kept up the fire while the rest stamped past me, until I was the last man again. The fire from the opposing hedgerow had slackened some by then, but I could hear the ominous

179

rumble of diesels in the distance. They were trying to find a route for the armored vehicles to get to us.

Up. Moving. The night air was burning in my lungs, tainted as it was with smoke and dust. The last week of fatigue was catching up with me, but I kept pushing, forcing my feet and legs to move, my head ducked down to try to present a slightly smaller target to the militiamen or EDC troops who were still shooting at us.

Down. No shot this time. I lay there, my chest heaving, my heartbeat thudding in my ears, sweat running down my face and soaking my fatigues despite the autumn chill in the air, as the rest continued the peel back. The good thing about that particular maneuver is that it can move very, very quickly.

Up again. We were almost to the end of the field. Another hedgerow stood between us and the nearest houses, but they had been blasted into wreckage and ruin by artillery, IEDs, airstrikes, or a combination of all three. Still, they'd provide more cover.

I found myself leading the way into the shattered neighborhood, reloading my rifle as I went. There were still a few rounds left in the mag, which went back into my chest rig, but I wanted that weapon in the best condition possible.

We were getting low on ammo. I did a quick count in my head as I stepped past the trees, my rifle up and scanning the half of the nearest house that was still standing. I had about three magazines left. Seventy-five rounds, not counting the five or six still in nearly-empty mags. About half what I'd infiltrated Slovakia with. I wished that we could get an airdrop, but hopefully, if we managed to link up with the Nationalists, they'd have some 7.62 NATO for us. Killian and his troops would be in trouble, though. Only the US Army was currently using the 6.8mm round; they'd have to scrounge weapons and ammo. And magazines.

Provided the Nationalists were willing to spare any. Which was, of course, provided that they agreed to help us.

The fire from across the field was only sporadic and poorly-aimed by then, but I could hear the diesels getting closer. They'd figured that we were going into the blasted neighborhood, so the vehicles were coming down the road toward us. We weren't out of the woods yet.

I got about five steps before I stopped dead, holding up a hand to grab Phil before he took another step. He started, looking at me, but I pointed at what I'd just seen.

It was hard to make out in all the rubble, but there was just enough difference in temperature that somehow, it had shown up in my fusion goggles. There was something half-buried in the collapsed brick of the wall, and a line running out from it all the way to the trees. The little nodules along that line would be the contact points. The house must have been hit the night before, or even earlier, and the Nationalists had been busy after that.

Rock, meet hard place. We had enemy troops behind us, armor coming up on our flank, more armor out on the other flank, which also happened to be an open field, and the Nationalists had seeded the ruins, which provided the only real covered and concealed route into the town, with IEDs. I spotted another one nestled in the pile of shattered masonry at the corner. I was sure that there were more pressure plates and tripwires set on the street nearby, and in the next building.

It made a fiendish sort of sense. From what we knew, the Nationalist forces in Vrbovè weren't large; while they constituted more of a reinforced company, as opposed to whatever small cell had been operating in Kuchyňa, they still weren't likely to have the heavy firepower and numbers of the big units out east, which had been largely formed around disaffected Slovak Army battalions. IEDs were a way of equalizing the battlefield. Anyone without extensive combat engineer support was going to go around the rubbled neighborhood, forcing them either onto the road, or out into the open field, which was probably being watched by dug-in machinegunners and RPG gunners.

And the difficulty of advancing along the road quickly became obvious as a flash lit up the night, followed a fraction of a second later by a concussion that shook the ground and just about knocked us all flat. The heavy *wham* of the IED detonation blasted leaves off the trees and bombarded the neighborhood with a blast of splinters, dirt, rock, and shattered asphalt, as an ugly black-and-orange cloud rose into the night sky. As the echoes of the blast died away, they were replaced by the fierce crackle of flames, what might have been distant screams, and then the harsh popcorn noise as the armored vehicle's ammunition started cooking off.

By then, the rest of the team was inside the treeline. The incoming fire had died away to nothing after that vehicle had been destroyed, and we weren't going to draw any more if we could help it.

Getting Bradshaw and the rest down into town without a balls-out firefight was going to be a good trick. But we needed to make contact with the Nationalists at the very least. We'd figure that particular problem out later.

But if I hoped that we had some breathing room, I was doomed to disappointment. With their advance halted by the IED on the road, the EDC or their lackeys weren't giving up.

I barely heard the distant *pops*, but the whiffling noise that began rising in pitch was unmistakable. And horrifying.

There was nowhere to go, not with those IEDs in the way. "Down!" I bellowed, suiting actions to words as I dropped flat and got as close to the ruined wall as I could, all too aware that there could very well be another cluster of 155mm shells behind it, just waiting for the right shock to go off, obliterating the rest of the bombed-out house, and me with it. But if I didn't have cover, those incoming mortar rounds were going to turn me into pink mist, anyway.

The mortars must have been pre-registered on the middle of the neighborhood. The impacts hit ahead of us, though they still shook and rattled every bone as they hammered into the ruined buildings and the street between them, close enough that each impact felt like being slapped against the ground by a gigantic hand. Dirt and debris were blasted skyward in ugly black fountains as the mortars hit and detonated, the sheaf forming a rough circle in the middle of the neighborhood. Maybe they hoped that we'd already penetrated deeper in.

I stayed as low and as small as I could get as the wall shuddered and quaked behind me, my teeth hurting from the ravening force of the detonations. For those few brief moments, I felt as helpless and alone as I ever have. When you're in a firefight, you have teammates, you have some control over your own fate. You can take cover, maneuver, shoot back. When you're under mortar, artillery, or air attack, about all you can do is try to find cover, hunker down, and pray.

I was doing a lot of that, right at that moment.

The mortars ceased, the echoes rolling out across the valley, and for a moment, everything seemed eerily quiet. Then the Nationalists responded.

Rockets roared out of Vrbovè with snarling, ripping sounds, streaking on bright tails of flame to the northwest and the south. I couldn't tell if it was counter-battery fire, or simply aimed at any of their enemies they had targeted, as retaliation for the mortar strike. It didn't matter. Hopefully, it kept some heads down while we worked our way farther in.

I was still worried about how we were going to make contact without being shot as infiltrators, but once again, I had to worry about burning that bridge when I got to it.

I wormed my way to where Phil was in a similar near-fetal position against the base of the wall, closer to the north corner of the house. "We've got to get moving," I said. "Watch for pressure plates, and hope they don't have any of them on command-det." If there was a trigger man sitting there with a switch wired in, and he decided that the ghillied-up figures slipping closer to Vrbovè were hostiles, we'd be paste. But there was no other way, except to try to withdraw and take our chances on our own.

But even aside from the logistical issues of trying to get to Poland by ourselves, going back the way we'd come wouldn't be a good idea. They'd be waiting for us. If they didn't just drop mortars on our heads, they'd move up with those armored vehicles that were sitting to the south to gun us down as we tried to get across the fields.

Like it or not, we were committed.

Phil got up slowly, looking carefully at everywhere he was about to put his foot, or his hand, and moved around the corner, toward the street.

He stopped dead almost immediately, looking around him. I stepped next to him, taking care of where I put my foot, realizing that it was going to be damned hard to spot tripwires in the dark, even with fusion goggles. A tripwire is a very thin line, and the grainy, grayscale phosphor could only focus at one distance. Let the wire be too close to focus on, and we'd never see it until it was too late, and we were chunks.

I could see at least three mounds of rubble that looked off; they hadn't fallen there naturally. Which meant they were packed with explosives and other nasty little surprises. I was pretty sure I could see the pressure plate strung out from one of them, but knowing what I did about these things, I thought it was entirely possible that that was the trigger we were supposed to see. Which meant there were others, that were probably better-concealed.

Or there weren't, on account of the time available to plant the IEDs, not to mention the training level the Nationalists had with such things. But the possibility was still there, and we couldn't afford to take the chance.

You take chances with explosives, you get dead. And you get your buddies dead. That much had been drummed into me as a Marine, long before I'd joined the Triarii.

Phil studied the street for a long moment, barricaded on the corner of the building, before he apparently decided on his route. He got to his feet. "Let me get about twenty meters ahead before you follow me," he whispered.

A roaring burst of machinegun fire thundered behind us. The enemy had foot-mobiles approaching again. "We might not have the time," I told him. "Just find us as safe a path through that as you can." *And please, Lord, don't let the locals spot us and decide to blow us up, just to be safe.*

With exaggerated care, he stepped out onto the sidewalk and started forward, threading a twisting path through the gauntlet of rubble piles. I saw him scan around him, then reach up to his NVGs as he looked down at the ground. He took another step, adjusted his fusion goggles again, then repeated the process. Slow and laborious, but given the threat, there wasn't any other way.

I looked back, but the fire had ceased. It seemed that either Tony or Dwight had issued a warning that had been heeded. For the moment.

Now we needed to get through before they mortared us again.

I hissed at Greg, who passed it to Jordan, and then, taking a deep breath, I followed Phil.

It was one of the most nerve-wracking movements I've ever done. The more I looked, the more IEDs I saw. They had all been camouflaged by piles of rubble or downed trees, but it had all been done hastily, so with a little effort, it wasn't hard to pick them out. And they were *everywhere*. The Nationalists must have been preparing for this for a long time. There was a lot of ordnance in that wrecked neighborhood.

Of course, they must have seen the writing on the wall as soon as Bratislava refused to honor the referendum that had called for a complete severing of ties to the EDC, after the new set of "working documents" had come out of Brussels a couple years before. This fight had been a long time in coming. They'd had time to prepare while their angry countrymen rioted in the cities and were promptly put down by half the Slovak Army, backed up by the EDC's "peacekeepers."

It couldn't have been more than a quarter klick to the end of the street, but that was a *long* two hundred fifty meters. There had to be an IED every ten meters. They'd been thorough. They didn't want anyone approaching that way.

But we finally got to the edge of the ruined neighborhood and the IED field, after what felt like an eternity. We hadn't received any more mortar or small arms fire from the northeast. Losing that armored vehicle, plus however many men on foot that we'd shot, seemed to have taken the starch out of the EDC for the night. I suspected they'd planned on steamrolling Vrbovè, and when it had proven to be a harder nut to crack than they'd expected, it had put them on their back foot.

Phil was crouched in the trees, well back from the edge of the field between us and the town proper. There was another hedgerow lining the road north of us, but I suspected that it was just as loaded with IEDs, and probably covered by machineguns and RPGs, or whatever recoilless rifles the Nationalists were using.

He grabbed me as I got closer. "There are heat signatures and movement across there," he said, pointing toward town. "I think they're maneuvering to block anyone getting through."

"Probably," I replied. "It's what I'd do." I knelt next to him, peering through the thick vegetation in front of us. This hedgerow was almost forty meters thick, so we had room to hide.

At least, until some trigger-happy Nationalist decided to do some recon by fire.

I felt a tightening in my guts. This was it. We had no partisan linkup procedures set up with the Nationalists. We probably should have made contact before infiltration and established them, just in case, but the situation in Slovakia was so messed up that not only did we not know how they'd react, but they had no way of knowing for sure that we were on their side. Slovakia was a hash of "immigrant" militias, Loyalists who had sided with Bratislava against the referendum, increasingly militant Hungarian militias in the south, politically hardline Slovak militias, Russian-backed Slovak militias, disaffected Slovak Army troops, and a whole lot of people stuck in the middle, just trying to survive.

And the US Army had stuck itself into the middle of that maelstrom, publicly supporting the EDC, which was hell-bent on crushing the Slovak Nationalists. I wasn't sure how *I'd* respond to an American making contact, looking for help, if I was a Slovak at that point.

But it had to be done. And that meant that I had to do it.

I took a deep breath. I didn't want to do this. I really, really didn't want to do this. It could very well end up being the last thing I ever did. Worse, it might not be, but it might still go very, very wrong.

I handed off my rifle to Phil and stepped out of the trees. Raising my hands, I called out, "*Dobrý den!*"

I waited to get cut in half by a burst of machinegun fire. Instead, I stood there, in the open, listening for the telltale noise of falling mortar rounds, for a couple of minutes before armed figures came out of the bushes and advanced toward me, their rifles pointed at my chest.

Chapter 18

Standing there in the open, staring at the muzzles of those two CZ Bren 805s, was probably one of the hardest things I've ever done. Including all the stuff that came later.

I discovered a long time ago that I'm not the kind to just lie down and die, or surrender. I'm not given to looking for fights just because—aside from joining the Triarii, which was explicitly looking for fights that needed to happen, but weren't; that's a whole other animal—but I won't back down from them if I know that I'm in the right. And I just don't like having weapons pointed at me.

But as far as I could see, this was the only option. It could mean that I was a dead man. It could mean that I'd be a prisoner for an unspecified amount of time before I was either bartered, years down the road, or shot in the back of the head behind some Slovak barn somewhere. That was out of my hands.

But that didn't stop the urge to suddenly yell for covering fire, turn, and sprint back into the hedgerows for my rifle. A threat is a threat, whether it's coming from hostiles, unknowns, or friendlies. These guys were currently unknowns, but that could change, real quick.

"I'm an American," I said as they got closer. Both men who were closing in on me were wearing civilian clothes under plate carriers laden with magazines and grenades. So were the half-dozen or so back behind them on overwatch. "I need to talk to your commander."

"American?" the smaller man, on my left, asked. His voice was thickly accented. "You do not look like American Army."

Meaning I wasn't wearing half my bodyweight in armor. I was in fatigues, chest rig, and a ghillie hood-over.

"I'm not," I told him. "I'm part of a special unit that came in to fight the Kosovars." It was true enough. And I knew that the Nationalists had no love for the Kosovars, the Turks, or the Syrians who had been pushed into the country by the EDC. "I do have some regular American soldiers with me. They survived the Germans' sneak attack on their base." I also knew, from the intel briefs, just how far the German-Slovak relationship had deteriorated since the EDC had started making demands based on economic blackmail. While it was up in the air just who was really running the EDC, the French or the Germans, a lot of the Nationalists blamed the Germans, especially since the majority of the EDC peacekeepers were Bundeswehr units.

The man studied me. "Where are the others?" he asked. His English, while accented, was clear and precise.

"They're waiting in the woods for me to make contact," I said. "Just descending on a town that's been surrounded by the EDC didn't seem like a good idea. We might get taken for the bad guys if we did that." The hackles were going up on the back of my neck as I anticipated another mortar barrage. They had to have drones up that could see this little palaver. "Now, can you either take me to your commander, or just shoot me and get it over with?"

The bigger man said something in Slovak, and the smaller man replied quickly, without taking his eyes off me. "Very well, American," he said. "Come with us." He glanced at the trees, but none of the Nationalists were wearing NVGs, so he couldn't see the rest of the team hunkered down in there.

I didn't glance back. Scott would hold their position. I still had my radio, though it was currently turned off. I could make contact if I had to.

I just hoped that this went smoothly enough that they weren't still stuck in there when the sun came up.

***

They escorted me back into the trees and along the back sides of a row of houses before coming to a technical that might have started its life as a Nissan or Toyota pickup, but had been

188

extensively up-armored with welded sheet-steel, with a vz. 59 machinegun on a swing-mount bolted to the cab. The smaller man, who wasn't pointing his rifle precisely at me anymore, waved at me to get in the back. That he did it with his off hand and not his weapon, I took as a good sign.

I'd barely settled on the tailgate before the gunner banged on the top of the cab with the butt of his knife, and we were rolling. The driver wasn't playing around, either. He gunned it, and if the vehicle hadn't been weighed down with all the improvised armor, I might have gotten thrown off the tailgate. As it was, I had to grab onto the edge of the bed to make sure I stayed in place.

It was a fast but winding trip into Vrbovè. The place had been half-smashed by the artillery and air strikes the night before. Entire houses had been blasted to rubble, some of them collapsed into the street, which was also cratered in places. As we twisted our way through the wreckage, however, I thought I saw more of the somewhat deliberate rearranging of the debris that we'd seen in the outer neighborhood. As we passed a machinegun nest burrowed into one of the piles of smashed bricks, I was sure of it. A few blocks down, two technicals had been stashed in the wreckage of a pair of houses, flanking the main road from the west. The Nationalists hadn't turtled after the hammering they'd taken. They'd been industrious, improving their positions in the wake of the destruction visited on them by the EDC.

I might have gotten glimpses of rocket batteries and mobile AA guns, but I noticed that every time I thought I did, we went the other way. The driver was being careful. Which was a pretty good trick, when you considered the fact that the whole town was less than four klicks square.

When we finally stopped, it was near the center of town; I could tell because the church steeple was still standing. The place had taken a pasting, and there was a massive hole blown in the church roof. I crossed myself briefly as I got off, and I could tell the short guy noticed. He waved me toward the light-colored building on the north side of the street, where a Slovak flag still waved defiantly. The windows had been covered over and sandbags stacked against the bottom of the wall. It looked like an artillery shell had clipped the corner of the roof before burying itself in the storefront next door and detonating. There wasn't a lot of that store left; the entire front of the building had collapsed.

The door was shut, but the little man banged on it with his rifle. A muffled voice yelled in Slovak from inside, and he replied in kind. After a moment, the door creaked open, letting a bit of red light out into the street. It was the only light source for a hundred yards, at least. The little man waved me inside, and I ducked through the door as he followed.

The entryway of what looked like it had been the police station had been turned into a defensive strongpoint. Sandbags formed two fighting positions at right angles to each other, aimed in at the door. The Nationalist fighters behind the sandbags were standing, one wearing a Slovak Army uniform, the other in civilian clothes, both holding older CZ vz. 58 rifles. There was a spotlight, currently dark, pointed at the door. They didn't have night vision, so they'd blind the enemy while simultaneously letting them see their targets, at least until the spotlight got shot out.

The short man brushed past them, waving as the one in the camouflage uniform saluted. I followed, since he seemed to expect me to. He turned sharply right, and we headed down the hallway.

Three doors down, he stopped and knocked. A murmur came from inside, and he turned and beckoned to me as he stepped through the door.

The office had been turned into a command center. The walls were lined with more sandbags, and there were wires running from several military-style radios up into a hole that had been knocked in the ceiling. Work lights had been set up, and I had to squint in the sudden brightness. With the window behind the building blocked off with sandbags, the Nationalists weren't quite so worried about light discipline in here. And the work lights probably made it easier to read the maps spread out on the desk in the center of the room.

The man standing at the desk was young, younger than me. He looked up, his face clean-shaven and slightly pudgy. His pale blue eyes weren't friendly, either. He straightened up as the small man said something to him in Slovak. I caught "American" in there somewhere.

He studied me for a moment. I know I wasn't exactly a friendly face; I still had camouflage paint on, and my hands were down at my sides but slightly cocked; I was really feeling the absence of my rifle right about then, and I was ready to grab just about *anything* to defend myself if this turned into a fight. Of course, they hadn't relieved me of my knife, but they hadn't thoroughly searched me, either. Which also could be a good sign.

"Who are you?" the blue-eyed man asked, as the shorter man took up a position off to my right, leaning against the sandbags on the wall.

"My name's Bowen," I told him. It only made some sense to be honest with potential allies. "I'm part of a special unit that was deployed to rescue the American that the Kosovars took hostage a few weeks ago."

"And what do you want from us?" the man demanded. "We will not surrender to Americans any more than we will to the French and German *bastardi* who unleashed the black-asses on our people."

"What do you know about what happened down south a few nights ago?" I asked.

"I know that the so-called 'peacekeepers' began attacking every one of our positions they could find," he replied bitterly, "and massacring anyone who lived nearby."

"I know," I said grimly. "We saw what they did in Kuchyňa." His expression flickered a little at that. The shadow of a frown touched his face.

"And no," I continued, "we weren't a part of it. We were already on the run." I proceeded to describe the destruction of FOB Keystone and the fights we'd had with the EDC and their proxy militias since then. "It seems that Slovenský Grob convinced the EDC that the US wasn't going to play along with their plan to pacify Slovakia," I said. "So, they decided to take us off the board. I'd think that would be nuts, but we haven't been able to make contact with anyone in the United States for days. Which means they hit our comm systems hard enough that they were confident no one back home would find out." I spread my hands. "Whatever you might think about Washington's policies about Slovakia, we have a common enemy now."

He just stared at me impassively for a long moment. I like to think that I'm a pretty cool customer most of the time; I've been in some pretty hairy situations, ranging from Africa and the Middle East to some of the nastiest urban war zones Stateside. But I was sweating. And it wasn't that warm in that room.

As I watched the man, I knew that I wasn't getting anywhere. I'd seen that look before. It wasn't disbelief, not quite. It was a closed-off, not *quite* hostile, but distinctly unfriendly look. He didn't give a damn if we were the last Americans in Slovakia. He'd already known what he was going to do as soon as he'd heard that I was an American, before I'd even begun to tell our story.

With a sick twisting in my guts, I struggled to keep my hands still as my mouth went dry and my mind switched into "who am I going to kill first" mode. I still had my knife, after all. And unless they shot me in the head, I could still cut a couple throats and take some of them with me.

Damn, this was a bad idea. But I hadn't had the imagination to think up another one, and nobody else had, either.

But before the command center turned into the scene of a short but bloody brawl, there was some commotion behind me, and someone else stepped into the room.

I stepped back and half-turned. I hadn't had my back to the door, I'd moved as soon as I'd entered to avoid that. But I needed to take another step to get out of the newcomer's way.

He was a big man, burly and white-haired. A thick mustache bristled above his lip, and he was wearing a Slovak Army field jacket, though stripped of insignia. He pinned me with a pale blue stare from within a mass of wrinkles that was remarkably similar to the younger man's as he stepped around the desk, then turned that same basilisk glare on the younger man, who stepped aside, his mouth working tightly.

The big man leaned on the desk on massive, gnarled knuckles as he turned his eyes back on me. "What is your name and rank?" he asked.

"My name is Matthew Bowen," I told him. Something had changed. I could *feel* the shift in the dynamic in that room. Whoever this old guy was, he wasn't somebody to screw around with. The other Nationalist fighters respected him. "My organization doesn't use conventional rank structures, but I am a team leader for a ten-man special operations team."

"Matthew," he said. His voice was deep and heavy, with a rasp that sounded like decades of cigarettes and slivovica. "My name is Jaroslav Rybàr. Tell me what you are doing here."

I repeated much the same story I'd told the younger man. Rybàr listened carefully, his face expressionless. I had no idea what he was thinking as he listened, but somehow, I felt that I was on somewhat firmer ground than I had been with the young buck. Somewhat.

No sooner had I finished speaking than the younger man spoke up with a rapid-fire stream of Slovak that I probably couldn't have followed even if I'd managed to study the language in any depth beyond a handful of phrases on the "pointy-talky" card that was stuffed in my chest rig. Rybàr turned his head slightly to listen, though his eyes remained fixed on me.

"My associate Skalický," Rybàr said, nodding toward the younger man, "reminds me that there have been infiltration attempts before. He is right. Do you have any proof of your story?"

"None beyond the men I have outside of town, and the bodies lying in what's left of FOB Keystone," I said. "Not to mention the smoking hulks of three armored vehicles just below Vyoskà peak."

He watched me thoughtfully for another long moment. Skalický started to say something else, but Rybàr raised a massive paw of a hand and he fell silent. "How many men do you have?" he asked, in the same low, rumbling monotone. His English was excellent, far better than Skalický's.

"About sixty left," I replied. "But we're getting low on food, and, more importantly, ammunition. We've been running or fighting with what we can carry on our backs for a week."

"You are not American Army," Rybàr observed.

"No," I replied. "I'm not. I am part of a special unit."

"Here for a hostage rescue mission, as you said," he rumbled. "Tell me, who was the hostage, and who was holding him?"

193

"He was an American soldier, being held by the Kosovars," I said. "We found him just before all hell broke loose. He's still with us."

"You came into this country to fight the Kosovars?" he asked, though I was pretty sure that I'd made that clear enough already.

"And anyone else holding Americans hostage," I answered. There might have been some bitterness that had crept into my voice. I was tired. "Especially since the Army was on lockdown after Slovenský Grob."

"Indeed," Rybàr said. He looked down at the map, the first time he'd taken his eyes off me since he'd bulled Skalickỳ out of the way. I didn't know if it was a good sign or a bad one. I was having a much harder time reading this ancient bear of a man than I'd had with Skalickỳ.

He looked up. "We could use sixty more men," he said. "But bringing them into Vrbovè will be difficult. The enemy has us surrounded, as you have seen. It was no small feat that you got as close as you did."

Skalickỳ started to protest in Slovak again, but Rybàr cut him off curtly. He stared at Rybàr for a moment, glared pure venom at me, then stalked out of the room.

"Filip is young," Rybàr explained. His tone had changed, subtly. "As the West presses to destroy our sovereignty, he has begun to listen to the voices calling for us to turn to Moscow for help. He is not alone."

Something about the tone of his voice made me ask, "How old were you when the Soviets invaded?"

He stared at me levelly, but there was something like respect in his eyes. "I was ten years old," he said grimly. "I will be cold in my grave before I ever trust a Russian." He looked down at the map again. "As I said, we can use your men, Matthew," he said. "But I should tell you that we are going to have to either break out of Vrbovè or die in place here. We put up enough of a fight to keep the French and Germans from taking the town so far, but our own supplies are dwindling." He pinned me with a stare. "We can help each other, but it will require your people to help us break out. That means attacking the cordon that

194

the EDC has put around Vrbovè, to open a gap that we can escape through."

That might be a tall order. "As I said, we're getting low on ammo," I told him carefully. I didn't want to shoot our delicate alliance in the foot, but I had to lay the cards out on the table. "And we don't have any anti-armor weapons. I'm not sure how much of a hole we can punch." *Not to mention that I'm not sure half of Killian's kids are up to it.*

But Rybàr didn't need to hear that. Not right then.

"You did not come in here alone," he said. "There was too much gunfire out in the no-man's land. How many of your men are still out there?"

"Nine," I replied. "The rest of my team."

He nodded. "Call them in," he said. "I will call our outer defensive positions and tell them to let them through. The recognition signal will be four flashes, answered by two." So, apparently, they *did* have some NVGs. "We do have some Matadors and RPG-75s, and enough ammunition to give you some. What caliber are you using?"

"7.62 NATO," I told him, as I turned my radio on. He nodded.

"We can spare some." He cracked a grin under his mustache. "After all, if your attack fails, then we might not get out either, eh?"

I tried to smile in return as I reached for my transmit button, but it was more of a grimace. I had sudden visions of a clever trap. We attack the cordon, get hammered, and then the Nationalists skedaddle and leave us in the breeze.

We'd linked up with the Nationalists, but right at that moment, I couldn't be sure that it wasn't a case of "out of the frying pan and into the fire."

195

Chapter 19

I was topping off the last of my magazines as I heard a vehicle rumble outside, and the door to the police station open. There was some commotion, but I finished thumbing the last 7.62 rounds in before stuffing the mag back into its pouch in my chest rig and turning to greet the rest of my team.

Rybàr had been as good as his word, offering me a crate of 7.62x51 ammunition as soon as I had called Scott and told him to move up and contact the outer defenses, with the assigned recognition signal. Apparently, that, at least, hadn't been a trap. The team was hustling into the police station, weapons slung, apparently unharmed. Scott handed me my OBR as I stepped out of the command center to meet them.

"Well, it was hairy, but I think we just conducted our first proper partisan linkup," he said. "We talked about this sort of thing for years in Recon, but I don't think we ever did it."

I just nodded as I took my rifle back and clipped the sling back on. I hadn't taken it off; it was looped around my shoulders underneath my ghillie hood-over. I pointed to the stack of ammo crates and Matador 90mm anti-tank launchers stacked in one of the side offices, that had been stripped and converted into an arms room. "Everybody top off," I said, before turning back to Scott. "Come on," I said, nodding toward the command center. "We've got a lot to figure out."

He and I stepped through. Skalický had rejoined us, though he was standing behind Rybàr with his arms folded, his face wooden. He still didn't like it, but he wasn't willing to cross Rybàr. Whoever Rybàr was, he had some weight behind him. Given that he was in his mid-seventies, that was saying something.

Rybàr himself was leaning over the map of Vrbovè and the surrounding area. There were markers on the map for the various EDC and allied units surrounding the town. I hadn't had a chance to really study their dispositions in detail before, but as I looked, the picture became clear.

Most of the enemy were concentrating on the roads, with the exception of what looked like two platoons of armor to the south. We'd already run afoul of the cluster of mech infantry squatting on the road leading toward Prašnìk, and had given them a bloody nose. But they apparently were backed up by AMX-10s, which would present more of a challenge. Of course, they'd been further bloodied by the IED that had blown up one of those vehicles, so they were at reduced strength, and, hopefully, rattled by the night's losses.

"As you can see," Rybàr said, in English, "The enemy has most of the roads blockaded, but they have left large gaps to the north. This is by design." He pointed to the road leading off the 499 to the northeast. "We have the routes to Sìpkovè heavily mined with artillery shells, anti-tank mines, and improvised bombs. They attempted to push in on us from that direction about eighteen hours ago, and took heavy casualties. When the militias fell back, French bomb disposal units attempted to clear the road, but we drove them off with mortars and sniper fire."

I was getting the picture. "So, that IED alley gives you a fallback route to the north," I said. He nodded.

"We have vehicle caches in Sìpkovè," he said. "They are not military vehicles, but they should suffice when mixed in with our up-armored trucks and the handful of scout cars that we have here in Vrbovè." He looked me in the eye.

"This is the plan," he said. "We will send more ammunition and Matador anti-tank rockets with you to take to the rest of your men. At…" he checked his watch, "0330, we will launch a diversionary attack on the cordon between Vrbovè and Stràže. We have sowed enough improvised explosives along that approach that any attempted counterattack should be severely slowed, if not stopped cold.

"At the same time, I need your men to attack the checkpoint on the road leading toward Prašnik. We will do the same; if we attack along the road, and your men attack from the flank, up the hill, we should be able to catch them in an L-shape. We will have SA-18s and the mounted Browning M2s to keep any air attack at bay.

"Once the checkpoint is broken, we can begin to move out to the north. We will link up on the road, and your men can load into the trucks."

"That's assuming that they haven't already reinforced that part of the cordon after we shot our way in through there, not to mention the IED that blew up that AMX," Scott pointed out.

"Of course," Rybàr replied. "Which is why we are sending ten Matadors with you, along with more rifle and machinegun ammunition." A faint, cold smile might have quirked his mouth beneath his mustache. "You will need it."

"I thought you said that you were running low on supplies," I pointed out quietly. It was a risk, calling him out like this, but I'll admit that I was nervous about this whole situation. And I'm no diplomat; that's why I carry a rifle for a living.

"We are," he replied. "But mostly the rockets and mortar bombs that are keeping the enemy back. And the anti-air defenses that are keeping the sky a little clearer. We have plenty of small arms ammunition; we have not needed it just yet. But when they come with armor, we need to have left."

"And what about the townspeople?" Scott asked. "Are we taking all of them with us?"

Rybàr didn't look happy. "No," he said. "We simply do not have the transport. But," he continued, raising a hand to forestall any objection, "we are not simply going to leave them to the enemy. They will be leaving the town when we do, to scatter to the other towns nearby. It is no guarantee that they will not be targeted, especially by the black-asses. But it is the best we can do."

I just nodded. It was true enough. Someone else might have objected to Rybàr's men making their stand in the town in the first place, as common as it had become in modern warfare. In my experience, it was often a case of using the local civilians as human shields.

But that was usually in the case of fanatical insurgents fighting for some ideology. Communists and Islamists, mostly. If

Rybàr and his men felt they were fighting for their country and their people against invaders on their soil, and given some of what had already happened at the hands of the militias and even the EDC in Slovakia, they may have fortified Vrbovè to try to *defend* the people there.

I was sure that, even if that weren't the case, Rybàr and Skalickỳ would insist that it was. And I had no way of knowing, one way or another. But the bitter truth is, when you're in a crack like we were, you can't afford to be too picky when it comes to allies.

Just don't make the mistake of trusting them *too* far.

"We'll load up and head out, then," I said. "Though we may need some kind of diversion; they're going to be on the alert now."

Skalickỳ had been getting agitated again, and spat something in Slovak. He was just being a dick at that point, because I knew he spoke perfectly good English.

Rybàr turned to look at him and said something gruffly in the same language. But Skalickỳ didn't seem deterred. He pointed at me.

"How do we know?" he demanded, this time in English, apparently to make sure that we understood. "Once we provide their diversion, how do we know that they won't simply run away? They are Americans. They've already sided with our enemies. 'Peacekeeping!' Agh!" He spat. "Keeping us under the 'European' boot under the guise of 'keeping the peace' that was already shattered by Berlin and Paris! Because how dare we take up arms to protect our country from foreign invaders and globalist extortionists!"

I just gave him a heavy-lidded stare. "Seems to me like you've got that kind of backwards," I said after a moment. "*We* came to *you* for help. I'd be a lot more worried about you lot letting us get stuck in and then running for it while we're keeping the enemy busy."

"Yes, *now* you need our help," Skalickỳ said acidly. "After your 'allies' turned on you. If not for that, you wouldn't care about our people being raped and murdered by the black-asses. You would be right there on the cordon, watching while they do it, making sure no one escapes!"

200

That pissed me off. I took a half a step toward him, my hand tightening on the pistol grip of my rifle. "Is that so, tough guy?" I demanded. "Remind me just *why* the EDC decided to sneak-attack the US peacekeepers here. Go on. Tell me." He stared at me angrily, his lips tightly pressed together. "Oh, now the truth ain't so convenient for your little narrative is it, fucker?" I stabbed a finger at him. "Americans stepped in to *protect* your people, and every American soldier in-country paid the price for it. Don't you *fucking* forget that."

Rybàr had stood with his arms folded across his thick torso, watching and listening impassively, letting it play out. His eyes were unreadable, but before Skalickỳ could summon up another verbal salvo, he lifted a hand to forestall any more argument. "Matthew is right, Filip," he said. "But there is another concern." He looked me in the eye. "Coordination. While timing can accomplish a great deal, I think you understand, as I do, that the fog of battle can create problems when attempting to coordinate such an attack as we have planned here." He shook his head. "One or two of you need to stay here, with me, so that we can be sure of communications between your people and mine."

While his tone was even and amiable, there was something in his eyes that made me wonder just how much he was telling the truth, and how much he was siding with Skalickỳ, and just wanted a hostage. Despite the, generally, noble stated goals of the Nationalists, they'd done dirt a few times in the last few months, which had eroded some of the sympathy for them among the US forces.

Let's just say that the "migrant" militias weren't the only ones with the blood of women and children on their hands.

But I had the lives of almost sixty Americans in my hands at that moment, and if making myself Rybàr's hostage was what it took to get them out, then that was what I had to do. I didn't like it. I *really* didn't like it. I doubted that he was going to disarm me, but one man with a rifle surrounded by hundreds with rifles and machineguns wasn't going to be much of a threat. If it came to it, I might take a few with me, but that would be the extent of it.

Don't get me wrong; if it came to it, I was definitely taking those few with me.

"I'll stay with you, then," I said, as Scott looked at me sharply. He didn't want to get into an argument in front of our newfound allies, but I knew that if we'd been in private, he would have asked me if I was out of my damned mind. Not unjustifiably, either, but desperate times call for desperate measures.

I turned to him, seeing the worry in his eyes. "Just make sure my ruck doesn't get left behind," I said. I checked my watch, then turned to Rybàr. "If we're going to kick this pig at 0330, then I need to get my men moving back to the linkup site." We had less than two hours.

He just nodded. I jerked my head at Scott to precede me out the door. He watched me for a second, a faint frown on his face, but finally turned and left the room.

I followed, though not without a last glance at Skalickỳ. There was no friendliness in his eyes. I made a mental note not to turn my back on Skalickỳ once the shooting started. Intel had picked up some faint whispers about Russian operatives in Slovakia, and if they'd gotten to Skalickỳ as thoroughly as it appeared, well. There was no love lost between Russia and the US in recent years, between clashes with Russian PMCs in Syria and Africa, and the consistent holding up of the Russian bogeyman as a political scapegoat for everything bad that happened Stateside for most of the last decade.

No, I would be keeping a very close eye on Filip Skalickỳ.

***

"This is fucking nuts, Matt," Dwight growled. "You know he wants a hostage."

"Yeah," I replied. I was leaning against the wall, mainly because I was tired enough that sitting down probably wasn't the best idea right at the moment. Not that I would have passed out for long; I had enough stress and anxiety racing around inside my skull that I'd wake right up again. Nor would any of my guys necessarily take much notice; they were all just as tired, and we were all too old and too seasoned to worry all that much about private-level leadership examples. I still had to lead by example, but a moment's weakness of the flesh, after all we'd been through, wasn't going to suddenly lead to a complete breakdown in team discipline. Cats and dogs living together, mass hysteria.

No, I was more concerned with the Nationalist fighters out in the hallway seeing it. My guys might forgive a moment's fatigue. We couldn't afford to let the Nationalists see any such display of weakness.

"I know," I continued. "And Rybàr knows that I know. But what other choice do we have? They could always side with Skalický and tell us that we're on our own. They might even be able to draw the EDC's attention toward our position, just to give themselves an opening to break out. All it would take would be one armed drone in the right place." I didn't know that they had any, but it seemed like just about everybody going into combat, whether state or non-state, had more drones than anything else anymore. "Believe me, I don't like it. I didn't exactly like handing Scott my rifle and 'surrendering' to their outer security, either. But once again, what other choice do we have?"

"We *could* just slip out and try to make it on our own," Reuben said. "These guys ain't angels, and if they're already borderline hostile…"

"We could," I agreed. "But how much farther do you think some of Killian's kids are going to make it on foot? Not to mention the wounded?"

That gave everyone pause. Dwight grimaced behind his salt-and-pepper beard, which accounted for most of the hair on his head. "Not far," he said.

"Bitches are *weak*." That was David, of course. Though he wasn't wrong. All of the females and about half the males had been flagging for the last couple of nights, cutting the distance we could cover almost in half. If the Nationalists had vehicles for us to ride in, it would help a lot. As things stood, if we tried to make it on our own, we'd probably end up having to go firm for several days to let everyone rest. We didn't have the supplies to be able to afford that. Furthermore, staying put for long was just going to get us spotted by a drone, after which we'd either be bombed, strafed, nailed with a HOT-3 from a drone, or surrounded and killed by militia or EDC regulars.

Working with the Nationalists wasn't exactly ideal, but it was the best option we had out of a plethora of shitty ones.

Scott finished topping off his last 25-round PMAG and straightened up. "Everybody set?" he asked. "If we're going to do this, we'd better do it quick."

The rest of the team hastily finished jamming mags or stuffing belts and started slinging the Matadors. The 90mm, disposable anti-tank/anti-door launchers were bulky, though they weighed about the same as the older 84mm AT-4s. They could do a number on an Infantry Fighting Vehicle, which was why I was glad enough to have them. Scott shouldered two, taking one for me, though I wouldn't be in a position to use it. They'd spread them around Bradshaw's section. None of us entirely trusted any of Killian's troops with one. They weren't trained on them, and there wasn't time to get them up to speed.

We weren't exactly trained on them, either, but we'd cross-trained enough that you could trust a Grex Luporum Triarius to pick up just about any weapons system and figure it out after a few minutes, if that.

"Let's move out," Scott said, looking down and checking that his radio was on, his headset in his ear. "Radio check," he murmured into his mic.

"Roger," I replied. I still had a couple hours of life on my battery. I hoped it would be enough. The Nationalists had batteries to restock our rechargeable battery packs, but we hadn't brought them; those were in our rucks.

The team filed out of the room, meeting up with the liaison Rybàr had appointed to get them through friendly lines, a fresh-faced kid by the name of Bartoš. As they passed, there were murmurs of "Good luck," or just a thump on the arm, which I usually returned, with bruising force in Dwight's case. The guy had hands the size of hams.

Jordan paused and looked me in the eye. We didn't always see eye-to-eye, but we were still brothers. He clasped my hand. "Stay safe, Matt."

I forced a grin. "I'm going to have all kinds of Nationalist meat-shields around me. You guys are the ones who need to be careful." His return grin was almost a grimace.

Scott paused for a long moment before he clapped me on the shoulder. "You'd better not let these sons of bitches kill you, you ginger bastard," he said. "Because you know that, no matter how hard you pray, you're not getting into Heaven if you die."

"Yeah, yeah," I replied with a half-smile. "I've got to have a soul for that." It was an old joke about my red hair and beard, but it served its purpose. "Don't worry. If it comes to it, I'll be sure to steal as many of theirs as I can to sneak in."

When he seemed like he wanted to stay, to protest, to insist that he or someone else stay, I punched him in the shoulder. "Get moving," I told him. "You're burning through our window."

He nodded, and turned and left the room. I waited a second, then went to rejoin Rybàr in the command center, listening carefully to the headset in my ear.

***

Less than ten minutes later, all hell broke loose to the southwest.

The initial *bang* of the first RPG-75 shot was almost lost in the sudden roar of small arms fire. The Nationalists were engaging the cordon on the 502, hoping to make the enemy think they were trying to break out there. A salvo of rockets roared off their rails only a block away, streaking on bright tails of flame to hammer at the tank positions in the hedgerows to the south.

The Nationalists might or might not have had drones, but they weren't using them for surveillance at the moment if they did. Given the antenna I'd spotted on top of the old police station, there was probably a reason for that. It looked like a drone jammer. And an expensive one. It might have once belonged to the Slovak Army.

Or, and this was in a way a more disquieting thought, it might have been Russian.

A few moments later, the sound of small arms fire intensified, and a heavy detonation shook the ground. A shell screamed by overhead with a howling, ripping sound that was audible even through the fortifications in the old police station. Which meant it had been low; probably a tank shell. The sounds of the firefight to the south turned into a steady thunder. The tanks were fighting back. Rybàr and Skalickỳ were listening carefully to the radios, issuing terse acknowledgements and orders.

Scott's voice crackled in my ear. "Deacon, Weeb. We're clear, moving up to rendezvous with Doomhammer." I'd almost forgotten that dumb callsign. We hadn't had a need to use it for most of the last week.

I passed the information along to Rybàr, who nodded and waved a hand to show that he'd heard me before returning his attention to the diversionary fight to the south. It sounded like things were slowing down; he was already pulling his people back. Skalický pointedly ignored me.

I just stood there, my hand flexing around my rifle's grip. I felt about as useful as tits on a boar hog, and it wasn't a comfortable feeling.

I just hoped that we could really get moving quickly, if only so that I could get back with my team and get back in the fight.

Chapter 20

It took longer than Rybàr had hoped to get ready to move, even with his subordinate leaders kicking and swearing at their men to get them moving. We needed to be well away from Vrbovè by the time the sun was all the way up, or we were going to have a hell of a time getting away at all.

From where I waited next to the Alligator 4x4 that was Rybàr's command vehicle, I scanned the sky above us. There were definitely specks of light moving up there, turning racetracks off to the north and west. Those would be the fast-movers, holding off only because of the SAM threat. And whether the SA-18s could reach that high was doubtful.

I really, really didn't want to get caught under another airstrike. But in this Brave New War, that might not be an option.

There were a lot of things that people like me, who had been trained in a military focused on counter-insurgency for decades, were going to have to get used to. Not having air supremacy was just one of them.

The diversionary fight down to the south had died away, though the tanks had tried advancing, only to stop when they lost a Leopard II to an anti-tank mine on the road. From what Rybàr had said, it was only a mobility kill, but the road was half-blocked, and the RPG-75 and Matador fire that had at least wounded another tank should have the effect of deterring an advance along the flanks.

At least for a while.

I glanced down at my watch, shielding the illumination with my hand. 0331. We were supposed to be kicking things off by now. I keyed my radio.

"Weeb, Deacon," I called. Rybàr had just walked up to the Alligator and was watching me out of the corner of his eye while he spoke softly into his own radio.

"Stand by, Deacon." Scott sounded more than a little stressed.

I glanced at Rybàr. "Our friends aren't going to stand by for much longer, Weeb," I said softly.

"Roger," was all he said in reply.

Rybàr was openly watching me by then, as the seconds ticked away. I checked my watch again. 0345.

I wasn't sweating. Not quite. But I wasn't comfortable, either. There were all sorts of ways this entire plan could go bad, and the perception that we weren't pulling our weight, regardless of the actual cause of the delay, was only one of them.

Finally, Scott's voice crackled in my earpiece again. He sounded harried and more than a little pissed. "Deacon, Weeb. We'll be in position in ten."

Another glance at my watch showed me that it was 0350. So, we were kicking this off half an hour late already. I couldn't help but feel a twinge of anger; I knew it wasn't my team behind the delay, and the odds that it was Bradshaw's section were pretty slim, too. Which meant it was the Army unit.

"Ten more minutes," I told Rybàr, keeping my voice even and level. He didn't respond at first, except to check his own watch.

"I have elements running behind schedule as well," he admitted. It was an olive branch, and for the moment, I was more than happy to take it. Fortunately, he'd detailed Skalickỳ to a different part of the growing column of rag-tag trucks, technicals, cars, and two MRAPs that were clogging the street around the church and the police station. "We will launch the attack in ten minutes."

Of course, there's always somebody who doesn't get the word. He'd barely finished speaking when a series of loud *thunks* announced the mortars going loud early.

Rybàr's head snapped around at the sound, as the rounds arced away with a fading, dopplered whirr. He looked pissed. I just keyed my radio. "Weeb, Deacon, you need to push. The mortars just went early."

208

If he swore—which I was pretty sure he did—he waited to key the radio until afterward. "Copy, Deacon," he said. "We'll do what we can."

Ten minutes doesn't seem like a long time, but once the shooting starts, it can be an eternity.

Rybàr climbed into the Alligator as the mortars started to hit with a rolling series of *crumps* off to the southeast, the flashes lighting up the sky behind the buildings. I followed suit; I didn't want to get left behind just because my guys couldn't get into position fast enough.

Rybàr was on the radio, rattling off more orders. Rockets were ripping away into the night, as the next mortar salvo went up. That one should have been aimed at the unit that Scott, Bradshaw, and Killian were facing. The noise of the heavy ordnance almost drowned out the stuttering roar and crackle of small arms fire along the edges of town.

Rybàr yelled orders, cranking down his window and sticking his Bren 805's muzzle out. I followed suit on my side, saying a quick prayer that my guys would make it through.

A moment later, as more flashes flickered to the south, accompanied by several heavy *thuds* and a long, ripping burst of machinegun fire, the column lurched into motion and started to push north, up the 499.

It was a little surreal. We were rolling like a regular convoy, while all hell broke loose around the edges of town.

It wasn't a swift or a smooth exit, either. The lead elements, about a block ahead of us, weren't rolling quickly, but were advancing by fits and starts, as if the drivers, or the vehicle commanders, were nervous about venturing too close to the growing conflagration off on the edge of town.

And the sound of that conflagration was starting to get worrying. A trio of loud *bangs* might have been either cannon fire or Matadors impacting. But the crackle and roar of small arms fire was only intensifying. I craned my neck to try to see, but we were still in town, with bombed-out buildings and rubble-and-sandbag barricades blocked my view.

Heavier fire thundered from the north. That definitely sounded like armored vehicles. More small arms fire. I was sweating, my fingers flexing unconsciously around my rifle. We still had three blocks left to get clear of the buildings, and the lead vehicles weren't speeding up. In fact, as a barrage of artillery fire suddenly screamed down out of the sky to hammer the north end of town, they stopped altogether.

Rybàr was yelling orders into his radio, shouting hoarsely to be heard over the earth-shaking thunder of the impacting artillery shells, that were throwing big fountains of smoke, dirt, and debris up above ugly orange flashes. One struck an already half-blasted house at the end of the street, sending an arcing cascade of shattered masonry and plaster out over the road before the remainder of the house's roof caved in.

"Deacon, Weeb!" I wasn't sure if Scott had just called me, or if I hadn't been able to hear him over the thunder of the arty.

"Send it, Weeb!" I yelled back, hoping that I could be heard over all the other noise and Rybàr's Slovak bellowing.

"The AMXs are down, but there's something else farther up the road that's got us under fire while the foot-mobiles are hunkered down and mag-dumping at us!" he shouted. "The artillery's hitting the Nationalists in town, but we're pretty well pinned!"

That was bad. It was bad enough that we were half an hour behind schedule, with the sun due up in less than two hours. If my guys couldn't move, they were going to get left behind and slaughtered.

"Roger," I acknowledged. I turned to Rybàr, who looked up at me, his handset still pressed to his ear.

"My men are pinned down by small arms and armored vehicle fire," I told him. "We need to take the pressure off them, somehow."

He didn't reply right away, and though I could see the wheels turning behind his eyes, my stomach clenched. This was it. If he decided to just go ahead and push, especially with that arty pounding his positions at the north end of town, then we were screwed.

In which case, I was going to go out there and rejoin my team, or die fighting the Nationalists to do it.

At that point, it had nothing to do with anybody's cause. It didn't even have anything to do with loyalty to Americans over

Slovak Nationalists. It was way more personal than that. That was my team. My brothers. I wasn't going to save my skin by leaving them to die.

Finally, though, he nodded. "We will have a narrow window between artillery barrages," he said. "They have not yet coordinated their batteries well enough to keep constant fire missions up. Take Sỳkora's section and move up quickly, link up with Hornick at the forward positions, and push forward to relieve the pressure! Sỳkora is in that MRAP, up there." He pointed. "He speaks English well, and is an aggressive fighter." I noticed, in passing, that Rybàr's accent got thicker under stress.

I must have hesitated for a moment. I know I was wondering if I was going to catch a bullet in the back if I ran toward the gunfire. Whatever happened, Rybàr caught it.

"Go," he said. "I need your men, and unless that strongpoint is broken, we will take heavy losses getting out of the town. Skalickỳ can complain later."

With an abbreviated nod of acknowledgement and thanks, I kicked the door open and spilled out onto the street, running toward the MRAP that Rybàr had pointed out. The column was completely halted by then; whether because of the heavy cannon fire that was starting to *crack* overhead or the slowly dwindling arty, I couldn't tell. Not that it mattered that much.

I climbed up on the running board and banged on the door. Or tried to. A fist against inch-and-a-half armored glass doesn't do much. Still the movement caught the vehicle commander's attention, and he cracked the door open.

"Where's Sỳkora?" I asked.

"I am Sỳkora," the young man with the wispy mustache, wearing a camouflage jacket and low-pro plate carrier replied. He had a Bren 805 across his lap.

"Orders from Rybàr," I said. "You and I are supposed to take your section and link up with Hornick, then push up and clear out the foot-mobiles in that strongpoint up ahead."

He didn't hesitate, but started getting out of the MRAP, forcing me to step down to the street in the process. "Good," he said. "I didn't want to sit here and wait for a shell to drop on my head." He turned toward the back of the towering armored

211

vehicle, barking orders in Slovak. A moment later, the rear door swung open, and more Nationalist fighters, in a similar hodge-podge of clothing and gear, piled out, while Sỳkora grabbed me and hurried toward the panel truck ahead, repeating the order.

"Come on," he said, "if we go up the main road, we will be sitting ducks. There is more cover this way." He immediately turned off to the west, heading around behind the row of houses just up a low hill. There were more trees, but precious little of what I'd call cover, aside from the houses. Vrbovè wasn't all that big, and we were getting to the end of it. But it was farther away from the area being pounded by the artillery, and his route put the houses between us and the impacts, so there was that.

We moved quickly, keeping as low as we could. I couldn't forget about those tanks to the south, but they seemed to be preoccupied with the RPG-75 and Matador fire, and were holding their positions. They also didn't seem to be firing on random foot-mobiles, either, which was good.

So far.

Sỳkora ran ahead, almost doubled over, down the line of fenced and walled yards, keeping as much as possible to the trees between the narrow fields out behind the houses. He wasn't bounding, except maybe to pause for a second before sprinting across a particularly open area. Time was precious, and speed was security.

While I ran, I keyed my radio. "Weeb, Deacon," I called between panting breaths. "I'm moving up on your right with a section of Nationalist fighters. Watch your fire to the right."

"Roger, Deacon," Scott replied. "Hurry up. It's getting hot here."

Sỳkora paused at the last house, and seemed to be talking to someone out of sight while I rushed to catch up. My back was aching and my knees were feeling every pounding impact with the ground. I hit a knee next to Sỳkora just as he finished talking with an older man, who was either Hornick or one of his lieutenants.

Given the wreckage of the house behind him, which was still smoking and choked with dust from the artillery shell that had blown about half of it off, I thought the odds that this guy was a lieutenant were better than even.

Sýkora turned to me and pointed. "We need to cross the road and work our way up to the reservoir," he said, his voice raised to be heard above the roar of the firefight ahead. Then we can strike their flank, and get close enough that they cannot drop artillery on us without hitting their own people."

I nodded. It was an old tactic. In Vietnam, it had been called "hugging." And it worked, provided the foot-mobiles weren't just Bosnian and Kosovar militia, and that the EDC actually cared about not dropping artillery on their heads.

What a hell of a mess we'd jumped into.

The artillery had ceased, though the smoke and dust were still drifting down out of the sky. Muzzle flashes flickered back and forth ahead, while brilliant, massive tracers from whatever was shooting farther up the road flashed overhead with earsplitting *crack*s. Hunched double, partially hidden by trees and the last few houses before the open fields that my team had crossed on the way in, we hurried toward the road.

Sýkora crouched near the road, though back in cover behind the corner of a bullet-pocked but otherwise intact house, and waved at one of his men. That one, humping a vz. 59, belts of 7.62x54 flapping around his chest and shoulders, ran forward. Sýkora issued terse instructions, and the machinegunner flopped on his belly at the corner, aiming his machinegun up the road, toward the flickers of the firefight between American and EDC forces. Another fighter, carrying one of the older vz. 58 rifles, stepped up over him, leaning out around the corner to add his own weapon to the covering position.

With the road covered, Sýkora pointed, and the first couple of Nationalist fighters dashed across the road.

If we were hoping that the fight would distract the enemy enough that they wouldn't notice us, we were doomed to disappointment. A rattling burst of automatic fire crackled down the road as the third man got halfway across, tracers flashing overhead. The fire went wild, but he threw himself the rest of the way across the road, landing badly in the ditch in a tangle of limbs and weapons. I thought he'd run smack into one of the first two.

The machinegunner opened fire in response, the staccato roar of the vz. 59 accompanied by a brilliant fireball spitting and flickering from the muzzle. The oncoming fire ceased for a moment, and Sýkora and I dashed across the road together.

We both dropped behind trees at the far side, as some sporadic answering fire started to spit from the shadows up the road. A tracer skipped off the pavement a few feet to my left, whining off into the night with a streak of red light. Several more bullets smacked into the tree bole above my head. I got my rifle around the side and returned fire, careful to aim just beneath the muzzle flashes that I could see.

More of the Nationalists were entering the fight, more rifle fire thundering up the road. The machinegunner was going to town, and as soon as another one got across the road, he flopped down in the ditch, propped his weapon up on the road itself, and added his own fire. They weren't well-coordinated; there were long stretches of silence, then both of them were firing at the same time, but they were still throwing enough metal to keep the enemy's heads down.

Then a burst of 25mm or 30mm fire ripped through the trees overhead, reminding everyone that we didn't just have to worry about the rifles and machineguns on the ground.

"Push!" I yelled, though it was likely that not all of them could understand me. I suited actions to words, hoping and praying that I wasn't going to find myself with my ass hanging out in the breeze in no-man's-land while the rest hunkered down and traded fire with the bad guys.

But as I dashed to the next tree ahead, even as a heavy-caliber cannon round blew a limb off with a shower of splinters that I had to duck my head to try to avoid, Sýkora was right beside me, moving to another tree just ahead and to my right, opening fire even before he'd settled down behind it.

Another Nationalist fighter ran up beside me as I squeezed off another shot at a muzzle flash in the shadows ahead. He had what looked a lot like an M203 attached to the underside rail of his Bren 805, and he steadied himself for a moment, then fired it. The grenade launcher went off with a loud *thunk*, just before a bullet smashed him off his feet. He dropped limply into the ditch beside the road, even as the grenade hit at the treeline ahead with a flash and a *thud*.

Then the machinegunners opened up again, raking the trees and the ruined neighborhood that we'd negotiated on the way in with long streams of green tracers. It was time to move again.

I dashed ahead, while Sỳkora stayed in place for a few seconds, yelling into his radio. A moment later, I threw myself down behind another tree, only a few dozen meters from the reservoir, and all hell really broke loose.

It seemed that the enemy had avoided most of the pressure plates inside the neighborhood, and the armored vehicles hadn't advanced far enough to reach any more of the IEDs placed along the road.

It also appeared that we had either been very, very sneaky indeed getting through that deathtrap, or else very, very lucky that the Nationalists hadn't decided that we were hostile.

Because the Nationalists apparently had that entire web of IEDs daisy-chained and rigged for command detonation.

I hope I'm never that close to that big an explosion ever, ever again. I was actually knocked flat on my ass as the entire world seemed to split open. The trees ahead were suddenly backlit by a flickering orange flash, which was actually dozens of artillery shells and improvised bombs going off at once. The shockwave blasted the leaves off the trees around me, showering me with debris where I lay on my side in the dirt.

My ears were ringing as I shoved myself up, looking for targets under the rising black mushroom cloud of dust and smoke. I sent up a wordless prayer that my team hadn't been too close to that. I was pretty sure that they were in the next hedgerow to the southwest, but there was always that chance, with the shift of the fight in our direction, that they'd moved up. And danger close for that daisy chain was probably damned near five hundred yards.

That fact was reinforced as more debris started raining down out of the sky on top of us. Brick, tile, fragments of less wholesome things, and smoking bits of metal started hitting the road and the ground, and I huddled close to the tree, hoping that its blasted trunk would absorb most of the shrapnel.

After that blast, the twin *booms* of a pair of Matador shots were almost little more than muted *pop*s.

I coughed; the air was thick with the smoke and dust from the chained explosions. "Weeb, Deacon," I croaked into the radio. At least somebody was still in the fight, judging by those distant detonations.

"Deacon, Weeb," Scott replied hoarsely. There was a lot of scratching in the transmission; whether it was damage or the fact that he was moving and panting I couldn't tell. "We're alive, but that was a little close. Some warning would be good next time."

"I didn't get any more than you did," I told him. "Are you clear?"

"Almost," he replied. "We're still taking some small arms fire from the houses at the north corner of the reservoir, but I think we can handle it and get past." Before he let go of his PTT, I heard a burst of machinegun fire; it sounded like Dwight or Tony was already getting after it.

"Roger," I replied. "We'll link up on the far side. Watch your step; remember, they've got that road IEDed to hell and gone."

"We're on it," he replied. "Out."

I let him go. The team needed to concentrate on the threat in front of them, and so did I.

Sykora appeared next to me. "We should have thought of that beforehand," he said.

"Yeah, well, you might have blown my guys up in the process," I growled. "Next time, tell me before you do that."

He looked at me for a second, as the shower of dirt and debris died away. "I did not know you had a unit back there," he said.

Well, that's running battlefield coordination for you. I realized that that was in no small part my fault; I'd assumed that Rybàr had given him the rundown over the radio, and I'd mentioned them in passing, but hadn't confirmed for myself that he was aware of them.

That was a gut-twisting realization, even as we turned northeast and headed for the road. The shooting had died down on the northwest corner of Vrbovè, and the way out was clear enough.

But I'd damned near gotten my team killed because I hadn't thought to double check that the friendly unit I was attached to were aware that my guys were downrange. I'd thought it was obvious, given the crossfire that was happening up there, but I'd been wrong.

Assumption is the mother of all fuckups, and I'd dodged that bullet by a hair. Fatigue or no, it wasn't a comfortable feeling. I'd missed something. And none of us were going to get any less tired as this went on.

I had to stay on top of it. Even as we moved toward the road, surrounded by the cloud of smoke and dust from the blast, which flickered with the muzzle flashes to the north as the other Americans drove toward the rendezvous point, I chewed the inside of my cheek until it bled, just to remind myself not to drop the ball again.

I could only hope that if I did, I would be the one to pay the price, and not my team.

Chapter 21

The linkup went fast; we piled bodies, wounded and able-bodied alike, into vehicles wherever they would fit, while the MRAP turret gunners kept pouring fire into the houses where the enemy were still hunkered down and fighting. Those had to be militia. There was no way that EDC troops were going to be that hard core, not from what I'd seen so far. After seeing those two Pumas get knocked out, EDC regulars would have been either hunkering down under cover or running for it.

It was because we were so spread out that I didn't find out that Killian had been hit until we stopped at a Nationalist vehicle cache in Hornà Streda.

***

Scott and I had dismounted to start picking vehicles. There were half a dozen big farm trucks and a couple of Alligators. I wanted to take the Alligators, but we were going to need the farm trucks, too. We had too many bodies, between Bradshaw's section, Draven's mortarmen, and the Army survivors.

We weren't dawdling. While the enemy had gotten a good shock during that breakout from Vrbovè, none of us were confident that we'd bought ourselves anything more than some breathing room.

Still, I had to get it off my chest.

As I was checking the fuel level in the first Alligator, and Scott was pulling the tarp the rest of the way off it, I said, "Look, Scott." I took a deep breath. It's never fun to confess your own shortcomings, particularly to the man you'd almost gotten killed. "That IED det. That was my fault." He looked up at me, frowning a bit quizzically. "I thought that Rybàr had told Sỳkora that you guys were out there. I got wrapped up in the fight and didn't make sure he knew." I didn't look at him. I didn't want to. I kept peering at the gas tank, even though I could see that it was fully fueled. I had to finally force myself to meet his eyes. "I fucked up."

Scott didn't say anything for a long moment, just shoving the tarp out of the way so that it wouldn't foul the 4x4 when we drove it out of the barn. "If I were gonna be an asshole," he finally said, "I might make a big deal about it. And I probably should, or I should if you were a wet-behind-the ears boot. But I know you better than that. And I'm in no position to throw stones."

He looked about as uncomfortable as I felt. "I just about dropped a JDAM on our own position once. Did I ever tell you about that?"

I shook my head. He hadn't. "Yeah," he said grimly. "I was the JTAC, calling fire on some militia who had us under heavy fire outside of Tripoli." I knew that Scott had been involved in one of the MEU interventions in the continuous hellstorm that was modern Libya. "Had two F-18s running racetracks overhead. I got excited and transposed a couple of numbers. Ended up dropping *behind* us, and only about five hundred meters away."

I winced a little, despite myself. A Joint Direct Attack Munition could be up to a 2000-lb bomb, and five hundred meters was definitely "danger close." "Anybody catch any frag?" I asked quietly.

"A couple of guys did," he admitted. "I think one of them is still carrying some of that around today. He won't talk to me." He went quiet, though both of us were still prepping the vehicles while we talked. We were grown men; we could do two things at once and both of us were well aware of the need for haste. "Point is, we've all fucked up at one point. Even Jordan, though he'll probably never admit it." I nodded. Jordan had an almost pathological need not to show weakness. It went along with the two-ton chip on his shoulder. "I've heard a couple stories about him, but I won't repeat 'em, not now."

"I wouldn't want you to," I said.

"And I won't repeat this," he said. "You've gotten it off your chest, I know it, and that's where it needs to stop. We're in too hairy a situation for it to get around the team, let alone anyone else. And for all you know, Rybàr *did* tell this Sỳkora guy, and he didn't hear it, spaced it under fire, or just didn't care until you called him on it. But the last thing we need right now is that seed of doubt in the team. It happened, we survived it, we learned from it, and we drive on. If it has to come out in the after-action once we've gotten out of Slovakia, we can hash it out then. Not before."

"Fair enough." It was why I was glad to have Scott as my assistant team lead. He was a level-headed guy who didn't think with his emotions. It was purely a flip of the coin, in my opinion, that had put me in the leadership spot while Scott got the number two slot. He'd do well with a team of his own.

Just then, even as I fired up the Alligator, the engine turning over twice before catching with a satisfying roar, Reuben came in, his ghillie hood thrown back, his face as dark with soot and dust as it was with camouflage paint. "Matt," he said, his voice tight and urgent, "Bradshaw needs to see you. Now."

Something about the way he said it made me sit up and take notice. "What's up?" I asked, as I swung out of the Alligator and stepped toward the door.

"I think you'd better come see," Reuben said, glancing at the Nationalists who were also rummaging around the barn, checking the other vehicles that would replace those that had been damaged or destroyed during the fighting for Vrbovè. I just nodded and followed him. Whatever it was, it was serious enough that we didn't want to air it in front of our allies just yet.

He led the way out into the sunlight. Clouds were moving in, and that light was getting wan. We were probably in for a storm soon. I hoped so; it would severely hamper the EDC's air assets, and give us some more breathing room.

Provided the Nationalists, with their demonstrably ragged training, didn't decide that they didn't want to go out in the rain. I didn't *think* Rybàr would stand for that, but I could see Skalickỳ causing problems, just out of spite.

The yard outside the warehouse was crammed with vehicles, most showing some signs of battle damage. We weren't going to be able to go low-profile, and given how many of those vehicles were thin-skins, that could make things dicier than they already were. Between a couple hundred Nationalist fighters and our sixty or so Americans, that made for a big convoy. I didn't know where the next Nationalist strongpoint was, but it couldn't be too close. I glanced up at the sky again, hoping for rain. Dumping, pouring, miserable buckets of it.

Reuben led the way toward one of the trucks, where a cluster of soldiers were gathered, in varying levels of kit, standing out among the Nationalists in their OCP cammies. Reuben started shouldering through the crowd, even as one of the Army NCOs, a younger Hispanic kid, started yelling at them to get out on security. It was broad daylight, and the town across the canal to our southwest wasn't entirely friendly. It wasn't exactly hostile, either, but the EDC and the Bratislava government would have eyes and ears there.

Jordan and Bradshaw were bent over Killian, who was lying on his side on the ground, his gear stripped off and his blouse mostly cut away. The side that Jordan was working on was drenched in blood, and another soldier was holding an IV bag above his head. There was a tourniquet cranked down on his arm, and a blood-soaked bandage was wrapped right beneath it.

Killian was pale as death, and his eyes were closed. It took a second before I could see that he was still breathing. He already looked like a corpse.

"What happened?" I asked.

Jordan glanced up, just for a moment, then returned his attention to his patient. "He took a bullet through the upper arm and into his side, just before we got to the column," he said. "It missed his heart and lungs, but it nicked his brachial artery. He lost a lot of blood before somebody got a tourniquet on him, and then it loosened up on the ride here." He pointed to the IV bag. "That's the third bag of saline I've put in him already. But it's not going to be enough."

He finished securing the bandage around Killian's chest, and then sat back on his haunches, his blood-soaked hands limp in his lap as he looked up at me. "I'm pretty sure he's going to lose the arm," he said. "I had to crank that sucker down to shut that artery off, and I'm not loosening it up again this side of a hospital. But the bad part is the blood loss. I'm pushing saline into him as fast as I can, but while it'll bring his blood pressure back up, we've got to get him to a hospital or he's gonna die."

I nodded. "I'll talk to Rybàr and Skalický," I said. I was already dreading that conversation. I knew that Skalický wasn't going to make it easy. I was already developing a pretty deep-seated dislike for the man. "Where's Warren?"

Bradshaw pointed. "He needed a minute. Not used to all the blood. Even now."

I nodded again, my expression tight behind my beard. I'd more than half expected Warren to be a royal pain in our collective ass, an overweight IT nerd of a warrant officer, out of his depth but still the ranking officer. Instead, he'd been remarkably low-key, essentially trying to pull his weight as a junior enlisted, acknowledging by deed if not word that he was out of his element.

But the bitter truth of it was that he *was* the ranking officer for these kids. And Killian's senior fireteam leader was standing there, staring at his platoon sergeant, looking sick.

I couldn't say that I blamed either of them. Sergeant Eckart had lost pretty much all his senior leadership in the space of a week. He was seriously out of his depth. This wasn't the way it was supposed to be; he'd never trained for this scenario. In a way, he was worse off than Warren, because he was *supposed* to be able to step up.

"Eckart, come with me," I told him, grabbing the black-haired young man by the arm and half-dragging him away from Killian. I steered him toward where Warren was sitting against the warehouse wall, staring into space with a sick, shocked look on his slack face. He'd picked up a weapon somewhere. I suddenly realized that it was probably Killian's.

"Warren," I said quietly. He didn't register immediately. "*Chief Warren.*"

He blinked and looked up at me, then scrambled to his feet. "Is Sergeant Killian…?"

I shook my head. "We need to get him to a hospital," I said. "Which means that we need to go have a chat with the Nationalist leaders. Since you're the ranking officer, and Killian's incapacitated, you need to come with me."

"I...don't know that I can do that," Warren said nervously. "I mean...we haven't gotten any orders from higher, and the last orders we had were to aid the peacekeeping mission, which meant suppressing the Nationalists. And it sure didn't include working hand-in-hand with Triarii. Don't take it the wrong way," he protested, as my expression darkened. "I'm not spitting in your eye. But you know what happened to Lieutenant Randolph after the Slovenský Grob incident. We could all be crucified if I make the wrong call here." He suddenly looked lost and alone. "And I don't even know where to start figuring out what the right call is."

"Warren, believe it or not, I know where you're coming from," I told him. "But right now is not the time to even worry about the political stuff. I don't know your politics, and at the moment, I couldn't possibly care less. I don't know Lieutenant Randolph, but if he has an ounce of honor in his body, he doesn't regret stepping up at Slovenský Grob a whit. Right now, your concern needs to be with these men's and women's lives, not with the impact on your or their careers. If we don't get Killian to a hospital, he's probably going to die. PFC Bond is probably going to die. Right now, their only hope is the Nationalists. And given what happened at Keystone, surrendering to the EDC is not an option. They'd just murder us all, or have their militia proxies do it. The Nationalists *probably* won't murder us." I jerked my head toward the Alligator where Rybàr was looking at a map on the hood, arguing with Skalický and several of his other subordinate commanders. "Come on. Worry about the rest of the Army later. We've got to worry about American lives *now.*"

He didn't know it, but I'd just essentially sketched out the Triarii's entire operating philosophy. Forget about politics and do what needs to be done.

He nodded slowly. He'd lost weight over the last few days of humping through the Little Carpathians, though he was still a bit doughy, and his endurance was still shit. But he came along, though he still looked nervous as hell. I considered telling him to straighten up and look like he was in charge, rather than show weakness in front of the Nationalists, but I was afraid that he might not know how.

Rybàr didn't look at us as we approached, but I know he saw us. Several of his bodyguards certainly did, stepping between us, their Bren 805s slung but held ready. I just stood and waited, my gloved hands crossed on the buttstock of my OBR as it hung on its sling in front of me.

Rybàr finished whatever it was he was saying, then issued a curt dismissal. Skalickỳ looked like he was going to stick around, but Rybàr waved at him and said something that sounded sharp, then waved at us. His PSD parted to let us through.

"Rybàr," I said by way of greeting. "We've got a problem. One of our guys got hit, bad. He's still alive, but he's lost a lot of blood. We need to get him to a hospital as soon as possible."

Rybàr nodded. "We have many casualties as well. But the only friendly hospital anywhere near us is in Nitra. It is a seventy-five-kilometer drive, and there are enemy forces between here and there."

"If we've got seventy-five kilometers to cover, then we're going to need to get moving soon," I said. The wind was picking up, and it had that damp chill that foretold rain. "If we're lucky, the storm will last most of the night and give us some cover." I felt a renewed bit of hope as thunder rumbled in the distance. A good thunderstorm would almost guarantee that the enemy couldn't get air over us.

"There will be enemy checkpoints on every major road," Rybàr protested. "Especially after what has happened. There are enemy forces blockading Nitra as we speak. It is the primary stronghold for the resistance in western Slovakia." He shook his head. "I agree, we need to get there, if only to treat our wounded. But I doubt we will reach it in one night."

But I was already thinking ahead. Thinking like a Grex Luporum Triarius. "They won't be expecting us to make a try for it, either," I pointed out. "We just got driven out of Vrbovè. But we took a hell of a bite out of them in the process." I stepped around to look at the map on the hood, even as the first few windblown drops of rain hit me in the face and spattered on the laminated map. "Look, if the weather holds, we shouldn't have to worry about enemy air too much. Even hardcore pilots won't be eager to take their birds up in this." Another grumble of thunder punctuated my sentence. "And if the enemy is as risk-averse as I think they are, they won't *let* their pilots fly strike or recon missions in a thunderstorm." So far, except for the armor support, which had gone a bit sideways for them, everything we'd seen suggested that the EDC regulars were hanging back and letting the militias do most of the fighting. And there was no way that they were trusting the militias with expensive strike fighters. Especially not when they didn't know where the mostly-Islamic fighters might drop the bombs.

"If we're worried about checkpoints, then that's what we have scouts for," I continued. "Send a vehicle or two on ahead, to radio back locations and alternate routes to get around them."

He looked at me levelly. "And what of the size of the convoy? There is no way to hide such numbers in the open countryside, and we will have to cross a great deal of it."

"Break the convoy up," I said. "Stagger vehicles in ones and twos, five to ten minutes apart. It'll require some coordination, but it's doable."

"And who do you suggest I send as scouts?" he asked. He sounded amused.

"Yes, my team is just about tailor made for that mission," I told him. "Look at it this way, if we do this, it should convince the naysayers among your commanders that we're on the same side."

He looked down at the map for a moment, chewing his mustache. Then he nodded. "Get with Jankovic to make sure that we can use the same radio frequencies," he said. "Can you be ready to move in thirty minutes?"

"We can be ready in ten," I told him. The rain was starting to come down harder, and it had gotten noticeably darker. "Where's Jankovic?"

He looked up and searched the chaos of the yard for a moment before pointing toward one of the MRAPs. "He should be at that vehicle. If you need batteries, he has them, as well."

I nodded, then paused. "Rybàr, this is Chief Warrant Officer Warren. He's the senior officer for the regular Army soldiers with us."

226

Rybàr seemed to get a little cold as he looked Warren over, and the warrant officer seemed to shrink a little. But finally, the burly Slovak stuck out his hand, and after a moment, Warren shook it. "You were at Keystone?" Rybàr asked.

"I was," Warren replied. His voice cracked a little, but he cleared his throat and drove on. "Which is why I don't have much gear."

"We can get you some," Rybàr said grimly. "We have plenty without owners." He stared at Warren for a moment, then looked at me. "There is some difference between your organizations," he said. "I do not know what it is, and for now, I do not care. You Americans came to my country to enforce the rule of a corrupt and morally bankrupt government which sold our people out to Berlin, Paris, and Brussels, backed up by a foreign invasion. But you have paid the price for your trust in the French and Germans. We have had our differences, but as far as I am concerned, we are now brothers, hunted by the same people. Maybe later we can be enemies again, but for now? All that is in the past."

"I'm...glad to hear that," Warren replied, a decided note of relief in his voice. "This has been a bit of a shock to us all, I think."

Rybàr nodded, then turned back to me. "Will any others of your special unit be staying with the convoy?" he asked.

There was a bit of emphasis on "special unit" when he spoke. He was still fishing, trying to figure out the lay of the land. The differences in demeanor, equipment, and display of competence between us and the regular Army soldiers were notable, and he was putting two and two together, slowly. I didn't know if any stories about the Triarii had made it to Europe. And I wasn't going to trot the name out until I had to. Why buy trouble? Not that Slovak Nationalists had any interest in internal American squabbles or the fragmentation and atomization that was happening over there. But it had been tamped down among the Americans as a non-issue for the moment, and I didn't want to pick at that scab. The US Army couldn't be counted on to be an entirely conservative organization anymore, and Warren's worries about backlash for working with us were very real.

Opening up that can of worms while we were still very much in a survival situation was a bad, bad idea.

"Yes," I said. "Bradshaw and Draven will keep their sections with the convoy." Rybàr hadn't been introduced to Draven yet, but the man was keeping his boys busy and keeping an eye on things while letting Bradshaw and I handle the face-to-face. Draven wasn't much of a people person. It was part of why he liked mortars; he rarely had to deal with the "hearts and minds" side of modern warfare.

"I would like to meet them, as well," Rybàr said. I nodded.

"I'll send them over," I said. "Right now, I need to go to talk to Jankovic, and we need to get rolling."

As I turned toward the MRAP, lighting forked across the sky and the floodgates opened, the rain pouring down in icy buckets.

Chapter 22

The storm was a Godsend.

Rain lashed the windshield hard enough that Phil had the wipers going as fast as possible, and it was still hard to see through the water spattering and sluicing across the glass. Aside from the lightning flashes, it was so dark that it looked like it was late evening, rather than midday. Not only was visibility cut way down, but the sheer volume of cold rain was going to severely degrade any thermal imaging, as well.

It worked against us a little, as well, but we were crammed into a blue VW Atlas, rather than the Alligator that I'd initially had my eye on. We wouldn't stand out, at a distance, anyway, as anything but a family trying to move around the countryside. Meanwhile, the technicals and AMX-10s, Pumas, Jaguars, and other armored vehicles being used by militias and "peacekeepers" were going to be easier to identify, at least at checkpoints. We had the advantage of being able to spot them as a threat sooner than they could determine that we were.

Not that we were *much* of a threat; five guys crammed into an SUV that really wasn't designed for five people of our size, even given Phil's sawed-off-runt status, much less with weapons and rucks. But then, we weren't supposed to be a threat; that wasn't our job at that point. Our job was to warn our people away from the actual threats.

The interior clearly hadn't been designed with a military application in mind; the seats were probably going to rot out, and the carpeted floor was sodden with mud and water.

It smelled like a mix of wet dog and rancid sweat.

None of us were talking much. We were all exhausted, spending what little mental energy we had left on keeping awake and alert.

No one had said anything about the breakout. It seemed to be understood that something had gone wrong, but everyone had survived, so it was shelved. If anything, the rest of the team, minus Scott, who knew the truth, were inclined to blame the locals.

If I was being honest with myself, yes, I should have double-checked. On the other hand, who sets off a daisy-chain of IEDs big enough to flatten a neighborhood without checking that there aren't friendlies around? And I *had* been on comms with Scott within earshot of Sýkora.

"Slow your roll," I told Phil, squinting through the water flowing in torrents down the windshield. It didn't quite *look* like a roadblock up ahead, but it did look like there might be...

There. Two boxy armored personnel carriers were sitting on the side of the road, about three quarters of a klick ahead. They were little more than dim, dark silhouettes through the rain, but they were definitely there.

I checked the map as Phil let off the gas and pulled over toward the side of the road. We were running dark, without headlights, and while it had kept our profile low, it had almost resulted in a head-on collision with a tractor a few miles back.

The plan was already going haywire. This was the third such checkpoint or laager site that we'd run across already, forcing us to go kilometers out of our way, though fortunately, we'd found routes higher into the mountains rather than pushing back west, into the open country. We were making progress, but we were definitely being pushed north, finding logging roads through the Carpathians, back trails that hopefully even the heavier vehicles could negotiate, while avoiding the enemy. There was no way we were going to get to Nitra in only seventy-five klicks.

I wasn't getting bent out of shape about it. I'd seen enough combat to know that that was the way it went. Plans look nice on paper, but rarely play out that way in real life, simply because no one can possibly predict all the potential obstacles. Human error, enemy movements, terrain that has changed or isn't quite what it looks like on the imagery, weather, mechanical failures…the list of things that could render a plan as written invalid was a long one.

As an old mentor of mine once said, "A plan is just a list of shit that ain't gonna happen."

I keyed my radio. We were getting to the point where we were really stretching the small handheld's considerable power, but our comms were still solid. "Flat, Deacon," I called.

"Send it, Deacon." Bradshaw's voice was faint and laden with static, but I could just make it out.

"Three APCs at," I rattled off the grid coordinates. "Troops inside or under ponchos tied to the hulls." They weren't in a hurry to go anywhere, not in that deluge. "Alternate turnoff at," and I rattled off another set of coordinates, about half a klick behind us. It hadn't looked like a great road, but it was a road, and it would be outside these guys' line of sight.

That was half of being a scout. You might not get a chance to get into the thick of it; you might be sneaking around in a civilian vehicle, trying not to be noticed and trying really hard *not* to get into a firefight. It sometimes felt more like running and hiding instead of fighting, but there's a time and a place for everything, and war isn't all kicking doors and slaying bodies.

Sometimes, it's just making sure that your own people don't walk into a trap.

"Roger," Bradshaw replied. "I'll pass it along."

While the Army's comms were screwed, and the nationwide cell service had been cut off, the Slovak Nationalists had some very smart people working for them. They'd cobbled together what amounted to cloned cell towers that were mounted on the MRAPs. They didn't have a lot of coverage, but they allowed the Nationalists to use encrypted text and voice apps on smartphones within a certain radius. It had drawbacks, but they were making it work for sending detailed information without needing to get on the radio for long periods.

Of course, we were out of range, so we couldn't use it.

Phil had stopped altogether, as another fork of lightning split the sky, followed a few seconds later by an earsplitting crack of thunder. The APCs were gray shapes in the dark and the

231

rain, and nothing moved near them as he hastily backed up until they disappeared into the gray sheets of falling water. Only then did he start to turn around, heading back toward that road we'd spotted. Some of the leading elements of the Nationalist convoy might beat us to it, but Phil had gotten pretty good at maneuvering the Atlas around obstacles. He'd get us back up front quickly.

Then we'd do what we'd been doing for the last couple of hours, ranging ahead and looking for the enemy and alternate routes around the enemy, while the rest of the Nationalists and Killian's—no, Warren's, now—unit followed, traveling in ones and twos.

I just hoped that the storm held, at least until dark.

***

It didn't. Neither did our luck.

The storm died away to scattered showers about mid-afternoon, leaving big breaks in the cloud cover and bathing the countryside in a patchwork of sunlight and shadow. It was pretty, but it wasn't welcome when it came to trying to get the better part of a battalion-strength element to Nitra undetected.

Especially when one of the MRAPs got bogged down in the fields south of Kovarce.

It shouldn't have come as a surprise. MRAPs weren't built for cross-country driving, or even much in the way of unimproved roads. They had been designed for the Main Supply Routes in Iraq, back when convoys on those MSRs were regularly being hit by increasingly large IEDs. On rougher terrain, they fared quite poorly, which had led to their replacement by MATVs long before I enlisted.

We got called back to hold security on the stricken vehicle. About a dozen vehicles were backed up behind it and couldn't move forward; the big vehicle was blocking the narrow dirt road. Some of the others could move around, but the problem was that there weren't many alternate routes around that spot. We were shielded by hedgerows from ground observation, but that wasn't going to last much longer with the weather clearing. The EDC had to know that we'd broken out of Vrbovè, and the hunt was going to be on.

232

From what I had observed so far, they weren't going to be eager to come to grips with us, either. They were going to try to spot us and hit us from the air. We had to get moving. I hoped Nitra had some serious air defenses. Rybàr's people had about six SA-18s left, and that was about it, barring the .50s. And they could be useful against helicopters, but not fast movers at altitude.

We were out of the vehicles, spread out along the hedgerow, watching down the road toward the red roofs of Sùlovice, while trying to scan the sky for drones, helicopters, or, worse, fast movers. Behind us, some of Bradshaw's men and a few of Killian's mech infantry soldiers tried to help the Slovaks get the MRAP unstuck. Draven's section was on security in the hedgerows. Glancing back, I saw clods of mud fly from shovels, while cardboard and plywood got wedged under the wheels.

We still had about twenty klicks to go to get to Nitra. And at the rate this convoy was moving, we *might* get there by midnight. If we were lucky. I scanned the sky again.

"Feels a bit like being a bug on a plate, don't it?" Phil muttered.

"A bit," I agreed. I was striving for British understatement. I felt exposed as all hell.

"You think they're going to send ground forces, or air?" Greg asked.

"You mean if they spot us?" I asked. "Probably fast movers, like they almost nailed us with up in the mountains."

"I don't think they want to get up close and personal, after the mauling they got in Vrbovè," Jordan said, echoing my own thoughts. "These guys don't seem very hard core."

"No, they don't," I replied. "Which was about what Intel said, based on recent events and the Kosovo thing. Most of 'em don't have the stomach for heavy combat. The EDC countries have been relying heavily on conscription for the last few years. Conscripts don't usually make badass fighters. *And*, heavy casualties don't play well back home, not when you've already got riots on the streets on a regular basis."

"And where they really need some savagery, they send the 'immigrants,'" Dwight grumbled.

"Meaning the black and brown guys," Jordan said. I felt myself stiffening a little, hearing the edge in his voice. Of all the times…

"Yeah, most of the time," Dwight replied bluntly. "Tells you something about them, don't it? Or were you gonna say it says something about me because I called a spade a spade?"

If there was one guy on the team who wouldn't put up with Jordan's touchiness, it was Dwight. And after a week of combat, forced movement, and a hell of a lot of sleep deprivation, this was the last thing we needed.

But Jordan didn't go on a tear this time. He had in the past. But this time, he just paused for a while. "Yeah," he said finally. "I guess it does."

I blew out a breath I hadn't realized I'd been holding. I didn't have to chew any ass or even just tell them to quiet down.

"Besides, what are you getting bent out of shape over these Muslim bastards for?" Dwight asked. "They're no different from the fucking Kosovars and Chechnyans."

Damn it, Dwight. Just let it drop, will you? We'd escaped a Jordan tirade, but it might have only been a brief respite, if Dwight kept pushing. And when Dwight got a burr under his saddle, he pushed

"I already said you were right, Teddy," Jordan growled. "Don't push it, or you'll stop being right."

Dwight snorted. But before he could get a head of steam going, Scott interrupted. "Looks like they're getting it out," he said.

I glanced back, thankful for the reprieve. Everybody was strung out and punchy. And with this bunch, strung out and punchy meant they were looking for a fight. Without the EDC and the militias obliging, the next step was internecine strife.

I had to crack down on it. I didn't like to have to, especially since I didn't have half the experience that a guy like Dwight did. Which didn't mean I wouldn't. It was my job. I'd crack heads if need be; I'd had to do it before.

The fact that Phil and Jordan still talked to me was a good sign that I'd done it right.

With a growl of engines, the MRAP surged up out of the hole that it had dug itself into, sending globs of mud flying from its wheels into the air. Hopefully we could get it back on a track that wouldn't bury it to the doors in the mud again.

Though as I looked around, that possibility looked a little slim. The only such route would be down the 593, and there were almost guaranteed to be roadblocks there. Unless the Nationalists had extended their reach farther north than we thought in the last twenty-four hours.

A runner came up, a young kid in mismatched camouflage fatigues, with an old vz. 58 slung over his shoulder. I watched him approach, wondering just how this was going to go, with no Slovak terp.

The kid got to us and looked around, confusion on his face. He was probably looking for rank insignia, and we weren't wearing any. I didn't really speak more than a few phrases in Slovak, so I just asked him, "What is it, kid?"

"I am looking for Team Leader Bowen," he said, in heavily accented but passable English. I suddenly felt a little ashamed, remembering some of Hartrick's stories about getting into Iraq and finding that some of the Iraqi kids spoke better English than the Marines had.

"I'm Bowen," I said. "What is it?"

"*Generàlporučik* Rybàr wants to see you, sir," the kid said.

That raised an eyebrow. I'd gathered that Rybàr had been military, and probably an officer, but while the specific rank was unfamiliar—I hadn't exactly memorized Slovak Army ranks before insert—it sure sounded important.

Of course, if he was with the Nationalist resistance, that rank probably didn't mean much to the Slovak Army anymore. But it told me something about the man that I hadn't known before.

I got up, my joints protesting from the beating they'd gotten over the last week, followed by long hours in a car, followed by crouching down on a knee in a hedgerow for the last hour and a half. "Let's go, then," I said. "Don't leave without me," I muttered as I passed Scott.

"I'll give you an extra ten minutes," he said. "Don't miss extract."

I glared at him, but he kept his eyes on his sector, a faint smile curling the corner of his mouth. Scott's ancestry was telling; he had a few wisps of filthy facial hair at the corners of his mouth and his chin, but that was about it, even after over a week.

The kid and I slogged through the muddy field toward the Alligator that was sitting about three vehicles back from the MRAP, which was now forging toward firmer ground, the driver twisting the wheel whenever it seemed to be bogging down. It took longer than it should have to cross the distance; the furrows made for treacherous footing, even more so after the soaking from the morning storm.

Rybàr was out of the vehicle, his own Bren 805 in his hands, scanning the sky as we approached. I followed suit. It was weirding me out that we hadn't seen any aircraft, or even drones.

Seeing us, Rybàr waved me over to where he spread a map out. He looked like he was going to spread it on the Alligator's hood, but reconsidered after glancing at the rainwater still beaded on the metal. He just held it up for me to see.

"We are almost within secure Slovak territory," he said. I noticed he didn't say "Nationalist territory." Of course, he wouldn't. The Nationalists believed they were defending Slovakia against foreign invaders and domestic enemies. "We have not yet reached the front lines, but we will soon. Notice the skies are clear?" He pointed at the clouds above us. "We have six batteries of S-125 SAMs around Nitra. The enemy learned the hard way not to try to hit us with airstrikes, at least not from helicopters or Tornadoes." I imagined the newer Typhoons were going to create bigger problems, but the Tornadoes were ancient, and intel said that the EDC might have about fifty in flying condition. That earlier thought about the EDC being worried about casualties was going to go triple for their fast movers.

Intel hadn't suggested that the Nationalists—or even the Slovak Army—had those kind of air defenses. But I had a sneaking suspicion, based on Skalický's apparent loyalties, as to just where the old SAM systems had come from.

"I have another favor to ask of you, my friend," he said. "You and your team are the most mobile and best-trained for infiltration. We are having communications difficulties; the

236

enemy is close, and has been jamming our radio transmissions more intensely around Nitra. They have had the city surrounded on three sides for the last three months.

"I need you to move in and make contact with our outer defenses and coordinate our entry into Nitra." He grinned jovially. I must have looked more than a little skeptical. "I am not asking you to go alone. I am sending Sỳkora with you again." He waved and called out in Slovak, and the young man—who looked a lot younger in daylight—came around the back of the Alligator. He nodded, and I returned it, wordlessly.

I didn't say that Sỳkora had almost blown up my team. That hadn't been entirely his fault, after all.

"I need you to hurry," Rybàr said grimly. "Some of my outriders have spotted drones at high altitude, outside of our countermeasure range. There are already ground forces moving toward us; I think the only reason they have not yet engaged us is that they are uncertain, and wary." He pointed toward the road to the north. "I take it you saw the hulks up there?"

I nodded. There had been three burned-out EBRC Jaguars up on the highway. At least, two of them had been recognizable as Jaguars. The third had been little more than mangled metal half in and half out of a massive crater blown in the side of the road.

He ran his finger down a line on the map. "This route should be reasonably secure. Unless matters have deteriorated further, there should be a scout unit here, in Dolnè Lefantovce. Sỳkora knows the passwords."

He put his hand on my shoulder. "I know that I am asking a great deal from you," he said. "You are not Slovak; this is not your cause. But we cannot help you unless we get into Nitra. You have seen the resources my cell has at its disposal now. Once we are inside the city, we can rest, and plan our next move."

Which had been my entire line of thought, going along with this plan. Heading for Nitra was kind of going in the wrong direction, unless we were heading back to Hungary. The Hungarians might take our stray American soldiers under their wings, but Poland was where the bulk of the other Brigade Combat Team of US Army Europe was stationed.

But we wouldn't make it to Poland alone, on foot, and with steadily decreasing supplies, not to mention a serious dearth of firepower. The Nationalists were our best hope.

Not that there wouldn't be griping. I could hear David and Jordan already, and I hadn't even told them yet.

"We'll get on the road in the next couple of minutes," I told Rybàr. I looked at Sỳkora. "It's gonna be a tight fit, so get in where you can."

Rybàr just nodded, and slapped me on the shoulder. Sỳkora looked a little nervous, but slung his Bren 805 and stepped up to join me. Together, we headed back to the team.

If this works, I might actually get a night's sleep tonight. I wasn't sure what that was even going to feel like.

Granted, I wasn't going to get my hopes up until we were inside Nitra, under cover, and someplace dry.

Chapter 23

The Nationalists in Dolnè Lefantovce weren't being particularly sneaky. There were two UAZs with mounted vz. 59 machineguns sitting right by the side of the road coming from the north. They could easily be pulled back into the trees, but apparently the scout force was confident enough in their artillery and SAM cover that they weren't too worried.

They probably should have been; if the EDC and their cronies could take out an American FOB, these guys wouldn't be much more than a speed bump.

Still, it provided us with a little advance warning that we were coming up on the rendezvous, so we stopped the vehicles and got out.

"Cocky bastards, aren't they?" Scott muttered as he joined me near the hood of my truck.

"Yeah," I replied, watching the two vehicles. They hadn't opened fire on us, at least, which either meant that they were under some decent fire discipline, or else they weren't sure whether we were friend or foe, and didn't want to light up other Nationalists. The fact that we weren't making any overtly hostile moves helped. "Just in case, I want you to keep Bravo back here to cover us," I told him. "Dwight, too. If things go south, I want both of those vehicles lit up like a Christmas tree."

"No worries," Scott replied. "Try not to get shot."

"No worries," I repeated. I looked over at Sỳkora. "Ready?"

He nodded jerkily. I didn't think he liked this situation. Not that there was all that much to like; making linkup with no comms and accompanied by foreign forces wasn't what I'd call fun, either.

I looked around at the rest of my element, gathered in front of the vehicle, standing so as to appear as non-threatening as possible, and waved toward the two vehicles. Spread out in a short line, weapons pointed at the dirt, we moved forward, keeping our pace easy and relatively nonchalant. I say, "relatively," because when you've been on the run and hunted for a week and a half, it gets hard to turn some things off.

We got closer to the two old Soviet UAZs, while the gunners and the men with rifles watched us. Most of them were in camouflage of some sort, ranging from old woodlands, to the Slovak pseudo-flecktarn, to American OCP/Multicam. The array of weapons was almost as eclectic. Fortunately, they weren't pointing them at us just yet. The gunners had their hands on their weapons, which were leveled, rather than pointing at the sky, but they still weren't pointed directly at us, not quite.

Sỳkora lifted a hand, keeping the other on his rifle, and said something in Slovak. After a moment, one of the soldiers, a burly man with a spare chin, lifted his own hand in greeting and replied in the same language.

By then we were barely fifty yards apart. Sỳkora stopped and rattled off a short speech in Slovak. The other man asked a question, and Sỳkora answered. The thickset man seemed to relax, his set expression breaking into a wide smile, and he spread his arms and said something jovially. It sounded like a greeting.

Sỳkora seemed to let out a sigh. He turned to me with a smile on his narrow face. "We are good," he said. "They are waiting for the rest of us."

I nodded, and keyed my radio. "Flat, Deacon. Tell the Big Hat that all's well." We were pretty sure our comms were secure, but broadcasting Rybàr's name still might not be a great idea. Greg had come up with the nickname "Big Hat" for him. It had stuck, even though I had yet to actually see Rybàr wear a hat.

"Roger," came Bradshaw's faint, scratchy reply. The bad guys really *were* cranking up the EM jamming around Nitra, if our radios were having a hard time getting through it, even this far away. After a long pause, he came back. "We're moving."

I glanced up at the sky, then shook the double-chinned man's meaty hand. I'd still feel a lot more comfortable once we got into Nitra.

***

At least, that had been my thought. Once we were actually there, that changed a bit.

We rolled into Nitra as one big convoy, having been held at the edge of the outer defenses by our escort of BOV armored vehicles.

Technically, we staged in Dražovce before moving southeast toward Nitra itself. But the scars of war were already visible. Several of the houses had been bombed or shelled, and smoke was rising from parts of the big Land Rover factory on the other side of the highway. Even as we started down the road toward Zobor and Nitra itself, artillery batteries on the hill above opened fire, the distant *thumps* of the reports muted in comparison to the ripping passage of the shells overhead.

The highway was studded with roadblocks, both the prepared kind, with concrete barriers, sandbagged bunkers, and machineguns and RPGs in evidence, and also more ad hoc arrangements, mostly tipped-over semi-trailers. Some of those were so blackened and pocked with bullet holes that they must have already been the scene of some fighting.

Smoke was rising from the southern edge of Nitra, though the white, red, and blue edifice of the castle appeared untouched as we rolled across the bridge between Zobor and Nitra.

The roads were empty of any civilian traffic. I didn't know if the Nationalists had evacuated the civilians before they'd strongpointed the city, a good three months before, but if they hadn't, the locals were definitely keeping their heads down. The only vehicles we saw on the road on the way in were wheeled BOVs, tracked BVPs, T-72 tanks, and an eclectic bunch of retrofitted technicals. It looked like a good chunk of the Nationalists had come from the Slovak Army, and had brought a ton of equipment with them.

That presented some hope. From what I was seeing, Nitra was going to be one hell of a tough nut to crack. Hopefully, that meant that we'd have a day or two to rest and refit before making our way north.

But that hope seemed to be fading as we got deeper into the city. More and more of the armored vehicles we passed seemed to be either digging in or falling back to more secure positions. I didn't pretend to know what was going on, but it looked an awful lot like the Nationalists were getting ready for one hell of a fight.

The defenses got thicker as we got closer to the castle itself. There were T-72s stationed on either side of the road as we turned up between the closely-packed buildings toward the castle, and more BOVs and technicals behind them. If the Nationalist headquarters was up there, they weren't taking any chances with their defenses.

The column halted at the base of the low hill where the castle sat, and I saw Rybàr and Skalickỳ get out of their vehicles, met by a knot of fairly well-equipped men in Slovak camouflage and dark green berets. It seemed that a lot of the Nationalists hadn't just come from the Army; they'd kept their uniforms and insignia. This was more division within the Slovak government than we'd been led to believe.

Rybàr looked back toward our vehicles as I got out. He waved at me to join him. I wasn't quite close enough to make out Skalickỳ's expression clearly, but he definitely didn't look happy, just going by his body language. He probably would have preferred if we'd been cut loose after getting clear of Vrbovè.

I walked over to join them. "The rest of our fighters will be assigned to defensive positions within the city," Rybàr said, turning to me as I approached. "We need you Americans to wait here, except for you and the other leaders. You will come with us to meet *Generàlporučik* Pokornỳ." He pointed over his shoulder toward the castle. "We have much to discuss, and not much time. It seems that the EDC forces outside the city have been reinforced while we were on the move. The command group thinks that an offensive is imminent."

I kept my expression carefully still. That was not what I wanted to hear. It sure as hell wouldn't be what Warren and the rest of the ad hoc Army unit now under his command would want to hear, either. They hadn't been particularly uppity, but they weren't eager to come to grips with the enemy, and they all seemed to be moving slower and slower. I'd been too busy to notice much, but their morale was clearly dropping, and resentment was festering, even as we ran for our lives.

"I'll get Bradshaw and Warren," I said. "We need medical help for our wounded."

His face went still for just a second. I felt a flash of anger. We'd fought beside them to break out of Vrbovè, and now he was going to hesitate when it came to giving medical aid to Americans who had helped his people.

But he nodded. "I will get my people on it," he said. "Right now, we need to meet with Pokornỳ."

It was probably as good as I was going to get. I nodded and turned back to find Bradshaw and Warren. Warren especially wasn't going to like this. I wasn't looking forward to that conversation.

***

Bradshaw was easy. He just nodded, issued some quick instructions to Watts, his assistant section leader, and came with me. Draven also just nodded and gave me a thumbs up. He'd stay back. Warren was a whole different proposition.

It took ten minutes of poking around the Army's trucks before we found him. He'd apparently delegated well, because while a couple of his young Sergeants were supervising care of the wounded and checking gear, there was no sign of him anywhere.

As we went from truck to truck, I was looking around, getting angrier as I did. A glance at Bradshaw showed his jaw was tightening and he was watching the Army soldiers with narrowed eyes.

"Hey, Sergeant," I said, grabbing one of the NCOs by the arm. The guy must have been in his mid-twenties, but he looked a lot younger to me, for some reason. "You notice something wrong here?"

He looked around. Half of the soldiers seemed to still be on the trucks. Some had gotten out to check the wounded, supervised by Jordan, Reuben, and a couple of Bradshaw's medics. Others were slumped against wheels or walls, helmets off and either talking quietly or zoning out.

When he didn't seem to get it, I picked his M37 up off the ground where it had been leaning against a tire and shoved it into his hands. "You might think that we're among friends, but you should have learned already that that can change any second. Get these kids up and on security. Now, where's Chief Warren?"

He frowned. He clearly didn't think there was any need to act like we were out in the field anymore; we were inside friendly lines. But if Rybàr was right, and we were in for a fight, there was no telling when it was going to start. This was no time to get complacent.

I could already tell that he wasn't going to act on what I'd told him. If only because I was the one telling him, and whatever had happened in the last week, I was just some scruffy contractor or something. I wasn't in his chain of command, so I couldn't tell him what to do.

"He's in his truck, over there," he said, pointing. His vague finger-wave could have indicated about three different vehicles, but it was better than we had before, and I could tell that he'd been sorely tempted not to tell us that much.

"Thank you," I gritted, and the two of us walked away. I could feel his eyes on my back as we went. I also noticed that I didn't hear him ordering any of his soldiers up and onto security.

Damn, I hope these kids aren't this stupid and intransigent if the EDC comes again.

Warren, it turned out, was in the last Land Rover, sitting in the back. And he was trying the radio. "Any American station this net, this is Chief Warrant Officer Warren," he called, as I opened the door.

"Turn that off," I told him.

He looked up at me. "We've got to keep trying," he said. "It's not in the open."

"If the EDC could successfully jam the SINCGARS net, don't you think they could listen in on it, too?" Bradshaw asked.

Warren frowned. "That shouldn't be possible," he said.

"Neither was jamming a frequency-hopping, encrypted net," Bradshaw pointed out. "I'd be willing to bet that there's some serious cyber warfare involved. Hell, you're an IT guy, aren't you? Shouldn't you be thinking of these things?"

"But, that's a *huge* breach," Warren said. "I mean, that's not just a hacking job. That's somebody actually leaking US crypto."

"Look, Warren," I said. "However it happened, it happened. We can't trust the comms. And right now, we've got a meeting with the Nationalist muckety-mucks. And since you're the ranking Army officer, you're expected."

He looked nervous. That seemed to be almost his default expression by then. "I don't know," he said. "What do they want to talk about?"

"From what Rybàr said, presumably the imminent attack on Nitra," I said. "Apparently the EDC forces outside the city got reinforced over the last day."

"Then I guess I should come," he said reluctantly, as he got out of the Land Rover. "We're going to need to get out soon if that's coming."

I didn't tell him that I suspected it wasn't going to be that easy. He'd find that out soon enough.

***

The castle was a mix of architectural and decorative styles from multiple centuries, but right at that moment, it was an armed camp.

Balconies had been turned into weapons platforms, windows were sandbagged, and armored vehicles squatted in the courtyard, including a pair of squat, tracked ZSU-23-4 Shilkas, self-propelled anti-aircraft platforms. *Russian* self-propelled anti-aircraft platforms. I hadn't known that the Slovaks even had any.

As we passed the two vehicles with their quad 23mm guns, I remembered Skalickỳ's insistence that the Russians would be better allies than Americans. I was starting to understand. And it wasn't a good feeling.

In fact, that castle was starting to look less like shelter, and more like a trap.

But the Nationalist fighters moving purposefully around the fortifications, carrying crates of mortar rounds and SA-18 SAMs toward the tops of the walls, paid us little attention. We got a few looks, but they varied from blank to faintly frowning.

Rybàr led us through a shadowed, arched passageway that went all the way through a three-story stone building, then up a curving walkway that led toward a bronze statue overlooking the city, with the main hall and cathedral on the right, and a smaller, white building on the left, topped by a round stone tower. A metal crucifix stood in the grassy courtyard, and as we approached it, I crossed myself. Rybàr glanced at me as I did so, and seemed to nod slightly.

Armed guards were stationed at the doors, and there were more sandbagged positions at the rail on either side of the statue, manned by men in camouflage and equipped with mounted .50 caliber M2 machineguns and multiple SA-18 SAMs.

I'd been kind of expecting Rybàr to lead us to the main hall, but instead he turned down the short flight of steps to the white building, which I saw was a museum. More sandbags had been set up inside the door and inside the windows. The Nationalists had been busy.

As we passed into the dimmed interior, I saw that they'd been busier than I'd thought. If the building had been a museum before the war, the displays had all been cleared away. It was a command post, now, lit by actinic work lights. Maps were up on plywood easels and spread across folding tables. Radios practically covered one entire wall, and laptops cast a bluish tint on the scene.

There was a constant low murmur in Slovak, all centered on the man leaning against the folding table in the center. From the looks of things, the plastic and aluminum contraption wasn't going to last much longer with his weight on it.

He looked up as we came in. He was massively built, and little of it appeared to be muscle. He had two chins beneath a round, flat face, with thick lips that seemed to be constantly parted. He was as pale as a fish's belly, despite the dark stubble on his head and his jaw.

For all that, he was wearing Slovak camouflage with the shoulder boards of a general officer. This must be Pokornỳ.

He and Rybàr greeted each other coolly. Even without understanding the language, it was clear that there was no love lost between the two men, despite—or perhaps because of—the difference in age.

They spoke quickly. Rybàr introduced us, though he did so in Slovak, only motioning toward the three of us. Pokornỳ looked at us, his face blank, his small eyes looking us over coolly while he breathed loudly and laboriously through his mouth. I could see the wheels turning as he scanned us, and I could tell that he wasn't happy to see Americans there.

I took an immediate and intense dislike to the man.

He turned back to Rybàr and spoke at some length. I couldn't follow it, but I was pretty sure I caught something akin to "Russki" in the mix. The sudden flicker of cold rage that crossed Rybàr's face for a split second before he clamped down on it at the word pretty well confirmed it.

Rybàr countered at equal length, motioning toward the map, the imagery on a laptop, and then at us. I didn't know exactly what the argument was, but I could tell that our future was currently teetering on a knife edge.

Finally, with a decided note of disgust in his voice and a faint, wet snort, Pokornỳ threw up his hands and turned back toward the map. For a moment, Rybàr just glared at the other man's back, then turned to us. "My friends," he said, "we are in a difficult situation here. I do not know if any of you speak Slovak, but *Generàlporučik* Pokornỳ is inclined to send you away as soon as possible."

"That's good, isn't it?" Warren asked.

I gritted my teeth. *Shut up, Warren.*

"Not as things stand right now," he replied. "The enemy has nearly a regiment of mechanized infantry and militia, with tank support, staged and ready to move on the city. Every report we have gotten suggests that they could start their attack as early as tonight." He shook his head. "You would not get far."

"But, then, why…?" Warren hadn't picked up on what I had.

"Pokornỳ thinks that the Slovak Nationalists should accept Russian help," I explained. "Which makes us an unwelcome complication. I'm guessing that American participation in the peacekeeping mission probably doesn't endear us to him, either."

"You are correct, my friend," Rybàr said. "I have made the case to allow you to stay inside the defenses for now. But…"

"But we need to lend a hand," I finished for him. "Otherwise, there's no call to waste valuable resources helping us."

He looked a little pained, but nodded. "I am afraid so." He stroked his mustache. "We have a common enemy, as you pointed out in Vrbovè. And you would have a long way to go. It seems that the EDC destroyed FOB Poole, as well. You would have to go all the way to Poland."

"Wait a minute." It was finally starting to dawn on Warren what was happening. "No, I can't do that. I don't have the *authority* to do that. Don't you understand? I am an officer in the *United States Army*. And the Army has *not* given me, or any other American, that I know of, orders that allow us to fight against the Slovak Army, or any EDC forces! We are here as *peacekeepers*!"

"Warren…" I started to say, but he turned to me, a mix of desperation and determination on his face.

"Look, Bowen, I don't know for sure who you are, or who you work for, but in the Army, we follow orders." His voice was shaking, putting the lie to his determined words. "And in the absence of orders, we are supposed to follow the last instructions received."

I kept my calm as I stepped closer, all too conscious that Rybàr wasn't the only one watching this interplay. Pokornỳ was watching, too, his piggish little eyes blank but alert.

"And if your last received orders are to hold security in a position that's about to get overrun?" I asked him quietly. "If they didn't include, 'Fall back when you deem prudent?'"

"This isn't the same thing!" he protested. "You're not talking about falling back, you're talking about fighting an urban battle against people who are ostensibly supposed to be our allies!"

"I would have thought that you'd have been disabused of that notion by now," Bradshaw drawled.

Warren's eyes flicked to him, a little too wide. I thought I understood what he was going through. He wasn't cut out for this. He wasn't trained for this. He was an Information Systems warrant officer. In the world he was used to, he wasn't ever *supposed* to have to deal with this kind of a situation.

248

And I had the sudden realization that if he tried to lead those young soldiers in combat, he was going to get them, and probably himself, killed. Not out of any malice, or necessarily negligence or incompetence. Simply because he wasn't prepared for it. And with that ad hoc, thrown-together bunch, it would be a disaster. And he knew it. But he couldn't bring himself to say that much; he couldn't allow himself, as the ranking officer, to show that weakness. So, he was falling back on orders and policy to try to cover for himself.

I wasn't sure whether to respect him or despise him for it. Maybe a little of both.

I turned to Rybàr, though not before meeting Pokornỳ's gaze just long enough to let him know that I wasn't going to be intimidated. "If my guys and Bradshaw's guys fight and Draven's lend a hand with the mortars, will that be enough?" I asked. "We're prepared for it. The regular Army soldiers aren't."

Rybàr looked slightly to one side, but he didn't turn all the way to look at Pokornỳ. He thought for a moment. "Yes," he said. "You have my word on it."

I blew out a breath I hadn't realized I'd been holding. "Good," I said. "We'll need to restock and try to get a little rest. Is there somewhere that Chief Warren's people can take shelter?"

He nodded again. "I will send Sỳkora with you as liaison," he said. "He will show you everything you need."

"Thank you," I said. I glanced at Pokornỳ. *No thanks to you, you fat fuck.* "How soon are you expecting the attack to start?"

Before he could answer, a distant growl turned into a ripping shriek overhead, punctuated by a series of rippling explosions in the city and up on the mountain beyond. One of the radio operators yelled out in Slovak.

"I would say it has just started," Rybàr said. "They just attacked our air defense radars.

"They are coming."

Chapter 24

It was a hell of an interesting movement to the forward positions.

The initial Suppression of Enemy Air Defense strikes had done their job well. Anti-radiation missiles launched from extreme long range had blown gaping holes in the Nationalists' air defense network. Pillars of black smoke marked where S-125 batteries had died. And in the wake of the SEAD mission, the air strikes were inbound. The distant, growling roar of jet engines could already be heard, even as loudspeakers mounted on vans blared warnings in Slovak, warnings that were probably unneeded, given the already concrete evidence that the attack was beginning.

But while the EDC's "Wild Weasel" aircraft had punched holes in the air defense network, they hadn't knocked it out completely.

We had taken vehicles the first part of the way, speeding through streets that were all but deserted, as partially blocked as they were by defensive positions. Bunkers, barricades, and sandbagged armored vehicles were stationed at chokepoints in concentric rings around the castle, though getting more closely clustered along the main thoroughfares. Presuming that Pokorný had been the mastermind of this defensive plan, he might be an asshole, and a puppet of the Kremlin, but he knew his stuff. Nitra was going to be a hell of a fight.

We were tearing down Pàrovskà Street, weaving through the web of defensive positions and, quite noticeably, avoiding certain sections of road that otherwise seemed fairly clear. I could imagine why. Barely slowing down, our driver yanked the wheel over and, tires squealing, turned onto Štùrova Street, speeding toward the open traffic circle ahead, and the mall beyond, where more columns of black smoke were rising into the air, as smoke trails streaked down out of the sky in the distance, the impacts of rocket artillery throwing billowing clouds of dust and smoke into the air at the edge of Mlynàrce.

None of us could do much more than cling to our seats in the back. The boxy MAN TG truck had been a civilian model before the Nationalists had pressed it into service, and hadn't really been set up for carrying passengers. I was pretty sure that the rough benches bolted into the box on the back hadn't been in there a week before, and to say that their installation had been hasty would be an understatement. I could hear the benches creaking and banging back there from the front seat as the truck swayed alarmingly through the turn.

I couldn't say that the driver's haste was unwarranted. He was a young, slightly pudgy kid, pale as death, gripping the wheel with white knuckles that made his otherwise pasty complexion look like a Caribbean tan. He was scared shitless, and given the low rumble of explosions, the shrieking howl of jet engines, and the flickering flames of ZSU fire from the mall parking lot ahead, he wasn't wrong. I'd thought I was jaded after what I'd seen over the last eight years, but even the nastiest dustups I'd seen in Africa with the MEU had been playground scraps compared to this.

A pair of tiny, triangular silhouettes appeared on the horizon, apparently coming right for us. The kid started to panic, but there was nowhere to go. There was a solid row of high-rise apartments with businesses between them on either side of the street. I pointed ahead and to the right, where there was an opening under the trees. I was pretty sure there was an armored vehicle under there, so it could be a target, but it beat being the only thing moving out in the open.

It had happened before I was born, but I remembered seeing video of "The Luckiest Man in Iraq." I had no desire to recreate that scene, as a lone car had sped across a bridge, running from a Coalition air strike during Operation Desert Storm, and almost not made it out.

The kid floored it, just as flickering antiaircraft fire, the tracers barely visible in the early morning, converged on the two

252

speeding silhouettes, accompanied by fast-moving, white smoke trails. They might have taken out the bulk of the S-125 batteries, but from what I'd seen so far, the Nationalists had a *lot* of SA-18s squirreled away in defensive positions. And there was no way to use anti-radiation missiles against heat-seeking MANPADs.

Both planes popped flares and jinked hard, but in trying to evade one of the man-portable SAMs, one of them ran headlong into a stream of 23mm tracers. The aircraft came apart in midair, fireballing with a distant *boom* that reached us a bare three seconds later, as flaming debris showered down on the town beneath.

Then the driver skidded us into our shelter under the trees, stomping on the brake and almost throwing me into the dash as he stopped abruptly behind a sandbagged T-72.

"Everybody out!" I yelled. There was no way I was going to get that kid to go any farther. And with the air attack already underway, it probably wouldn't be smart to try to push any farther in a vehicle, anyway.

Slamming the door open, I dropped out of the cab, dragging my rifle and a small haversack with me. We'd left our rucks behind; they were too heavy and bulky, especially if we were going to be fighting in close quarters and falling back. But several of us had grabbed small sacks and packs, stuffing ammunition and grenades into them. I had an extra three hundred rounds of 7.62 NATO and four weird, ribbed, pear-shaped URG-86 grenades stuffed in the sack.

I'd also ditched my ghillie, leaving it stuffed in my ruck. It wouldn't do much good here.

Sýkora had apparently been semi-permanently designated as our liaison, and he seemed to be resigned to it. He and three more of his men had been in the truck with us, with the rest of his unit riding in the trucks behind us with Bradshaw.

He looked around. "Come on!" he yelled, as he pointed toward the buildings. "There is a rally point nearby!"

He was almost drowned out by a thunderous explosion, as one of the vehicles in the mall parking lot ahead was struck by either a missile or a guided bomb. An ugly, black-and-orange fireball boiled up on the other side of the trees as another arrowhead shape flashed by overhead, spewing flares while hissing, white smoke trails sped after it.

We ran in a loose column, trying to get close to the side of the apartment building, heading for the south side of the traffic circle. The building didn't provide a lot of overhead cover, but it would help. A direct hit on the roof might well drop it on us, but anything other than a direct hit on our side would probably be survivable.

I can't say that I'd ever really expected to be dodging bombs and artillery fire in an Old World urban setting when I signed up for the Marine Corps, all those years ago. Strange, how the model of war we'd grown up with in the post-9/11 world had suddenly taken a turn toward an older form of warfare, that we'd all been assured was a thing of the past.

Reaching the apartment building, we huddled at the base of the wall for a moment as another flight of fast-movers roared by overhead. Another one was hit by a SAM and curved off to the south, trailing black smoke and losing altitude.

I had a pretty good idea where Sỳkora was heading; I'd looked over the map, too. There was a marshalling point and assembly area in an ag equipment store on the southwest side of the traffic circle. Getting to it was going to be interesting, though, since we had to cross an open street to reach it, with residential houses in the way.

But after a moment, the airstrikes on the mall parking lot seemed to be over. There were still explosions in the distance, but our little pocket of Nitra seemed to be quiet. I nudged Sỳkora, and we got moving.

That didn't mean we got complacent. We paused at the edge of the street, scanned the sky above, and ran for the next bit of cover. Unfortunately, there wasn't much; we were right on the edge of the traffic circle, with a clear enough view of the smoke still billowing out of the mall parking lot ahead, accompanied by the roar of flames, what might have been dim screams and slightly louder shouts, and the popcorn crackle of 23mm ammunition cooking off.

So, the pause only lasted for the briefest moment, just long enough to make sure we weren't about to run right into an armored column, before we were dashing for the assembly area and command post. It wasn't a long way, but with the amount of firepower flying around, it sure felt like it was a lot longer than a hundred yards.

We pounded up the pavement and across the grass, toward the glass-fronted businesses. The glass had mostly already been smashed out, I imagined reduce the frag if a nearby bomb blast or artillery impact shattered the windows. In its place were more sandbags.

These guys had been busy.

Of course, they'd had almost three months to fortify the city. The peacekeepers and Loyalist Slovak Army had tried to smash the Nationalist resistance early, but had been bloodied at Galanta, after which the Nationalists had fallen back to Nitra. Earlier attempts by Loyalist forces, even with peacekeeper backup, to enter the city had been rebuffed by direct fire and IEDs. It had become to the Nationalists what Fallujah had been to the Sunni insurgents in Iraq, back when I'd been a kid.

And now, it seemed that the EDC was going to try to recreate Operation Phantom Fury in Nitra. Only this time, there were Americans on the defenders' side.

Sýkora was yelling out the countersign, even before the sentries dug in at the entrance to what had once been a farm store could yell the challenge. The kid *really* didn't want to get shot by his own side, which was a risk when he was accompanied by a bunch of foreigners in unfamiliar fatigues and carrying unfamiliar weapons.

Especially given the Nationalists' already rocky view of Americans, since we'd technically been on the peacekeepers' side until recently.

The countersign was apparently enough for the men at the front of the store, as Sýkora waved us forward, and we hurried inside.

I looked around. The agricultural equipment store had been stripped, all of the sales counters and products carried off who knew where. Stacks of ammunition crates, storm cases full of weapons and munitions, and more crates of medical supplies filled the bulk of the old store, while dim red lights shone from the CP near the back. There were knots of men in all sorts of camouflage, or civilian clothes, with a similarly diverse assortment of chest rigs, plate carriers, helmets, and rifles. Sandbags lined the walls, but there was little to no overhead cover to speak of. A single direct hit on that place, and everybody inside was dead.

I was already itching to get out and get somewhere better hardened.

Sỳkora stopped in the entryway, looking around as his eyes adjusted to the dark. Then he pointed, and led me toward a map table in the center of the CP.

A short man with a pointed face and a slight gut was leaning on the table with one hand, holding the handset of what looked like an old Soviet field telephone to his ear with the other.

He spoke rapidly in Slovak, pointedly ignoring us until he got a reply, then snapped something else, then slammed the phone back in its cradle before looking Sỳkora up and down with a sour, disapproving look on his face. I didn't understand the Slovak word he snapped out impatiently, but I could recognize the tone. *Who are you and what do you want? Can't you tell there's a battle on?*

Sỳkora spoke quickly, motioning to us, as well as the Slovak fighters he'd brought. The sour-faced man looked us up and down, his narrowed eyes taking in every detail of our features, our clothing, our gear, and our weapons. I was sure he didn't miss the sour smell of a week and a half in the field, or the dirt, grime, and camouflage face paint ground into our pores and the lines in our faces.

"This is *Major* Kysely," Sỳkora said. "He is in command of this sector of Mlynàrce, controlling the main approach along Bratislavskà and Štùrova streets."

Kysely was watching us, his eyes narrowed and looking rather less than impressed. Given what we were capable of, I suspected that that was his default expression when he wasn't sure what to do with what he'd been given. He spoke briefly, and Sỳkora answered. "I told him that you are American Special Forces, and that you are here to help defend Nitra. He has heard about the attacks on your bases outside Zilina and Lozorno."

I glanced at Scott. Did every Nationalist in this country know more about what was going on than we did?

Probably. They had information networks that we simply hadn't had time to build. And the Army wasn't in the business of building such networks, especially when a good chunk of the locals resented their presence in the first place.

"Where do you need us?" I asked Kysely. Sỳkora was already acting as translator, and I'd learned a long time before that if you're talking to the Big Man, you talk to the Big Man directly, instead of to the terp.

Kysely eyed me for a moment, then motioned us closer to the map table. He started pointing and speaking in rapid-fire Slovak, while Sỳkora translated. Given how fast Kysely was talking, I suspected we were only getting a brief summary, but it was better than just doing pointy-talky and hoping that some tiny glimmers of information got through.

"He wants to keep you back here," Sỳkora said, as Kysely's finger pointed to positions flanking the traffic circle. "There are already teams in place at the forward positions, and the enemy is already moving into the town." He turned a little paler at that, and visibly swallowed. "They will be falling back as the enemy advances, and will pass through our positions here. He says that there is no time to push to the forward line."

I glanced at Kysely. He had already turned away impatiently, snatching up the field telephone again and rattling orders into it in Slovak. As bad-tempered as he seemed to be, I couldn't blame him. This was quite possibly one of, if not the primary approach route an attacker would take to clear the city. He had a lot of responsibility on his shoulders, and couldn't waste time with a bunch of foreign fighters who had no Slovak and no clue about the city or its defenses.

"All right," I said. "Fine. Show me where he wants us, and we'll get split into elements and get set."

Kysely looked up at me. I didn't know if he understood my words; he didn't seem to speak enough English to articulate his orders in the language, but he might still know enough to understand what was said. But he picked up on something in my voice. A flicker of some indefinable expression crossed his face. I got the impression that he still wasn't too happy about having us there, if only because we were Americans, but he wasn't going to turn away extra guns to fight the EDC, their proxies in the militias, and the Loyalists.

He quickly pointed to three spots. "He says these buildings have been fortified, and have more weapons and initiation systems for the explosive traps."

I nodded. "Tyler, we'll take this one," I said, tapping the farthest away, on the other side of the circle. It wasn't as far forward as it might have been, but given that the building closest to the enemy was a gas station, I was going to take that as a win. "You can split your guys between the other two."

He nodded, turning to look around the crowd stuffed into the command post. "Allen! You take 3rd and 4th Squads, and get over to this three-story on the corner. The rest of us will move to here and set up."

A distant rumble sounded, barely audible over the radio noise and mutter of voices inside the marshalling area. It was a ways off, but after the air strikes, I didn't think it was far enough.

"Let's move," I said. "I don't think we've got a lot of time."

Chapter 25

The building hadn't been as well fortified as Kysely's headquarters, but it was still useable as a strongpoint. Plastered concrete walls were going to be hard to penetrate with small arms, anyway, and there were sandbags stacked against the windows, at least on the ground floor.

We got to the front door after one of the longest, most nerve-wracking sprints across open ground I could remember. After the airstrikes, it really didn't feel good to be out in the open, and it didn't get much more open than running just under two hundred yards across a traffic circle. We didn't bound. We ran flat-out, lungs starting to burn by the end, boots pounding on the pavement and gear beating against our chests. Dwight and Tony both fell behind early, only catching up once we reached the corner of the building. Dwight was red in the face, visible even past the bits of camouflage face paint still clinging to his skin, and breathing hard. He was getting along, and he was built like a powerlifter, anyway. Running had never been Dwight's strong point.

We'd stopped at the corner, and Phil and I moved toward the door, which faced southeast, away from the enemy. We still moved carefully; neither of us wanted to get shot by friendlies, or, rather, allies. We still weren't sure exactly where we stood with the Nationalists.

Of course, we hadn't gotten cut down by machinegun fire crossing the traffic circle, so there was that.

"Friendlies!" I yelled toward the door. "*Priatel'*!"

"Come, Americans!" a heavily accented voice yelled back. "Quickly, before the planes come back!"

I looked back and signaled the rest of the team to follow, as Phil and I pushed toward the door, passing in front of sandbagged windows with narrow firing slits between the sandbags. I glanced up, but it didn't look like the upper stories had been so fortified, but at least they had good fields of fire from the ground level windows.

There was a big man just inside the door, with a Bren 805 in his hands. He was so massive that the rifle looked like a kid's toy in his mitts. He wasn't even looking at us, but peering at the sky past my shoulder as we mounted the steps.

"Hurry," he said. "They are using explosive drones against the forward positions."

That got us moving. I knew the last thing that I wanted was to be in the open when some drone operator with an itchy trigger finger flew a glorified model airplane packed with Semtex overhead.

We ran up the steps and inside. The big man shoved the doors, which had been covered in what looked like bomb blankets, closed, then shoved more sandbags against them. They wouldn't stop an assault for long, but the whole point was to kill the assaulters before they got to the door.

The building had been some sort of government office, but unlike the farm store, it hadn't been stripped. Instead, the desks, computers, file cabinets, chairs, and everything else had been shoved against the walls, away from the windows, aside from the desks that were being used as firing platforms for the three vz. 59 machineguns I could see from just inside the foyer. The place didn't seem packed; I could only count four men from where I stood, including the giant who'd ushered us in through the door.

"We are glad to have you here," the big man said, sticking out his hand. From the looks we were getting from a couple of the men in the larger office space, that appreciation might not have been quite as unanimous as he made it sound. "I have ten men here, and *Major* Kysely thinks that the enemy will come down Bratislavskà first."

"Is everybody on the ground floor?" I asked.

He nodded. "It is all we had time to harden," he replied.

260

I nodded as well, looking around as he led us through the office space. There were trees around three sides of the building, but he had machineguns set up with fields of fire to the north and west, even where the trees made it difficult to see more than a dozen yards. There were RPG-75s and Matador launchers set up near the western corner, but even they wouldn't be enough if a full armored column came up the road.

Of course, from what I'd gathered from Kysely, this was only supposed to be one of several fallback positions. It had sounded, based on his explanation of the forward elements falling back through our line, that a staged, defense-in-depth had been planned. Which meant that we had a fallback position as well.

"We only got the wavetops," I said. When he looked a little confused, I explained, "We didn't get a complete briefing. Just told to come here and dig in. What's the plan?"

"Oh," he said, nodding. "We hold here while the forward defenders fall back through our lines, then fight until we get the order to fall back, or we run out of anti-armor weapons." He pointed southeast. "Our fallback position is the Dynamik building, three hundred fifty meters that way." He pulled a municipal map out of his plate carrier, and traced the line along the roads that would be our route. "We must stick carefully to the route and stay off the main roads."

I nodded. At that point, I expected that most of the parked civilian vehicles we'd seen on the way out to the front were probably VBIEDs. It would not be healthy to run down that street under fire.

After looking around again, I frowned. "You don't have anyone on rear security?" I asked.

He looked at me as if I'd said that the sky was green. "The enemy is that way," he said, pointing to the northwest.

I sighed. "Yeah, I know that. Doesn't mean that they can't pull a fast one. What if they get past one of the other positions and come around the flank?"

"I'll take the door, Matt," Dwight said. He was still breathing hard and was leaning against one of the desks that had been pushed to the wall. "I don't really feel like moving for a bit, anyway." He took a deep breath. "I'm getting too old for this shit."

"That's what we've been trying to tell you, Dad," David said, as he peered out one of the firing slits at a sandbagged window.

"Shut your damn mouth, Peanut," Dwight said, though he was still blowing hard enough that it lost a lot of the growl it might have had.

I gave him another look, feeling my brows knit slightly. Dwight had been sticking it out, but he'd been slowing down a bit the last couple of days. He was a beast, strong as an ox, but he was past fifty, and the prolonged movement and combat was clearly starting to take its toll. I just nodded, though. It didn't need to be commented on.

What were we going to do, anyway? There was nowhere to fall back to, no safe haven where we could rest and recuperate. It was fight, or die.

Dwight wouldn't give up. I knew that much about him. Hell, he'd stopped bitching, and that worried me more than anything else. He was grumpy old bastard, but he was husbanding his strength for the fight.

We were all strung out. I could see it as I looked around. Jordan was tight-lipped as he watched the Nationalists who were studying him with varying degrees of curiosity and a bit of hostility. Given how many of the "immigrants" who had been forced on Slovakia were Somalis and other Africans from the Sahel, I expected that they didn't have a lot of affection for black people. I just hoped that the fight at hand kept that whole nest of snakes under a rock, because Jordan was way too strung out to keep his temper under control if things got racial.

All of us were wearing the same beat-down, hangdog expression. It wasn't depression, not really. We'd been concentrating too hard on staying alive to think too much about how bad our situation really was. It was just exhaustion. The only one who didn't seem like he was carrying an extra fifty pounds that nobody could see was Greg. True to his character, he had found a group at one of the firing slits, and was trying to strike up a conversation, asking for the names for things in Slovak. Greg was just too friendly for this business.

"I'm going to take a look up top, is that all right?" I asked the big guy. I wanted a better look at the situation, and without drones of our own, that was going to mean getting some elevation.

"The windows are not sandbagged up there," he said, sounding a little uncertain. "It is not as safe as down here."

"Not as safe, maybe," I said, without adding that staying safe wasn't going to win the battle. "But I want to see more. I'll stay away from the windows; I've done this before."

Even as I said it, I had a sudden flashback to a year before, just before I'd gotten my own team. Hartrick and I had climbed an abandoned building just outside one of the no-go zones in Detroit, to run overwatch for a relief convoy after a rash of bombings downtown had killed dozens and left half the city without food or water when the truck drivers had refused to venture past the suburbs. That had felt similar, setting up well back from the window with a pair of 6.5 Creedmoor RPRs, watching for the gangs to try to hit the responders. The convoy drivers hadn't known we were there, but they hadn't complained later, either, after we knocked a hijack operation back on its heels with aimed fire.

I could still picture the blood spatter on the windshield of the old Corolla, and the shocked expression on the face of the right-seater, just before I snuffed him out, too.

The big man still looked a little doubtful, but he nodded. I'd hoped that he'd decide that we projected enough of an air of professionalism, despite our bone-crushing fatigue, that he wouldn't get in our way too much. Apparently, we'd succeeded.

I beckoned Chris to come with me. I didn't want to take too many up with me, but Chris was a bit better at long range than Phil was.

We mounted the steps, climbing two at a time. I don't know about Chris, but I was simply forcing my body to do what I wanted it to at that point. I was struggling to keep my breathing deep and even by the time we hit the third floor.

Nobody had done anything up there; the offices were still set up, if abandoned. The computer screens were dark, but it still looked like things had just been closed down for the weekend.

I realized I had no idea what day of the week it was. Hell, I wasn't sure what day of the month it was.

The windows, fortunately, weren't all that large, and were set high enough off the floor that I could crouch down and look out from just over the sill. Unfortunately, there was a good-sized tree, the leaves turning bright yellow, right outside, obscuring a good chunk of my field of view.

Not all of it, though. I could see the smoke rising from the burning ZSUs in the parking lot across the traffic circle, and see some of the tracers ricocheting high over the edge of town, punctuated every once in a while by the billowing gray-and-black cloud of an explosion. The fighting had already kicked off.

I got up and moved back, letting my rifle dangle on its sling as I grabbed a desk and started pushing it toward the window. Chris joined me, and we got it up against the wall. I had to stack some books as a rest, but I got my rifle set up so that I could use the scope with a fair degree of stability.

Movement flickered above the fighting. I couldn't make out just what I was looking at, not at first. Whatever it was was too small. But a moment later, the dark speck dove toward the ground and disappeared. A few seconds after that, a small, muted *boom* sounded, and a dark wisp of smoke and dust rose into the sky,

The big guy downstairs hadn't been kidding. The enemy were using kamikaze drones against Nationalist positions.

Not that they were a particularly new threat. They'd been common weapons for at least a decade by that point. But it's one thing to know that. It's another to know that the enemy has them in the air, over your head, poised to blot you out in a puff of smoke and fire.

Another explosion, a much bigger one, rocked the town. A huge, gray mushroom cloud rose up above the roofs. That wasn't a drone; that had to have been an IED.

Even though I'd told the big guy that I just wanted a better view of the situation, I was looking for targets. Anything we could do to slow the enemy advance down was going to help, and from my position, I could knock off enemy infantry with only a slim chance of being detected.

As I'd told the big guy, I'd done this before.

But as the weapons fire and explosions to the north got more intense, there was no sign that either the Nationalists were falling back, or that the enemy was breaking through. I'd gathered that the plan was to fall back by stages, whittling the EDC and the Slovak Army down block by block, street by street. But I didn't know what the signal was to retreat, and it was looking and sounding an awful lot like a pitched battle out there, rather than a holding action prior to breaking contact.

Two more massive explosions rocked the building, the shockwaves rattling the window in front of us. A moment later, half a dozen drones, just that I could see, made their suicidal dives, blasting more of the Nationalists to bits. Or attempting to; I'd gotten a better look at one of them, and they weren't large. They couldn't carry the same payload as a HOT-3 missile or a Hellfire, so it was entirely possible that they might be venting their fury uselessly against hardened positions. I hoped so.

Nevertheless, it was apparent that *somebody* was taking a hell of a shellacking out there.

***

After another hour, things started to die down. No Nationalist forces had fallen back. One of the Slovaks from downstairs came to the top of the steps and yelled. I thought he was asking if we were still alive, which was a bit asinine. If one of those drones had hit the building, they'd have known it downstairs.

Still, we at least had a breather for the moment. I tapped Chris and we left our hide site, following the Nationalist fighter downstairs.

"What did you see?" the big man asked.

"Lots of explosions and kamikaze drones," I replied. "But nobody falling back, and nobody getting through, either."

He nodded. "They led with foreign militias," he said. "They did not do well."

I could imagine. Most of those militias were heavy on the jihadist fighters, and they liked a lot of spray-and-pray, and didn't often use cover that well. Running out into the middle of the street with a PKM under the arm and dumping half the belt seemed to be their favorite maneuver.

I'd seen it in Africa, and I'd seen it again in Detroit and Philadelphia. And too many other American cities.

"Now what?" I asked.

"The militias fell back after taking heavy losses," the big man said. "*Major* Kysely said that the forward elements are staying in place for now."

I nodded. "So," I said, "Now we wait."

It was the way of combat. Nothing ever goes entirely according to plan, and just when you get keyed up to fight, the fight goes somewhere else.

Not that it wasn't going to come to us eventually. It would. We just had to take the breather without losing the edge.

Because it wasn't a reprieve. It was a breather. Nothing more.

Chapter 26

It stayed quiet longer than I'd expected, given the intensity of the initial bombardment.

Sure, we still heard the echoing crackle of small arms fire and the occasional explosion. But the stretch of Bratislavkà Street that we could see remained empty. We still stayed away from the unshielded windows; the enemy's kamikaze drones could still be spotted from time to time, and every once in a while, a distant *thump* marked when somebody hadn't been quite careful enough.

Of course, I was pretty sure that the Nationalists had a few of those, as well. I wondered how many of them they were expending before the next push came.

The day dragged on, and time slowed to a crawl as we watched the approaches, and each other.

The language barrier kept us from interacting much with our Slovak counterparts, but that wasn't all of it. There was some tension there, as if they weren't sure of us. Some openly seemed to resent our presence, looking at us with disdain when they had to look at us at all. While on an intellectual level, I kind of understood, given that American forces had been backing up the "peacekeeping" forces that had been hell-bent on crushing Slovakian sovereignty, and, in some cases, had protected the militias that had committed atrocities against the local populace, at the same time, it pissed me off. Whatever had happened before, the EDC and their cronies and proxies were as much our enemies as they were the Slovaks'. And we were there, defending *their* city, when we could be running for the border.

While we didn't have a lot of choice—helping with the defense was a necessity of the immediate situation, and the price we had to pay for their assistance in getting to Poland—the fact that we were still stepping up, only to get the stink eye from some of these guys, didn't play well with my temper, which was already worn raw by exhaustion and combat stress.

And I wasn't exactly alone.

Two of the Slovaks manning one of the vz. 59s at the corner were glancing over at where Jordan, Phil, and I were sitting against the wall. One of them murmured something to his comrade, and they both looked pointedly at Jordan.

"You gonna let them eye-fuck you like that, Jordan?" Phil asked.

Oh hell. Phil had apparently recuperated enough to get his mouth back up and running.

"I mean, I sure wouldn't," he continued. "Looks to me like they're wondering if you're a Somali or some shit."

Jordan, somehow, apparently hadn't noticed the looks. Which was a little surprising, given how sensitive he could be. He looked over at the two Slovaks.

"The fuck you looking at?" he demanded.

Dammit, Phil.

Before I could interject, though, Reuben spoke up from across the room. "Let it go, Jordan, for fuck's sake." He looked across the room at us. "Why do you keep letting other people jerk you around like that? You can't change your skin color, and you can't change the skin color of other assholes these guys might have dealt with. You keep letting other people knock that chip off your shoulder, and eventually you or somebody else is gonna get hurt, who doesn't need to be."

"Yeah, when your mom dies from getting beaten up by skinheads, then come talk to me," Jordan snapped. "Until then, mind your own business."

"Really, motherfucker?" Rueben turned away from his firing position, getting genuinely pissed. And being the massive dude that he was, when Reuben finally got pissed, he got a little threatening. "Get the fuck over yourself. You think you're the only one who's ever lost anybody? You think you're the only one who's ever been picked on for the color of his skin? I've had it with this race bullshit you're always shoving in everybody's face.

You're not fucking special, so quit picking fights with your own fucking team because you can't control your fucking emotions."

Jordan's face had gone rigid. Despite my own mounting anger, I could tell what was going on. It had nothing, really, to do with Jordan's eternal touchiness or even Reuben's intense dislike of identity politics.

We'd been sitting there waiting for a fight, keyed up and ready to slay bodies for hours. The longer the fight was delayed, the more strung out we were getting, and on top of the hellish last couple weeks, it was straining the team to the breaking point.

I needed to do something, and quick. "Shut the fuck up, all of you," I growled. "You know what? Push. All three of you."

Phil looked at me with a little shock. For a moment, nobody said anything.

"What?" Phil asked.

"You fucking heard me," I snarled. "You jackasses want to start a fight in the hide, you've obviously got some nervous energy to burn off. Do pushups."

Phil glanced at Jordan, who was taken aback enough that he returned the look before looking back at me. I wasn't generally a martinet; I knew that I didn't have the background or the experience that some of my teammates did, so I tried to keep it low key and congenial. But I'd had enough. And I was the team lead. This entire lash-up was my responsibility, and I'd be damned if I let it come apart because discipline slipped due to fatigue and stress.

"I'd do it," Tony drawled. "Matt's got his mad-dog eye going."

That seemed to snap them all out of it. Tony never said much—hence his callsign of "Chatty"—but that meant that when he did open his mouth, people tended to listen, if only out of surprise.

Still looking a little shell-shocked, Phil leaned his rifle against the wall, got down on the office floor, and started doing pushups. He slowed almost immediately; extended combat ops weren't great for maintaining certain kinds of upper body training. Jordan did the same, more slowly. Reuben was already cranking them out.

The two Slovaks had watched this entire interplay with visible interest. I looked over and met one of their eyes.

"You want to join 'em?" I demanded.

The big guy, whom I'd found out was a former Slovak Army *Nadporučik*, or lieutenant, named Biskup, said something wryly in Slovak. Both men hastily diverted their attention to their sector.

I let the three push for a couple minutes, just long enough to get the message across without wearing them out. That could be counterproductive at that point. "All right, get up," I said. I waited until they were back upright before continuing.

"It's been a rough couple of weeks for all of us," I said. "No argument there. But you know what? *I don't care.* This isn't the fucking Army. We don't get to fall apart because the going gets tough. Just because the Army cats sat down on their butts in the rear doesn't mean shit to us." I pointed to the northeast. "You idiots want to explain to the enemy that you need a few minutes to get a schoolgirl spat out of your systems?" I spat on the floor. Impolite, maybe, but I was just disgusted enough that I didn't give a damn at that point. "Grow the fuck up and remember where the hell you are."

I stood suddenly. I could *feel* the rage thrumming in my veins. I needed to get back upstairs and take another look around. I needed to move, to *do* something. Truth be told, I was just as strung out and itching for a fight as the rest.

Chris joined me as I headed up the steps. I ignored him; I didn't want to talk. Chris seemed to sense that; he held his peace.

We got up to the third floor and moved low along the floor to our previous vantage point. Only then did I realize that Biskup had come with us.

"It is hard for all of us, I think," he said softly. "The waiting."

"Yeah, well," I said. "My guys should have known better."

"So should mine," Biskup replied. "Some of them have come from other cells, though. Some of them from Russian-supported cells."

Something in his voice made me turn away from the window to look at him. He met my gaze evenly, and nodded. "You should be careful," he said.

I nodded, grimacing sourly, as I turned back to the window. The tensions with Russia had been ratcheting up over the last few years, between actual Russian influence operations, expansionist moves in the Baltics, and certain people stateside finding the very existence of such operations to be a convenient scapegoat for *everything* happening that they didn't like. I couldn't help but suspect that the MGB was rubbing their hands every time an American politician pulled "Russia" out of their ass to blame somebody who didn't like their latest cockamamie scheme to waste more money. It only fed the Kremlin's own finely tuned paranoia.

And that paranoia had to have been passed on to their proxies in Europe, as well. Who knew what the American peacekeepers had been accused of during cell meetings and planning sessions?

A rippling series of explosions that lit up the dimming horizon suddenly jerked me out of my reverie. A crackling roar of small arms fire was followed by a distant but unmistakable rumbling and squealing. It was the shriek of well-worn metal rubbing together.

Tracks.

"Heads up down there!" I barked down the stairs. "Incoming!"

I got down behind my rifle, finding the scope with my eye and scanning the darkened Bratislavskà Street ahead, watching for movement.

For a long time, there wasn't much. Drones circled and swooped above the industrial and commercial section of Mlynàrce ahead, while flashes and flickers of tracers preceded *booms*, *thuds*, and harsh *cracks*. There was a lot of fighting going on out there, but none of it had reached us, yet.

But it did seem to be getting closer.

I heard a crackle of an electronic voice behind me. Biskup had a radio to his ear; apparently the Nationalists had managed to get some kind of comms up, though they might well be transmitting in the clear, using code phrases. I didn't know, and right then wasn't the time to ask.

"The lead elements are abandoning their positions and falling back," he reported. "They have taken heavy losses. The recognition signal will be blue chemlights." He paused, listening. "The Army is coming. They are bringing tanks and BVPs, with infantry moving ahead to clear out anti-tank teams and IEDs, and hunter-killer drones in support."

I just nodded, keeping my eye on my sector. The drones would be used to try to neutralize any pockets of resistance, and lacking that ability, the infantry would push into the buildings to clear them, unless resistance was too heavy. In that case, the tanks and BVPs, which were a Czechoslovakian version of the Soviet BMP fighting vehicle, would bring heavier firepower to bear.

At least, that was what I gathered. There had been a time, not long past, when international sentiment would have negated that kind of use of firepower. Western forces were expected to minimize collateral damage, which meant precision-guided munitions and careful raids.

Given that the EDC had been using increasingly savage jihadist militias as their proxy forces in Slovakia, it was apparent that the old rules no longer applied. Never mind the artillery barrages that had preceded the assault.

More flashes. More grumbling thunder of explosions. A massive fireball rose into the sky; I doubted that was a cannon shell. More likely, the retreating force had had a nice, big IED prepped to cover their retreat.

The shooting died down a bit as the forward elements disengaged. I could see drones swarming around the buildings ahead, but I held my fire. Shooting one of them down might just give away our position and draw more of them to that window. It was time to be patient and wait.

A blue chemlight appeared through the smoke still drifting off the wrecked air defenses in the mall parking lot. A pair of figures came running through the trees, pausing behind the boles to cover their comrades, who ran past them and across the traffic circle. I noticed that they were avoiding the gas station to the north, and could imagine why.

272

Their route wasn't the best they could have chosen, though; the traffic circle was wide open, and the drones had penetrated deeper into the city. Movement caught my eye, and I shifted my sight picture to find the drone that was even then stooping on the running men.

Chris and I both fired at the same time. One of us missed. The other caught the drone in the wing and sent it spinning into the ground, where it detonated.

We missed the second remote-control kamikaze, though. It plunged down and blew up a foot above one running Nationalist's head. The sudden, ugly black puff shrouded the carnage, but as the smoke cleared, there were three bodies lying on the grass, motionless. The other four Nationalist fighters kept running. There wasn't anything they could do for the fallen men, anyway. And staying in the open was a recipe for disaster.

A half-dozen drones were suddenly buzzing nearby, searching for the source of the shots that had dropped one of their number. I had to wonder how many drone operators the EDC had working, or if these were the new, semi-autonomous ones that all the tech magazines had been wetting themselves about lately. If the latter, they were going to have a hard time finding us. Bots still needed very strict search parameters, or else they locked up.

The guys with the blue chemlight made a run for it. Another drone stooped on them, but got shot out of the sky from the other side of the traffic circle. The last of the forward fighters disappeared between the buildings to the south.

It had all happened with nightmarish rapidity. The drones were small targets, especially in the dying light and drifting smoke that hung like a pall over Mlynàrce, and they moved fast.

We stayed still, as much as the situation made me want to move, to maneuver, to go out and take the fight to the enemy, to do something to help those guys out in the open. But that would have been suicide.

So, we waited and watched, as the drones patrolled, circling around above our heads, looking for us.

After what might have been a half an hour, I started to see more movement down by the road.

Getting on my scope, I scanned until I spotted a human silhouette down by the trees on the side of the parking lot across the traffic circle. The man was wearing a helmet, body armor, and carrying a rifle. Probably not militia, then. Slovak Army. I doubted that the EDC themselves would be leading the charge.

He paused, holding up a hand to signal a halt, taking a knee next to the tree, and I almost lost him. But after a moment I thought I saw why he'd stopped. And why it had taken them so long to advance that far.

He was pointing, and a moment later a small, tracked robot moved forward, a manipulator arm poised above its chassis. He thought he'd spotted another IED.

So, they were advancing carefully, sweeping for IEDs as they came. That was a good idea. Except when the enemy had overwatch on the IEDs themselves.

"Chris, you seeing this?" I asked.

"Yeah," he replied.

"Biskup, how many IEDs are in that area?" I asked, without taking my eye from the scope.

"IEDs?" he asked.

"Bombs," I clarified. Apparently, the Slovak lieutenant's knowledge of English didn't extend to US military acronyms.

"Ah," he said. "There are several at that intersection, and the petrol station is rigged with many explosives." He paused. "There are two, I think, that are supposed to be obvious."

I nodded faintly. It wasn't a new tactic. Set an obvious trap to force the enemy into the less-obvious one. "Well, shall we make it even more obvious?"

My finger was already tightening on the trigger as I spoke. Any step to slow the enemy advance down would help.

My rifle *cracked*, and a moment later, the robot hitched a little in its movement, plastic blasting away as the bullet punched a hole into its electronic vitals. It wasn't hardened, then. Good.

Chris had fired at the same time I had, and the pointman slumped to the ground behind the tree.

The nearby drones were suddenly swarming more closely, and it was making me nervous. We had the window open to facilitate shooting, and if one of those things flew in…

I fired again, putting another bullet into the bomb robot as it hitched forward. That must have hit something vital, because it suddenly stopped and didn't move again.

For a long moment, everything stopped; no more infantry showed themselves. I glanced over, to see that the man Chris had shot had been dragged out of sight. They were there, but they were being smart; they didn't know exactly where the shots had come from, but they had some idea, and they weren't exposing themselves.

Then the sloped, sharp-edged prow of a BVP infantry fighting vehicle loomed around the curve, the rattle and squeal of its tracks reaching us faintly from two hundred yards away.

"Oh, shit," Chris muttered. While it wasn't a tank, that 30mm cannon could still do a number on our position, especially since we hadn't fortified it with more sandbags.

But Biskup was grinning. "Perfect," he said. He had something in his hand, and pressed a button.

Something on the side of the road blew up with a puff of dust and smoke and an ugly *thump*. The BVP rocked, sparks flying from its flank, and slewed to a halt halfway across the street. The commander's hatch opened and a figure bailed out, just as the vehicle started to burn.

I didn't see anyone else make it out.

There was a momentary lull after that, but it didn't last long. While no more infantry or vehicles showed themselves, the drones over the traffic circle suddenly went nuts.

"Down!" Chris yelled, and the three of us were suddenly trying to cram ourselves under the desk as a drone dove at the window.

Three drones hit the side of the building. The one aiming for our window almost killed us. If the operator, or the AI, had been just a little more precise, it would have.

Instead, it clipped the open window with a wing and smacked into the window frame before detonating. The heavy, tooth-jarring *thud* of the explosion shook the room, and fragmentation pattered against the walls, but we'd gotten low enough and had enough of the desk between us and the explosion to avoid the worst of it. I still felt a fiery sting in my leg, and had to reach down and check that it hadn't clipped anything that was going to leak too much. My hand found the rent in my trousers and the piece of viciously hot frag underneath it, and I was able to pull it out myself, though it hurt like the devil to do it.

We stayed down, contorted into painful positions against the base of the wall as we tried to stay as small as possible, waiting for the other shoe to drop.

But it didn't. Whether they didn't have enough drones to try to clear out the whole building, or they just weren't exactly sure where the snipers or trigger man were, no more suicidal RC airplanes came at us.

My paranoia was finely-tuned enough that I just *knew* that the enemy were moving on us while we had our heads down. It's basic combat tactics. So, I forced myself to get up, levering my OBR up over the shrapnel-pocked desk, and got back on glass.

Just in time to see the front of one of the buildings that Bradshaw's guys had occupied disappear in a blast of grit, smoke, and fire as a tank shell blew half the wall apart.

I didn't have a great view, so I had to hear about what Bradshaw did later.

I didn't see him grab three Matadors and charge out of his own hide site, despite the protests of his Slovak counterpart. Nor could I see him take a knee in the middle of Ôdora va Street, calmly take aim at the T-72 that had just shot at his boys, and slam a 90mm HEAT round into its flank. He dropped the tube, grabbed another one, and shot the BVP behind the tank, even as the giant plume of flame—which I *could* see, even through the dust and smoke—shot up out of the T-72's turret.

The Slovaks and other Triarii opened fire on the advancing enemy to cover the crazy American as he dashed toward the wrecked building, still lugging the third Matador.

I couldn't see him start hauling mangled bodies out of the remains of the building's front, helped by blood-smeared and shell-shocked men, even as more maneuvered out to provide covering fire. I did see the blast as he got his third armored vehicle kill of the evening, though. The flames rose like a roman candle above the parking lot.

***

"Deacon, Flat." Bradshaw's voice was almost unrecognizable, hoarse and scratchy.

"Send it, Flat," I replied.

"Štùrova Street is blocked," he reported. "They're trying to maneuver around it. We've had to fall back to the marshalling area." He paused for a moment. "I'm down four guys."

I could hear the pain in his voice, as hard as he tried to hide it. It had been a hell of a blow, and he'd lost men on this op already. If I remembered the numbers right, his section was down to about two thirds strength.

"Roger," was all I said in acknowledgement. Bradshaw understood. We could mourn the men who died later. Right now, we had a battle to fight.

And I could already hear the squeal and rattle of tracks on the other side of the trees, in the mall parking lot. With the left flank having fallen back, we were now Target Number One.

Chapter 27

I pulled back from the window and turned to Biskup. He was still down on the floor, while Chris and I had popped back up to be able to see and shoot.

"We need to relocate," I said. "Fast. If they've already got this building targeted with drones, they're going to follow up with something heavier, soon enough."

He didn't argue, but started toward the stairs, keeping low. "There is a trench just past the corner," he said. "It leads to a better street crossing."

I hoped that that street crossing had some cover, but even if it didn't, we were out of options.

We just about flew down the stairs as another flight of drones slammed into the top floor. At least one made it through the open window, the *thud* of the explosion shaking the entire building as shrapnel sleeted through the air and shredded everything in the office we'd just vacated. Smoke, dust, and whirling debris boiled down the stairs after us, and we dropped onto the ground floor in a hot, choking black cloud.

"Everybody out!" I bellowed. "They've got us zeroed!"

"This way!" Biskup yelled, grabbing Chris by the arm as we started toward the door we'd come in through. "There is a back door!"

We hustled after him, joined by his Slovak Nationalists, who were lugging the vz. 59s and a collection of AKs, Bren 805s, and vz. 58s.

Biskup threw the door open and plunged out, which might not have been the wisest course, but as a tank shell obliterated the room we'd been using for overwatch, clearing the immediate area outside the door suddenly seemed to be a lot less of a priority. We followed, even as a sharp *crack* sounded behind us.

Biskup was already down in the trench that had been hastily scraped in the ground behind the building, leading across the yard in front of the neighboring office building, running in a half-crouch. There wasn't anything to do but follow him.

The trench wasn't that deep; it might have gone down about four feet. Which was better than nothing, but it only provided so much cover, and running bent over gets taxing very quickly, especially if you're already running on fumes beforehand. But we got to the crossing, which was partially covered by a hasty barricade set up with cars flipped on their sides and the liberal application of barbed wire, just before a missile streaked down out of the sky above and smacked into the already burning building we'd just vacated.

I hadn't heard a fast-mover or a helicopter, so my guess was it had been launched by a high-flying, stealthy drone. Something small enough that the remaining SAM teams would have a hard time spotting it before it delivered its payload.

Biskup paused just before the crossing, scanning the sky overhead. I did the same, but neither of us could see the UAV that had launched on the building. Fortunately, there were a lot of trees that hadn't dropped their leaves yet, so we had some overhead concealment. Less than we might have liked, but there was nothing ideal about this situation. The EDC wanted the Slovak Nationalists crushed with a quickness, and they were expending a *lot* of firepower to do it.

Fortunately, they seemed to have assumed that their plans were going to work as they'd drawn them up, which was why we'd managed to slow them down as much as we had already.

"That noise," Biskup said quietly. "That must have been one of the mines at the edge of the circle." I nodded. It made sense; the Nationalists had probably sowed the treeline around the edge of the mall parking lot with anti-tank mines and similar nasty surprises.

Without waiting for any further acknowledgement, Biskup got up and dashed across the street, keeping low behind the barricade. A moment later, I waved at Phil to follow him, only crossing myself once Phil and another one of Biskup's guys were across.

It was hardly the first danger area crossing I'd done, and far from the widest. It still felt far more dangerous than anything I'd done before. No danger area I'd seen in Africa, or even the no-go zones Stateside, had ever had tanks and drones hunting me as I exposed myself.

Still, I got across and found a reasonably covered spot near the two-story apartment building on the other side, taking up security as I waited for the rest of the team and the Nationalist fighters to cross.

I was pleasantly surprised that we all made it without being fired upon. Maybe the enemy thought they'd gotten us with that drone's HOT-3 missile. I doubted it, but things had to be pretty confused in the EDC/Slovak headquarters by then. The Nationalists had already bloodied the offensive badly, just in the first few hours of the push.

From there, we started bounding from house to house, in twos and threes. It was dark, and all the lights in the city were out, except for the lurid orange glow to the northwest, from burning buildings and burning vehicles. It was an eerie, hellish scene, even in the white phosphor glow of my NVGs, as we moved through what had clearly once been an affluent, modern neighborhood, while the industrial area beyond burned, along with the bodies of those who hadn't made it out of their steel tombs.

We paused in the trees, just before crossing Pàrovskà Street to the VBC building, which had been sandbagged up inside and outside. They'd hardened it as much as possible, including boarding up the top windows to keep the flying glass down. Unlike our previous position, there would be no mistaking this place for anything but a strongpoint.

If this went on much longer, there wouldn't be a building standing that wasn't a strongpoint, even if it had been blasted halfway to rubble. The Nationalists seemed entirely willing to turn Nitra into a miniature Stalingrad.

Not that I could blame them.

Biskup called ahead on his own radio, and only after he got a response did he stand up and wave us forward.

He'd gotten halfway across the street when a buzz penetrated my battered hearing.

I grabbed Phil and threw him back down, even as I lifted my rifle, searching for the drone. There. It was already on its dive, and I knew I was probably too late as I snapped the weapon to my shoulder and took a snap-shot, barely using the sights at all.

By some miracle, I hit it, and it spun out of control. But it was already on its terminal dive, and it exploded six feet off the ground, shrapnel sleeting into Biskup as he ran. He crumpled in a heap on his face, blood quickly darkening his camouflage fatigues.

Two of the Nationalists were already running down the steps to grab him. I swept the sky with my eyes and my rifle, but the drone seemed to have been a singleton. That time. There was no telling that there weren't another two dozen just around the corner, already zooming in on the sound of the explosion.

"Move!" I was yelling at the other Nationalist fighters as well as my own team. "Get off the street!"

Of course, Dwight didn't entirely heed me, instead taking up a position near my and propping his Mk 48 against a tree, covering up the street in the other direction. "I'm getting too old and slow," he growled, "I need a breather."

Being Dwight, his fatigue and age had little to do with it. He wasn't going to run for cover while I was out there with just a rifle, covering the rest from the drones.

Still, especially with Chris and Scott helping herd the Slovaks, we got everybody across in seconds, crowding into the VBC building. "Matt!" Scott yelled from the doorway. "Turn and go!"

I thumped Dwight on the shoulder. "Let's go, old man," I barked. "Don't let me beat you to the door."

Dwight heaved himself to his feet and sprinted. He was still pretty quick for a man of his size, but I could still outdistance him quickly. I didn't. There was no way in hell I was running to cover and leaving Dwight in the open.

We got to the door as I thought I heard a dopplered buzzing behind me. "Move! Get to cover!"

The entryway had been turned into a firesack; there were sandbagged positions at the doorway itself, then another set just a couple yards inside. We dove for the second set, even as the Nationalist soldiers in the entryway lifted what looked like a makeshift armored door, cut out of half-inch steel.

The door rang like a bell, flame and smoke spurting around the edges, and one of the Slovaks yelped, snatching a bloody, mangled hand back from the edge. Smoke poured in, but the door had done its job. The drone had vented its fury on the outer entryway, instead of shredding us inside.

Jordan moved up to help the wounded man, while the rest of us got ourselves sorted. It was too late for Biskup; one of the Nationalists was pulling a jacket over his face. He hadn't survived the drone strike that had felled him.

Seeing that there wasn't room in the entryway for us, I pointed toward the south end of the building. "Jordan, we're going to see if we can't help out down this way," I said. "Catch up when you finish with him."

Jordan, absorbed in his task, just waved a blood-smeared hand to tell me he'd heard.

The rest of us moved down the hallway, looking for a place to set in and wait for the next blow to fall.

***

But it didn't, at least not right away.

We could still hear sporadic gunfire and explosions, but they came in short bursts and sudden, single reports. From our vantage point, Štùrova Street was still clear, except for the half-dozen cars and buses we could see, including one bus that had been parked across an entire lane. I could only imagine how much explosive had been crammed into those buses. After what I'd seen, the Nationalists hadn't left anything on the street without a purpose.

Still, it had been over an hour, with no follow-on attack forthcoming. I didn't think that we'd hurt the enemy badly enough to make them give up, but it definitely seemed like they were reworking their plans.

We'd set up shop in a ground floor office, with two windows facing down Štùrova Street toward the enemy positions.

It was big enough for the whole team, plus the half-dozen Nationalist fighters who'd already been occupying it.

"Scott," I called, turning away from the slit left in the sandbags stacked against the window. He hurried over. "Let's go to fifty percent," I said. "Nobody drops gear or takes their boots off, but if we can get a little bit of sleep before the next push, let's do it." We'd been moving and fighting for a long time, and as we'd seen just a little while before, it was taking its toll. "I'll take the first watch, so get the rotation started, then you go down, too."

He looked like he was going to object, but I stopped him. "My team, my call, Scott. Just set it up and get some rest."

He nodded heavily, and turned away as I looked out at the deserted street, dimly lit by the distant flicker of the fires.

In less than five minutes, half the team was down, finding any semi-comfortable spot. Dwight started snoring like a runaway chainsaw in moments.

***

I let them sleep for just about two hours. The time mostly passed in silence; none of us who were still up were in a talkative mood, not after all that had happened, and what was sure to happen again soon. The stillness and lack of activity immediately started to get to me, and by the time I shook Scott awake, my eyes were aching, and every fiber of my being was ready to fall down and sleep for a week.

It took a minute for Scott to get coherent enough to start waking the rest. After that, I made sure the others who'd stayed up went down before I finally found a stretch of floor with a sandbag to use as a pillow, wrapped my rifle sling around my arm, the OBR against my side, and closed my eyes.

***

I was back in Baltimore, on some hit that I knew I should remember, but somehow didn't. Everything was just slightly off. I knew it was Baltimore, but it looked like Seattle.

Phil and I were at the door, ready to breach. Dwight, Scott, Reuben, and Tony were on the cordon. I looked at Phil, who had his rifle leveled at the door, and gave me the nod. I pivoted and donkey-kicked the door.

It cracked, but held. I kicked it again. It still didn't open. I could hear movement and yelling inside. I kicked it a third time, and it still held shut. Then a burst of gunfire tore through it and blew Phil off his feet with a spray of blood.

I kicked the door again and again. For whatever reason, I just kept trying to get the breach open, even as Jordan dropped, blood spurting from a bullet wound in his throat.

A drone dropped out of the sky and blew Dwight and Reuben to bloody doll rags. I kept frantically kicking the door, frozen in place otherwise.

The sound of an armored vehicle rumbled down the street, shaking the entire house, which now suddenly looked like my parents' place. A T-72 was rolling down the streets of Baltimore, fire flickering from its coax PKT machinegun. Bullets tore Scott and Tony to pieces, and tracked up onto the porch, searching for David, Greg, Chris, and I.

***

I forced my eyes open. My heart was pounding. I stared at the ceiling, or what I could see of it. There wasn't much light inside the VBC building.

I struggled to breathe slowly and deeply. Just a dream. *Just a dream.* We were still alive. Despite everything that had been thrown at us over the last week and a half, we were still alive.

But for how much longer? Even as relief that the dream had been nothing more than that flooded over me, the real depth of our plight came crashing back down. We were in the middle of a besieged city, surrounded by enemies and not-quite-friends. The entire city had been laced with explosives. And the nearest real friendlies were a long, long way away.

Lord, I don't want to fail. Please, please, whatever happens to me, don't let me die letting my guys down. I know it's selfish, but if we're going to die, please let me go first. I don't want to watch that for real.

It took a long time to get back to sleep. The vivid images of my teammates and brothers getting shot to pieces wouldn't go away. I think by the time I finally drifted off again, it was probably less than thirty minutes before Scott was supposed to wake me up.

I awoke to the sound of distant gunfire.

"Flat, Deacon," I called, as I rolled to my knees and levered myself up off the floor. Everything hurt, and I wasn't exactly bursting with energy, either.

"Send it, Deacon." Bradshaw sounded worse than I felt. I wondered if he'd gotten any rest, or if he'd been engaged all night. It was starting to get light, the darkness no longer quite so impenetrable. I suddenly felt guilty. If Bradshaw had been fighting, while my team and I had been sitting here resting...

"Do you have eyes on the fighting to the south?" I asked. I could see smoke rising that way, but little else.

"Negative," he replied. "We've been firm just off Kollàrova Street since we fell back. But it sounds big. Like they shifted their axis of attack to the south."

Before I could respond, there was a sudden crash of heavy-caliber fire off to the east. It sounded like tank guns. Several of them.

"Deacon," Bradshaw said, with a growing urgency. "That came from behind us."

There was some commotion toward the east side of the building. I got up and hustled over there, looking for somebody in charge.

"You are the Americans?" an accented voice asked. I turned, my hand still on my rifle, just in case. But this guy, who looked about in his forties, with a thick mustache, had his vz. 58 slung and was wearing a full Slovak Army uniform, though with the Nationalist armband around his sleeve.

"We're some of them, yes," I answered.

"We need to be ready to fall back to the north," he said. "The enemy broke through with tanks up Cintorinska Street. They have targeted any possible strongpoint with drones, and have been blowing up our car bombs with tank fire."

"I've got men on the south side of Štùrova Street," I protested. "We can't leave without them."

"If we do not leave, we will be the next to be blown to pieces," the shorter man replied. "Are you coming?"

I looked toward where I'd heard the tank fire.

"Not without my boys," I told him.

"Suit yourself, American," the man said, turning away. "But there is not much time left."

I turned back toward our little redoubt. "Scott!" I bellowed. "Get everybody up and ready to move! We need to break Bradshaw out of that pocket before the EDC and the Loyalists close the noose!"

Chapter 28

Of course, trying to break an armored pincer movement with a ten-man team is far more easily said than done. I was wracking my brain to figure out a plan, even as we gathered what little gear we'd put down, along with an RPG-75 or Matador for each man. The weight would slow us down, but we needed every bit of punch we could get.

And it still wouldn't be enough. I knew that.

But I didn't see another way out. I was dead tired, and the nightmare of watching my team get cut to ribbons in front of me haunted my thoughts as we prepped, and Scott and I pored over the map, trying to figure out how to attack this. We were too few. We were all going to die.

And yet.

I couldn't leave Bradshaw and his guys to die. I wouldn't. Even if it meant going in alone. Even if it meant I failed, and died before I could get them out. Better that, than to turn tail and save myself.

And the truth was that even as I felt like I was demanding that the rest of the team commit suicide with me, I knew that if I spoke up and made it a volunteer-only mission, they'd take it as an insult. We were Triarii. We were a Grex Luporum team. We didn't leave our brothers behind while we ran for safety. Every one of these men, even Jordan at his testiest, or Phil at his most mouthy and assholish, would throw themselves at Hell itself if it meant going after a comrade in trouble.

Even if it meant dying.

I didn't want to go out there. Out there, with the killer drones, and tanks, and airstrikes. I didn't want to die. The thought of it was twisting my guts as we worked, as I stared at the map and drew a complete blank as to just how we were going to do much of anything besides go out in a blaze of glory, maybe to be remembered by a few of the Slovak Nationalists, and hardly anyone else.

Scott wasn't looking at me; he was staring at the same map with a fixity that told me he was thinking much the same thing.

"Americans?" a heavily-accented voice asked from the doorway. I looked up to see a positively ancient-looking man, his beard snow-white beneath salt-and-pepper hair poking out from under a Slovak Army helmet. Like the burly, mustached man who had refused to help a few minutes before, he was carrying a vz. 58.

"Yeah," I said heavily. I didn't want to get in another argument with a Nationalist who didn't want to stick around.

"You are going out there?" he asked, pointing to the south, where the crackle of small arms fire was getting more intense, punctuated by the dull, heavy *thuds* of explosions.

I straightened up. "That's right," I said, as the team's eyes turned on him, hands not far from weapons. Every eye was on the crusty-looking old bastard, but he didn't take his eyes away from me, even though I got the distinct impression that he was well aware that he was the center of a lot of not-too-friendly attention.

He nodded. "Then we are coming with you," he said, motioning toward the doorway behind him. My eyes flicked over his shoulder, and saw the group of men, young and old, in a variegated collection of civilian clothes and camouflage, armed with just about everything from Bren 805s to old bolt-action Mausers. "This is our city. Those are our friends and family down there, not just yours," the old man continued. "Besides, no Slovak patriot should pass up the chance to kill more of the traitors who would sell their own country." He looked like he wanted to spit on the floor.

I looked over the group. They were rag-tag, but then, so were we. And they had more spine than our own Army did.

Maybe that was uncharitable. But we were down here fighting, while Warren and the others were sitting up there, refusing to engage the same people who had wiped out their own comrades, worried about political repercussions. There was bound to be a *little* bitterness.

"You're more than welcome," I told him. "We can use every gun we can get."

Something clicked. *Guns.* I might have an idea.

I ushered the old man over to the map. "Do you have radio contact with your artillery?" I asked. I hadn't heard much Nationalist artillery firing during the last day, though there had definitely been some. I didn't know how much had survived the air strikes or counterbattery fire.

"We can reach the Fire Direction Center, yes," the old man said. Clearly, he was more than just a militiaman who'd been called up by the Nationalists. Either he was former military, or he was a really fast learner. "I do not know how many batteries they have left."

"We might only need one," I said. "Can they preregister on these points, here?" I pointed out the three intersections I wanted targeted.

He peered at the map for a moment before calling one of the younger men over. The blond kid was lugging a radio, and handed the old man the handset. He spoke over it in Slovak, listened, then started to rattle off numbers. He was giving the coordinates. He looked up at me.

"Do they shoot now, or on command?" he asked.

"On command," I replied. I had a hunch that we were going to get one shot at this, and if the artillery fired too early, we were going to be out of position.

He spoke quickly into the handset, then handed it back to the kid, with a curt order that was unmistakable in tone, if not in language. *Stay close to me.*

Gunfire erupted from the east side of the building. A moment later, the building shuddered with a horrific *crash*. Dust billowed through the hall, and I thought I saw cracks in the wall as dust and debris sifted down from the ceiling.

"That's our cue, boys," I said, snatching the map up and shoving it in my chest rig. "Either we get out there and kill them, or they're going to bring this building down on our heads and kill us."

"Out the back," the old man snapped. "There is more cover there."

"You heard the man," I said. "Let's go."

Phil was already moving, hitching the RPG-75 higher up on his shoulder. Phil wasn't all that big, which meant he had less shoulder than, say, Dwight or Tony, to carry stuff.

We had to weave through the office spaces, making our way past more piles of desks, chairs, and electronics, as another hit on the building made the entire structure shudder ominously, aside from the shock of the initial impact. The dust and smoke in the air were getting thicker, and more and more of the Nationalists were joining us, bailing out of the VBC building before it collapsed under the hammering of 125mm shells.

There were already Nationalist fighters outside, in the parking lot on the north side of the roughly U-shaped building, along with a couple of ancient-looking, hastily up-armored trucks. One of them had a familiar antenna mounted on the roof of the cab, and I breathed a little easier. It looked a lot like the one I'd suspected was a drone jammer on the move out of Vrbovè. Hopefully, that meant we didn't have to worry so much about kamikaze drones blowing us up.

Provided they were remote-controlled, and not bot-controlled. That could get a little more dangerous.

Almost a dozen Nationalist fighters were crouched behind one of the trucks as bullets smacked into the armor, some with loud *bangs*, some ricocheting off with vicious whines. More rounds *snapped* overhead, smacking into the VBC building, breaking glass and smashing plaster and concrete, and we ran for cover, most tactical movement or formation forgotten for the moment.

A burly Slovak with a PKM leaned out in front of the truck's grill and ripped off what sounded like half a belt, the chattering roar momentarily drowning anything else out, spent brass cascading out onto the pavement to join the pile already there. Given that he was hip-shooting it, I doubted that he'd hit anything, but he'd kept some heads down, and given me a chance, as Phil, Greg, Tony, Chris, and I ran to the truck, to see a bit of what we were up against.

292

There was an armored vehicle squatting on the roadway behind the high-rise, just barely visible as a dark green shape through the trees and a handful of civilian vehicles. Men on foot were scattered between the trees, trading fire with the Nationalists while taking more fire from windows in the upper floors of the high-rise.

I was pretty sure the only reason that that vehicle hadn't already blasted the two up-armored trucks was that it simply didn't have that good a shot. It was barely visible around the corner, and seemed to be trying to maneuver, but having a hard time with the tight spaces.

I leaned out past the guy with the PKM and took a snapshot at a silhouette beneath the nearest tree. I might have missed, but he ducked, and I got a better look at the lay of the land.

"We've got to take that vehicle out," I yelled, even as PKM Guy leaned out and blew off the rest of his belt. I slung my rifle, cinching the sling tight, and pulled the Matador off my back.

I just needed to not get shot while I lined up the armored vehicle.

Of course, Tony and Dwight were way ahead of me. Tony went flat under the truck, and Dwight pushed to the back, similarly dropping to the prone and setting his Mk 48 on the bipods. Tony having been in position first, he went to work first.

There is something vaguely awe-inspiring about watching a pair of well-trained machinegunners synchronizing their fire. I'd gotten pretty good at it in the Marine Corps; being an 0331 kind of meant you either had to be able to run a machinegun like a virtuoso or you weren't suited to your MOS. But Tony and Dwight were better than I ever had been.

Tony's burst had barely ended when Dwight's ripped into the treeline. When Dwight let off, there was almost no pause before the roar of Tony's 48 picked back up again.

Frankly, they made the Slovaks look like amateurs.

Of course, I didn't have the time or the inclination to just admire their work. They didn't have the ammo for me to dawdle, either.

I sprinted to the tailgate of the truck, where I knelt and prepped the Matador. It was fairly simple, and the directions for arming and firing were laid out in a helpful graphic affixed to the side of the tube.

Down on one knee, I eased an eye out, over Dwight's shoulder, to locate my target. I got a better view from there, even though it was still half-hidden by a tree. It was wheeled; probably a BOV infantry fighting vehicle, not far off from a Stryker.

A bullet ricocheted off the truck next to my head with a loud *bang* and a nasty buzz, even as I pulled my head back. Dwight reacted immediately, despite the rhythm he had going with Tony, shifting his hips slightly to move his point of aim and ripping off a ten-round burst at the tree where the shooter was crouched. Bullets tore into the trunk, spewing splinters and bits of bark from the impacts, but I couldn't see if he'd hit the Loyalist soldier.

Short term, it didn't matter. He'd forced the man to put his head down, and that was my opening. Shouldering the Matador, I stepped out, dropped to a knee, and bellowed, "*Backblast area clear!*" as I leveled the sights on the boxy, dark green hull ahead of me.

I took a split second to steady my aim, then I squeezed the trigger. The rocket crossed the gap in an eyeblink, the *whoosh* of its motor lost in the jarring *wham* of its impact.

The vehicle rocked as the flash of the detonation momentarily engulfed it. When the smoke cleared, the BOV was burning fiercely, and the infantry were falling back, though in good order, firing bursts of covering fire as they dashed from tree to tree, avoiding the blazing hulk of the stricken BOV as the onboard ammunition started cooking off.

One of the things drummed into us as Triarii is that once you have the initiative, you've got to hold onto it. Attack, attack, attack. Dropping the spent Matador tube, I swept up my rifle and dashed forward, the weapon in my shoulder as I dropped prone behind a tree and got on sights, my finger already tightening on the trigger as a Slovak soldier, turning and spraying a burst back toward me, filled the aperture.

It was a hasty shot, so I only hit him in the shoulder. He staggered, thrown halfway around by the impact, and I dropped him with a follow-up shot that was so quick that I really didn't have time to think about it.

I hadn't issued orders, or yelled some inspiring war-movie, "Follow me!" I'd just acted. But training makes up for a lot of talking, and the rest of the team was moving with me, the Nationalists catching up as they figured out what we were doing. Chris pounded past me to another spot, taking cover right at the corner of the high-rise, while Tony and Reuben joined him. Cover was at a premium out there; the trees provided most of it, and few of them were that large.

I heaved myself to my feet and moved up quickly. There was a row of underground storage units or garages ahead, on the other side of the trees, beneath yet another high-rise apartment building. Even as I took cover, taking a shot at another Loyalist soldier who had turned to fire back at us, a tank round or missile hit one of the upper floors of the high-rise with a deep *bang*, sending debris cascading down into the street. The man who'd shot at me flinched away from the rain of deadly fragments, and I shot him, sending him spinning to his face on the pavement.

Unfortunately, while I had good cover, I was on the wrong side of the burning BOV. Cursing under my breath, I ran around it, feeling the heat beating against my face as I went, joining the rest of the team and a handful of Nationalist fighters at the steps leading up to the parking lot on the outside of the bigger high-rise attached to the VBC building.

The stairs provided some good cover, at least from fire coming from Štúrova Street. I looked around, spotted the oldster from inside, and waved at him to join me. He grabbed his radioman and ran, doubled-over, to join us.

"Can you call a fire mission on that intersection?" I asked.

"Yes," he replied, "provided the artillery has not moved too far to avoid the drones or counterbattery fire."

He didn't wait for my acknowledgement, but grabbed the handset and rapped out fast, clipped orders in Slovak. A moment later, he looked up. "Shot," he said.

I hadn't known that the Slovaks used the same verbiage for fire missions that we did. Or maybe he'd done some work with the Americans a long time ago, maybe in Afghanistan or someplace, and had learned there, and was just translating so that we'd understand.

The round came down out of the sky with a tearing hiss, and struck the red tile roof of the old, elegant row houses across the street. The old man was immediately shouting adjustments into the handset, and while I couldn't understand the rapid-fire Slovak, I knew roughly what he was calling. *Left fifty, drop ten, fire for effect.*

There was too much weapons fire rattling and thundering south of Štùrova Street for me to hear the reports of the howitzers or multiple launch rocket launchers up on the hill, but the scream of the incoming shells was distinct enough, even though the rattling and squealing of treads had told me that the Loyalist commander on the ground had identified the threat posed by that single artillery shell and had ordered his vehicles to scatter. They hardly had time, though.

The battery commander had been thinking. While the spotting round had been a regular high explosive, the full barrage detonated high in the air with a curiously muted series of *pop*s.

A split second later the intersection, and a good chunk of the buildings around it, disappeared in a rippling cloud of explosions, the overlapping detonations sounding like the crackle of the popcorn popper from Hell.

The subsequent detonations of tank magazines cooking off only added to the conflagration.

"Flat, Deacon!" I yelled into the radio, trying to be heard over the catastrophic noise that was echoing up and down the street. "The intersection is cleared, you need to head straight north to link up with us!"

"We would," Bradshaw replied, "but a mech infantry unit just pushed up Hollèho Street and has us pinned down! If we try to push out, we're going to get slaughtered."

Dammit. "We'll see if we can take some of the pressure off," I replied. I turned to the oldster. "Our guys are pinned down by another unit that pushed up Hollèho Street," I told him. "We need to flank that unit and get those guys out."

"Another artillery strike?" he asked.

"No, I think they're too far inside danger close," I replied, momentarily pulling the map out of my chest rig. "We'd be just as likely to kill our guys as the enemy." I spread it out where he could see it, and pointed out my plan quickly. "We'll cross here, get to the south side of these row houses. My team will set up there and hit them down this street, while you push past us and hit them another block to the south." I was cursing the openness of Nitra at that point. It had made that artillery strike go well, but it made it hard as hell to bottle anyone up. And reduced the amount of available cover.

But the old guy nodded. "There are improvised bombs here, here, and here," he said, pointing. "They should have been detonated when the enemy penetrated that far, but either the trigger-men were killed, or they abandoned their posts and ran. I know where the backup triggers should be."

"Good," I replied. I'd been in enough shitty guerrilla wars to know that I should hate even the idea of IEDs, but when you're outmatched, any advantage becomes a useful one. "Are your guys going to do it, or are we?"

"My men know the city better," he said. "You shoot, we will blow them up."

I nodded. "We don't have much time." I turned and quickly briefed my team on what we were about to do, in as few words and as little time as possible. It also gave the oldster time to pick his team and get ready to move.

"Bring the AT launchers, too," I said. "Bradshaw said mech infantry, so they've probably got BVPs, BOVs, or both." Or Pumas, if the Germans had come in with the Slovak Army, but this column seemed to be entirely Loyalists.

Then there was no more time to dawdle. I got up and led the way out onto the devastated street.

It should have been a lot more of a hair-raising crossing than it was. Smoke was drifting thickly down the street, and footing was less than ideal, given the debris and smashed asphalt under our boots. But the artillery barrage had done its job well, and anyone still north of the row houses was probably too shell-shocked to try taking a shot at us.

That didn't mean I took my time. I put my head down and sprinted as hard as I could for the south side of the street, probably setting a personal record for speed with gear and weapon.

297

I had aimed for the narrow street between row houses, and came out of the smoke to pause and take a knee behind a tree. The wall next to me seemed to have been unscathed by the fighting, so far, and was covered in blue graffiti that I couldn't read.

My pause lasted just long enough to make sure that I wasn't about to run into a long burst of machinegun fire. There were still a few vehicles parked along that street, but how many of them had been rigged as bombs, I didn't know. I did know that I didn't want to loiter too close to any of them for too long.

I started down the side of the street, my weapon up and ready, moving fast without running. Phil was on the other side, covering the angles that I couldn't see, while I did the same for him. We headed quickly down the street, the rest of the team falling into a staggered column behind us.

I kept glancing back as we went, checking as the rest of my team and the Nationalists entered the street. Several of the Slovaks quickly disappeared into the building on the right, behind Phil and Greg. I hoped they were the triggermen.

We got to the end of the street without meeting any opposition, though the rattle of small arms fire, punctuated by the *chunk, chunk, chunk* of heavier stuff, was intensifying as we went. Bradshaw and his boys were in a bad way, and we needed to hurry.

The street ended in a T-intersection, with trees on one side and a blocky, gray-and-orange building on the other. Phil paused at the intersection, and I held my corner until David came up and popped it, allowing me to move across the street and join Phil, Greg, and Jordan. Greg and Jordan still had RPG-75s, and from what I saw as I crossed, we were going to need them. There were squat, angular, dark green shapes squatting at the end of the street ahead, about a hundred forty yards away.

I dropped prone in the street, getting behind my rifle and preparing to cover the RPG gunners. We were still completely undetected, from what I could see; the Loyalists' entire focus seemed to be on Bradshaw and his Nationalist companions.

"Go," I hissed. Greg had slung and cinched down his rifle, and had his RPG-75 in his hands, as he dashed forward to the next corner, where the row houses opened up on a sort of courtyard between them, Jordan on his heels. Phil had headed farther out into the street, moving to my left and getting down beside me behind his rifle.

That was when we got spotted, and everything went to hell.

One of the Loyalist soldiers happened to look over his shoulder. We were close enough that I could see his expression through my scope, and saw his eyes widen as he swung his Bren 805 around toward us. He was just a little too slow; he had been facing the wrong way and Phil and I were already on sights. Our shots blended together into a single, harsh *crack*, and he dropped like a puppet with its strings cut, his helmet half blown off by Phil's round.

Then a full half-dozen Loyalists, who had been crouched behind the BVP squatting at the intersection, turned and started shooting.

From where we were lying, we had good shots, and didn't have to move much. I shot one, hitting him high in the chest, and he staggered, but apparently was either a tough bastard, or was wearing body armor, because he didn't go down. I shot him again, and was a little too high. The round tore out his throat in a spray of blood and he fell.

I'd barely let the trigger reset before I was settling on the next one. Double tap. I saw him fall and shifted to the next, as bullets flew so close overhead that I could actually feel the shockwaves, and others spat up chunks of asphalt to right and left.

Then Greg apparently decided that enough was enough, and took the chance. He leaned out, leveled his RPG-75, and fired.

It was a decently long shot for an RPG, but while Greg might come across as a little goofy at times, he knew his business. The round flew straight and true, and smashed into the BVP's flank just as the turret got almost all the way around.

The vehicle shuddered as the round hit it with a resounding *bang*. For a moment, smoke poured out of the hole, and it didn't seem like it had done much, though it certainly had given the soldiers on foot pause; the incoming fire had slackened considerably as they'd dived for cover. Then the BVP started to burn, flame pouring out of the turret, which had halted as soon as the round had hit.

Then half the street ahead seemed to just disappear.

The concussion was enough to shake the ground where we lay, and shattered glass was cascading down onto the street to the right and left. The shockwave, pushing smoke, dust, and debris, washed down the street toward us, and I barely got my head down fast enough to protect my eyes. It rolled over us, sandblasting any exposed skin and plucking at our clothes.

I picked my head up as fast as I could, searching the swirling murk ahead for the enemy. It was doubtful that any of them were in much shape to fight after that, but I wasn't willing to bet my life or the lives of my team on it.

"Damn!" I heard Greg yell. "I didn't think the warhead was *that* big!"

"It was the IEDs, moron," Jordan said.

"I know that, you killjoy," Greg replied, as he got down on a knee at the corner with his rifle.

I ignored them. "Flat, Deacon," I called. I sure hoped that they hadn't been too close to that blast. That had been way bigger than I'd expected. Bits of brick and debris were still raining down out of the sky.

"Deacon, Flat," he replied, his voice sounding strained. "This is getting a little old."

"Sorry, we were a bit out of time," I told him. The shooting had died down to almost nothing. "And we're not collocated with the triggermen. You should be clear enough to move by now."

There was a renewed rattle of machinegun fire, and the *bang* of another RPG or Matador from somewhere out there, on the other side of the miasma of smoke and dust. "Roger," he said. "We're moving."

I could already hear more armored vehicles maneuvering, the rumble of diesels and rattle and squeal of tracks. We had accomplished what we'd set out to do, but we were still extended well past the line of resistance, and needed to move before we got cut off, just like Bradshaw had been.

I got up and spotted the oldster crouched behind the corner behind me. He was waving frantically. I ran to him, taking a knee next to him and Tony, who was covering back the way we'd come. Smart man. He'd missed out on the fight, but he knew that if we got taken by surprise by a flanking movement, we were done.

"We just received a transmission from *Generàlporučik* Rybàr," he said. "The east flank is collapsing, and the second attack from the west is coming through." That was the flank that we'd already had to fall back from. "He is ordering all who can to disengage and fall back to the castle."

Chapter 29

The shock of that massive chain of IED blasts had bought us a bit of a breather, but as my hearing cleared, I could pick up the indications that we were still awfully close to being cut off. The rumble of armored vehicles and the crackle and thunder of weapons fire was getting louder to our left and our right. We had to move, or this little breakout was going to be stillborn.

As we ran back up the narrow lane, peeling to the inside to maintain cover back down toward the south, just in case the enemy tried to come back at us from behind, I tried not to think about how much explosive might have been packed into the cars along the side of the street, or buried under the trees and sod on the inside of the curbs. "Go big or go home" seemed to be a Nationalist motto when it came to IEDs.

We reached the edge of Štúrova Street, but had to hold our position. While the mech infantry column had been stopped in its tracks, a force of technicals and militia, backed up by a platoon of Pumas, had advanced up the street from the traffic circle after breaking through the western flank. Bullets were skipping off the pavement and the stucco sides of the row houses, and a burst of 30mm fire pulverized the corner, sending smashed brick, plaster, and glass cascading down onto the sidewalk.

Chris had his Matador on his shoulder, but the oldster pointed at him and shook his head, yelling something in Slovak. He had his radio handset held at his shoulder, and I got the message. So did Scott, who was closer, and grabbed Chris by the back of his chest rig and pulled him back from the street corner. A moment later, we heard the ripping scream of the first artillery round, followed by the heavy *crump* of its impact.

"Chris!" I yelled. "Spot the impact!"

He ducked his head out into the street, then quickly drew it back. The incoming small arms fire had slackened considerably; even the jihadis who made up most of the foreign militias in Slovakia knew what incoming artillery meant, and didn't want to be out in the open when it came down on their heads.

"Left ten, fire for effect!" he yelled back.

I turned to the oldster, but he was already shouting the adjustment into the handset.

I'd been expecting another cluster munition barrage, but that wasn't what we got. Either the howitzers were running low, or they were otherwise occupied, or they were relocating to avoid EDC and Loyalist counterbattery fire.

Or they'd already been destroyed.

Anyway, the hissing roar coming down out of the sky had a noticeably different tone from the ripping noise of the howitzer shells. And even though I wasn't the target, it made me want to curl up into a ball and stuff myself into the deepest hole I could find.

Multiple launch rockets were often launched with targeting along the lines of "pulverize everything in that grid square."

Even sheltered by the buildings that lined the lane, we got rocked, as the rockets rained down on Štúrova Street. Shockwaves and the sheer, mind-numbing assault of noise slammed at us around the corner, and we could *feel* the front of the row house next to us smashing down into the street.

"Danger close" was simply par for the course in this fight.

As the echoes faded, and we huddled against the wall to try to avoid the rain of smoking debris that had been thrown up into the sky, Tony suddenly opened fire down the lane to the south, even the staccato thunder of his Mk 48 sounding muted after that catastrophic hammering. "We've got to move!" he yelled.

I looked back. Figures were darting from tree to car to tree down at the other end of the lane. I pivoted, snapping my OBR to my shoulder and caught one with a snap shot as he dashed toward a parked van. He fell on his face on the pavement and didn't move.

"Get cover out on the street and start pushing across!" I yelled. "RPGs and machineguns first, east and west!"

Chris was already moving, ducking out around the corner with his Matador, a Slovak Nationalist with a PKP joining him. Several more Nationalists took the other corner and immediately opened fire. I looked over just in time to see one of them shoulder his RPG-75, and I blanched.

"Chris!" I screamed. *"Get down!"*

The oldster saw the same thing at the same instant, and his bark in Slovak arrested the man with the RPG-75. He looked back, to see that Chris and the Nationalist with the PKP were right in his backblast area. He dashed farther out in the street, dropped to a knee, and leveled his RPG-75 at his target, which I couldn't see.

Then a burst of machinegun fire cut him almost in half before he could fire. He slumped to the debris-littered pavement in a welter of blood and shredded viscera, his finger tightening spasmodically on the RPG's trigger, sending the rocket haring off to impact against the front of the row house off to the west as the backblast blew more dust and debris down the street.

"Shit!" Chris pivoted, grabbing the Nationalist machinegunner and physically throwing him out of the way, and leveled his Matador. He paused for a split second to level the weapon and fired, the rocket streaking away almost too fast for the eye to follow.

The *wham* from around the corner announced that he'd hit what he was shooting at, just as the Nationalists opened fire with rifles and machineguns.

The oldster was grabbing my sleeve. "We have to move!" he shouted. "Now!"

"Go!" I yelled back. "We'll bring up the rear!"

"Make sure you come with us!" the old man replied, giving my arm a hard squeeze.

We didn't know each other from Adam. For all I knew, he was another Russian sympathizer, like Skalický or Pokorný. For all he knew, I believed in the EDC's peacekeeping mission, and was only helping the Nationalists for the sake of my own skin. But when you fight next to a man, even if you don't know him, a bond gets built. It might only last until the end of the fight. But it's no less real for all that.

"We'll be there!" I replied, pushing him toward the street. "Get moving! And try not to drop any more arty on our heads!"

He grinned, then started marshalling his men for the dash across the street. It was going to be a long one, even if the actual distance was only about forty yards. But when you've got a crossfire ripping down the street, and armored vehicles coming behind it, forty yards gets to be a long damned way.

The Nationalists crossed fast, even as Dwight and two of the Slovak machinegunners laid a withering storm of fire down the street to cover their movement. Scott, Tony, David, and Reuben were laying the hate down the lane behind us, while Greg and Jordan covered the ravaged west side, where some of the jihadis were starting to poke their heads out of the devastation left by the rocket barrage.

We were in a crack, and no mistake.

I'll admit, despite that bond, I still worried that the Nationalists were going to get to the other side of the street and keep going. But the old man got them to covered positions and started laying down covering fire for us.

"That's it!" I yelled, pulling one of my last high-concentration smokes out of my chest rig, pulling the pin, and tossing it down the lane behind us. "Time to move!"

As the grenade popped and started spewing thick white smoke, rapidly filling the lane and obscuring us from the enemy, I got up and started moving. The rest were doing likewise, firing final bursts at the bad guys down the street before getting up and surging forward.

I felt every brutal mile and every sleepless night as I dashed across that forty yards of hell. The smoky air burned in my lungs and my legs felt like lead, even as I tensed, waiting for the bullet or shell that was about to take my life. We ran spread out but as one unit, trying to get across that kill zone as quickly as possible, before the enemy could zero in and kill us, even as the oldster's PKMs and vz. 59s raved and roared to keep the enemy's heads down.

We made it, gasping for breath at the far side, plunging past the Nationalists' position. The oldster immediately started pulling his men back from the street and chivvying them up the narrow, tree-lined lanes to the north.

Together, we fell into a staggered column, keeping our rear security as tight as we could, and retreated toward the castle.

***

It wasn't a rapid break-contact drill of rushes and bursts of covering fire the whole way. We linked up with more Nationalists and Bradshaw's battered infantry section another block to the north.

"Damn, am I glad to see you guys," I said to Bradshaw, as we set in briefly at a barricade formed of sandbags, barbed wire, and a tipped-over truck.

"So am I," he said wearily. "I've about had it with danger-close artillery, though."

I winced. "How close were you to that last barrage?"

"Not so close that any of us took any real frag," he said. "Frankly, it saved our asses; we just about ran headlong into that group, and were under some heavy fire when they just fuckin' *disappeared*. We'd broken contact from that last bunch of mech infantry to the south, but moved too quick heading north. Lost a couple of the Nationalists right off."

The oldster came to join us, along with Kysely, who looked considerably older, dirtier, and more battered than he had just a day ago. "They are coming up Pàrovskà," the oldster said. "They are moving more slowly; the mines and improvised bombs have made them cautious. There is another column moving up Štefànikova trieda. So far, they are pacing each other, and there is another delaying force set up there. If they fall, we will have to set the charges here to delay and fall back before we are cut off."

I was scanning our surroundings. The street was tight, most of the buildings touching each other, with few alleys to provide escape routes or ambush sites. As thorough as the Nationalists' preparations had been, they hadn't had time to knock holes in all the walls to turn the buildings into tunnels.

They might have been hoping to get through the battle without the city being a total loss, too.

There was a bit of tree-covered low ground to the west, but getting back onto this side of the barricade would be difficult, if not impossible, and Janka Kràl'a Street, at the end of the block behind it, had been turned into a nightmare of victim-actuated IEDs and concertina wire. Getting through that would be just as dangerous for us as for the enemy. No, we were going to have to stick with the Nationalists' plan and hold at the barricade until we got the signal to fall back.

I didn't like it. Grex Luporum Teams aren't trained to be die-in-place elements, short of a true *in extremis* situation. We were light, fast, mobile hunters. Our job was to get in, kill everybody who needed killing on the target site, or else call in enough fire to do it remotely, and get out. But the situation was what it was. We could either adapt and overcome, or we could die.

I wasn't big on lying down and dying.

I hunkered down behind the overturned truck as we heard the low rumble of diesels and the rattle and screech of tracks approaching. That sounded big. The drones had been cleared out of the sky; the closer we got to the castle, the more jammer trucks the Nationalists had deployed. So, at least we didn't have that to worry about anymore. But if the Loyalists were landing with tanks...

They were. The low, ugly, dome-turreted shape of a T-72M1 was trundling up the street, its 125mm smoothbore turning toward us as it tracked along the curve of the road.

If you've never been downrange from an enemy tank, you can't really understand the sheer terror of facing one of those things. It's one thing ambushing one from the flank or behind with a rocket or an IED. But the frontal armor is always the thickest, and if its main gun is pointing at you, you're looking right at the very maw of death itself. The size and power of the growling, steel beast becomes secondary at that point.

Two rockets *bang*ed out from the barricade, a Matador and an ancient 135mm, wire-guided Konkurs. The Matador glanced off the front glacis and detonated against the high rise off to the west. The Konkurs, on the other hand, hit right at the turret ring.

The tank momentarily disappeared in a puff of black smoke and flying sparks, before something bigger blew, and the entire turret was blasted skyward, looking for all the world like a gigantic frying pan flying through the air. It came back down halfway on top of the burning chassis with a catastrophic, deafening *clang*.

Against that, the machineguns tearing up the infantry to the flanks seemed like popguns.

Then the Nationalist triggerman next to me mashed the lever of his detonator, and half the street behind the destroyed tank disappeared with a flash, an ugly blast of smoke and frag, and a tooth-rattling *wham*.

Kysely nodded, standing up behind the tipped-over truck as the dust and smoke whirled around us. He spoke quickly.

"We will set the charges here to delay and fall back to the next position," the oldster translated. The triggerman was already doing something with the actuation circuit for the next row of IEDs, embedded in the truck, set in piles of rubble alongside the columns holding up the overhanging second story of the blocky Evis Hotel, and inside the doors of the red-tiled store across the street. When they went off, this entire block was going to be a very unhealthy place to be.

We hoped that it was going to take the Loyalists, the EDC, and the militias a long time to move up to clear the barricade out. They'd taken punishing losses so far. And to get to the barricade, they were going to have to go past the dead hulk of that tank and the waste that had been laid of the column behind it. None of those sights were going to make them eager to press forward.

We picked up and started moving up the street, leaving the triggerman to finish setting the charges.

***

The square in front of the Nitra Gallery wasn't the Nationalists' last stand. Not quite. Nitra castle still loomed above, wreathed in smoke but defiant. It had clearly taken a couple of hits as the airstrikes had resumed, but the EDC's planes were staying at higher altitudes, with a corresponding loss of accuracy in their bombings. That was a two-edged sword; smoke and dust

309

rose from residential neighborhoods where bombs had gone astray.

Not that the EDC cared about Slovak civilians. If they had, they wouldn't have unleashed jihadi militias on the countryside.

The square had been turned into a fortified staging area. Two T-72s were sandbagged up, their main guns pointing down the primary approaches, their 12.7mm commander's machineguns pointed up at the sky. There were even two ShKH Zuzana 2 howitzers similarly fortified, their 155mm tubes on direct lay. Anything they hit, especially at the ranges involved there, wasn't going to live.

The rest of us had set up in the Gallery itself, the windows sandbagged, watching and waiting for the next push.

Smoke was rising in a hundred places above the city. Even from the second floor, where we had gathered with some of Kysely's Nationalists, we could see high-rises that were only half-standing, entire sides collapsed into rubble. Some of that was from EDC bombs and Loyalist tank fire. Some of it was from Nationalist artillery and IEDs.

I could see helicopters circling to the south, lean, predatory shapes that would be a threat as soon as they closed in on us. There were still plenty of shoulder-fired SAMs and a few heavy machineguns up in the castle, that would make the airspace plenty dangerous for the helos, but they had more standoff than most of the AA weapons we had remaining had effective range.

"Damn," Scott muttered. He and I were crouched under a sandbagged window, and he was peering out through the firing slit. He looked drawn and haggard, beneath a thick layer of dust and soot on his face. I guessed that I looked much the same. My beard felt like it was about half grit. "What are they waiting for? Why don't they just come and get it over with?"

Personally, I was plenty glad for the break, but I understood his point. There comes a time where the waiting only stretches already strained nerves, and the anticipation becomes worse than the hell of combat itself.

"There you are, my friends." I turned to see Sỳkora coming toward us from the stairs. "I have good news." He squatted down between us, staying below the slit. "*Generàlporučik* Kràl sent *Generàlporučik* Rybàr a message, just a few minutes ago." He grinned, his teeth white in the blackened grime on his face. "The Loyalists have had enough. They are standing down. They are not surrendering, yet, but they are falling back to the edge of the city. It seems as if they are not happy with the Germans letting them do most of the bleeding against their own countrymen."

"Are the EDC forces going to sit down for that?" I asked.

He shrugged. "Probably not. But it sounds as if they do not have the strength they would need to take the city by themselves. It sounds as if the German commander is furious, and the black-ass militias even more so, but what can they do?"

"Those jihadis can still do a lot of damage," I warned him. "There'll be stay-behind elements, the really young, stupid, hard core *shahid* types. It's going to take weeks to root them all out." And the Nationalists might not have weeks. I didn't say that part.

Before he could respond, one of the heavy machineguns outside started pounding, spewing tracers up into the gray, smoke-choked sky. The growing rumble of jet engines rose to a shriek. We all got low, praying that the Gallery wasn't the target. Though we'd probably never know what hit us.

Bombs struck below, the thunderclaps of the detonations sounding almost like the world was splitting apart. It was a noise you felt, more than heard. It vibrated through every bone.

I glanced out. One of the Zuzana 2s was burning. Craters pocked the square, and one of the T-72s was smoking, its back deck partially mangled. Several of the sandbag redoubts that had been set at the mouths of the approaching streets had been obliterated, smashed bits of what had once been men scattered amidst the blackened debris at the edges of the bomb craters.

The helos came next, but the bombs hadn't quite done the trick. As rattled as he had to have been, the other T-72's commander was on point, and was already swiveling his turret to the south as the Tigers swooped toward the square.

The 125mm smoothbore thundered, a blossom of flame spitting from the muzzle, and the lead Tiger just disintegrated in a fireball, whickering bits of fuselage and rotors fluttering toward the ground a mere five hundred feet below. The others quickly dove for the rooftops, banking away and fleeing as the wreckage burned, adding to the pall of smoke that lay low over Nitra.

Chapter 30

We stayed in place until nightfall, waiting to see if the unspoken truce really was going to hold. I had no illusions that the EDC was going to let it stand; hell, Bratislava wasn't going to let it stand. It was only a matter of time before Kràl was relieved for cause, the Loyalists reinforced, and another push was made.

But as it got dark, it finally started to look as if we had a breather, if only for a few days.

Only once we were fairly confident that the offensive wasn't going to kick off again in the next hour or so did we start back up to the castle.

Once our guys were set in a small cottage, getting their mags reloaded and finding some much-needed chow, Bradshaw and I headed for the field hospital first, looking for Killian.

The hospital had been set up in a lower building, set into the hill just beneath the museum that had been turned into Pokornỳ's command post. The walled courtyard in front of it was crammed with vehicles, and even as we hiked up toward the gate, another Nationalist ambulance came roaring up the lane and turned in the gate. The back doors were hanging open, offering a glimpse of mangled, bloodied bodies wrapped in bloodstained bandages. The Nationalists had hammered the Loyalists badly, but they'd taken a mauling, themselves.

It was inevitable, given the amount of firepower and explosives being thrown around in such close quarters. It was a sobering sight, nevertheless.

We followed the ambulance in, and as the Nationalist soldiers started offloading the wounded, without saying anything, the two of us stepped forward and started helping out. That wasn't why we were there, but the need was there, and Bradshaw and I were of the same general temperament.

I stepped up to help a man who was missing a foot, mangled meat and splintered bone hanging down from a shredded pantleg, a cinched-down ratchet strap around his upper thigh acting as a tourniquet. There was also a reddened bandage wrapped around his forehead and one eye; he probably wasn't going to ever see out of that eye again.

We limped inside with the rest of the casualties. At that point, it didn't matter that the man missing a foot and I probably didn't speak the same language. We'd probably fought in entirely different parts of the city. None of it mattered. I found a medic, who pointed to a bare spot on the floor, and I helped the wounded man down, checking the tourniquet as I did so. A moment later, a young woman with dark hair held back with a bandana pushed me aside and started assessing the man's wounds. I straightened up and looked around.

The place looked like a scene out of a World War II movie. Wounded and dying men covered just about every flat surface, and there were more coming in as I watched. Harried medics and young volunteers were rushing from casualty to casualty, assessing and triaging. Even as I watched, an ancient-looking, white-haired man straightened up, leaning away from the man he'd been working on, settling back on his haunches. His shoulders slumped and he hung his head, before stripping off his blood-smeared gloves and crossing himself. I followed suit, even as I kept scanning the long room.

I was looking for Killian, but I spotted Warren first. He was sitting down on a cot, his elbows resting on his knees and his head down. I started weaving through the rows of wounded toward him, Bradshaw joining me as he stepped away from the stretcher he'd helped carry into the hospital.

Warren looked up as we approached. We must have been quite the pair of apparitions, blackened by dust and soot, still kitted up for combat. Warren was still filthy from our fighting retreat through the mountains and away from Vrbovè, but he hadn't been out there in Nitra. He'd lost weight, his cammies and the plate carrier he'd acquired on the way now fitting far better than they had at first. His face was drawn, his eyes bloodshot. He had an M37 leaning against the cot next to him.

My eyes shifted from him to the cot. The shape lying on it had been covered by a poncho.

Warren nodded, his face slack, his eyes glimmering. It took him a moment to get the words out.

"Sergeant Killian died two hours ago," he said. He looked down at the still shape under the poncho. "They tried, but he'd lost too much blood. They said he must have kept bleeding, that maybe there had been an internal bleed, too."

I looked down at the cot. There wasn't much of anything Jordan could have done. There wasn't anything any of us could have done, not with an internal bleed in a combat situation. The only hope we'd had had been to get him to surgery. But we hadn't been quite fast enough.

Even when you've seen death, it's still hard to accept that, no matter how hard you try to stave it off, every man has his time. Killian's had come, whether we liked it or not.

Warren looked back up at us. "I don't know what to do now," he said, his voice barely above a whisper. "I'm not a combat leader. I'm the ranking officer, but I have no idea what I should do." He looked back down at Killian's shrouded body. "I guess that I figured as long as Killian was there, we could figure it out. But now…"

I didn't think he was talking to us at that point.

"Warren," I said. He didn't respond, but kept staring at Killian's corpse. "*Chief Warrant Officer Warren!*"

That snapped him out of it. He blinked and stared up at me, his eyes wide, the tracks of tears in the dirt on his face.

"I'm sorry that Killian's dead," I said, and I meant it. "He was a good dude, and he was solid when things went to shit." I scanned the other American wounded. There were fewer still among the living than I'd hoped. And I didn't see the girl who'd lost her leg in the airstrike among them, either. I felt a pang at that. I'd never liked seeing women get hurt, and it was one reason I'd always been uncomfortable with the women in my platoon in the Marine Corps. One of many. "I'm sorry that all of them are dead.

"But you can't fall apart because Killian's not here to lean on anymore," I said, turning my stare back on Warren. I was sure I looked like hell; I hadn't had a chance to look in the mirror, but I could imagine, just judging by what Bradshaw looked like. My face blackened by smoke, dirt, and debris, my eyes bloodshot orbs set between lines of black. "You're the ranking officer, like it or not, and these kids are going to need you to act like it. We're not out of the woods yet."

He stared down at his hands, then nodded silently. "You're right," he said, though his voice shook a little, and he looked back at Killian's body one more time, as if begging for advice. Finally, though, he heaved himself to his feet, picking up the M37 as he did so. I suspected it had been Killian's rifle. He only had about three magazines left for it. "Did we win?"

"We won a breather," I replied. "But that's it." I nodded toward where Bradshaw was checking on his own wounded. "We need to go talk to Rybàr. Once Tyler's done."

Warren nodded jerkily, then looked down at the floor again. After a long moment, he said, "Bowen…" He hesitated. He still wasn't looking at me. "I…I should have made a different call." He swallowed, hard. "We…we should have…we should have done something."

"Yeah, you should have," I replied harshly, still watching Tyler. He'd lost a third of his section since Borinka. It was only through the grace of God that my team was still intact. It was hard to accept Warren's apology, when we'd been out there fighting and dying while he had stayed up here, mostly secure, with his troops, waiting.

"Sorry" didn't quite cover that.

He still didn't look at me, but kept studying the blood-stained flagstones on the floor. Tyler finished talking to Wolfe, who'd had his forearm shattered by a bullet, and stood up, meeting my eyes and nodding. It was time.

"Let's go," I said, taking a deep breath and trying to push away the sudden flash of anger at Warren.

I almost didn't say it. But I forced the words out. "Can't change what's already happened. Just got to do better."

He looked at me for a moment, searching my face as if he wasn't sure what to make of that statement, but I was already heading for the doors, ignoring the dull throb of the cut in my leg. It hadn't killed me yet, and it wasn't likely to. I didn't think we had all that much time. We needed to talk to Rybàr and find out what our next move would be.

And whether it would be with the Nationalists' help, or in spite of them.

***

It took a while for the three of us to find Rybàr. He wasn't in the command post, and Pokornỳ looked considerably less than enthused to see us. He stared at us with those piggy eyes, breathing through his mouth, until we left, looking for his far more amiable counterpart.

We had circled almost the entire castle before we finally found him, up in the cathedral's bell tower, scanning the edge of the city with thermal optics and talking on three different radios at once. It was a tight fit up there, but we made it up.

"You survived," he observed, glancing over at us as he raised his binoculars again, looking south.

"So did you," Bradshaw replied, deadpan. If Rybàr caught the hint of accusation in Tyler's voice, he didn't show it. I glanced at Bradshaw. He was holding it together, but it was clear that he was hurting. Having lost four more men fighting for a city that wasn't ours wasn't sitting well.

Of course, expecting a septuagenarian to be out on the front lines with the young bucks was probably a bit of a stretch. I wondered a little at Rybàr's age. He'd probably been retired, and had left his pension behind when the civil war had started.

"What do you plan to do now?" Rybàr asked, still peering through his thermals at the edge of the city. They had to be just about the only way to see anything, between the darkness and the pall of smoke still hanging low over the city.

"First thing is rest, if we can manage it," I said grimly. "Most of us are dead on our feet." I almost regretted my choice of words; too many of Bradshaw's boys were flat dead.

He nodded. "Of course," he said. "We all need rest. I only hope that we can get the chance." He lowered the thermals and looked at me for the first time. "Talk to Sỳkora; he can show you where the other Americans, the regulars, stayed during the battle. It is reasonably secure."

317

I nodded warily. "Reasonably secure" could have more than one meaning, under the circumstances. I was sure the Nationalists weren't too happy about having Americans sitting on their hands while the Nationalist stronghold was getting pounded to rubble.

"We already found it," I said. "The rest of our men are there now." He nodded, his eyes to the thermals again.

"But I would caution you," he continued quietly, "to be ready to move quickly, before you rest."

I frowned, and felt more than saw Bradshaw's stare get slightly sharper. "Pokorný?" I asked.

"Yes," Rybàr replied. "I strongly suspect that he sold his soul to the Russians a long time ago, before even this current crisis. But even if he is only using them as allies of convenience, he is very proud, and has a strong hatred for all the 'peacekeepers' who came into our country to force us to follow the dictates of the EDC. He will not want it to get out that he defended Nitra with American help."

Not that we were any kind of lynchpin, but I see his point. "You think he's going to try to make us go away?"

"He might," Rybàr replied. "He should have his hands too full at this point, but he can be a vicious, vindictive man. Do not underestimate him."

"So," Bradshaw said, "we still need to plan on getting out of here and heading for Poland."

Rybàr nodded again. "Yes," he said. "I should be able to get you transport in the morning, or the next day." He fixed us both alternately with a steely gaze. "Do not make the mistake that I am being soft-hearted in sending you out of the country," he said. "I can still use you here, and as you have seen, this war will use men up. But whether your countrymen know it or not, you are now as much at war with the EDC as we are. And American resources will help us. Alone, eventually the EDC will manage to break the Nationalist movement." His gaze suddenly got far away. "We have already lost more than we could afford, here."

"We'll be ready in the morning," I told him. I glanced at Warren, who had been standing back by the ladder, being very, very quiet. He stepped forward, straightening to attention.

318

"I'll make sure my soldiers are ready, as well," he said. He looked at Bradshaw. "We'll hold security tonight." He swallowed. "We've had more time to rest."

I had to hand it to him; that took some balls. My estimate of Warren went up a notch. The guy I'd initially taken him to be would have kept hiding behind his rank and his fears of political and career repercussions. But maybe, something about sitting in that hospital, watching Killian and several other of his soldiers die, watching the casualties come pouring in, listening to the hammering of artillery, airstrikes, tank fire, and small arms fire down in the city, had changed something in him.

I hoped so. Because we still had a long way to go to the border.

"What few reports I have received are saying that the peacekeepers are still out in force in the countryside," Rybàr said. "But if the word spreads to the rest of the Loyalists in the Army about what has happened here, they will be considerably weakened. Speed should get you to the border with reasonable safety, especially if we pick the route carefully."

He stood, stretching his back. "We will speak more about it in the morning, my friends," he said, shaking Bradshaw's and my hands. "I will not forget what you have done here. What you have sacrificed. *Slovakia* will not forget. You have my word."

Neither of us had much to say to that. We were too tired and strung out. We just shook his hand before turning and heading back down the ladder.

***

Greg had the HF radio set up when we got back down below, to the red-roofed cottage where most of Killian's soldiers had been put, and the rest of the Triarii had now joined them. And he had a look on his face that immediately woke me up. Greg didn't look that grim. Ever. He held out the handset. "It's Kidd," he said. "You'd better talk to him."

I grabbed the handset. "Pegleg, Deacon." I didn't bother with the unit callsigns; we all knew who was who, and under the circumstances, I'd probably end up screwing it up, anyway. Damn, I was tired.

"Deacon," Kidd said heavily. "I've got some bad news." He paused, as if trying to figure out how to say it. "We finally got an HF shot back to the States. We don't have a lot of details, but it's bad. Really bad.

"Somebody hit us at home, Deacon," he said. "And I'm not talking like September 11th. Orders of magnitude worse, from what the Colonel told me. At least sixty percent of the grid is down, hard. Attacks on infrastructure. Mass-cas attacks in multiple major cities, mostly the ones that haven't already turned into battlegrounds. There are rumors that the President's dead. Enough transport hubs have been hit that cargo's at a standstill. Which means the cities are starving."

I closed my eyes. It wasn't as if things had been good before we'd left. Now, with the US at war, whether it knew it or not, it sounded like two-thirds of the country was going from civil war to post-apocalyptic wasteland.

"The Colonel's moving fast," Kidd continued, without waiting for my acknowledgement. "The areas we had already partially secured are doing all right, mostly. But it's still a relatively small part of the country." He sighed; I could hear his breath gust against the mic.

"So," I said. "That's why they figured they could get away with wiping out the American FOBs in Slovakia. They figured they had us licked already. And they're not far from wrong."

"Oh, they're wrong," Kidd snarled. "We're definitely on the ropes, but we're not down yet. The Colonel made that *abundantly* clear." He paused. "It's just going to take some time before we can really hit back effectively."

"We're heading for Poland with the Army survivors in the morning," I told him. I still felt numb; the shock and horror of the last two weeks, coupled with my own bone-deep exhaustion, were keeping me from really, fully processing what he'd told me. It all seemed very distant, very abstract at that point. "What's your plan?"

"We've officially made contact with the Hungarian government on behalf of the Triarii," Kidd replied. "They are already pissed about what's going on right on their border. We're hearing that Budapest has formally recognized the Nationalists as the true government of Slovakia, and that Hungarian Army units are deploying to the border to reinforce the Hungarian militias. We're moving up to join them tomorrow. I don't think we can get to you quickly, though. Slovakian airspace is still extremely non-permissive."

"Don't try," I told him. "The Nationalists are going to try to get us to Poland, and there's a lot of Slovak Army and EDC forces between you and us. I'm pretty sure that the last major US bases in Europe are in Poland, and *somebody*'s going to have to link up with them and help get things sorted out." I realized that I was probably going to get stuck doing a lot of liaison stuff with the Army in the near future, and stifled a groan. "And Poland's probably going to be just about the only place we can land more troops and equipment." Of course, there was Italy, that had rejected the EDC several years before, but that was an even longer haul.

"Good luck, then," Kidd said. "Not much else we can do."

"No, there isn't," I said. I took a deep breath. Kidd was my senior, but he sounded downright shell-shocked. "We're not out of this yet, Pegleg. Remember that."

"I'll try," he said, a touch of the old acid in his voice. "Pegleg, out."

I handed Greg back the handset. He was watching me, his eyes a little wider than usual. "Like I told Kidd," I said, "we're down. We're not out."

He nodded. "I know," he said. Greg was optimistic like that. Even after what we'd just been through. "It's just…I never expected to live through a *Fallout* game, you know?"

"None of us did," I said, finding a spot against the wall. I looked up at the ceiling. "We were taught from when we were kids that those days were over, never to come again. Even in the face of every bit of evidence to the contrary."

Despite my exhaustion, it wasn't easy, getting to sleep that night.

Chapter 31

It was still dark when a hand shook me awake.

I was alert immediately. I hadn't slept soundly, and when I'd finally drifted off, it was to more hair-raising nightmares. Opening my eyes to the dark hell of reality was almost a relief, after what I'd seen behind my eyelids.

The shape above me was hard to make out, but a moment later, Scott said, "Sỳkora's here with Rybàr. Says it's urgent."

I sat up, only to find that as lightly as I'd slept, it hadn't kept my body from stiffening up. I groaned. Everything just *hurt*. My eyes felt like they had ground glass in them. I still got up on my feet and followed toward the front door.

Two angular, six-wheeled Tatrapan personnel carriers were sitting on the road outside the cottage, their engines rumbling. Rybàr and Sỳkora stood at the base of the steps outside the door.

"Come," Rybàr said, "I know it is early, but you need to leave, now."

"What's up?" I asked, as Scott went back inside to roust the rest out. Warren was already assigning who was going on what APC among his own men.

"I just received word," Rybàr said, "that the First Division of the European Defense Corps crossed the border from Austria four hours ago."

I frowned. "The European Defense Corps?" I asked. "You mean that show unit they built out of the old Franco-German Brigade?" That didn't sound right, particularly not given the grim way that Rybàr had said it.

"That was what they masked it with," he said darkly. "For four years now, just like the Germans did before the last war, they've been building a larger force in secret. There have been rumors, about compounds on German and French military bases where no one is ever allowed, and regular units being denied training areas for no reason, only to hear live fire on those same training areas."

I hadn't heard any of that intel, but I supposed it made sense. I knew enough about the EDC to consider them the biggest pack of utopian sociopaths on the planet, but that didn't make them stupid. They'd wanted a military force capable of bringing the rest of Europe to its knees ever since Macron and Merkel had been talking up the idea of an EU Army, and when that misbegotten idea had shown how worthless it was in Kosovo, being built on the hollowed-out shells of the Bundeswehr and the Armee de Terre, they must have decided that some other path was necessary. While the Bundeswehr and the Armee de Terre had been using active conscription for the last several years, trying to get their strength up, this sounded like something different.

"How big is this force?" I asked. "I need to know everything you can tell me about it."

He shrugged. "We haven't gotten any information that is really certain," he said. "I have heard that they have only one division, about the size of the French Foreign Legion. I have also heard that they have as many as five. The force coming against us is only one division in strength, but it is more than we have to oppose it, even if the entire Loyalist remainder of the Army joins us."

It was hard to make out his expression in the pre-dawn darkness, but I tried. "And you're going to stay here and fight, anyway?" I asked.

"This is my country," Rybàr replied. "I will not flee. Not without a fight." His teeth flashed in the dark. "Do not worry, my friend. I have no intention of making a futile sacrifice. If we cannot smash them in an open battle, we will become partisans and bleed them slowly. But now, your escape to Poland is even more important. We need help. We need American help."

I nodded, numb. I couldn't tell him that that help might be a long time coming. Not until I knew more. Colonel Santiago was a mean son of a bitch, as well as being smart as hell and determined when it came time for it. Once he figured out that the EDC had been involved in the terrorist attack on the US—and at that point, I had no doubt that they had been—he was going to find a way to make them suffer for it.

But getting the forces into Europe to do that was going to take time. Time that Slovakia was going to spend under the boot. There was no getting around that. And I didn't want to tell Rybàr that.

Not that he'd necessarily rescind his help in that case. He might, but I felt that I'd gotten to know him well enough to trust that he wouldn't. But at zero dark thirty, outnumbered and surrounded by men who had just had the daylights blasted out of them, who might or might not really be friends, didn't seem like the time or the place to say that.

Rybàr waved another man over, who was wearing green coveralls and a tanker helmet. "This is *Major* Medved," he said. "He will be leading the unit that will escort you to the border." He shook my hand and clapped me hard on the shoulder. "Good luck, my friend." I gripped his hand firmly and nodded. While I knew that his first concern always would be the Nationalist cause, we would have been dead a long time ago without Rybàr's help. He nodded back, returned Medved's salute, and hurried off with Sýkora in tow.

I shook the *Major*'s hand. "We've got another thirty or so men coming out," I told him. The Tatrapan's were already looking pretty full.

"We have two more BOVs and an old OT-64," he said. "It should be enough, though it will be tight quarters." He turned and started walking up the road, even as Scott and the rest of the team started coming out of the house. I waited for Scott, took my ruck, which was somewhat lighter by then, from him, and started up the road after Medved.

Up at the crest of the hill, the rest of the little convoy was waiting, engines already rumbling. At the head was a single T-72. The crews were aboard, though the hatches on the BOVs and the OT-64 were open. Medved paused at the lead BOV and waited, as my team and I caught up.

"Reporting says that the road is clear at least as far as Hronský Beňadik," he said. "But there are still drones and aircraft up. You Americans need to try to stay out of sight as much as possible; all my men still have their Slovak Army uniforms. We should be able to slip through most checkpoints as Slovak Army, particularly after what happened here." He grinned tightly, with little humor in the expression. "We have captured enough Loyalist deserters, along with those who came over to us in the last couple of hours, to be fairly certain that the state of the Loyalist Army is very bad right now. A mixed convoy just trying to get to Zilina will not be out of place."

I nodded, waving at the rest to start loading the vehicles. Everyone had freshly-filled magazines and their weapons in their hands. We'd made sure to load back up before we'd gone down for the night. "What's the planned route?" I asked.

He pulled a map out of his pocket and spread it on the BOV's hull, pulling out a small green-lens flashlight so that we could see it. "Here is Nitra," he said, pointing. "Most of the territory to the north and east has been mostly controlled by us for the last few weeks. The EDC and the Loyalists pushed in from the west and south, but were unable to penetrate far onto our eastern flank, and not at all into the mountains to the north." He traced the line of the R1 Highway toward the hills to the northeast. "We should be able to move quickly along this road," he said. "The biggest threat on that route is from the air, and the EDC took severe aircraft losses in the fighting here. They will be cautious about risking more aircraft. Once we reach Hronský Beňadik, we can make contact with the cells there and get updated reporting about Žarnovica. There was a Loyalist mechanized infantry company holding that city, last we knew." He let his hand fall. "From there, we can determine the route north that will present the least opposition."

I nodded, as I looked back at the rest of Bradshaw's men. Draven was with Bradshaw; he'd folded his section in with the other infantrymen for the moment. My team was loaded up, and Draven and Bradshaw looked like they were the last of theirs.

Bradshaw gave me a thumbs up. "We're ready to go when you are," I told Medved.

"Let's go then," he said. "As you Americans say, 'We are burning daylight.'" He laughed. It was still dark, without even the beginnings of dawn showing in the east.

I was too tired to join him. I just swung my ruck off my shoulders, chucked it into the crowded back of the BOV, and swung up behind it, finding a cramped seat next to Tony, the ruck almost keeping me from finding any place for my feet. I leaned out and pulled the hatch shut, and Scott, across from me, dogged it. A few minutes later, the vehicle lurched into motion.

We were on our way.

***

Medved wasn't wasting time. While we had little to no visibility in the back of the BOV, a fact that I hated with every fiber of my being, I could paint a bit of the picture just from the way we were moving. And boy, once we finished the series of twisting turns that got us out of the castle and then through the maze of blasted rubble and wreckage-strewn streets of Nitra, we were *moving*.

I suspected that the T-72 was the limiting factor for our speed; all the other vehicles were wheeled, and could probably do something close to sixty miles an hour on the open road. That tank could do maybe thirty-five. But from the feel of it, we were doing every bit of that thirty-five miles per hour once we got on the highway.

It was a dark, cramped ride. I couldn't see anything; the BOV didn't have windows or vision blocks for the rear troop compartment. We could only sit and endure, hoping that we weren't about to get turned into burned meat in the mangled remains of the vehicle when a HOT-3 missile hit it.

David was asleep almost as soon as we started moving, his head lolling against the back of the seat, his mouth hanging open. Dwight just tapped his fingers against his Mk 48's loading tray cover, his eyes fixed on nothing about six inches in front of his nose.

Reuben was sitting closest to the gunner, and had his head craned to look out the top of the turret, peering at the sky.

His lips were moving; I didn't know if he was praying or just reciting something, or even talking to himself to pass the time.

Tony had his eyes closed, but was so still that I was sure he was awake. It didn't surprise me. Tony was quiet and meditative. It was his way.

Jordan was off in his own little world, as aloof as ever. He was covering it well, checking over what was left of our team med gear, but clearly, somebody had said something that pissed him off.

Or maybe he was processing what we'd just been through, and I was reading too much into his silence and focus. The trouble was, he'd been on such a hair-trigger for so long that I couldn't tell anymore.

Greg was sitting closest to the driver, and kept trying to engage him in conversation. It didn't seem to be going very well, but that wasn't dampening his spirits.

It was a little weird, watching it. Greg had been the first to find out, if not the details, at least the severity of the situation back home. He was the nicest of us by a long shot, and had just witnessed the most intense urban fighting any of us had ever seen. And yet, he was still being cheerful and friendly. It took knowing the man, knowing what he'd gone through himself, to see why. Greg had just about had his head blown off by an IED. He'd skated so close to death that it was entirely likely that nothing would ever quite faze him again.

Phil, on the other hand, wasn't looking so good. He was staring at infinity, somewhere past David's shoulder, his face set in a blank look of dread. He wasn't even trying to get a rise out of Jordan.

Phil was a big talker, and he certainly was competent enough to get on a Grex Luporum team, but he wasn't head and shoulders above anyone else. I could easily replace him on point with Chris. That fact had never shaken his self-confidence, though. He was a bit of a legend in his own mind, and always had been.

Facing the unmitigated hell that had been Nitra, and finding out just how bad the war was going, a war that we hadn't even realized had reached that stage until a few hours ago, had apparently shaken him more than anything else ever had.

Chris had his head down, a red lens headlamp illuminating the tiny New Testament he always carried with him.

Scott was doing the same thing I was; scanning the troop compartment and checking on the team. He met my eyes as I looked over at him, and one corner of his mouth quirked upward. It wasn't quite a smile. It was an acknowledgement that we were thinking on the same track. I just nodded my head tiredly.

We rode on in silence, the only sounds the rumble of the diesels, the growl of the tires on the pavement, and the occasional chirp of the radios up in the crew compartment.

***

After a long while, we slowed, and then lurched to a stop. A terse burst of Slovak came from the radio up front, and the commander replied. Then we just sat there and waited.

There wasn't really room to move my OBR to point it at the hatch. But the gunner didn't seem overly agitated, and I couldn't hear any gunfire. Hopefully, we were in Hronský Beňadik, where Medved had planned on linking up with more Nationalists.

Someone knocked on the rear hatch. He had to be using a hammer or a crowbar, otherwise we never would have heard it. Scott reached over and unlatched it, letting it swing open as he lifted his own OBR to lay it across his knees, the muzzle pointing out the open portal.

I squinted in the sudden morning sunlight; I hadn't realized until then just how dark it was inside the vehicle in comparison to the countryside. Medved was standing there, his tanker helmet under his arm and his brown hair in wild disarray, along with a man I didn't recognize, wearing a tracksuit under an ancient AK chest rig and carrying an equally ancient and battered-looking vz. 58. Actual AKs seemed to be in short supply in Slovakia, which seemed strange after seeing them all over Africa, not to mention in more than a few PRA hands Stateside.

We were sitting on the road, with a Y intersection just behind us. Low, tree-covered hills rose to the north and south, with the town, mostly one-story, stucco houses with peaked, red tile roofs, lining the single main road. A church with a red onion dome steeple loomed just to the north.

"This is Kristiàn," Medved said, gesturing toward the man in the tracksuit. "He commands the Nationalist forces here." From what I could see, the Nationalist forces in Hronskỳ Beňadik amounted to maybe a couple dozen militiamen. This wasn't a large village.

But I got down from the BOV, trying not to wince and hobble as my stiffened muscles and joints protested, and shook Kristiàn's hand. He nodded to me, his grip firm, and spoke rapidly to Medved.

"He says that there have been some skirmishes in Žarnovica," Medved translated, "but that the Loyalist forces there are reluctant to risk their necks fighting. The word of the cease fire in Nitra has already passed here, so he does not doubt that it will have reached Žarnovica by now. *Kapitàn* Zima will be nervous, but I think he will be more likely to try to wait things out. If he can avoid an engagement while the direction of the Loyalist Army gets determined, he will."

I frowned. "That sounds like a lot of 'hopefully's," I said. "I think we should stop short. My team will disembark and recon the town before we move in."

But Medved shook his head. "No," he said. "A normal Loyalist unit would not do that. Zima might not want to risk getting in a fight, but even he won't fail to notice if we act strangely, and offloading a reconnaissance element before approaching what should be a friendly unit will be very strange."

I assented, though reluctantly. Part of it was because I simply didn't like the idea of trying to roll through an enemy position while riding in a wheeled steel coffin. Part of it was because I really didn't know Medved from Adam, and it had already been made clear that some of the Nationalists weren't thrilled with American help. I sort of trusted Rybàr to have picked a trustworthy commander to lead this little trip, but there was always the possibility that he'd chosen poorly.

But, ultimately, we were stuck. The only other thing to do would be to dismount and continue the next one hundred thirty klicks on foot, and without any real hope of cooperation from the Nationalists.

We'd never make it. Not with our numbers, or with Warren's kids in tow. And, worse, it would destroy any rapport we had with the Slovaks. And we'd need that alliance, along with the one with the Hungarians, if we were going to stand a chance of hitting back at the EDC.

We'd been hurt. Worse than I think the US had ever been hurt before. And despite my paranoia and exhaustion, I knew I had to keep that in mind.

The concept of the "Strategic Corporal" had been discarded by the Usual Suspects in the echelons of command by the time I joined the Marine Corps. The Powers that Be didn't want mere NCOs making decisions that would have far-reaching strategic and geopolitical consequences. Of course, tightening the top-down leadership's grip didn't keep those consequences from happening anyway, but that didn't have much to do with their thought processes.

But here I was, a GL team leader, having to make these decisions that would directly impact the American war effort, whatever form it ended up taking, for years to come.

I shook Kristiàn's hand again, and climbed back into the back of the BOV for the next leg of the trip.

***

We stopped again almost an hour later, but this time, while there was some chatter over the radio, Medved didn't come back to talk. Just judging by the time that had passed, I guessed that we'd come to Žarnovica, and Medved hadn't wanted to risk having his American passengers spotted by breaking seal.

I had no choice but to take it as a good sign that we kept on rolling after that, instead of getting into a firefight.

I tried not to think about the possibility that we'd been sold out, and were on the way to a prison camp, as the miles stretched away behind us and we headed deeper into the mountains.

Chapter 32

The forest on the south bank of the Vah River was so thick that we had to push right to the edge of the road to get eyes on the bridge.

It wasn't the main bridge into Bytča. That was about a kilometer to the west, coming off the main highway. For obvious reasons, we were still trying to avoid major thoroughfares.

It had been a fast run north. Medved hadn't stopped for anything, though he admitted, after I brought it up when we halted in the hills above Hrabovè, that we had taken some fire going around Prievidza. It seemed that that city was a free-for-all between the "immigrant" militias, Nationalists of both pro-Russian and strictly Slovak stripes, and EDC peacekeepers. We'd managed to avoid getting entangled, but he couldn't promise that the EDC aircraft overhead hadn't noted the column of armored vehicles pointedly avoiding the conflict.

But we'd made it clear, and had covered the rest of the distance in about four hours. That was almost four times what it would have taken in a regular civilian vehicle, but military vehicles sacrifice speed for ruggedness and armor.

Frankly, I was thankfully surprised that the T-72 hadn't thrown a track.

The entire trip had been conducted buttoned up in the armored vehicles, and now, as non-ideal as this range to the objective was, I was just happy to be out of that steel coffin and back on the ground, on my own two feet, where I could maneuver and take cover instead of sitting and waiting for the bomb, missile, tank shell, or mine to blow me to crispy bits inside a steel box.

Another storm was rolling in. The sky overhead was leaden, and the wind had picked up. That was good, since we'd seen several drones circling above the city as we'd approached through the trees, but most of them were too light for that kind of turbulence. They'd cleared out, recalled by their controllers, leaving the sky mostly clear. Which meant we only had to worry about detection from the ground.

There were two BVPs that I could see on the north end of the bridge, and there might have been two more behind the buildings that obscured our view of the intersection beyond it. So, there was at least a mechanized infantry platoon watching the smaller bridge. Which meant there were probably more watching the bigger one.

We had to get across. Poland lay only twenty-five klicks as the crow flies from us. The only other ways across the Vah meant either going northeast to Zilina, past the ruins of FOB Poole, which would have been a bad idea, since Zilina was also the headquarters for the EDC's 2nd French Contingent, or southwest to Povàžka Bystrica.

We'd picked Bytča because Kristiàn had told Medved that two companies of the 11th Mechanized Infantry that were holding the bridges and the surrounding countryside had publicly declared their allegiance to the Nationalist cause, shortly after hearing about the fight for Nitra. Which, if true, meant that we had a friendly crossing.

If it was true. That was the question.

"What do you think?" Phil whispered. He and I had moved up to the edge of the road, leaving the rest of the team about fifty yards back in the trees. We were too close as it was; I knew that every extra body I had up there was going to increase the chances that we'd get spotted.

"Hard to say," I replied, still watching the BVPs through my binoculars. It was early afternoon, but the clouds made it look like evening was coming on. "They're still flying the Slovak flag, but so are the Nationalists. And if they just flipped..."

"I really, really don't like this complete lack of partisan linkup procedures," Phil muttered.

"You and me both, brother," I replied. I lowered the binos. "Let's head back."

We eased back from the edge of the road and started slipping through the thick forest. It was as bad as anything I'd had to thrash through in northern Virginia; the trees weren't all that tall, but they were very close together. The vehicles were parked on a road on the south side of the hill, about a mile behind us. They were going to have to get on the road to approach the bridge; there was no way they were making it through these woods.

But we hadn't gotten ten yards before my earpiece crackled with Scott's voice.

"Deacon, Weeb," he hissed. "Are you moving back?"

"Roger," I replied, taking a knee and signaling for Phil to halt. Scott wouldn't be asking for nothing.

"Did you move off to our west?" he asked.

"Negative."

"Then watch yourselves," he said. "We're hearing movement to the west; sounds like anywhere from five to ten foot-mobiles."

I swore silently. If Scott had wondered if it was us, that meant that they were coming between Phil and I and the rest of the team. Which could get dicey. At the very least.

I signaled Phil to go flat, but he had heard, and was already halfway there, crawling back under a low tree. I followed suit, pointing my rifle toward the west. We were still just in our fatigues and chest rigs; none of us had bothered to get our ghillie hood-overs back out of our rucks. That might have been a mistake, though I'd hidden in plain sight in just cammies before.

Then we waited.

It didn't take long before I heard what Scott had heard. Footsteps rustled in the leaves and grass under the trees. A twig snapped. Low voices murmured in what sounded like Slovak.

Slowly, the first man came into view, barely twenty yards away. He was dressed in Slovak Army camouflage and gear, carrying a Bren 805. The man behind him was identically dressed and equipped. They were clearly patrolling. But whose side were they on?

It wasn't a new problem. The days of uniformed armies and clear-cut factions seemed to be long over. It was made worse in Slovakia with the split in loyalties, and the apparent shifts within the Loyalist Army after Nitra.

When Medved and I had briefly spoken before this little leader's recon, he had mentioned that we'd gotten a lot farther, a lot faster than he'd expected. Entire Loyalist units seemed to be standing down. We'd passed abandoned checkpoints, or checkpoints where the unit was still there, but had pulled back and hunkered down. The entire country seemed hushed, waiting.

Nitra had been a pivot point. It remained to be seen just what would come of it, especially with the EDC's 1st Division moving in from the west. But for now, the central part of the country seemed to be holding its breath.

The patrol came closer, more men filing through the woods. They were about as spread out as was reasonable in that sort of close vegetation, with about one to two yards between them, moving in single file. They weren't all that tense, and some conversation was going on; they weren't trying to be clandestine like we were.

About five yards away, the lead man held up a hand to call a halt, and they took up positions, on a knee, while the leader pulled a radio out of his vest.

Well, this was a problem. We were both low and behind trees, but we were so close that all it would take was one glance in the wrong direction and we were made. Of course, I was sure that between the two of us, we could take most of them out in the first couple seconds, but it would be a near thing.

I had my sights trained on that lead man, my finger resting lightly on the trigger, my thumb on the selector. It would take a fraction of a second to flip it to *Fire* and put a bullet through him and into the man behind him. The stack had turned out that way; I had two for the price of one. And yet, I didn't want to shoot him, not if he turned out to be a friendly. The problem was, I wasn't sure at that point how to find out without getting shot.

Hell, if we startled these guys from five yards away, it was probably going to be a firefight no matter whose side they were on.

Just as I was resigning myself to staying as stock-still and silent as possible, hoping that the patrol moved on without spotting us so that we could link back up with the team and plan from there, Scott's voice hissed in my earpiece again.

"Deacon, Weeb. If you can't reply, just listen. Làska thinks that he's picked up the Loyalist net on his radio, and wants to try to call them." Làska was the young scout that Medved had sent up with us. He hadn't been willing to leave the entire mission to us, not that I could necessarily blame him. "If they're on our side, he'll try to arrange a linkup."

I couldn't reply. At that distance, we'd be made if my stomach growled.

A moment later, the lead Slovak's radio crackled with what sounded like Làska's voice. The pointman looked startled, and looked back at his number two man, who didn't seem to have any answers for him.

He lifted the radio and spoke into it. I couldn't understand the words, but the tone was easy enough to make out. *Who the hell is this and what the hell are you doing on my net?*

Làska spoke rapidly, while the Slovak pointman interrupted twice. I still couldn't follow the conversation. But it didn't seem especially acrimonious. In fact, the longer I watched them, the more I figured that these guys were desperate for somebody, *anybody* to show up on their side. These guys were looking like cornered rats, and it wasn't a good look.

Which only intensified my intent to stay still and silent, avoiding looking directly at any of them—for some reason I've never been able to understand, you really *can* feel it when somebody is staring at you, particularly when they're only five yards away. They were jumpy and scared, and more than likely to open fire at anyone or anything that surprised them.

Finally, the pointman said something that sounded final, though it was a mystery to me whether it was good final or bad final. He then switched channels on his radio and made another call.

Come on, move on first. It was really starting to hurt, staying stock-still like that. My knee was in an odd position, and it was going to lock up.

337

But he spoke briefly with whoever was on the other end, then stuffed the radio back in his vest and stood up. He spoke rapidly to the rest of the patrol, two of whom sounded like they were objecting to something, but he shouted them down and pointed back downhill toward the bridge and the town.

Unfortunately, downhill meant walking within three feet of my position.

I tried not to breathe. I tried to stop my own heart, because the beating sounded loud as hell, even as old boy's boots crunched in the leaves and fallen branches. Only at the last second did he turn aside, just a little, to find a better way through the thick vegetation. The others followed, filing past about four feet away.

None of them looked down at their feet or saw me where I was huddled under the low-hanging branches of a sycamore. They went right by me, not one spotting me despite the fact that I could easily have tapped any of them in the shin with my rifle.

It wasn't the first time I'd seen it happen. It didn't make it any less unnerving.

I still didn't move while the crunch and rustle of the patrol got farther and farther away. Finally, I couldn't hear them at all, but I still stayed where I was, barely daring to breathe. Only when I hadn't heard anything for at least a minute did I start to move, shifting my leg to relieve the growing pain in my knee.

Phil let out a long, shuddering breath. "Holy shit," he whispered.

"Yeah." I slowly, carefully, and most importantly, *quietly* got to my feet, moving out from under the tree and scanning the woods downhill and to the north, where the patrol had disappeared. I couldn't see anything, but I pointed uphill and farther to the southeast, signaling Phil to get us as far as possible from that patrol before we moved in to rejoin the team.

Without another word, and as soundlessly as possible, we headed back up through the woods. We didn't have any way of knowing just how that conversation had gone, and at that point, I wasn't willing to risk the noise to call Scott and ask.

We'd find out when we got there.

***

Làska wasn't exactly a fountain of information. All he could tell us, as we crouched there in the forest, was that the team leader had said that he needed to contact his superiors. Which was about all that could be hoped for; there was no way that a simple patrol leader in a Slovak Army mechanized infantry platoon was going to be authorized to make official contact with anyone without his superior officers' input. No matter whether the 11th had gone over to the Nationalists or not.

And, I reflected as we headed back to rejoin the convoy, even if they had, how would they know that our Slovaks were Nationalists, and not Loyalists looking to punish them for turning their coats?

There are few wars more complicated than civil ones. And that's saying something.

**

We were back in the weeds, this time with a couple of old Carl Gustavs that Medved had brought along. I was, frankly, surprised that we even had the ammo for them. The Carl Gs had been getting phased out of the Marine Corps when I'd been in, after far too short a tenure.

We were there as backup, as was the T-72, which was sitting on the road about a klick to the east, with a clear shot at the far end of the bridge. Neither Medved, Bradshaw, Draven, or I were eager to take chances. Somewhat to my surprise, Warren had been on the same page. He didn't have his troops down in the brush with us, but they were armed and on the alert, ready to do what they could.

Unfortunately, against BVPs on the bridge, that wasn't much.

The lone BOV with Medved aboard rolled toward the south end of the bridge and halted just before moving out onto the span. Medved popped the commander's hatch and climbed out, dropping to the pavement and stepping out onto the bridge.

The two BVPs at the other end didn't move, but a man in uniform stepped out to face Medved.

"*Imrich?*" the man at the other end yelled.

"Alojz?" Medved replied.

The man at the far end started walking toward the center of the bridge. I kept him in my scope, while Chris, next to me, kept his Carl G pointed at the one BVP we had a shot at. This could still go south awfully quickly.

Medved advanced to meet the man. When they met at the center of the bridge, they stood apart for a moment, then shook hands and bear-hugged each other.

"I *think* that means we're good," Greg said.

"I hope so," I muttered.

A moment later, Medved turned and waved the BOV forward. The armored vehicle rumbled onto the bridge, and we started breaking down and moving toward the road. The rest of the column was already starting down the road toward the bridge, the crew of the lead BOV having apparently called over the radio that we were among friends.

I still glanced at the sky. The wind was still gusty, and the clouds lowering, but the storm hadn't materialized quite as I'd hoped. There was still the very real chance that we'd be observed by a drone, or even a manned aircraft.

The second BOV rolled to a stop at the bottom of the hill, and we piled in. The rest of the column was already trundling across the bridge, Medved's T-72 at the rear. Medved himself had walked to the far end with the other man, who appeared to be a friend.

They were waiting when we reached the north bank. I got out, joined by Warren, Draven, and Bradshaw coming from the Tatrapans.

Medved was grinning with some evident relief as we walked up, all of us still geared up and armed. Even Warren, somewhat to my surprise. I glanced at the man. Physically, he'd hardened up considerably since we'd pulled him out of the wreckage of FOB Keystone. That was inevitable; days on end of hardship and exertion on little food and less sleep will make the laziest butterball turn lean. There was a new determination in the set of his face, though, even though when I looked in his eyes, I could still see the look of a man who was out of his depth and knew it.

"This is *Kapitàn* Alojz Suchỳ," Medved said, his arm around the other man's shoulders. Suchỳ was a slight man, with a hawkish face and pale eyes. "We went to officer training together."

It was an inevitability of civil war. Of course there were men among the Nationalists and the Loyalists who knew each other. There were probably men on either side who were members of the same family.

"The rumors we heard were right," he went on. "The 11th has refused any further orders from the EDC puppet government in Bratislava or the EDC itself. They are holding the bridges here in Bytča for the Nationalist cause."

He sobered, then, and looked north. "There's more, isn't there?" I asked.

Medved nodded. "It looks as though a battalion-sized formation of EDC tanks and mechanized infantry have moved to occupy a line from Makov to Čadca. Apparently, some forces from Poland have already pushed across the border, and now the EDC is trying to seal us off from Poland.

"It will be a fight to get out of here, my friends."

Chapter 33

It was dark, but the clouds that we'd hoped would cover more of our approach were rapidly receding into the east, leaving the sky clear and studded with stars overhead. They were crystal clear; the lights were all out in Vrchrieka, and the column, now consisting of our mixed unit of Americans and Nationalists from Nitra, as well as an entire company of the 11th Mechanized Infantry, was blacked out. Not that it would keep us from being observed if the enemy drones had thermal imaging—which I was sure they did—but it was a standard precaution.

My team was gathered at the back hatch of one of the Tatrapans. Bradshaw, Draven, and Warren had joined us, along with Medved and Suchy. We had our fusion goggles down and switched on, our mags full, and were getting ready to leave.

Under different circumstances, we might have left our rucks behind. They were heavy and cumbersome, and we wouldn't need what little sustainment supplies we had left in the firefight ahead. But most of that stuff had been cleared out and stacked in the BOV we'd been riding anyway. The rucks were full of a much more lethal cargo.

"You realize that this is only going to work if they're really spaced out like we hope they are?" Warren asked. "And if they've got all their drones concentrating on the north."

Scott and I glanced at each other and nodded. "That's why we move carefully and slowly," I said, "and recon every gap before we move into it." I nodded toward the north. "We've got some good concealed approach routes along the hedgerows between the fields. We should be able to see any problems before we get to them."

"That's a lot of 'shoulds,'" Warren said.

"This is the nature of the beast, Warren," Bradshaw put in. "There are risks in combat. There comes a point that you've got to accept them, accept that you've done about as much as you can to alleviate them, and push through, even knowing that you might not come out the other side." His voice sounded hollow; I could tell that he was thinking about those of his men who already had taken those risks and come out the losers. The men who hadn't made it out of the Little Carpathians, or out of Nitra.

I still wasn't sure how my team had, so far, gone unscratched. We were weary, beaten down, and shell-shocked, but so far, none of us had died.

It couldn't last, and I was afraid that our streak was going to end here.

There was an entire battalion between us and Poland. Five companies; two of tanks, three of infantry. And they had air support; we'd heard helos growling in the distance already. Against that, we had one Grex Luporum team, about two-thirds of a Triarii infantry section, reinforced by a mortar section without mortars, a rag-tag, platoon-sized element of US Army soldiers, some of them wounded, and about two companies of mixed Slovak Nationalist troops. We had sixteen BVPs, two BOVs, two Tatrapan APCs, and a single T-72 tank.

That wasn't what I would call an even match.

Which was why my team and I, with Làska and another three Slovak scouts, were going out ahead of the column, in the dead of night. We were going to try to even the odds a little bit.

I looked around the team. "Everybody ready?" I asked. I got a series of nods and monosyllabic grunts. Nobody, not even Phil, seemed to be feeling all that chatty.

Bradshaw stepped over to me. "Watch yourself, brother," he said softly. He stuck out his hand and I gripped it. He turned the handshake into a brief, one-armed bear hug, and then stepped back.

Warren was waiting as Bradshaw stepped away. He didn't seem to quite know where to look, though his expression wasn't the clearest through the white phosphor tubes of my fusion goggles. They were focused on a point about a hundred yards away, so he was a little blurry.

"I…" he started. "Part of me thinks I really should be going with you."

"No," I said, with a chuckle that honestly didn't have much humor behind it. "Don't even think it, Warren. You're not ready for this kind of op. Might never be."

He nodded, looking down at the ground. "Maybe, once we get to Poland…"

"Worry about the next step after Poland once we're in Poland," I told him. "Your boys and girls are going to need you to keep your head in the game, and to focus on the fight we've got right here." I blew out a sigh. I was too damned tired for this, too tired and beaten up to be mentoring a man who was at least five years my senior. "You might not have been trained for this, Warren, but you've got a couple of good NCOs. Listen to them, and follow Bradshaw's lead. He'll keep you in line."

He nodded again, finally looking up at me. He wouldn't have seen much besides the boxy housing of my NVGs. "Good luck," he said.

"You too." I looked around. My team was all waiting, standing with rifles in hand, looking at me.

I'd never expected to be in this position when I'd joined up with the Triarii. Being only the middle of the pack, experience-wise, but having an entire team, not to mention the reinforced company presently relying on my team, looking to me to give the word. It was sobering. Always had been sobering, ever since Hartrick had called me in and told me that I was taking over the team as he moved to a different billet within the organization.

But sobering or not, it wasn't time for woolgathering. "Let's move out," I said. I waved at the hill to the north, and Phil turned and led out, moving past the BVP that was parked and rumbling at the edge of Vrchrieka, moving toward the dark mass of the forest.

***

It was just over a klick to the treeline at the edge of the fields. It hadn't been a straight shot; there were clearings to avoid, and our chosen hedgerow was well off to the west from Vrchrieka.

345

We crouched in the shadows of the treeline, watching the fields and the scattered lights of Vysokà nad Kysucou on the far side.

My fusion goggles were showing bright white spots well separated from the lights. Closer inspection made out the blocky shapes of German Pumas, with the smaller heat spots of human figures on foot nearby. None of them were moving at the moment, but they were there, and from the heat signatures coming off the armored vehicles, their engines were running.

They were also stationed in a perimeter around the town, rather than in the middle of it or on-line to the north, facing Poland. Which was not unsurprising, but was going to make the approach more difficult. While armored vehicles in general aren't great for visibility, I was pretty sure that the Pumas had thermal sights, like the US Army's M5 Powells, and they were holding security, their 30mm cannons aimed out at the fields.

We could hope that the gunners weren't paying that much attention, given the hour. A glance at my watch, carefully shielding the green glow with my hand, told me that it was just after 0200. And if this had been a regular Bundeswehr unit, that would have been a pretty good bet. Discipline in the regular EDC forces had been pretty lax for a long time.

But if these were ED Corps troops, and if Rybàr's intelligence was accurate, we couldn't take that chance. They might be just as disciplined as we were, if the EDC's trainers had really been as professional and focused as Rybàr had suggested.

Next to me in the bushes, Phil pointed up at the sky. I followed his finger, and spotted the moving speck in the sky. It was hard to see; it was small, it didn't have much of a thermal signature, and it wasn't showing lights. But there was just enough ambient light coming from the town that our fusion goggles had managed to pick the drone out.

From there, it was easy enough to spot the other three. They appeared to be flying racetracks, circling above the hills north of the town. I was surprised that there weren't more, especially focusing on the south, given that the Bytča garrison had gone over to the Nationalists.

There was no avoiding the drones, but fortunately, they were far enough away that we might be able to use the hedgerow

346

after all. Especially since it was on low ground between fields. Which also meant that it was going to be wet as hell, but physical discomfort was getting to be the least of our worries.

I would have preferred to use the drone jammer still mounted to one of the BOVs, but that would have meant moving the vehicles up more closely than we wanted to at this stage, and alerting the enemy that something was wrong with their drone coverage.

That was the same reason we couldn't set up a diversion to cover our movement. Setting off a bomb at one end of the town would certainly get them looking in that direction, but it would also alert them that somebody decidedly unfriendly was in the neighborhood.

There was nothing for it. I tapped Phil on the shoulder and pointed down into the hedgerow. He quietly rose and started in.

We were committed.

The hedgerow was less of a hedgerow than it was a beech and pine thicket, with soggy ground at the lowest point. We were soon thrashing through vegetation so thick that I doubted the enemy could have seen us if they'd driven right up to it. I know I couldn't see much, between the thickness of the trees and bushes, and the lay of the fold in the land. We still moved carefully, staying low and scanning ahead constantly. I didn't object to Phil's constant halts to look and listen while crouched down in the little draw, even as our time slipped away.

Compromise is failure, and we'd probably get everyone else killed along with ourselves if we screwed this up.

We had just about a klick to go to reach the road. The line of trees took us uncomfortably close to one of the Pumas and the squad of EDC soldiers either bedded down or on watch near it, but the drones in the sky overhead meant that we didn't dare come out from under the trees until we had no other choice.

That point was going to come, but by then I hoped to be close enough to the town that we'd get lost in the noise, dismissed as just another group of EDC troops on the ground. If the drone operators were even looking that close to the town itself.

It was a long slog, the worst part being when we came to a much thinner stretch of trees, that had looked a lot thicker on the imagery. To make matters worse, there was a small farmhouse right on the edge of the trees. If someone was awake in there, or the enemy had posted sentries, or they just had a dog that started barking...

But we slipped past without being detected, plunging back into the thicker strip of woods leading most of the rest of the way to the outskirts of town. By then we could hear the growl of the nearest Puma's idling engine, almost drowned out by the more distant, but louder, snarl of helicopter rotors.

Finally, we got to the end. The nearest Puma was rumbling about two hundred fifty yards away. But we were out of cover; the trees stopped at the edge of the railroad tracks that paralleled Highway 487.

I put my hand on Phil's shoulder, watching the Puma stationed on the road. It was awfully close, but our options had been limited. I could also barely see its prow; I probably wouldn't have even noticed it for sure if it hadn't been for the two men with rifles who had wandered partway down the road toward us before turning around and heading back.

I stayed in place for a long moment, taking in the lay of the land and what I could see of the enemy dispositions. I thought we could dash behind the nearest house without exposing ourselves to that armored fighting vehicle, but I wanted to be as sure as possible before we moved.

After a couple of minutes, I was as confident in our route as I was going to get. I pointed it out to Phil as best I could with hand and arm signals, and he nodded after a moment. He got the gist. I turned back and passed it on to the rest of the team.

Then Phil stood up and started toward the nearest house.

He didn't dash. Didn't run in a half-crouch. He walked normally, upright, just like we'd patrolled through the woods and over the hill. No hurry, just moving from place to place with some purpose and alertness.

That was deliberate. In the event we got spotted, we knew that everyone with a weapon still in the town was an enemy. The EDC didn't. Even if they were pretty sure that there shouldn't be a patrol out that way, they would have to check.

That would give us the momentary advantage we needed to break contact and run for it.

A good infiltrator doesn't sneak in a way that would appear suspicious. If there's an unavoidable chance of being spotted, he acts like he belongs there.

We'd gotten a lot of practice at that in places like Portland, San Francisco, Chicago, and Baltimore.

In fifty yards, we were out of sight, disappearing into the shadows of a two-story farmhouse with a peaked roof. The road ahead of us looked clear. We started to move more carefully, weapons up and scanning for contact as we moved toward the road itself.

There wasn't a lot of cover at the road itself. There was no sidewalk. Some of the fences had concrete bases, but were otherwise just built of wire or pickets. The houses, most of which were timber and plaster, were set back from the road, and those that weren't had fenced front yards.

Frankly, even in the dark, the town looked less European than anywhere else we'd been in Slovakia. If I hadn't known that we were less than seven klicks from the Polish border, I could have sworn we were in Idaho or Montana.

We paused, still partially sheltered from the road by a small, boxy house with a flat roof and a porch that faced east instead of the road to the north. It wasn't ideal, and I knew that if anyone inside looked out their window, we were screwed. But it was all we had to work with.

Of course, I suspected that the local Slovaks weren't going to be in a hurry to alert the EDC invaders who had occupied their town of something strange, provided they didn't simply dismiss us as more EDC soldiers patrolling.

I didn't want to speak. I just signaled, tapping my shoulder and pointing to the ground. We started dropping rucks, taking turns to avoid dropping security. Just because we couldn't see any enemy troops on the road didn't mean they weren't around the bend.

I pointed to Phil, David, Jordan, Chris, and Reuben. Scott would cover the rear with Greg, Tony, and Dwight. Dwight had already dropped his ruck and moved ahead, to where he could see down the road to the west, dropping prone behind his

Mk 48 and settling in to cover that direction. Tony was setting up pointing the opposite direction.

With security set, the rest of us, weapons slung and laden with the IEDs and initiation systems we'd pulled out of our rucks, started moving toward the road.

We were going to make sure that the enemy couldn't reinforce Vysokà nad Kysucou when the column hit it.

Most of the IEDs weren't that large, being about the size of a large coffee can. They were still heavy; shaped charges embedded with copper cones to make Explosively Formed Projectiles aren't exactly light.

We worked quickly, both because time was of the essence—Medved wanted to try to punch through just before dawn, which was getting closer with distressing rapidity—and because we didn't know just when a security patrol was going to come down the road. The EFPs needed to be placed carefully, snugged into the ditch on the side of the road with the inverted cones pointing up and inward. Then the initiation system, thin wires with small contact points at regular intervals, was wired into them and threaded across the road to the other side.

We had to be sneaky with the initiators. The idea wasn't to hit the lead vehicle first and then leave the rest of the IEDs ahead of it, essentially useless. We had them daisy-chained, with the initiation system at one end. By the time a lead vehicle rolled over the contacts, the bulk of an enemy formation should be inside the kill zone.

The IEDs wouldn't kill everything. There was a good chance that more than a few would miss. We tried to avoid pointing them at buildings, but there was going to be some collateral damage.

I just told myself that we had no other choice but surrender and execution. I hoped that God would see it the same way.

I hoped that most of the civilians had already headed for the hills when the tanks and IFVs had showed up.

With the IEDs set and armed, we moved back to our staging area and picked up our rucks again. Scott pulled Dwight and Tony back in, and I pointed to Phil. He started across the road, making for the woods behind the houses to the north.

We dashed across in pairs, no longer as concerned with looking normal. We hadn't been made yet, which told me that the drones weren't watching the town itself. And we were still way too close to those IEDs. I wanted some standoff. Besides, we still had half a dozen more in our packs, that needed to be set on the other side of town, about a mile to the east.

We hurried through the thick pine and fir woods, our packs noticeably lighter, and came quickly to what might have once been a clear-cut. There were still strips of woods standing, but there were straight, rectangular clearings between them.

With time getting short, we didn't get too sneaky. Phil turned north and pushed uphill until we had enough trees between us and the town that we could cross the open area without too much risk of being spotted. Only then did we turn east again, heading downhill, moving quickly from tree to tree.

We'd gotten so fixated on avoiding notice from the perimeter around the town, and the trees were thick enough, that we didn't even see the small farmhouse squatting in a clearing a good three hundred yards farther north than we'd expected, until Phil burst through the trees and found himself facing it, about fifteen yards away.

And the half-dozen EDC soldiers looting the farmer's chicken coop.

The EDC soldiers had frozen at the same time Phil had, and I caught up with him on the inside of the treeline to see the tableau of six men, all but one with their rifles set aside, their hands full of chickens, and Phil, almost frozen, but already starting to bring his weapon up.

The one with the rifle yelled and snapped his rifle to his shoulder. I shot him, the *crack* of the report echoing across the hills in the quiet of the night. His head snapped back, dark fluid splashed against the chicken coop, and he dropped.

The other five dropped the birds and dove for their rifles, but Phil, Greg, and I were already shooting. Bullets smashed through heads, ribs, lungs, and stomachs. In seconds, it was all over, the last of them gasping out his final breaths with a horrible gurgle. The chickens had gone berserk, flapping away with squawks drowned out by the rifle reports.

351

But it was too late. The echoes of the gunfire were still rolling across the valley.

We were made.

Chapter 34

Phil was still rooted to the ground, his weapon pointed at the bodies of the men we'd just gunned down. I could hear his ragged breathing; he wasn't panicking, but he was definitely rattled by the close call. On top of everything else that had happened, Phil wasn't doing too good.

"Let's move," I told him, stepping up next to him, my own rifle pointed at the darkened house. We had a little time; I doubted that the soldiers down below would immediately think that their men had been ambushed. It was more likely that they'd shot up the farmhouse themselves. However, that didn't mean they wouldn't send someone up to check it out, anyway. And once they found the bodies, the hunt would be on.

Not to mention the fact that, intervening hill or not, Medved and the others had to have heard that burst of gunfire. They were going to be on their way; Medved had made that clear enough before we'd left.

Bradshaw would probably have shot him if he hadn't.

Half-pulling Phil, I forged across the lawn and into the trees, my rifle held muzzle-high, scanning the sky overhead as I realized that the enemy didn't need to wait until another fireteam or squad could come up and investigate the gunfire. They just had to reroute a drone.

Unfortunately, we didn't have quite as much time as I'd hoped.

Phil saw the straggler first. He had turned to look back toward the house and the chicken coop as we pushed for the trees, and suddenly stopped dead, throwing out a hand to grab me before hurling himself backward, dragging me with him. I felt the bullets *snap* past my nose before we landed in a heap behind the coop.

I was on my back, weighed down by my ruck, which was light*er*, but still not *light*. I scrabbled backward, the rucksack acting like an anchor, keeping me from moving far. More rounds kicked up dirt near my boots, and I pulled my feet back, which didn't help me get my balance any.

Greg pushed past me and opened fire in return, leaning out just past the corner of the coop and hammering a fast series of five shots back at the town. But when he pulled back and reached down to help me up, he was shaking his head.

"He's running," he said, breathing hard. "I didn't get a clear shot."

I gripped his hand and heaved myself up, the rucksack threatening to drag me back down until I got my feet under me. "Let's move," I grunted. "We need to get under cover *now*."

I could already hear the faint buzz of motors above us. The drones were coming, drawn by the gunfire. The initial burst of fire might have been the soldiers murdering the house's owners, but the second series of shots would have told anyone paying attention that there was trouble up on the fringes of the town.

Jordan was already hauling Phil up. "I don't think we're going to get close to the road, now," he said.

"I doubt it," I agreed, as we pushed into the forest "Plan's out the window. Medved's going to be moving. We need to break contact and get into position to support the rest when they come up." I was already forcing my tired brain to think ahead, even as the buzzing in the air got louder, and I started to hear the rumble of engines down below. The EDC was moving, responding to the contact on the north side of their perimeter.

I pointed uphill, and Phil started moving, the rest of us falling into a rough V formation behind him.

The hill was getting steeper and the trees thicker. On one hand, that was an advantage; thicker trees meant a better chance to hide from the air. On the other hand, it was slowing us down, especially being as tired as we were, and the enemy was coming. And they were, presumably, better-rested than we were.

Footing was getting treacherous, and we were getting spread out through the trees, but we kept moving. Phil was lagging; I was gaining on him despite my exhaustion. His shorter legs were working against him. As I glanced back, I got a glimpse of a ragged mob of eight more heat signatures moving through the trees. The burly one that was Dwight was noticeably falling behind.

The buzz of a drone was getting louder. It didn't sound quite like the kamikazes that the enemy had been using in Nitra, but I couldn't be sure. It wasn't like my hearing was the best anymore. Worse, I could hear the growl and rattle of a Puma IFV behind us. It wasn't going to be able to follow us into those woods, but let the gunner get a glimpse of a thermal signature, and the trees weren't going to do much against that 30mm.

I paused, the breath heaving in my lungs and my quads on fire, turning back to make sure that Dwight didn't fall too far behind.

Then the world exploded.

I can't say I heard the strike. I saw it as a sudden blinding flash, felt it like a hammer to the skull. Everything went black for a moment.

Everything was still black when I opened my eyes, but I quickly realized that was because I'd been thrown on my face, with my ruck over my head, holding me down. My NVGs were digging into my eye sockets, pointed down into the dirt.

Remembering the explosives in the pack, I hastily scrabbled for the quick releases on the straps and yanked on them, freeing myself only to just about slide down the hill into a tree. I caught myself, though unfortunately with my rifle rather than my hand. I had to check it by feel as I got up, since my fusion goggles were still askew, but it didn't *feel* like the scope was broken. I'd put it through worse.

I snatched the goggles up so I could see. My ears were ringing, every sound deadened as if I was underwater. My ruck was smoking, and I quickly heaved it downhill and away from all of us, in case something was about to blow. It didn't get nearly as far as I wanted it too, but I needed to assess the situation, and it hadn't blown up yet.

The HOT-3 missile had missed; if it had hit, I'd have been dead. We all would have been dead. I'd seen up close and personally what a Hellfire could do to a small unit in a small area, and the HOT-3 wasn't all that different.

It had blown half a dozen trees apart, one of them having fallen almost on top of Phil. He was flat on his back, not moving. Neither was Greg, a few yards away. Greg was halfway under the top of the tree, which had been partially denuded of branches and needles by the blast.

Downslope, though the sound was muted to my traumatized ears, Dwight opened fire, the bright flash of his Mk 48's muzzle blast flickering in the dark. A moment later, David joined him.

Push the fight. Hartrick's mantra went through my mind without my even consciously thinking about it. Phil and Greg might be dead. They might be alive. But if we got overrun in the next couple of minutes, it wouldn't matter for either of them.

I skidded down the hill, almost bouncing off of a tree in the process, Jordan not far off to my left. Neither of us were moving all that well; the HOT-3 might not have killed us, but the near-miss had still been a hell of a shock.

I stumbled against a tree, whipping my rifle up as I spotted a glowing thermal shape dash toward another tree off to the right and downhill. My first shot missed, smacking bark off the tree he'd just ducked behind. It was a bad shot, and I knew it even as the trigger broke. It wasn't because I'd knocked my scope off zero when I'd hit the tree.

Rifle and machinegun fire rattled and roared in the woods, echoing between the trees, muzzle flashes briefly lighting the night. Then it all turned into insignificant noise as that Puma opened fire with its 30mm.

The gunner didn't have much of a target, which was the only reason that none of us got pulped. Massive shells hammered through the trees, exploding trunks and shattering branches, showering us with splinters and smashed bark even as the shockwaves slammed at us. I dropped flat, getting as small as possible behind a tree, my hindbrain gibbering and telling me that now was the time to curl up in the fetal position and hope it all went away.

But I couldn't listen to the animal part of my brain. I knew it. So, I popped out from behind the trunk, shot the EDC soldier who was charging uphill under cover of the Puma's fire through the skull, and started crawling forward.

I wasn't just advancing for the sake of advancing. I had seen a fallen rucksack with an RPG-75 sticking out of it, lying against a tree a few yards down the slope. I didn't know whose it was; Chris, Reuben, and Scott had all been carrying the 75s. All I knew at that point was that that tube sticking out of the ruck was our only hope against that vehicle.

Of course, I was probably going to die before I could kill the Puma. The small arms fire was getting thicker, bullets *snap*ping past my head, smacking into tree trunks and kicking up gouts of dirt and leaves around me, and no matter how much return fire Tony and Dwight could put down, we were still getting pinned down and suppressed by that damned cannon.

All this damned way, just to die in the woods six klicks from the border.

Movement caught my eye; down on my belly, I was going to be hard-pressed to get a solid look at anything through the NVGs, as the mount and the weight bore them down toward the dirt. I rolled halfway on my side, snapping my rifle up just in time to hammer two shots into the man running toward me from the flank, just as he fired over my head.

He hadn't been aiming at me. I heard Dwight grunt, and then his Mk 48 went silent.

I rolled back over. Dwight was down on his face. He wasn't moving.

The 30mm had ceased fire for a moment, but I kept crawling toward that ruck. It was barely three meters in front of me...

Another 30mm shell blew up the tree over my head, showering me with smashed bits of wood pulp, splinters, and broken branches. I tucked my head as the debris cascaded down on me, waiting for the top of the trunk to drop down and brain me. But it fell behind me, crashing down through the branches around it with a noise that would have been catastrophic if not for the 30mm rounds blasting its cousins to splinters around it.

Finally, throwing caution to the winds, I got up on all fours and scrambled the last couple of yards to the ruck.

Letting my rifle dangle on its sling, I ripped the RPG-75 out of the rucksack and prepped it as fast as I could by feel. Not being terrifically familiar with the weapon, I fumbled it a little, even as I crouched as low as I could. Tony was still in the fight; I could hear him hammering away, the muzzle flash flickering off to my left. Other rifles were still blasting away, so we weren't alone.

Hoping and praying that I'd armed it right, I rose up, found that I couldn't see through the sight with my NVGs, spent a precious second trying to flip them up before ripping the skullcap mount off my head, and shouldered the AT launcher. I couldn't see much; it was dark as hell under the trees, but that 30mm muzzle blast was pretty impressive, especially from so close. The real trick was going to be hitting it without hitting a tree trunk.

"Backblast area clear!" I yelled hoarsely, and fired.

The *bang* resounded deafeningly across the hillside, almost simultaneous with the blinding flash of the impact. The Puma was so close that I didn't even hear the *whoosh* of the rocket.

There was a moment's quiet after that deafening report. Then a jet of flame blasted up out of the top of the Puma's hull, and it started to burn in earnest.

I dropped the tube, snatching up my rifle with one hand while I pulled my NVGs back over my head with the other, but instead of opening fire, I ran bent double to try to avoid the sporadic small arms fire that was now starting back up the hill in the aftermath of the Puma's death, to Dwight.

He was clearly dead. Even without being able to see him clearly, I could tell. The bullet had ripped his throat out, and he was limp and unresponsive. I had to heave him off the 48 so that I could pick it up. It felt like there was still half a belt in the soft-sided drum, or "nutsack." I braced the gun against the nearest tree trunk, pivoted around it, and ripped off a fifteen-round burst at the handful of flickering muzzle flashes to the right of the stricken Puma.

Scott was suddenly by my side. "We've got an opening, Matt!" he screamed over the roar of gunfire. "We've got to break contact and move!"

I knew he was right. But right then, I didn't want to leave that spot. I didn't want to leave Dwight behind. I didn't know if Phil and Greg were alive, but I didn't want to leave them, either.

I'd left the dead after the airstrike that had destroyed Killian's vehicles. I hadn't liked it, but I'd done it. I had to do it now. But I didn't want to. Right then, I was ready to stay there with Dwight, even if I died, too.

I wasn't thinking straight. Not that I was aware of it at the time. All I knew was that my head hurt, along with the rest of me, that Dwight was lying there next to me and couldn't move on his own, and that the people who'd killed him were down that hill, and if I kept fighting, maybe I could kill them, too.

Scott fired a fast series of pairs from the other side of the tree. "Damn it, Matt!" He fired twice more. "We've got to move!"

"Dwight's gone," I replied, between bursts. It didn't make a lot of sense, saying that then. It didn't make any difference in the context of what Scott was saying. Dwight was dead, but that didn't change the fact that we needed to break contact or we were going to get flanked and wiped out.

"And if we don't move, we're all going to join him!" Scott yelled. "Come on, Matt, snap out of it!"

Maybe that was what I needed to hear. Maybe I was finally shaking off a little of the concussion from the drone strike and the shock of firing that 75. Maybe my guardian angel was smacking me in the back of the head, telling me to listen to my ATL.

I fired another burst, then got up and turned. The only thing to do was lead. There was no chance to plan and coordinate in that chaotic hell of a firefight in the woods, in the dark. "Moving!"

I ran up the hill. Or, I tried to. Weighed down by the machinegun, my own rifle and ammo, and up a steepening slope, it was more of a lumbering jog. But I got a few meters uphill and found another tree to get behind, dropping to a knee and checking that I wasn't about to put a burst into Scott's back before I dropped prone, laid the 48 on its bipods, and fired, holding down the trigger for a ten-count, the muzzle blast spitting flame and throwing up dirt and leaves in front of my face.

Scott and Tony moved, as more rifle fire echoed from above and to my flanks. At least some more of the team was still alive. I fired another burst as the two of them labored past me, shifting my hips to play the stream of bullets back and forth across a widening sector of fire as Tony and Scott got out of my way.

Then, just as I was about to get up, realizing that I'd left the reloads with Dwight's body, and that I had maybe a quarter belt left, a new sound suddenly changed everything.

The *wham* of a 125mm cannon firing echoed down the valley, followed almost immediately by the *boom* of a Puma dying.

Medved had arrived.

Chapter 35

That 125mm thunderclap seemed to have shocked the entire valley into stillness. At least for a moment.

The EDC infantry, already stunned by the destruction of their armored support, fell silent for a moment before they started falling back. They were moving in good order; if anything, they were moving back better than we were. They were bounding back under cover of their compatriots' fire, even as all hell started to break loose to the south.

I heard a 30mm cannon start pounding away to the south, only to be silenced by another crash of 125mm fire. What sounded like two anti-tank missiles roared out over the fields, and sporadic small-arms fire started to rattle and crackle from the town as well as the distant treeline.

"Deacon, Flat," Bradshaw called.

"Flat, Deacon," I replied, gasping for air as we kept moving. The Mk 48 was really starting to weigh me down. "Be advised, the east road is not blocked. I say again, the east road is not blocked."

"Copy," he replied. "Are you near that burning hulk up on the hillside?"

"That's us," I replied. "We're going to try to keep moving east, break contact, and then hit them from the rear, down the next draw over."

"Hold what you've got," he said. He might have sounded a little exasperated. "Get to a defensive position and go firm. If we know where you are, we're not going to accidentally shoot you."

He was right. I was too rattled, too drained, and I was probably concussed. We were already in a bad position; the enemy was between us and the friendlies. That put us downrange of every weapon the Nationalists had. If we hunkered down and stayed in place, we could still do some damage, without risking a friendly-fire incident.

I looked up. There weren't many rocks around there; that part of the Carpathians was old, and the slope was smooth except for the trees. But there was a thicker stand of pines or firs up above, about fifty yards to the north. It wouldn't stand up to missile or cannon fire, but it was better than nothing.

"Phil!" I had to yell for him twice before he looked back, and I pointed toward the stand of trees. "Three-sixty, right there!" He nodded, and forged toward the stand of trees, and I followed, my OBR beating against the backs of my legs as I struggled uphill.

I got about halfway there before turning back, taking a knee with one foot braced against a tree, the nearly-empty Mk 48 pointed back downhill as I searched for targets.

The rest of the team was struggling up the hillside to my right and left; I recognized Tony by his bulk and the machinegun in his hands, David from his smaller size. I risked a look around, since the fire from the base of the hill had died away to almost nothing, and got a quick count. I only counted seven, including myself. Had we lost two more? Had we made it all that way only to be gutted here, at the end?

Tony reached a tree just uphill and to my left, and set up. "Set!" he gasped. I heaved myself to my feet and started slogging up toward the stand of trees.

It took far too long to get there. The staccato thunder of the fight down to the south and the rising growl of rotor blades to the north only added to the sense of urgency. But I pushed through, finally reaching the stand of trees and struggling to get set without my boots sliding out from under me. "Tony!" I yelled. "Turn and go!"

Tony wasn't moving quite as fast as I had been, but as he lumbered up the hillside, I got a better picture of the overall situation, and our position. The stand of trees was in such a position that I could get a clearer picture of the entire valley than I'd been able to farther down.

The first thing I saw was that my fears hadn't come true; there were nine of us either already set or moving to the stand of trees. We'd lost Dwight, but so far, he was the only one we'd have to bury. Or simply have a service for; I wasn't sure we were going to be able to go back for his body. He'd join the other unburied dead, both Triarii and regular Army.

The squad we'd been fighting had fallen back into the town, leaving quite a few bodies behind them. But they were the least of our worries at that point.

I could see the T-72, the BVPs, and the BOVs spreading out across the fields from the narrow, unimproved road leading over the ridge from Vrchrieka, their distinctive outlines blazing white in my thermals. Medved had pushed the tank out onto the higher ground just to the west of the draw we'd used to cover our approach, and was laying waste to anything that tried to shoot at him. So far, the element of surprise seemed to have worked to our advantage; it seemed that the EDC was worried about incursions from Poland, and probably thought that they'd gotten hit by a Polish recon unit. There was certainly no love lost between the Poles and the EDC; Warsaw had cut away from the dying corpse of the EU before the European Defense Council had been officially formed, and had, by then, enough military power on the German frontier to make it abundantly clear that trying to force them back into the fold was going to be a very bad idea. Being right at the end of the Fourth Balkan War, the EU had gotten the message. Their own forces had been badly handled by the Serbs and Kosovars both, and they knew that they didn't have a good chance against the Poles in a stand-up fight. So, despite the fact that the 11th Mechanized had gone over just to their south, their entire focus seemed to be on the north.

The 11th's BVPs were staying in the trees, hammering at anything that looked like a hardened position with 30mm fire. Their Spigot launchers were elevated, too; they were hunting any armor that might try to stick its head out.

But the dynamics of the battle were already shifting. I couldn't see the east road, but I could see the west, and reinforcements were already coming from Makov and Varechov potok.

There were too many trees and houses in the way to get a full picture of the column that was working its way up the road, but I could definitely identify Pumas and the lower, wider silhouettes of Leopard 2 tanks. One T-72 wasn't going to last long against that, if our IED ambush didn't work out quite as well as we'd hoped.

"Flat, Deacon," I called. "Be advised, we have eyes on enemy reinforcements coming from the west. Estimate company strength, Pumas and Leopard 2s."

"Roger," Bradshaw replied. There was a pause, presumably as he passed the information on to the Slovaks. "How far are they from your block?"

I peered between the trees. "I think the lead elements should hit the initiator in the next two minutes," I said. But even as I let my thumb off the transmit switch, I felt a sinking sensation in my guts as I watched what was unmistakably a tank section veer off the road, pushing between the scattered houses and toward the fields. The tanks weren't going to get caught in the ambush. And they were out of range of our remaining RPG-75s.

But before I could send Bradshaw the warning, the lead Puma hit the initiation system strung across the road.

For a moment, the western suburb of Vysokà nad Kysucou disappeared in a strobing flash and blast of smoke and debris. The stuttering detonations shook the ground beneath us, and the shockwave made the trees bend and wave as it washed over the hill. As the smoke started to clear, we could see intense, flickering points of light through the murk, as vehicles burned and men died.

In the aftermath, I mashed the push-to-talk button. "Flat! Tell Medved…" But it was too late.

Enormous muzzle flashes pulsed at the far side of the still-dispersing cloud of smoke and debris. The reports of the tank guns rippled out across the valley like the world's biggest hammer hitting the world's biggest anvil. Four streaks of bright light, all that could be seen of the sabot rounds, slammed into the T-72.

The tank disappeared in a bright flash and an ugly puff of smoke. The turret blew off and soared into the sky, coming back down on the burning hulk a moment later with a crash that seemed like little more than a tap after the cacophony of Medved's death.

One of the BVPs launched a Spigot. The anti-tank missile streaked across the field, barely visible as a tiny point of flame in my fusion goggles, and slammed into the easternmost Leopard 2 with a resounding *bang.*

The German tank returned fire a moment later, and the BVP burned. The missile must have hit the front glacis and failed to penetrate the armor.

The other vehicles were trying to scatter, the BOVs ducking into the draw while the BVPs and the Tatrapans ran for the trees. Another BVP died, transfixed by another streak of white and briefly vanishing in a flash and a cloud of smoke, the *wham* of the impact drifting across the valley to us.

There was nothing we could do but watch. We had no air support, no artillery. The enemy that was killing our brothers in arms was out of range of the handful of anti-tank rockets we had left.

But that wasn't going to stop me. We were probably all going to die. I'd be damned if I sat still and just watched it happen.

I dropped the Mk 48. "Have we got any 75s left?" I thought briefly of my own ruck, somewhere down the slope in the trees, but I hadn't packed an AT launcher, either an RPG-75 or a Matador. I'd loaded up on EFPs, which weren't going to help at this point.

Scott looked around, but David answered the question. "We've got two and one SA-18."

The SAM wouldn't do squat against tanks, but I wasn't willing to drop it. "Drop everything but the launchers, weapons, and ammo," I rasped. "We're going to go down there and kill a couple of those tanks."

It said something about the mental state we were all in that nobody objected. We were moderately safe there in the trees; the enemy had fallen back at the same time we had. Going back into the fight was only piling risk on top of risk.

But, despite the little squabbles that often arose, we were Triarii. And there were Americans, including other Triarii, on the far side of that valley, getting cut to pieces by the same bastards who had murdered thousands of other Americans not that long ago.

None of us were going to be able to look ourselves in the mirror again if we ran for it and left those men to die. Even if we could get to the border without being spotted from the air and intercepted.

There was a rustle of movement, almost inaudible as the battle raged down below, as those still carrying rucks dropped them, and the last RPG-75s were pulled out. I left the Mk 48 where it was; there weren't enough rounds left in the nutsack to make it worth the weight anymore.

Another Spigot raced across the fields. They'd do better if they volley-fired them at the tanks, but the BVP commanders seemed to have lost a lot of their coordination with the loss of Medved's tank and the two BVPs that had already been destroyed. The ATGM smacked into a house, missing the targeted tank entirely, just as the Leopard 2 fired again, its main gun belching fire. That answering tank round missed, though; the BVP driver wasn't holding still for anything, which may have been why the gunner had missed in the first place.

"Ready," Scott said. He had an RPG-75 on his shoulder, as did Reuben and Chris. I got up, my rifle back in my hands.

"Let's go."

The truth was, the way things were going, we probably weren't going to manage to do much more than avenge our fallen. We had a good seven hundred yards to go to get into a firing position.

But we had to try.

Phil and I led out, the rest falling in behind us. But we hadn't gotten far before Phil stopped, throwing up a fist.

I wasn't sure what had made him halt; I scanned the smoke-shrouded forest around us, seeing the burning Puma that we'd killed, along with some of the more distant hulks of the vehicles that had run into the IED ambush.

I heard it then. The rising growl of rotors. The helicopters were coming.

"Get that SAM!" I hissed, though we only had the one, and there was definitely more than one bird coming. Greg turned and started back up the hill toward our little redoubt.

Rockets howled by overhead, the smoke trails dimly lit by their exhausts, and slammed into one of the BOVs that had sheltered in the draw. The vehicle fireballed, then started burning fiercely. A moment later, two pairs of Tigers swept by overhead, their rotor wash lashing the tops of the trees, the snarl of their engines vibrating the ground.

We dropped flat, to a man, without a single command or signal to do so. It's hard to say whether it's worse to be under air attack, or facing armor on foot. The same sense of helplessness applies in both cases.

We could still fight; small arms fire against helicopters had been taught since Vietnam. And we would fight. I didn't know of any case where massed small arms fire had actually managed to shoot one down, but damn it, we were going to try.

"Spread out, take cover, and get ready to shoot!" I yelled. It wasn't as if stealth was going to help much at that point.

We weren't going to get a shot at the tanks. They were too far away, and there was no way we were going to close that distance quickly, not with enemy helos overhead. *Sorry, guys. We tried.*

The two pairs had split, banking off to west and east, ready to take the remaining Nationalist vehicles in a pincer. Greg was coming down the hill, panting and skidding on needles and fallen branches, dragging our one SA-18 MANPAD with him.

Then one of the Tigers exploded.

The flash caught me completely by surprise. One moment, the helo was stooping on the BVPs below, the next it was a fireball raining bits of fuselage and shattered rotor blades on the fields beneath. His wingman tried to bank away, but exploded a split-second later.

Two arrowhead shapes roared by overhead as the second pair of Tigers dove for the deck and ran for it. I could feel the crackling thunder of the jets' engines in my chest as they streaked past, their single engines bright points of light in the dark. At the same time, I heard another set of jet engines growling in the distance, getting louder by the second.

The second flight of F-16s fired a rippling cascade of rockets at the Leopard 2s that had been murdering the Nationalists from the south side of the road. Fireballs and spouts of dirt and smoke billowed up into the night sky, followed a moment later by the hammering *thuds* of the rocket detonations.

More noise was reaching us from the far side of the hill, more explosions and what sounded vaguely like tank gun fire. More planes went by overhead, this time the bigger, twin-tailed forms of F-15s, while heavy, dragonfly shapes beneath pounding rotors started to lay rockets into Vykorà nad Kysucou itself.

The Poles must have heard the fighting and decided to join the party.

"Deacon, Flat," Bradshaw called. I breathed a sigh of relief at the sound of his voice. "Warren's got comms with an American unit commander from BCT 7. They are hitting the EDC formation from the eastern flank, moving west across the fields. Watch your fires in that direction."

"Roger," I replied. "I hope they do the same."

"We've passed on that you're up there," he said. "They'll be watching, but you might want to turn on some IR strobes or something. Those Hind pilots might not be sure that you're friendlies."

That might not be the best idea, under the circumstances; I was pretty sure that the EDC troops had NVGs, as well. But we had to do *something*.

I had just dug my strobe out of my chest rig and flicked it on when Phil grabbed me and pointed.

A ragged group of figures, carrying rifles, were moving out of Vysokà nad Kysucou below us, pushing northwest and toward the trees. They weren't in much of any kind of formation, and they were moving fast. They looked like they were running for it.

The only one not carrying a weapon was the little man in the middle.

The Americans and Poles were unleashing holy hell on the EDC formations to the east of town. The Leopards 2s to the west—those that had survived the F-16s' first pass, that is—were pulling out, fleeing down the road toward Makov. We suddenly had no targets within range.

Except for that group down there.

"Let's move," I said. "If they fight, kill 'em. If they surrender, maybe we can get some intel out of 'em."

We spread out, weapons up, and started slipping through the trees. It was as if, suddenly having been given some renewed hope by the American and Polish attack, we'd gotten our second wind.

Some of the EDC soldiers were still looking around them. One of them looked up as we swept down toward them and let out a yell, snapping his rifle to his shoulder and opening fire. The muzzle blast flickered in the darkness, and bullets smacked into a tree above Greg's head as he ducked behind the trunk.

We responded with a ragged volley, flame flickering in the woods. Bullets smashed men off their feet even as the group turned and dropped to a knee to return fire.

They reacted with admirable alacrity. One grabbed the unarmed man and forced him flat, while the others ran for trees or any bit of cover in the dirt they could find.

I shot one who was trying for a tree just barely too far away. I tracked in toward him as he dashed toward it, catching him with a bullet high center chest just before he slammed into the trunk and slumped behind it, his rifle clattering off the bark as he fell. Quickly tracking toward the next man, I had to duck behind a tree myself as he fired at me, the first round going past my ear with a harsh *snap*, the next one ricocheting off the trunk with an angry buzz.

Then Tony about cut him in half with a burst from that Mk 48.

Two more dashed from cover, trying to get out to our flank. Three of us fired at the same time, and they dropped. One kept moving for a while, but he was curled in the fetal position around the bullet hole in his guts, screaming his lungs out. He wasn't a threat anymore.

The unarmed man was suddenly yelling, in a language I couldn't quite make out. The gunfire had stopped, which was when I noticed that a lot of the sounds of combat in the distance had also died down.

I peered around the trunk of the tree. The unarmed man was standing up, his hands held on his head. He barked something at the men next to him, who dropped their rifles and followed suit.

We moved down toward them, weapons leveled, fingers hovering close to triggers. I wasn't sure this wasn't a trap; I'd seen it happen before. But nobody pulled a grenade or was lying in wait with a rifle pointed at us. The wounded and dead were scattered across about twenty yards, and we moved through them carefully, kicking weapons away from hands until we came to the man with his hands on his helmet.

I couldn't see a lot of detail in the fusion goggles, but he wasn't nearly as heavily geared up as the others. He did have a pistol, which he had unloaded and laid on the ground at his feet. He also had a small pack on his back.

He didn't resist as I tied his hands behind his back while the rest of the team either secured his two surviving soldiers and set security. "Who are you?" I asked, as I cut the pack off his back and started rummaging through it. There was a laptop and several maps inside, along with what looked like survival gear, a radio, and extra food. I wasn't sure if I could expect an answer, but the man replied in a faint British accent.

"I am Captain Blithe, 3rd Company, 2nd Battalion of the 3rd Mechanized Regiment, EDC 1st Division," he said.

"What's on the laptop, Captain?" I asked, looking up from the pack at him.

"You can't expect me to answer that," he replied.

"Maybe," I said, turning him around. "It's going to be a long war. May as well make it as easy for yourself as you can."

"I don't think it will be," he said in reply. "I daresay it's already over. This little victory of yours won't count for much."

"We'll see." But while I wasn't indulging in false bravado, a part of me wondered if he wasn't right. It wasn't like we were in a good spot as a nation, and Poland wasn't the most strategically advantageous position to fight from.

But we'd fight. One way or another.

Of course, I could have pointed out that his bravado was a bit misplaced. The company commander running away from the fight was hardly the sign of a robust fighting force.

370

But I was too tired. I'd hand him over to the BCT commander and the Poles. Let them get what information they could out of him. We'd make sure we got our hands on it, one way or another. The Triarii had friends high enough that we could make that happen.

We were all in the same fight now, anyway.

The thunder of gunfire and rockets was dying down. Smoke was drifting across the valley below us, but the fighting seemed to have started petering out. With the last of the prisoners secured, it was all over but the linkup.

Epilogue

Dwight lay under a poncho, accompanied by far too many other bodies.

Part of the lumber yard just north of the railroad tracks in Turzovka had been set aside for the dead. It seemed that our intel hadn't been completely accurate; while we'd heard that there had been cross-border incursions to the north, the Poles and elements of BCT 7 had pushed across the border after they'd discovered the destruction of FOB Poole, and secured Turzovka. They'd been probed by the EDC, but that had been about it until the previous night.

Now, in the aftermath, as many of the dead as possible had been retrieved from the battlefield around Vysoká nad Kysucou, and laid out for identification and burial.

David was taking Dwight's death hard. The two of them had verbally sniped at each other since the team had been formed, but now that Dwight was gone, the hole he'd left had made it really seem like the running joke about him being David's dad had had some truth to it. He'd been a grumpy old bastard, and hardly the fatherly type, but he'd been around a long time, as a Marine and then as a contractor before he'd joined the Triarii. He'd seen a lot, and he took loyalty to his team seriously. Hard-headed common sense had been his stock in trade, and we'd miss him.

The nine of us left were gathered around him, though the poncho was still up over his face. We knew what Dwight looked like. We'd rather remember him as he'd been alive, rather than the blood-spattered, bluish corpse that he was now.

"Matt!" I turned to see Bradshaw and Warren waiting at the door. I held up my hand. Bradshaw nodded. He understood. He still had more of this to do, himself.

Together, we lifted the body and carried it. It was rough; Dwight hadn't been a small man, and the poncho he was wrapped in didn't make it easy to carry his bulk. But we made it work. We had to. We owed it to Dwight.

The grave had already been dug, under an oak with its leaves turning yellow. We struggled over to it, and set him down for a moment.

I stood over his body, trying to find the words. That was when the Polish chaplain saw us and started over.

He'd already said the funeral Mass for the dead. He was praying over as many of them as he could as they were lowered into the ground in the already-crowded cemetery between the lumberyard and the river. The Americans didn't have a Catholic chaplain, but of course the Poles did. He didn't speak much English, but he motioned to Dwight's body. I nodded.

The prayers were in thickly-accented Latin, but I could follow most of them, praying along as much as I could. We committed Dwight's body to the earth, while we begged God to have mercy on his soul.

Then we buried him. It was a long way from Virginia, but there was no way we were going to be able to get him back Stateside for a funeral anytime soon.

As the rest of the team took turns covering the grave, I turned back and rejoined Bradshaw and Warren, where they stood respectfully waiting. Bradshaw's face was drawn and his eyes were haunted; his section had gotten through the battle at Vysokà nad Kysucou without taking any more losses, but the men they'd lost since this had started still stung.

"Well?" I asked quietly.

"He accepted the orders," Warren said. "Not gracefully, but he accepted them."

I nodded. General Reeves didn't have a good reputation from what I'd heard already; he was a political general and thoroughly married to the "New Army," which was just repeating the mistakes of the old with more gusto. He couldn't have been happy about having to work with the Triarii.

But he didn't have a lot of choice in the matter. While the Amphibious Ready Group and the 6th Fleet in the Med had made contact with the Hungarians and started probing Slovakian airspace, and we had sporadic contact with the *Abraham Lincoln* Carrier Strike Group in the North Sea, American assets in Europe were damned thin at the moment. We had a copy of the first "Letter of Marque and Reprisal" issued by the US Congress in over a century, that I knew of. The Triarii were independent of the Department of Defense, but now had full top cover to prosecute the war in Europe and wherever else it was flaring up on behalf of the United States.

Because Slovakia wasn't the only place. The Chinese had moved against the 7th Fleet in the aftermath of the attack, and there were more strikes in Central Asia and along the southern border of the US. Contact had apparently been lost with several advisor units working in Iraq and Syria. It really wasn't looking like the EDC had acted alone.

We still didn't know exactly who was behind the cyber attack that had crippled most of the country, but we had our suspicions. Whoever had spearheaded it, it had clearly been coordinated with as many enemies of the US as possible.

"He's not happy with me, either," Warren continued, looking a little sheepish. "After all, I was supposed to refuse to have anything to do with an 'illegal organization of right-wing terrorists.' His words. Apparently, getting cut off and slaughtered would have been preferable. He's *really* not happy that I defended you, even before I knew about the Letter of Marque."

He was looking a little worried. The political consequences of his decisions were coming around, and I realized that while they hadn't mattered while we'd been fighting for our lives, now his career could well be torpedoed for doing what had needed to be done.

"Well," I said, "if they do decide to cashier you, you could join us. You'd still need some serious train-up, but I'd say you got some not-insignificant OJT on the way here."

He nodded, his mouth getting a little tight. "Thanks, Matt."

I clapped him on the shoulder before turning back to finish helping to bury Dwight. "Like I told that Limey bastard we captured," I said, "it's going to be a long war. We can use all the fighters we can get, political generals be damned."

THE STORY CONTINUES IN:

HOLDING ACTION

MAELSTROM RISING BOOK 2

From the Author

I hope you've enjoyed this first entry in the *Maelstrom Rising* series. It's a bit of a return to form for me, being something of a spiritual successor to the *American Praetorian* series that came before it. While that series went in a direction that I hadn't quite expected when I began it, this one is going to go where I had initially planned the AP series—a full-blown, multi-axis, asymmetric global war.

Escalation is only the first chapter in that war. There's a lot to come. To keep up-to-date, I hope that you'll sign up for my newsletter at www.americanpraetorians.com—you get a free American Praetorians novella, *Drawing the Line*, when you do.

If you've enjoyed this novel, I hope that you'll go leave a review on Amazon or Goodreads. Reviews matter a lot to independent authors, so I appreciate the effort.

If you'd like to connect, I have a Facebook page at https://www.facebook.com/PeteNealenAuthor. You can also contact me, or just read my musings and occasional samples on the blog, at https://www.americanpraetorians.com. I look forward to hearing from you.

Made in United States
North Haven, CT
28 October 2021

10659289R00225